Book 2

of

The Ingenious

Trilogy

The Ingenious

and the Heart of Shattered Glass

J.Y. Sam

This is a work of fiction.
Names, characters, organisations, places, events, and incidents are either products of the author's imagination, or are used fictitiously.

www.jysamofficial.com

Paperback ISBN: 978-1-8382436-3-0
Hardback ISBN: 978-1-8382436-5-4
eBook ISBN: 978-1-8382436-4-7

First edition

DEDICATION

To Franco, Isabella, Marco.

ACKNOWLEDGEMENTS

Once again, my family – Franco, Isabella, Marco – have all been wonderful in putting up with me when my mind was so often cocooned in a completely different world, writing!

I'm completely indebted to Beth Moyse for joining me on my writing journey – it was reassuring to have her with me as I teased out book 2 into coherent chapters. Her grammatical acuity, friendship, and little cheers of encouragement have been invaluable! Especially when I doubted myself, which was often...

Thank you too to Mary Sergeant for proofreading to catch all those elusive little errors – and also to her husband, John, for lending her brilliant mind to the project! As well as dear Atsuko, enlisted as a last-minute proofreader, who has encouraged me and my little writing journey from the start. It's truly humbling to have such kind and generous friends. (And I hope my never-ending tweaks and additions, haven't undone all your good work...)

So grateful to Kamila and Iwona (and Beth too!) for running their artistic eyes over the book cover that David Prendergast put together beautifully from my stream of never-ending changes.

And a big shout out to all the wonderful beta readers for your willingness to read the book and give me your honest and thoughtful feedback – it has helped enormously in polishing the manuscript into something I hope you can be proud of too. Your support and advice is greatly valued, believe me!

And as always, I thank my God, for the undeserved kindnesses he gives us all, every single day...

SYNOPSIS OF BOOK 1:
The Ingenious and the Colour of Life

Project Ingenious, a secret government experimentation programme, was put together to create child prodigies from the genius genes identified by Dr Axel Kendra. Together with Professor Harald Wolff, a renowned genetic scientist, Project Ingenious produced seven babies in time – each named simply by a different letter of the Greek alphabet. But the significant loss of life, both of unborn foetuses, as well as the mothers who bore them, troubled the scientists deeply. Explaining this to the powers that be, they were ordered to continue despite the dangers, hinting that their families would suffer if they refused. This behoved Dr Kendra, Professor Wolff, and their colleagues, to escape with the seven Ingenious infants, burning down the laboratories to cover their tracks, as well as to ensure that the experiments stopped.

The scientists, the children, and their families, went into hiding, taking on new names and scattering around the globe – careful to conceal their true identities, and their genius.

18-year-old Jake Winters' older sister had been missing since her participation in Project Ingenious, and Jake has for years been trying to find out what happened to her – but he too disappeared mysteriously. In turn, his girlfriend, Calista Matheson, a natural genius in computer sciences, started digging around to discover what had happened to her beloved Jake. But this put her in danger, and Professor Wolff managed to save her from an assassination attempt.

She is taken within the Professor's unusual underground safe-house, Avernus, where he lives with his guide dog, Acuzio, and a deaf, nameless man, called the Chauffeur.

Seventeen years after the project started, an assassin was sent to kill the youngest Ingenious child, 13-year-old Jemima Jenkins. Professor Wolff, now blind, immediately sends his guardians to bring two of the Ingenious children into safety, teenagers Milly Bythaway and Tai Jones, together with Milly's father, Brian, and Tai's kittens. Tai was discovered living on the streets, abandoned by his mother. The other Ingenious children's whereabouts were known only by Dr Kendra, but so far the Professor has been unable to locate him.

Calista, the Chauffeur, Tai, and Milly, become good friends – and Calista helps the Professor create a supercomputer with state-of-the-art components, in the hope that it will help them track Jake's last movements, as well as locate – through facial recognition technology – both Dr Kendra and the missing Ingenious children. Calista soon discovers that Jake kept highly-secure files on a dark web server, and after hacking into them, she finds that the files are video recordings of the senile mutterings of an old man in a care home. He turns out to be Dr Kendra. Immediately they bring him into the safety of Avernus, together with his wife, Gaia, who is saddened to learn that the Professor is blind, and his wife and son are now dead. The Professor is disconcerted that his dear friend, Dr Kendra, has been suffering from Alzheimer's for some time, not least because he is also unable to divulge the whereabouts of the missing Ingenious children. Stacks of notebooks in his care-home room are discovered to be about his last scientific experiments before his mental health declined: the cure for dementia. Dr Fargo, a family friend of the Professor's, is called in to complete Dr Kendra's own cure, together with genius Milly Bythaway.

Meanwhile, the Professor is able to locate Tai's missing pet, a female Doberman called Dog – and is astonished to find that the abilities of both Tai and Milly are more than just intellectual: Milly is able to project images into people's mind, and Tai not only has a special connection with animals, but can also see people's thoughts and feelings as mesmerising displays of colour.

Breaking news, however, reports the unusual phenomenon of seven Oxford University students falling sick, each having a rare cancer-like virus. They were all in the same Genetics class. Professor Wolff cannot ignore the unsettling similarity with Project Ingenious. A telephone call from the Prime Minister confirms his fears. The PM tells the Professor that he had received an anonymous message asking for Professor Wolff to hand himself over, together with 'the children', in exchange for the cure that will save the Oxford University students' lives. If not, the virus that infected them will be spread further.

A stricken Professor decides to hand himself over, but not the children, in the hope that he can negotiate with the perpetrator. But Tai and Milly run after him, joining the Professor at the Thames Barrier rendezvous. When a midget submarine arrives, two thugs emerge, and they take the Professor and the children inside. But no cure is left for the Oxford students.

Transferred to a larger submarine – the Professor awakes, blind, confused, and stricken, only to find that he is alone with the perpetrator, who brazenly admits to infecting the Oxford students. A lengthy discussion makes the Professor realise the man has a blatant disregard for the sanctity of life, and is a psychopath. The Professor, in a fit of rage, triggers the switch on the underside of his shoe – transmitting a signal back to the UK to initiate a missile strike, the Professor's b-plan.

But when the Professor is reunited with Milly and Tai, he immediately regrets what he has done. Tai holds the Professor's hand as they contemplate their last moments, and to the Professor's amazement, he finds that he can see, through Tai. They stare out of the viewing glass, into the beautiful depths of the sea as they wait for the missiles. A blue whale swims up to them, and Tai is able to read the whale's thought-waves; he sees the whale's memories of her life, ending with the moments she peered through each viewport of the submarine – suddenly realising that the submarine has escape pods. The first missiles rain down on them, and their locked door is opened, whereupon they immediately run from room to room to locate the escape pods, only to discover an emaciated teenage boy strapped to a trundle bed. They free him, and at last manage to escape in one of the pods – shooting out into the water. But a missile explodes nearby, hurtling them against a large rock and splitting the pod open. To his shock, Tai finds himself on the seabed, in the freezing water. He spies Milly, the Professor, and the boy – but knows there is no time to save them all; the swim to the water surface alone is beyond reach. As he passes out, his mind detonates with a single thought-wave. SAVE US.

A great shoal of sharks had gathered around. They circle the four, creating vortices which lift them off the seabed – and the sharks immediately push them up with their snouts and swim at great speed toward the surface. The four are left floating there, two of them face-down, before the sharks swim away. The lone whale had also been affected by Tai's thought-wave, and she swims closer, rolling underneath and surfacing with them on her back. In time, a helicopter flies over and rescues them.

Faraway, in a remote village in China, a young Chinese girl, Li Mei Hui, lives a hard life as a farmer's wife. She is haunted by distant memories of a childhood in another country. Despite her simple life, she shows herself to be extraordinarily gifted, building – with the help of local villagers – a beautiful and ingeniously-designed house that is admired by all. She uses it to home children whose parents are forced to leave to find work in faraway industrial towns. Mei Hui had been sold into marriage, but the sudden death of her drunken and lazy husband, as well as a terrifying attack in the night, an attempt to kill her, help her to discover an incredible ability of being able to read people's hearts: whether they are good or bad, genuine or false. Amazingly, Jake Winters and Jemima Jenkins turn up at her house. It transpires that Jake had managed to save Jemima, and they immediately went into hiding. Together they followed Jake's leads to find his sister, taken from Dr Kendra's senile mutterings – bringing them to China in search of Mei Hui.

Jemima is able to speak near-perfect Chinese, and tells Mei Hui of Project Ingenious. Mei Hui realises she must go back to London with them, despite being saddened to leave her children; she arranges for them to be cared for by a neighbour who has a good heart.

Back in London, Jake and Calista have a touching reunion. In time, Jake quizzes the Professor about his sister, Kara, but the old man only vaguely remembers her as there had been hundreds of project participants.

They discover that the boy rescued from the submarine was also an Ingenious child, the first, the Alpha: 17-year-old Karl König. He had been tortured by the psychopathic perpetrator, and everyone sympathised with him – except for Acuzio, the Professor's guide dog, who growled at him.

Strange things begin happening in Avernus, but the news that Karl is dying from a genetic mutation eclipses everything. They acknowledge too the possibility that the other children, including Milly and Tai, have the same disease as Karl, which will cut short their lives. Milly has already started having head-splitting migraines.

The Professor has a sleepless night worrying about the children – but as he passes Karl's room, he freezes when he hears the voice of that psychopathic man in the submarine. It is Karl, mumbling in his sleep! Realising that it was him all this time, the Professor quickly locks the door.

The next morning Karl finds himself waking up with his hands in cuffs, chained to the bed. The Professor tells him that he knows who he is – and Karl admits everything. He wanted to kidnap the other Ingenious children, to use them as guinea pigs for the cure that he'd been developing for himself. He had nearly completed it, but it is now too late, his death is imminent. The Professor offers to help finish working on the cure with him – they might still be in time. But Karl refuses. If he dies, Karl reasons, why should they live? He wants them to suffer as he is.

The next day, the Professor desperately asks Tai to look into Karl König's mind, to find out the details of the cure. But Tai, who is terrified of the boy, is reluctant. They come up with the idea of Jemima, Milly, and Mei Hui joining Tai for support when connecting with Karl König's mind. It is their only chance. And they put it into operation.

But when they enter Karl's mind, which appears as a barren arctic tundra, they soon come across the Doomsday Vault – Karl's protective barrier, in his mind, for the cure. But it is impenetrable, and the four teenagers regroup, deciding instead to go deeper into Karl's past, right from the beginning, to try and alter his memories, and change his heart, in the hope that he might voluntarily give them the cure.

In doing so, they discover the biting reality of what happened in Project Ingenious, and see the making of a psychopath. They relive Karl's coldblooded memory when he ordered the murder of his own parents. But Milly, Tai, Mei Hui, and Jemima persevere in weaving new memories into a new past – righting all the wrongs. His mind edited, his life rebooted.

After Karl eventually wakes up, he seems to be a changed person, genuinely caring, and voluntarily offers Milly the details of the cure. However, the discovery of his father's pocket watch – whom he had assassinated – makes Karl question his very sanity. Eventually, he commits suicide, to everybody's shock.

Jemima sits down with Jake, explaining to him that when they had gone through Karl's memories, they also discovered what had happened to Jake's sister. She had died within the project, and her ashes buried in a field filled with cornflowers.

Jake visits the field, accompanied by Acuzio the dog. He sobs as he sits at the field's edge, clutching his sister's cardigan. Acuzio sniffs it, then suddenly turns and flies through the field, running to the exact spot where he had smelled that same scent. He starts digging frantically, and Jake follows him, only to find his sister's necklace in the loamy soil. Jake brings the cornflowers that had been growing there back home.

The teenagers within Avernus begin to return to normal life, until the Professor is told that Tai's mother has been found; the train she had been on months ago to visit her ailing father, had crashed, and she has since been in a coma. No-one knew her identity, until recently. Tai rushes to the hospital, where she is near death. He sees the colour of life glowing around her, but it is fading as her life-force ebbs. He grips her hand and sobs, desperately willing with all his might for her to live. He doesn't want to be alone. To his surprise, the colour around her becomes suddenly brighter, and more vibrant – and she arouses from her coma, much to everyone's surprise. Medical staff rush into the room to tend to her, and one of the nurses asks Tai if he is the patient's father. Tai catches his reflection in the mirror, his skin is wrinkly. He looks old. He feels weak. And realises that his own colour of life is pale, and barely there...

Back in Avernus, Dr Fargo and Milly had already given Dr Kendra his own cure for dementia, but it had not fully worked, giving the old man only random moments of lucidity. Kendra is now in his room, rocking in his chair, to and fro. He mutters incoherent babblings as usual, until he stops, and begins talking about one of the Ingenious children being where 'the black meets the white'. And that they must get to her quickly, before *he* comes... His wife, Gaia, asks who he is talking about. And Dr Kendra tells her: their father.

DRAMATIS PERSONAE

Acuzio – Professor Wolff's male guide dog, a husky.

Alma Morales – mother of Saffron Morales. Married to Ignacio. The couple set up an animal shelter by the Rio Branco river, in the Amazon jungle, and live there with their daughter.

Anne Fitzsimmons – mother to Jeremy Fitzsimmons 3rd. Married to Maxwell (Max) Fitzsimmons.

Brian Bythaway – father of Melody (Milly) Bythaway (third Project Ingenious child). His wife, Savannah Bythaway, died of cancer when Milly was nine years old.

Calista Matheson – a natural genius, who learnt computer sciences from her boyfriend Jake within a matter of months, and surpassed even his skills. Now 18 years old.

Chauffeur – Professor Wolff's chauffeur. He is deaf and mute, and communicates with the Professor through tactile sign language.

Chiara Wolff – Professor Wolff's wife who died together with their son, Christian, when their house went on fire sometime after Project Ingenious ended.

Christian Wolff – Professor Wolff's son. He died at 12 years old, together with his mother, Chiara, when their house went on fire sometime after Project Ingenious ended.

Cyrena Fitzsimmons (19th century) – wife of Jeremy Fitzsimmons 1st. Her family are landed gentry, but she is disowned by her parents for marrying a lowly farmer.

D1 and D2 – agents working for Professor Wolff. D agents are intelligence operatives, in comparison to the V agents, who work in the field.

Dog – Tai's adopted female Doberman, a stray. When her puppies died, Dog fostered kittens: Olly, Pasha, Max, Treacle, Missy Mop.

David O'Connor – chief of the security detail in charge of protecting Dr Vassiliev.

Edward Masterson (Sir) (19th century) – married to Molly Masterson (Lady). The couple had their portrait painted by the renowned but mysterious artist, F. Jaffrey.

Eligio – an Amazonian curandero, a tribal healer, skilled in the knowledge of natural medicines from the jungle.

F. Jaffrey – the pseudonym under which Jeremy Fitzsimmons 1st painted. His real identity has never been revealed to the general public.

Fargo, Dan (Dr) – son of eminent scientist Professor James Fargo, known for his work on gene therapies. Called in by Professor Wolff to complete Dr Kendra's cure for Alzheimer's. He is also consulted for general medical matters.

Fidelia Fitzsimmons (19th century) – daughter of Cyrena and Jeremy Fitzsimmons 1st. She is a twin with her brother, William.

Gaia Kendra – Greek wife of Dr Kendra. Changed name to Adrienn Laszlo after escaping from Project Ingenious.

Georgina Whyte (Georgie) – love interest of Jeremy Fitzsimmons 3rd, and the subject of the dragonfly girl painting.

Gerard (Gerry) – part of the special ops division, enlisted by Rory Sanderson, the Prime Minister's head of security. They accompany Calista, Jake, and Jemima Jenkins on their mission to the Amazon jungle.

Ignacio Morales – father of Saffron Morales. Married to Alma. The couple set up an animal shelter by the Rio Branco river, in the Amazon jungle, and live there with their daughter.

Isaiah Fitzsimmons – grandfather to Jeremy Fitzsimmons 3rd.

Jake Winters – a computer whizz, and boyfriend to Calista Matheson. His older sister, Kara, participated in Project Ingenious, but Jake has since discovered that she died during the project and was buried in a field of cornflowers. Now 19 years old.

Jasmine – super-computer built by Calista Matheson.

Jemima Jenkins – seventh and last Project Ingenious child (Omega). English. Now 14 years old. She is a mathematics genius, and soon discovers a most unusual ability, to do with discerning the remaining seconds of a person's life.

Jeremy Fitzsimmons 1st (19th century) – the first in the Fitzsimmons family line to display unique mind abilities. He came from a poor, farming background, and married his childhood sweetheart, Cyrena. He became a famed but mysterious artist who painted under a pseudonym, F. Jaffrey.

Jeremy Fitzsimmons 3rd (21st century) – descendent of Jeremy Fitzsimmons 1st.

Karl König – first Project Ingenious child (Alpha). German. Died when he was 17 years old.

Kendra, Axel (Xeli) (Dr) – renowned scientist known for his work on mapping the human genome and identifying the genius genes. Partnered Professor Wolff within Project Ingenious. Married to Gaia Kendra. After escaping from Project Ingenious, they changed their names to Dr Laszlo and Mrs Adrienn Laszlo.

Lyubova (Lyu-Lyu) – Dr Vassiliev's beloved Siberian molly cat. She and Dr Vassiliev have an enduring love for each other, and are near-inseparable.

Maxwell Fitzsimmons (Max) – father to Jeremy Fitzsimmons 3rd. Married to Anne Fitzsimmons.

Mei Hui Li – sixth Project Ingenious child (Sigma). Chinese. Now 15 years old. Has the ability to read hearts – how good or bad, false or genuine, a person is.

Milly Bythaway (Melody) – third Project Ingenious child (Delta). English. Now 16 years old. She has a photographic memory, is able to remember everything she reads, and can learn new languages easily. Her special power is that she can implant images into people's minds.

Molly Masterson (Lady) (19th century) – married to Edward Masterson (Sir). The couple had their portrait painted by the renowned but mysterious artist, F. Jaffrey.

Peter Davids (Dr) – cancer expert consulted when Oxford University students contracted deadly virus.

Parry-Johansson (Ms) – tour guide and art advisor, specialising in painter F. Jaffrey's work.

Prime Minister (PM) – referred to by Calista as Boz, or Bozza.

Rory Sanderson – the Prime Minister's head of security. He is Scottish, married, and has a three-year-old son. Sceptical about the Ingenious teenagers, until an encounter with Jemima Jenkins.

Sabu – the last remaining black jaguar cub. His parents died of a strange disease, which he too has contracted.

Saffron Morales (Saffie) – second Project Ingenious child (Beta). Brazilian. 16 years old. Has the ability to absorb the abstract feelings and emotions of other Ingenious children, even at great distance. Also has a special way with animals. The isolados tribesmen call her daughter of Mother Earth.

Savannah Bythaway – mother of third Ingenious child, Milly Bythaway. She died of cancer when Milly was nine, after knitting Milly a precious beanie hat. Milly constantly hears her mother's voice in her head.

Tai Jones – fifth Project Ingenious child (Theta). Jamaican. Now 15 years old. He is a simple boy, but has the ability to see people's thoughts and feelings as colourful auras. Also has an unusual connection with animals. After discovering his mother in hospital in a coma, and willing for her to live, he inadvertently misused his powers to revive her, making himself old and close to death in the process.

Tyaishia Jones – Jamaican mother of Tai Jones (fifth Project Ingenious child).

V1 – male middle-aged agent working for Professor Wolff. V agents work in the field, are skilled in the ways of ninjutsu, and often referred to as ninjas. V1 was killed on the same day that agent V3 was attacked.

V2 – male agent, believed to be in his thirties.

V3 – female older agent. V3 was attacked by thugs in an alleyway, and has since been in a coma. Milly feels responsible for her injuries, because she planted the spy camera that was discovered by the assassin Penny Thompson, which consequently led to the agents being drawn into the trap.

Vassiliev, Vadim (Dr) – stern cat-loving Russian scientist, brought in by Dr Fargo to work on and complete Karl König's cure.

Viola – grandmother to Georgina Whyte.

William Fitzsimmons (19th century) – son of Cyrena and Jeremy Fitzsimmons 1st. He is a twin with his sister, Fidelia.

Wolff, Harald (Harry) (Professor) – genetic scientist who led Project Ingenious together with Dr Axel Kendra. After escaping from Project Ingenious, he changed his name to Johan Hindemith. He became blind sometime afterward.

CONTENTS

'People judge others by what they look like,

but I judge people by what is in their hearts.'

1 Samuel 16:7b

Contemporary English Version

PROLOGUE

1839. One could say that Jeremy Fitzsimmons had everything a man might wish for... except for one rather unfortunate thing.

His wife, Cyrena, was beautiful, kind, patient, understanding, and whilst always a lady in every way, and the mistress of Oakley Hall, she had an exuberance and passion for life that seemed to infect everyone she touched. They had two perfect children – young master William, who was thoroughly sensible and serious for his tender age of 13, yet not averse to flashes of playfulness and joy, which were in no small part due to his playful, joyful twin sister, Fidelia. They all got on swimmingly.

And unlike other households where the servants were very much beneath their employers, and considered as mere slaves, their 25-strong staff – half of whom had been with Cyrena's kinfolk for as long as she could remember – were always treated as extended family, with civility and generosity, much better than were their equals in other households. In fact, it would be fair to say that the staff and the Fitzsimmonses really cared for each other. Some might even use the word 'love' – that of the familial, endearing kind, a quality that was not entirely inappropriate in this instance.

Jeremy Fitzsimmons was completely devoted to his family and staff, and finding himself lord of the manor through marriage to his wife, took very seriously his role as estate owner. And the land was extensive.

They delegated most of the estate work, for it was not their forte, to a capable and experienced manager whom they trusted, with explicit instructions that tenanted and yeoman farmers were treated fairly, and that the poor, or those who fell on hard times, be found work, either as paid labourers with the farmers, or on the building or grounds of Oakley Hall – for there was always work to be done, indeed it was never-ending –

to balance the lack with their surplus, and to ensure that no-one in their holdings starved, not even for a day.

And in this way, the Fitzsimmonses' reputation spread so greatly that people from far and wide uprooted entire households in order to settle on their estate. It seemed that everyone connected to them and/or their land prospered. Even the family's own fortune augmented in every way; their bank manager, Mr Thurston of the National Province, was very pleased indeed.

One might therefore ask what on earth could Jeremy Fitzsimmons' misfortune be? Surely the man wanted for nothing.

It was something that had developed gradually through his childhood, much to his parents' increasing alarm. He started out a golden child. As a baby, his blue eyes sparkled liked topaz, flaxen hair so fine as to be reminiscent of a cherub, pale skin the colour of freshly churned butter. He was such a handsome infant that people gasped when they saw him for the first time. Over the years he grew into a respectful and bright yet intense boy – and at six, manifested a love of art and painting that fair made his parents burst with pride. His sketches of people were not the usual potatoes with stick arms and legs, normal for others his age, but fine pieces that revealed his keen eye for detail, a light-handed penmanship, and a unique sense of interpretation that hinted at even the great masters' oeuvres. Still-life was sketched with verve and flourish, and his paintings had a quality that hushed the observer with stunned admiration. Both he and his family knew immediately that he had found his true metier as an artist.

But even as his artistry developed, so did the mole that appeared on his upper left cheek when he turned 15. It started out so small and insignificant as to be mistaken for a freckle. Yet over time it bulged and blackened, and both physician and apothecary had to be called upon – they prescribed every known salve and liniment, to be applied thrice a day, morning, noon, and night. Yet, despite this, it still grew and grew, so that by the time he was 20 it had taken over most of his face. Gone were his golden good looks, to be replaced instead by coarse features, thick eyebrows that had knitted together, and patches of whiskered skin that defied shaving and abrading. And whenever shaving was attempted, the whiskers just seemed to regrow even thicker and tougher than before. In time, and with heavy hearts, he and his parents reluctantly resigned themselves to the fact that nothing could be done to remedy the disfigurement. It was something he and they must live with – so sad for a young man that craved society and acceptance.

It was perhaps fortunate that his childhood sweetheart, Cyrena, had known Jeremy since they were three, and having grown up with him, she saw only his gentle nature, his sweetness, and his good, kind heart. She had been in love with him right from the beginning, and neither the decline of his handsome visage, nor the sadness that tinged his hushed conversations with her, affected the deep feeling she had for him in the slightest.

Their wedding was a small ceremony, attended only by immediate family and the closest of friends – not more than a dozen in total. But as Jeremy gazed upon the lovely, blushed face of his bride, whilst they grasped each other's hands as if their lives depended on it, he took in every detail – her muted amber eyes, the curl of hair that had teased out from under a crown of forest flowers, the quiver of happiness in her lip – and he felt his eyes dampen with tears. Could it really be that love was strong enough to overlook such a brutal physical disfigurement? Yes, yes, and yes again, he thought to himself triumphantly, as he slipped the wedding band on her finger.

But yet still, it was not to be a bed of roses. Their union meant the immediate dissolution of Cyrena's bond with her own family. Her parents in particular could not approve of their privileged daughter marrying below her status – a farmer's son, a simple tiller of the soil – but especially because the betrothed was so obviously 'hideous'. They were unable to see beyond the surface, beyond position. It was like asking the colour-blind to appreciate a lustrous, flaming sunset. Impervious were they to his superior character, his decency, and that he made Cyrena feel as though she were the most precious, most loved person in the world. To Cyrena, it was a painful but necessary sacrifice to sever ties with her family, for she loved them dearly, but could no longer endure their constant and abrasive criticism of her husband, their vehement disapprobation.

Yet the young couple allowed nothing to dampen their happiness, a happiness that was solidified by the birth of their at first unexpected but then eagerly anticipated twins.

Years later, when a governess took over their schooling, Cyrena busied herself with a start-up fashion-designing business, whilst Jeremy continued with his painting. The former executed her designs with more than a little maladroitness, whilst the latter excelled with dynamism and creative brilliance. And because Jeremy Fitzsimmons shunned society – or rather, society shunned him – he worked under a pseudonym, 'F. Jaffrey', whose name and reputation became known in varying circles as a mysterious, yet masterly, artist. All of which made him even more sought after. Such was the abundance of engagements that bookings had to be made many years in advance.

His fame and reputation spread like wildfire, which was due in no small part to his rather unconventional and extraordinary methods. People did not need to sit for him for hours and days and weeks, fidgeting, scratching noses, and balancing on aching derrières, as was the usual way.

Sir Edward and Lady Molly Masterson soon experienced this for themselves when the enigmatic F. Jaffrey visited them at their country house in Oxford. He arrived cloaked both in the darkness of night and a hooded mantle that shrouded his face. He brought none of the wares of his trade – no brushes, no easel, no canvas, pigments, or oils. Nothing. The elderly couple though were not surprised by this, for his curious ways were spread around in hushed tones. Lord and Lady had been awaiting his visit with nervous anticipation and excitement – she in her Chantilly lace-edged gown with wide petticoats (even though it was de rigueur to have narrower ones these days) and he in his best tweed hunting jacket.

When Jaffrey entered their large drawing room, they saw that he was an impressive figure. His natural poise gave nothing away of his poor farming background. His gait, as he drew closer, was assured. The men shook hands – it was a lingered handshake, with the visitor placing one hand over both of theirs, several seconds too long for comfort. They were warm hands despite his travelling for hours through the winter snow. And even in such close proximity, the dim candle-light illuminated only the tip of his beard.

After the exchange of pleasantries and introductions, Sir Edward passed him a glass of port that had been warming by the fire. He lifted an eyebrow. 'Will you not take off your coat, sir? True, it is freezing outside, but in here it is warm. Or do you not feel it?'

Jaffrey took a sip of the port before answering. 'It is perfectly warm, Sir Edward, and a beautiful house I might add. But I prefer not to linger. That is the way I work, take it or leave it.'

Lady Molly hastened to say, 'We take it!' For she was eager to have the great F. Jaffrey paint them.

Sir Edward harrumphed, nodded, and returned to his wife, who was already sitting in the position in which she wanted to be painted – after having plagued her husband to death for days and weeks about the perfect aspect. The old man stood next to his wife in exactly the way they rehearsed, the coupled glanced at each other, and then turned toward their guest, who was already downing the last of his drink. He smacked his lips. 'That is exceptionally good port!'

'It is my own,' Sir Edward said with pride. 'And you shall certainly have a bottle or two before you leave.'

Jaffrey put down the crystal glass, and drew closer, studying them, studying their surroundings. 'I thank you,' he said, though his tone revealed that he was already deep in thought. After several minutes he said, 'Do you have any special requests?'

'Yes,' piped up Lady Molly. 'I want my dear deceased Westie sitting here, by my side.' She waved in the direction of her ankle. 'Maverick was his name. I will let you have his portrait before you leave.'

Jaffrey held up his hand. 'No need,' he said. 'I already know what he looks like.' Husband and wife glanced at each other, puzzled; there were no portraits of the dog hanging in the room or hallway. 'Please do not ask,' he answered before they said anything. 'I just know. And how large would you like the canvas?'

The old man gestured toward the far wall, which was completely bare. 'The largest size you can do, to fill that area, there. It has been empty for far too long.'

'And please make me look good!' said Lady Molly, turning to glance at herself in the side-wall mirror and patting back her hair. She was not a vain woman, but she wanted the best painting of herself for posterity.

Jaffrey had heard the request too many times. 'I paint only the truth,' he said rather firmly. The Lady was about to say something, but he added smoothly, 'And as you are clearly an elegant woman, Lady Molly, there should be no problem there.'

The old woman couldn't help but flutter a coquettish little laugh. 'Make that *three* bottles of port!' she told her husband.

'Yes, yes,' growled the old man, eyes narrowing. 'But when you say you paint "only the truth", what exactly do you mean?'

The assured stranger faltered briefly. 'I... I mean that there is purity and truth in my paintings. I mean to say, they cannot lie.' He changed the subject quickly. 'My terms are that you will be sent the portrait in five months. I take my time because I put everything into it. The cost of £200 must be paid to the courier on delivery.'

'£200!' coughed Sir Edward. 'My goodness! That is more than an entire year's wage for some. Nay, two years' worth.'

His wife gently kicked his brogued feet. 'We accept!' she said.

'But... but what if we don't like it?' protested her husband. They both stared at Jaffrey.

'I assure you, you will like it,' he told them in no uncertain terms. 'I have never had a client return my work. You will see... I would like to point out too that I am not asking for any advance. But if you harbour any doubt, tell me now.'

'No, no – we have no doubt. And we accept your offer,' repeated Lady Molly firmly, her eyes sliding sideways to her husband – a sign that he dare not cross her.

The old man ground his teeth and acquiesced. 'Very well,' he mumbled, suddenly needing a stiff drink himself.

Jaffrey swept his eyes across the scene one last time – slowly, purposefully. Absorbing every object to the tiniest detail, every nuance of light and shade, colour and texture. 'That settles matters then. It was a great pleasure to meet you both. And if you don't mind, I shall bid you good night and take my leave.'

'Is that it?' asked the wife holding out a hand; she was not ready for him to go. 'No sketches, no... Daguerreotype?'

Her husband looked at her. 'What on earth are you talking about woman? Sounds like gobbledygook!'

She threw the man a withered look. 'Have you not heard the latest, dear? A Daguerreotype is one of those new-fangled contraptions that can take little lifelike pictures. It's wondrous!'

Jaffrey turned back round to face them. 'I do not use any such device...'

'Then how can you paint our portrait?' she asked, baffled. 'You've made no sketches.'

'Simply put, I have an excellent memory. Now, if you don't mind, I have a long journey back home.'

'Yes, yes of course,' said Lady Molly thoughtfully.

Her husband rang for the butler, who came within minutes. He was told to bring three bottles of port for their visitor, and then escort him out. Jaffrey nodded courteously toward the couple before leaving – and just like that, he was gone.

Five months later, a huge muslin-wrapped parcel bound with cord was delivered to their mansion with great fuss and upheaval and shouting of instructions. Four servants heaved and panted as they brought it inside and propped it against the bare wall, where it was to be hung. Lord and Lady Masterson stood aside with bated breath as the cord was cut and the muslin unfolded.

When the cloth dropped to the ground revealing their full-length life-sized portrait, Lady Molly gasped and stumbled back, a trembling hand lifted to her mouth. Unbelieving eyes swept over the stature of their perfectly painted forms, their expressions, the detailed embroidery on her silk dress – even the way her husband lifted a single eyebrow. Their figures were not in rigid stances, but in a state of flux; a stray moment captured in time. And the colours were beguiling. Muted cadmium and chrome yellow, alizarin and Scheele's green, amongst others – all rendered with a delicate cast of light that made the colours glow. By their feet on the floor sat their beloved Westie, Maverick, licking his mistress' extended hand, as he had often done. Around his neck was the red tartan collar that he used to wear, half hidden under bright white fur.

As she registered all these beautifully captured details, Lady Molly gasped again and again, and nearly fainted – caught just in time by her husband, who quickly deposited her on the chaise. Her lady in waiting and other servants cried out and rushed around her, fussing, and someone brought some smelling salts. They fanned her copiously, and at last, she sat up, and stilled her beating heart. 'I'm fine, I'm fine,' she exclaimed, shooing them away. She wanted to see the picture again, and they divided like parting waters. She took in the astounding painting for several minutes more, eyes flitting over every inch, every detail. 'You see, Ed? You see,' she told her husband. 'It is worth *five times* the amount we paid.'

For once, Sir Edward agreed with her unreservedly. He removed the monocle from his eye and pocketed it. His eyesight was failing, still, it was good enough for him to appreciate in silent wonderment the masterpiece set before them.

•••———————————————————•••

1966. 127 years later, inside the National Portrait Gallery of St Martin's Place, London, a blond 14-year-old boy stood in front of the same large portrait. The colours had darkened – the dog's fur now a murky raw sienna.

The teenager looked small against the vast canvas, as he stared up at it with open-mouthed awe. Behind the boy stood two bodyguards, and just in front was a woman, his own personal guide, dressed in a plaid flared skirt, a mohair twinset, and pearls. Her beehive up-do was perfectly styled with not a hair out of place. The boy reached out a hand to the painting, magnetised by it, his legs straining the rope stanchion.

'No touching,' the guide told him anxiously. Then she remembered who she was talking to. The son of a billionaire. 'Please,' she added respectfully. She eyed the Polaroid camera hanging around his neck; of course he had the latest, most expensive gadgets. The guide cleared her throat before continuing her discourse. 'This portrait is one of the renowned 19th century artist's most famous works. We've since discovered that F. Jaffrey was a pseudonym – and until now, nobody knows the real identity of the artist behind these wonderful paintings. All we know is that he was a rather mysterious man.'

She waved a hand toward all four walls of the exhibition room. 'All these pictures you see here represent, not a curated collection, but rather the entirety of his known works, most of which are on loan by the owners. However, Jaffrey was a prolific painter, and we estimate that his complete oeuvre numbers around three hundred. So the majority of his paintings are missing, and our art investigators are none the wiser as to where they can be, or who could have them.'

Continuing on, they made their way around the large room, picture by picture – and she highlighted features of each painting, the artistry, and the 'sui generis' nature of the artist's style. Her enthusiasm was infectious, and though the boy was barely a teenager, he listened with rapt attention and respect.

Eventually, she glanced at her watch. 'Shall we move on? We've got a lot more to see in the gallery.'

The boy hesitated. 'No,' he said. 'I just wanted to see these paintings again. So I think we'll go now. Is that okay?' He held out his hand, like a little gentleman, and, hesitantly, she shook it. He lingered in handshake a few seconds too long for her comfort. But the guide was thrown, wondering why the boy was cutting short their tour, perhaps she had said or done something wrong. But the boy told her, 'Don't worry,' with a knowing look. 'You haven't done anything wrong, Ms Parry-Johansson.'

She was relieved. 'Oh, good, thank goodness!' she breathed, though she couldn't remember telling him her name. Then she realised she'd forgotten *his* name.

'My name is Jeremy,' he told her, reading her mind. 'Jeremy Fitzsimmons.'

'Knowledge of the past and of the places of the earth

is the ornament and food of the mind of man.'

Leonardo da Vinci

PART 1

1 UNRAVELLING

'Tyaishia!!!' shouted Tai's mother in her thick Jamaican accent, her voice hoarse from incessant sobbing. 'Ty-ai-shia!' she croaked, and then hiccoughed, which surprised even her. She reached for another tissue and blew her nose, making it even redder than before. Just weeks ago, she had awoken from a long coma, only to find that her son had come down with a very strange and frightening illness, and not only that, she was then told that her ailing father had died whilst she was comatose. She hadn't been able to stop crying since.

She sat by Tai's bed now, within the underground safehouse they called Avernus, in almost the same way Tai had sat next to her in hospital weeks before. She herself was still weak despite her miraculous recovery. Red eyes shadowed with dark circles were stark against freckled cafe-au-lait skin. She watched as her son slept. Tai was on his side, with his back hunched, the deep wrinkles on his face were incongruous, his hair streaked grey, and the skin of his hands was sagging and marked with liver spots. She wondered to herself, eyes wild with disbelief, how could her normally fresh-faced 15-year-old son look even older than her? She looked up at Brian who was standing on the other side of the bed, red-faced. She was angry with him for pronouncing her name wrong, angry with the doctor, angry with the world! She felt like she'd been dealt three jokers from the same pack of cards that was her life, one after another, even though there were only supposed to be two. She eyed the cup and saucer in his hand. 'And why d'yuh English always tink tea is di answer t'everyting?!' Her voice was raw in anger.

Brian started to say something, but then decided against it. He placed the tea on the bed-table, mumbled 'Sorry' – and quietly left.

She stared at the empty doorway through which he disappeared, and suddenly realised how thirsty she was. Sliding the saucer closer, she slurped the tea. It was creamy sweet, with condensed milk; he'd remembered the way she liked it. She pulled another tissue from the box, wiped her eyes, and then threw it in the bin at her feet. It was piled high with tissues.

In the kitchen, blind, old Professor Wolff was patting a hand inside one of the cabinets. He thought for a moment, then opened another cabinet and felt around inside that one too. 'Jasmine!' he called out to the air, even though there was no-one in the room. 'Where have all the cups gone?'

'There should be 50 cups, Professor,' came a smooth female voice from thin air. It was the artificial intelligence persona of the computer, they called Jasmine, that controlled and automated Avernus. 'There are currently seven humans in Avernus, so there should be plenty of cups to go around,' she told him. Which of course was useless to him.

Annoyed, the Professor closed the cabinet door and began feeling around the work surfaces. 'Well, they've disappeared! All of them!' he grumbled. He soon discovered that there was a whole stack of dirty dishes, cups, and cutlery in the sink, and he stopped and heaved a deep sigh. He went over to a different part of the kitchen, felt for a glass and a bottle, and poured himself some wine. He practically inhaled it.

He knew very well that he was falling apart. He recognised the signs. The last time it had happened was just over 10 years ago when he tore through the charred, smoking wreckage of his burnt house, coughing hard, eyes stinging, and heedless of his own safety. Only to find horrific remains... The next thing he knew, he was waking up in a strange hospital bed, distraught not only from grief, but also to find that he was blind.

He poured himself another glass. He wanted to sit, but with all the newcomers to Avernus, nothing was in its place. He had bumped and tripped and stumbled so many times across things that ought not to have been there, things that should have been returned to their original position, that should never have moved in the first place!

'Professor?' came Jasmine's voice, making the old man jump. 'My sensors detect that your heartbeat and pulse have quickened. Would you like me to call Dr Fargo to give you a check-up?'

The Professor hung his head resignedly. 'No,' he said, muffled.

'I'm sorry, I did not hear. Can you repeat?'

He looked up suddenly. 'No!!!' he shouted, and smashed his fist on the surface, realising too late that he was still holding the glass. It shattered in his hand, and a wet sensation of both warm and cold seeped between his fingers. He let go, and shards of glass tinkled on the marble worktop. 'Aaargh!' he cried, and he crumpled to the floor, his hand extended, blood dripping silently onto the floor.

There came the sound of heavy footsteps, and someone running to his side. It was the Chauffeur. He lifted up the old man from the floor without a word, being both deaf and mute. Carefully picking off the glass from the Professor's hand, he then pulled him up and guided him to one of the seats. He caught movement at the side of his eye, and turned to find Acuzio, a handsome husky, bounding into the room, and the Chauffeur quickly lifted his hand to him. The well-trained dog immediately stopped in his tracks, and when the Chauffeur swung a flat hand down toward the floor, instantly the dog sat and waited obediently. There were bound to be glass splinters on the floor, and with everything else going on, the last thing he wanted was for the dog to get injured too.

He tended to the Professor first, cleaned his hand with disinfectant, and bound it in gauze. Then he cleared the work surface and swept and wiped the floor. At last, he pulled up a chair in front of the Professor, who was sitting with slumped shoulders. The Chauffeur took his unbandaged hand and began signing on it – a series of touches, strokes, and taps. *About you, I'm worried*, he told him, his face creased with that very anxiety. *You're not eating, and I can see you're not sleeping.* He signed dark shadows under his eyes, and mimicked being tired and exhausted. *I know, many problems. But you must be strong. You, we all need. You, we need!* He emphasised the last signs decisively, his expression a blend of pleading and frustration.

The Professor barely comprehended, his mind in a fog. But the Chauffeur stubbornly repeated the signs again and again. Finally snatching his hand away, the old man closed his eyes. Then, at last, he nodded weakly. And the Chauffeur smiled sadly. He sat back, the chair scraping noisily though he did not know it. He turned around, flicked a finger at the dog, and Acuzio immediately came to his master, whining with concern. The dog began licking the fingertips that were poking out of the bandages, and the old man just sat back and let him.

Within the two-storey high library that was called the BC, Dr Kendra was sitting – bewildered – on one of the sofas, with his wife Gaia behind him, and 15-year-old Mei Hui to his side, grasping his hand between both of hers. Mei Hui's eyes were closed, deep in concentration, and she sat there for what seemed like an age, though it was not so long. Her features flickered in minute ways, eyes moving under creased eyelids, twitching lips drawn in a thin line. But in the end she let go, and sat back, defeated. She shook her head, silky hair swishing lightly. 'I cannot find out anything,' she said in disappointment. 'I... I do not have the same ways with the mind that Tai has. His abilities are much stronger. Also, Dr Kendra's mind is... muddled. The only memories I can see are recent ones at those times when he could understand, when he could think clearly. I cannot see further into the past. It is like... looking into water that has been agitated with mud.' She wiped her forehead with the back of her sleeve, in the same way she used to do when working on the farm in China. She sighed deeply. She missed the children she once looked after, missed her parents. She was frustrated too.

Gaia's expression was one of resignation. Her once-brilliant husband was now little more than a vegetable, riddled with Alzheimer's disease that seemed to get worse by the day. Ironically, before he had succumbed to it, he had been an eminent and respected scientist working on a cure for dementia, though an imperfect one – and now, after being administered his own cure, it only resulted in brief and unpredictable flashes of clarity. Locked away in that mind were the identities and whereabouts of two children born to Project Ingenious – who up to now they still hadn't been able to find. Mei Hui Li, Milly Bythaway, Tai Jones, Jemima Jenkins, and the ignominious Karl König, who had committed suicide several weeks before, were five of the seven Ingenious children.

Mei Hui, with her innate and extraordinary ability to peer at recent memories inside people's minds, had been trying to find out where those two missing children were, but in vain.

'You did your best, dear,' Gaia told Mei Hui, who was clearly frustrated.

'It was worth a try.'

Mei Hui smiled briefly. 'If only–' she started. She wanted to say if only Tai was all right – because he had an amazing ability to read people's minds like a book, and could even transfer his thoughts, his will, into them. Mei Hui was sure he would easily have succeeded where she had failed. But somehow Tai, when visiting his comatose mother, and after mentally willing for her to get better, had suddenly 'aged' and degenerated physically, at the very same time as she stirred awake. It was incredible, unbelievable, disastrous. Mei Hui caught a choke in her throat and fought to control her emotions. The 'if only' line of thought, she knew, was a useless one, resolving nothing. It was a loop of reasoning, ad infinitum, that never went anywhere.

'I know,' said Gaia softly. 'We're distraught over Tai too. He was...' she stiffened, correcting herself. 'He *is* a remarkable young man.'

Mei Hui looked at Gaia and the vacant Dr Kendra as she thought about Tai. He was like a brother to her – and his 'illness' was breaking her heart.

16-year-old Milly Bythaway was elsewhere. Elsewhere both in body and mind. She entered the dimly-lit room once more. It was her haven, a cocoon that shielded her from the outside world. She hummed quietly to herself, carefully carrying a cup of tea. It was hot, and so she passed it from one hand to another, trying not to spill it. She glanced at the sleeping figure lying on the bed, inert and straight, and carefully lowered herself onto the bedside chair. She took a sip of the tea, but gasped when it burnt her tongue. Absentmindedly, she looked around, then got up and placed the cup on the sideboard amidst all the other things.

Returning to her seat, there was a <u>small pile of daisies</u> on the bed next to the woman's arm, that Milly had left earlier – and she hunched over them now, making little slits in each stalk with a fingernail, silent with concentration. She strung the daisy heads through the slits, to make a chain. Her fingertips were stained with black, which in turn left smudges on the delicate white petals.

Milly felt hot, and she made to push back the beanie hat on her head – only to find that it was not there. Her heart cracked with a dull ache, and she sighed, and then returned to the daisies. At last she completed the chain, and she held it up in satisfaction. It was fragile and pretty, despite the blotches. Milly got up and reached for the head of the sleeping form, placing the delicate circle gently around her crown. The girl stood back to admire her handiwork, then rearranged it a tad, and stepped back again. It looked lovely on the comatose agent, V3, even though the old woman's face was horribly slashed with cuts, scars, and bruises. Milly had combed out her fine white hair into a fan on the pillow, and in her mind the agent looked serenely beautiful. Pleased, the girl leaned forward and gently kissed the woman's cheek, before leaving the room. She suddenly felt thirsty and wondered where she had put her tea. Yet again, she had forgotten that it was on the sideboard, amongst the sea of other cups – all full to the brim and stone cold.

•••————————————————————•••

Rory Sanderson, being Scottish, was used to speaking his mind – yet he hardly ever crossed his boss. After all, his boss was one of the most powerful men in England – but this time he just had to say something. 'But, sir, she's a *child*,' Rory told him squarely. 'Just turned 14. I really don't think she should be joining us on the mission.'

The PM stopped and stared at him with small, beady eyes. 'Jemima Jenkins may look cute and innocent and childlike, Sanderson – but make no mistake, she is more intelligent and more crafty than you and I put together. Actually, than the entire cabinet put together.' The PM looked at him with that sideways thoughtful stare that he did, before turning to leave. But then he stopped. 'I suggest you keep an open mind. You might even learn a thing or two.' He turned and left.

Sanderson watched him walk away, and sighed with frustration. He continued walking along the hallway, and then twisted the shiny brass door knob to one of the Downing Street COBRA rooms, stepping inside. They had been given access to use it by the boss himself, in light of the secrecy of their mission. Six of his best special ops men were sitting around a rather grand meeting table quietly talking amongst themselves, all in dark suits, whilst three teenagers were dressed in jarringly bright colours. The sore point in question, Jemima Jenkins, among them. Her curly blonde hair and rosy cheeks did indeed make her look insanely cute, detracting from the fact that she was a child prodigy and mathematics genius. Jake and Calista were sitting next to each other, with Jemima standing casually next to Jake, leaning an elbow on his shoulder – she considered him to be her best friend even though there was a four-year age difference, and he and Calista had been steady for years. Calista was, at that very moment, eyeballing Jemima with disdain. Though she ought not to have had anything to worry about; while Jake was handsome in a delicate, refined way, Calista herself had a savage beauty that stopped most men in their tracks. The couple were made for each other.

Rory Sanderson coughed to get everyone's attention and spread out a large map on the table. 'Erm, if I can have your full attention please,' said Sanderson, glaring at Calista. 'I trust you've all read the brief sent to you in advance.' He turned back to the map. 'Now, the one clue we have from Dr Kendra is "where the black meets the white".' The ailing Dr Kendra had, in a rare moment of lucidity, revealed that the sixth Ingenious child was somewhere in the Amazon, before his mind faded again to the Alzheimer's disease. Sanderson tapped at a specific point on the map with his index finger. 'We've found a place that exactly fits that description, here, in Manaus, the capital of Brazil – where the dark, almost black, waters of the Rio Negro, meet with the sandy-white waters of the Solimões River. It's a well-known tourist attraction because the confluence of rivers creates a very visible divide between black and white waters. So I'm confident Manaus is where we need to start looking for our POI–'

Jemima excitedly threw her hand up, as if she were in a class at school, saying, 'I'm guessing POI stands for...'

'Person of interest,' answered Sanderson with a withered look. 'Now, where was I... right, the city has a population of over two million, and all we know about the POI is that she's female, and around 16 to 17 years old. That's it. So be prepared to do a lot of intelligence work, a lot of digging.' He looked at his men. 'Each of you will need to reach out to local IS's or IB's...' He ignored Jemima who had put her hand up again. 'For *those* not in the know, that means intelligence sources or intelligence bureaus... I'm hoping they'll collaborate. Check out all the schools, clubs, social places, and see if anyone fitting her description stands out as being particularly...

gifted.' He glanced at the teenagers. 'Calista, Jake, both of you will need to infiltrate local information servers to see what you can find there – with the utmost discretion, mind. We don't want to aggravate anyone, especially since the boss'll be asking for local government's collaboration.' Sanderson glanced at Jemima who was brimming with excitement to see what role she might play, but he turned away. 'Erm, and the rest of us will just have to keep eyes and ears open, and... not get in the way.' He cleared his throat. 'We'll be flying out to Manaus at 05:00 tomorrow, arriving around 23:00, when we'll settle in and get a good night's sleep before starting investigations early the next morning. We'll be using the PM's special jet, and the flight will take about 18 hours with one refuelling stop. I would say pack just the essentials for a tropical climate, but enough for several weeks, since we don't have much to go on...'

Undeterred, Jemima bounced up and down. 'So exciting!!' she squealed. 'I've always always ALWAYS wanted to go to the Amazon.' She clapped her hands with joy. 'You know, they say that the Amazon jungle is so vast that it's referred to as the "lungs" of the earth? Fascinating isn't it?'

'Nope,' murmured Calista under her breath. She caught Sanderson's attention. 'Are you sure Bozza said *she* should come?' she asked, nodding toward Jemima.

Sanderson blinked awkwardly. 'If you mean the PM, he was very clear.' Though his own expression showed his own disapproval.

Jemima glanced from one to the other, unfazed. 'I'm an asset to the mission,' she told them candidly. 'I can learn new languages in days, sometimes hours. I'm a probability expert, so I'll be able to mathematically pinpoint the likeliest possibilities, saving heaps of time from following dead ends. And...' she stopped to think for a moment.

'And you're an imp!' mumbled Calista under her breath, at the same time as Jemima said, 'I'm super clever!' beaming.

Jake shot Calista a warning glance. Then he turned toward Jemima. 'Jem, it's just that, well, not that you'll be a liability, but...'

'It could be dangerous,' finished Sanderson.

Jemima thought about this. 'Manaus is a city isn't it? So it's not like we'll be going into the wilds of the jungle or anything.'

'I'm talking about the actual *person* we're looking for,' said Sanderson. 'Let's put it this way... Karl König had us all duped, didn't he? We all thought he was a bit of a lost soul, and he made everyone feel sorry for him. But it turned out that his exceptional mind was also exceptionally twisted. He thought of himself as the greatest intelligence on the planet, and would stop at nothing, even murder, to get what he wanted. So, do you see now why we have to prepare for every possibility?'

Jemima fell silent for a moment, but her optimism was unfailing. 'I bet *this* Ingenious kid is good!' she said obstinately.

Sanderson visibly deflated. He started folding up the map. 'Let's hope so,' he said. 'For all our sakes.'

There came the sound of a vibrating phone, and Sanderson pulled his out, saying simply, 'Chas.' He listened to the man's urgent words, and then glared sternly at the teenagers. He put away his phone, beckoned them to follow, and quickly rushed out of the room. They were led to the operations room, filled with rows of desks and computers, where most of the workers were crowding around the large screen at one end of the room. A news reader, a stern-looking man with sallow skin, was speaking urgently. The words 'Breaking News' slid along the bottom of the screen in red.

'...seven Oxford students, all of whom were studying Genetics when they came down with the same sudden onset cancer. They all died within days of contracting the disease. Dr Peter Davids, the cancer expert who was consulted by the scientific council formed to investigate the disease, has now stepped forward saying that there are striking similarities with – and therefore, he believes, a connection between – what he alleges is a secret government project, code-named "Project Ingenious". Dr Davids claims that the project was formed to create babies genetically engineered with a genius gene. Seven in total. When asked what grounds he had to substantiate such a claim, he replied that he personally knew someone who had worked as a nurse in the laboratories, but is now retired. He alleges that the nurse, on seeing the news about the seven Oxford University students, immediately confided in Dr Davids–'

Sanderson was already on the phone to the news channel, speaking at length with urgency and barely-suppressed anger to someone high up. When he finally put down the phone, his face was bright red as he turned to the screen.

Just seconds later, the news reader suddenly faltered mid-sentence, went quiet as he listened to someone in his earpiece, and then stopped. 'I'm sorry, I'm just getting an update,' he said, thrown. 'Right, er, I've been told we need to repeat at this stage that those claims are completely unsubstantiated, and um they have neither been confirmed nor denied by Downing Street, who have yet to comment.' Glancing down, he swiped his tablet uncertainly, and then looked up again at the screen. 'Now, on to other news...'

When the teenagers turned round to Sanderson, he was shaking his head, vexed. He called across to the colleague that had alerted him. 'Chas, bring in Dr Peter Davids for questioning right away!! Oh, and see if you can find out who the hell this nurse is too!'

The man didn't need to be told twice. Going back to his desk, he started making phone calls.

'This is disastrous!' Sanderson told the three teenagers as they gravitated around him. 'That idiot, Davids, has made Project Ingenious public. The PM is not going to like this at all!'

Jake raised an eyebrow. 'That's an understatement.' He glanced across at Jemima who had gone very quiet. Drawing closer, he put an arm around her. 'You okay, Jem?'

Jemima started to nod, but then stopped, and shook her head.

Jake squeezed her shoulder. 'Nobody knows you're an Ingenious kid. And besides, we're not going to let anything happen to you, okay? I'm sure it'll blow over soon.'

Jemima sniffed. 'Y-you're right. Thanks.' But then she thought for a moment, looking worried. 'Only... things leak, don't they? And we don't know how people will react if...' She stopped, changed her thought. 'When I was little, one of my favourite films was "Beauty and the Beast", but I always hated the part where the villagers turned on the Beast,' she said, looking up at Jake. 'It's human nature isn't it? For people to be afraid of – even hate – the things they don't understand.'

There was nothing Jake or anyone could say to that.

Jake squeezed her shoulder again, and kissed her head of shiny golden hair. She somehow smelled of both peaches and innocence.

2 LEONARDO IN DA HOUSE

Later that day, Jemima was in the kitchen at Avernus setting up equipment that looked very much like a chemistry experiment.

Donning safety glasses, she used a Bunsen burner to heat up and bend long, thin glass tubing. Then she clamped together a round-bottomed water-filled Florence flask to a laboratory stand, with, at the other end, an upside-down glass funnel encased in a paper filter, inside a second flask. All connected with glass tubing and sealed with rubber stoppers.

Dr Dan Fargo came rushing into the kitchen only to stop in his tracks when he saw Jemima's apparatus. 'What on earth are you doing?' he asked, drawing closer.

Jemima flashed him a grin and positioned the Bunsen burner underneath the water-filled flask, and then spooned brown granules in the other flask. 'Making the best coffee you ever tasted!'

Fargo raised an eyebrow. 'There *is* a coffee machine you know…'

'No there isn't,' said Jemima, leaning elbows on the table and cupping her face as she watched the water boil with keen interest. 'It broke. Hence, this little makeshift invention…' Before long, the water evaporated from the first flask, bubbled into the second one, where she mixed the coffee grounds into the boiling water, and then turned off the Bunsen burner. The vacuum that was created soon pulled the filtered coffee back into the Florence flask – and when it finished dripping, she put on oven gloves, detached the flask, and poured half into an insulated travel mug, and half into a cup. After screwing the top onto the mug, she handed it to the doctor. 'Here you go! A straight black Americano to go. And I defy you not to love it!' she said excitedly.

The doctor smiled and took the container. 'You know how fussy I am when it comes to coffee…'

'I defy you!' she repeated, beaming.

'I'm late, so I'll tell you my verdict later,' he said, already on his way out. 'And thank you!!'

The doctor rushed along several corridors, calling out, 'Jasmine, what time is it?'

'It's 13:08, Dr Fargo, and you are late for your rounds with nurse Hale. She is waiting for you in the medical room.'

He rushed through several dimly-lit corridors until he finally reached an open door that glowed with light. Inside he found not only the nurse, but also Professor Wolff sitting on a gurney. She was unwrapping blood-stained bandages from his hand. She sucked in breath. 'That does look sore, Professor,' she said, stooping closer to inspect it. 'Thankfully it's not very deep.' She looked up to find Dr Fargo entering. 'Ah here's the man himself! Dr Fargo, the Prof cut himself on some broken glass. Do you want to take a look?'

The doctor glanced over her shoulder. 'No, I'll let you handle it. She's got a much better bedside manner than me, Harry!' he quipped with a smile. But the Professor did not answer. The doctor sat down and took a sip of the coffee. It was good! But then he noticed the Professor's grim expression. 'Is everything okay, Harry?' Again, the old man did not respond.

The nurse took advantage of the fact that the Professor was blind, and she gently shook her head at the doctor, before cleaning the wound and putting on fresh gauze and bandages. Finally, she said, 'All done! Now I think I'll leave you two to have a chat.' She patted the old man's arm gently, before shooting a knowing glance at Dr Fargo.

The doctor put the coffee down, and gently sat next to him – the gurney creaked in protest. 'What's wrong, Harry?'

Silence.

Dr Fargo realised he needed to do the talking. 'It might be a bit of a stab in the dark, but I think I understand. You've been through a heck of a lot. Karl's... suicide, the death of V1, V3 still in coma. And now Tai.' The doctor looked down at the floor, trying to find the words. 'I honestly can't imagine what you must be feeling. But... well, I just want you to know that you're not alone. And I'll do anything I can to–'

'Eleven years...' said the Professor finally. He caught a choke in his throat and looked up – his blank, red-rimmed eyes staring just to the side of the doctor. 'Eleven years ago, today, my wife and son died.' He pronounced every word slowly, starkly. The weight of them hung in the air. 'Killed!' he said forcefully, making Dr Fargo jump. 'Murdered in cold blood!'

'Do you... know that for sure?' asked Dr Fargo cautiously.

The Professor closed his eyes and heaved a juddered sigh. 'Yes, I do. The fire happened a year after we fled. And before that, years before, when I tried to talk with the heads of Project Ingenious, tried to shut the whole thing down because of the *tremendous* cost to human life, I was told in no uncertain terms that if I valued my family, and my life, I needed to keep going...' The Professor baulked and turned away. 'And they got away with it,' he said quietly, seething. 'They got away with murder. And... and I want revenge. They have to pay for what they've done.' He was clenching his fists, making the pain in his hand throb even more. But he didn't care.

'I'm sorry, Harry,' said Dr Fargo. 'But this thing that you've been harbouring all these years... it's eating away at you. And my concern is that if you don't let go, it'll hurt you more than it hurts them.'

'Let go?!' said the Professor, as if he'd mentioned the absurd. 'And how do you propose I do that, hmm? The only resolution is to excise the evil. Cut it out. Like cutting out a cancerous growth, a malignant tumour. Only then will the world be a much better place.'

Dr Fargo stiffened. 'Are you suggesting murder, Harry?'

'I'm suggesting the execution of justice.'

'And will that make you feel better? Becoming like them?'

'I... I won't know till it happens,' the old man sniffed. 'But I think it might.'

'I beg to differ,' said Dr Fargo, suddenly sad that his dear friend was so consumed with hatred. 'I have a feeling that it will only make you feel worse. Much worse.'

'Then we must agree to disagree.'

The doctor sighed. 'That we must...' he said quietly, trailing off. He had known and admired the Professor for decades, since the time when he was a respected and well-known geneticist, when he could see. And even after the Professor became blind, he was still one of the most insightful men he knew, who had an uncanny knack for seeing far beyond the obvious. But now, now that he was alone, and empty, after years of simmering with rage, was he becoming blind in other ways too? Blind to his own faulty reasoning, blind to what hatred was doing to him?

In time, Dr Fargo stood up and looked around for where he'd put his coffee. It was on a shelf next to a neat row of box files. He reached for it, and left. Leaving the Professor alone with the bitter company of his rage.

•••————————————————————•••

Mei Hui and Milly were in the BC, playing with the kittens, though not in the usual way one would play with cats – throwing little tinkly balls, or dragging string for them to pounce on. The girls were experimenting with Milly's newfound 'ability'. She had discovered weeks ago, whilst reminiscing with her father about family photos, that she could put images and memories into other people's minds. And she practised doing this now with the young cats. Their adoptive mother, named 'Dog' by Tai, for lack of inspiration, quietly watched over them.

The girls had placed five different objects about five metres away and a ruler's length apart: a cup, a pen, a screwed-up ball of paper, a book, and a paperweight. They sat on the floor cross-legged, with the powder-ginger Missy Mop and her striped brother, Treacle, nestled in Milly's legs, while black Max with his white socks, grey-striped Olly, and the rather round marmalade Pasha were with Mei Hui. Milly gently tapped each of them on the head in quick succession with an index finger, implanting a different image in their minds. The fluffy little creatures immediately stopped what they were doing, as if they'd just thought of something, and then began looking around. When they saw their given object, they scrambled out over the girls' legs and proceeded to bounce over to them in straight lines. Their mother, who was lying on the floor, perked her head up and followed their progress with interest.

As they neared their targets, both Mei Hui and Milly became more and more excited, and when Treacle reached the screwed-up ball of paper first, Milly raised her hands in triumph. 'Yay!!' she shouted. 'Treacle's won!! Which means we're at a draw, three wins each.' The kitten began batting the paper with its paw, starting a chase with the others.

Mei Hui frowned. 'No, it is not a draw. You have won only two games. I have won three.'

Milly stopped, puzzled. 'Oh yeah. Okay… so, best of seven?' She started to get up, but Mei Hui asked her, 'Are you okay, Milly?' – and she sat back down. 'I'm fine!'

'It is just that… your memory is usually flawless. You have an encyclopaedic knowledge, but you just got a simple score wrong.'

Milly glanced from the kittens to Mei Hui. 'I'm okay, honestly. Just didn't think.'

Mei Hui paused, finally accepting her answer. 'Fine,' she said. 'We can do best of seven.'

Just then, they heard a shout from outside in the corridor. Dog had already jumped up and was bounding out, and the girls followed her. They ran around several corners until they reached the source of the noise, close to their bedrooms. The Chauffeur was making loud guttural noises with his throat, clearly upset, while Brian – Milly's father – was trying to calm him down.

'What is it?' asked Milly, with Mei Hui behind her.

Brian motioned to the wall. 'Graffiti,' he said, glancing from the Chauffeur to Mei Hui. 'All over the wall. Someone's got hold of a black marker and gone mad.'

The girls stepped back to view the wall in its entirety. It was covered with cursive, neatly written script – yet there was something odd about the writing.

Brian tilted his head. 'Is it… is it English?' he asked, confused. He went closer to inspect it. 'Actually, it looks like Italian, but *weird* Italian.' He scratched his head; something was bugging him.

The Chauffeur – a neat freak – was visibly upset that the wall had been vandalised, even though it was beautifully handwritten and perfectly executed, so that each quote was centred in a montage. He disappeared to get some bleach and cleaning cloths, huffing as he went.

Brian stepped closer and rubbed one of the letters with a finger. 'It's permanent marker as well.'

Mei Hui followed him, inspecting the words close up. 'It looks like it's written back to front.'

Brian had an idea and disappeared around the corner for a few moments, to get something from the bathroom. A shaving mirror. When he returned, he held it up to the wall, and looked at the words in the reflection. 'It's mirror writing!' he said triumphant. He read some lines out loud:

'*Chi poco pensa, molto erra.*

La saggezza è figlia dell'esperienza.

Una volta che abbiate conosciuto il volo, camminerete sulla terra guardando il cielo, perché là siete stati e là desidererete tornare.'

His pronunciation was good. 'I did Italian at uni,' he said, always happy whenever he could make use of the language.

'So what does it mean?' asked Mei Hui, curious.

'Ah, right – it means:

He who thinks little, errs much.

Wisdom is the daughter of experience.

For once you have tasted flight you will walk the earth with your eyes turned skywards, for there you have been and there you will long to return.'

To Brian, it all seemed so familiar somehow... And then he remembered, gulping nervously. 'It's <u>Leonardo da Vinci</u>!' he said, astonished. The hand holding the mirror dropped by his side, and he quickly turned to look in the same direction that the Chauffeur left. 'I, er... I think I'll go and help the Chauffeur get the cleaning stuff,' he said, and quickly scuttled after him.

Mei Hui glanced at Milly, who was standing further back, near the turning of the corridor – half in shadow, hands thrust casually into her jean's pockets.

'It is strange, isn't it?' said Mei Hui thoughtfully, her eyes scanning the full expanse of wall with quote after quote. She counted that there were 15 of them, and they were all written meticulously.

Dog, who had been sitting quietly, stood up, sniffed the wall, and then went over to Milly.

The girl had a blank expression on her face as she pulled out a hand and stroked Dog's head casually. Her fingers marked with smudges of black ink.

The next morning, Dr Fargo was with Tai, giving him a check-up as quietly as possible; his mother was still sleeping in a corner of the room, snuffling lightly.

Tai was sitting up, slumped, and staring blankly ahead, eyes half closed. He looked frail, withered, and pale, as if dried and bleached by the sun. Gaia came in with a breakfast tray. 'Oh, I'm sorry–'

'No problem!' whispered the doctor, tilting his head toward Tyaishia.

'Ah, I'll be quiet,' Gaia whispered as well, leaving the tray on the bed-table. She stood back, hands on hips. 'How are you Tai?' she asked softly.

The boy turned his head slowly toward her, eyebrows slanting almost apologetically. 'I feel... tired. Everything aches.' His voice was lower and huskier. Even the way he blinked seemed painful.

Gaia nodded, concerned. 'Sounds like rheumatism or arthritis,' she said, stretching her fingers open and closed. 'I've had it for years myself, in my hands and wrists especially. It aches even now. Horrible isn't it, but I have to say you're doing amazingly well!'

Tai didn't feel as if he was. He glanced at the doctor. 'What we were talking about before... can you tell me?' he asked in earnest. 'I want to know.'

Dr Fargo had taken his blood pressure, and was scribbling the results in a chart. He looked at Tai, and gave in. 'It... it's difficult to predict. But with all the readings, I would say that... physically, your body is the same as that of a 65-year-old,' he said, eyes creasing with concern.

Tai nodded slowly, though he felt more like 165. Dull eyes glossed over the food in front of him – he was only mildly hungry, but even the thought of lifting the spoon to eat the porridge seemed a task.

'But I've got good news!' Dr Fargo told Tai, determined to keep upbeat in this extraordinary situation. 'We've been able to recruit Dr Vadim Vassiliev to work on the cure for you and the others. He's the best of the best in the field of genetic disease and curative therapies – and we are very lucky to have him. It took a while because of all the, er, red tape... but he was flown over from Russia three days ago, and settled in a secure location by the British government. He's gathering a hand-picked team, and they're setting up custom laboratories as we speak. Karl's scientific expertise was incredible, complex, ground-breaking – and Dr Vassiliev is the one person in the world who has the expertise and the know-how to be able to complete the cure for your disease. And I'm very, very hopeful that it can also help with... with whatever's happened to you, Tai.' He smiled kindly. But then he thought of something. 'I've been meaning to ask. How on earth did this happen? Understanding might help.'

Tai's eyes slowly slid across to his mother's sleeping form. He watched her quietly for several seconds, tenderness softening his features. 'Ma,' he said, dampness glistening in his eyes. 'They told me she was dying. So... when I visited her, held her hand, I willed and willed with all my might for her to get better. I...' he looked down briefly, silent tears slipping over mottled cheeks. 'I wanted her to wake up, wanted her to live.' His softly-spoken words were like tumbling feathers.

Gaia melted and hugged him. His frame was skeletal, barely anything there. 'You gave her part of you, Tai,' she sniffed, pulling away. 'You didn't realise, but you gave her life.'

Tai stared at his mother's sleeping form, as she lay slumped in the armchair, a blanket pulled right up to her chin. She was snoring.

He had made the ultimate sacrifice, even though he had no idea what he was doing. His mother was a strong and often scary woman, but Tai did not need to wonder whether she really loved him or not, despite her flaws and her hot temper, her moods and her depression – because he knew, and had always known, that her love for him was so fierce that she would die for him.

And it was because of that unuttered, unbreakable bond, that Tai in turn had responded with the same strength of feeling toward her. Though he hadn't realised what he was doing. Such was his naivety. The boy's love for his mother had cost him dearly.

3 THE HALF MAN

Jake wandered along one of the corridors, carrying a large plant pot with a mass of delicate blue flowers in his arms, preoccupied and mumbling to himself. Jemima came across him as she was walking back to her room, intending to finish packing. She stopped and examined the flowers. 'Oh no! They're wilting,' she said, concerned.

'Aren't they! I've tried everything to keep them going, but they still look really sorry for themselves – so I thought I'd try putting them somewhere with a bit more light, like–'

'The pool room!' said Jemima at the same time as Jake. She touched one of the leaves, stroking it thoughtfully. It felt fuzzy and prickly.

'What's wrong?' asked Jake, noticing her faraway look.

Jemima blinked and looked up at him. 'I... er, nothing.' She smiled. 'Come on, I'll help you find a nice spot for them.'

The teenagers had the habit of swimming early every morning, not just for the exercise, but to lap up the serene beauty of the room – with a water feature cascading down the furthest wall, and a transparent ceiling that was also the bottom of the small lake above. Koi fish flitted in peach-gold flashes through the lake water – and the Ingenious children had discovered an unusual side-effect of their abilities in that the fish were drawn to them, like iron filings toward a magnet, following them around as they swam.

They trailed after Jemima now, as she and Jake walked around the pool, feeling for any draughts and looking up at the light filtering through the lake water above. She at last settled on a ledge in one of the walls that was both shielded by a lush Areca palm, as well as benefitting from a cast of sunlight. 'Here!' she proclaimed, looking from the ledge to Jake who had just caught up with her. 'They'll get sunshine most of the day, and it's not too draughty from the aircon.' She took the pot from Jake, who didn't let go because it was heavy – and together they placed it carefully on the ledge.

He stepped back to admire it. 'Hope they do better here,' he told her.

Jemima felt somehow drawn to the flowers – the vibrant ragged blue petals contrasting with the deep green stems. She stroked one of the leaves. 'They're gonna do just fine. I think.' And then she stopped again.

'What is it?' asked Jake. 'You look kinda funny.'

'I... I don't know how to explain it,' she said thoughtfully. 'I just feel odd every time I touch them. And... I know this is going to sound bizarre, but numbers keep popping up in my head.'

'Huh!' said Jake, eyebrows raised. 'I think you've been spending too much time with your nose buried in maths books all day.'

Jemima shrugged it off and play-punched his arm. 'Well, maths books are a gazillion times better than *Celeb* magazine!!'

Jake spluttered. Gossipy celebrity and fashion magazines were not exactly his thing. He only browsed through them together with Calista because she loved them so much, and he was trying to take an interest in the things *she* enjoyed, like any good boyfriend. 'It's more interesting than you think!' he said defensively. 'You should try reading one. You, er, might learn a thing or two about fashion,' he said cheekily, eyeing her scruffy jeans and sloppy blue jumper.

Jemima punched him harder.

'Ow!! That really hurt,' he cried, drawing back and holding his arm.

She began walking away. 'Boohoo!' she smirked, sticking out her tongue at him before leaving.

Jake watched her go, then turned back to the pot of cornflowers. They somehow looked brighter than before. He hoped that it wasn't just his imagination, hoped that it was a good sign. He leaned in and kissed one of the flower heads softly. 'I'll be back as soon as I can,' he told them with a hushed voice. 'So don't die on me...' He caught a choke in his throat. *She* had died a long time ago. Kara, his sister. Her ashes buried in the field, in the soil beneath the flowers, their roots absorbing her. 'Just... stay alive,' he said firmly. He stared at them one last time, before leaving.

•••——————————————————————•••

The Chauffeur, Gaia, and Dr Kendra were having a heated conversation in the den, in near silence. Or rather, it was mostly the Chauffeur signing to the doctor, trying to talk to him in a huff – his usually pale face was bright red. But the Chauffeur was getting more and more frustrated as it became clearer that Dr Kendra wasn't taking anything in. The old man just sat in his armchair – a vacant expression on his face as he hummed quietly to himself.

After a while, Gaia held the Chauffeur's arms down, stopping him from signing. The Chauffeur tried to shrug her off, but she kept firm hold. When he stilled, she eventually let go and signed to him: *No good. He doesn't understand. His mind... it's not there. It hasn't been for a long time.*

The Chauffeur looked from her to Dr Kendra, vexed. There was so much he wanted to tell him. But it was no use, he had left it too late.

Just then, Calista came running into the den, wide-eyed and anxious. 'Chauffeur!!' she cried, panicked, and tapping frantically at her bare wrist. 'The time! Bozza's coming in an hour. We need to start prepping now!!'

Earlier that day, Calista had bumped into the PM on her way out of Downing Street, and as usual she'd talked nearly non-stop to him about the mission to the Amazon, and how wonderful it was to have Jake back, even if he did bring with him that little blonde gremlin. And she told him that, thanks to the Chauffeur, she'd mastered the art of cooking. Well, she'd mastered ramen soup noodles at least. And to think she used to be crazy about pot noodles! Then she went into intricate detail about how the secret was in simmering a soup stock for hours to get maximum flavour out of the bones and meat and vegetables, with ginger, star anise, and other spices, to give it that umami depth. It was delicious! And he definitely had to come round to try it sometime.

The PM nodded copiously as he listened to her talking at a hundred miles an hour, eyes magnetising now and then to his wristwatch. He had a ton of matters of national importance on his agenda still to get through – and here was Calista chattering on about noodles. Feeling slightly desperate, he blurted out, 'I'd love that!' And then added, 'When there's an opening in the diary, of course.'

His secretary – who was standing next to him, and smiling at Calista – said, 'Actually, there's an opening tonight, sir.' She winked at Calista. They had already become firm friends, comparing nail varnish colours, and giving each other make-up and hair tips.

'You'll come?' she asked the PM with imploring eyes, and he melted.

'Yes, yes, of course I'll come,' he said, making a mental note to cancel his night off. He had been hoping to catch a film with his wife, and have his favourite dinner of bangers and mash, and maybe even a slice of Victoria sponge. But it would have to be postponed.

Calista turned to the secretary, 'You're invited too, Bev – tonight at seven okay?'

The secretary shook her head regretfully. 'Sorry, babe, but we've already been invited by the in-laws – or should I say, the outlaws!' The two started cackling hysterically.

Calista had an after-thought and turned back to the PM. 'Oh, and Boz, bring the missus. She's gonna love my food!' She ruffled his messy ash-coloured hair on impulse. 'And… you can bring wots-'is-chops if you want.' She said this a little hesitantly, she had never really liked babies. They were loud, noisy, demanding.

The PM raised an eyebrow. 'Do you mean my son?' he asked, trying to finger-comb his hair back into place.

She nodded.

The PM made another mental note to ask his wife. Even though he wielded immense power as England's political leader, *she* was the boss at home…

And so, that evening, the PM came with his wife and son to Avernus, bearing gifts of custard tarts baked by the Downing Street cook, flowers, and a bottle of wine. Despite a red-faced Calista working herself into a frenzy preparing everything with the Chauffeur beforehand, they eventually sat down to bowls of delicious noodles, in a flavoursome broth, garnished with slices of tender pork, shiitake mushrooms, green vegetables, and a perfectly cooked egg. The PM and his wife declared it was the best ramen they had ever eaten, and Calista beamed at the Chauffeur sitting next to her.

But the Chauffeur, who was usually greatly pleased when everyone enjoyed their food, was instead troubled and distracted. When the dishes were cleared, and everyone was sitting around chatting quietly to each other, Calista caught the Chauffeur's attention, and signed to him. 'What's wrong?'

The Chauffeur huffed, and glanced across at Dr Kendra sitting in his wheelchair. Gaia was taking care of him as usual, putting a glass of water to his lips for him to drink, then tenderly wiping the sides of his mouth with a napkin. The doctor's expression was deadpan, eyes staring straight ahead, completely blank. He had deteriorated rapidly in the last few weeks. *I'm frustrated*! signed the Chauffeur frantically. Calista looked confused and shook her head – she'd learnt a few signs, but not enough to understand. He took Calista's hand and led her across to Gaia, tapping the woman's shoulder. When Gaia turned, he signed to her: *My story, I want to tell* – and he pointed at Calista.

Gaia looked at him, surprised. *Now?* she signed back, flustered, glancing around at the others.

The Chauffeur followed her gaze to find that everyone had stopped talking, and were one and all watching them.

He repeated his signs to them as well. *My story, I want to tell!* he told them defiantly.

Gaia interpreted. 'He wants to tell you his story,' she told the guests apologetically.

The PM nodded his understanding. 'Please, don't mind us,' he said, graciously. 'The poor chap is clearly troubled.'

Gaia indicated to the Chauffeur to go ahead, and he took her hand and kissed it in thanks. They stood opposite each other. His cheeks burnt red hot as he thought for a few seconds, glanced at Gaia, and then launched into a flurry of signs. Eyes sparkling, impassioned facial expressions, and emitting gurgles of emotion from his throat. Gaia interpreted out loud for everyone.

I was born as a half, the Chauffeur told them.

He paused, took a deep breath, and continued.

The other half of me – my twin sister – had the better deal. He looked at Calista – her lovely, expectant face reminded him so much of her. *My sister, she was so beautiful – made your heart stop. She had a captivating smile, and infectious laughter. She found even the smallest things fascinating. Her skin was like porcelain, grey eyes, and wild hair the same colour as a buttercup. Unlike me, she could hear. And people were drawn to her.*

The Chauffeur seemed to come alive as he explained, like a mime artist acting out a drama.

If I were born whole, just me, I would have been lost. But my sister led me, throughout our childhood. I followed her around like a puppy. She lit the way ahead, like a flame in a dark tunnel. She too had no name, because when we were born, we had been abandoned by our birth mother. Not in a nice clean hospital, where people could find us, look after us. No! She left us in a dirty drain, on a night raging with storm, in the middle of winter. Without even something to wrap around us, something to keep us warm and dry. We were tossed away, and left to die. I was told that when they found us, we didn't even have the energy to cry.

Over the years we were looked after by many different people and families – I lost count of the number of homes we stayed in.

Different people called us different names, but they were not our names.

They soon realised I could not hear and could not speak. I had stopped my ears to shut out the world. And I also had nothing to tell it. I only had eyes for my sister, my beloved sister. But in time, for some reason that I still do not understand, she was taken away from me! The Chauffeur extended his arm, reaching out to someone who was not there, a pained expression on his face. But he quickly snatched his hand back, closed his eyes briefly, and continued signing – slower now, as if each movement wracked him with pain.

Suddenly my world was empty, dark. I was lost. I was just 10, but didn't want to live a minute longer. Not without her. Mute, I could not call for her, could not cry for her – deaf, I was unable to listen for her return... Instead, one night, I locked myself in the bathroom, filled the bath to the top, and slipped my head under the water. I watched the air bubbles from my mouth drift up, like heaven was calling them. Calling me.

Of course, it did not work. They smashed open the door and pulled me out. They made sure that in the next house, they only had showers, and all the sharp knives were out of reach. Again, I was passed from place to place. No-

one really wanted half a boy that could not hear, could not speak.

Time passed, and entire silent years came and went. Slowly, so slowly.

One day, I was surprised to come back from school to find Dr Kendra and Gaia, waiting in the sitting room. I remember Gaia's smile – it lit up the whole room.

Gaia put a hand on the Chauffeur's arm, overcome. She took a deep breath and signed to him. *I want to tell them the story from here,* she said. And the Chauffeur paused, but then nodded. She managed to compose herself, and continued signing for the benefit of the Chauffeur, even though he could read lips. She wanted him to understand every detail of what she was about to say. He already knew the story as a child – scraps gleaned here and there – but she wanted to tell it now in its entirety, hoping that his understanding as an adult would give him resolution.

Gaia signed and spoke out loud at the same time: *My brother and his wife had adopted the Chauffeur's sister. The adoption agency didn't tell them she had a brother... They had no idea. They could not conceive, and desperately wanted a child. My sister-in-law especially. As soon as they saw the little girl, they fell in love instantly. They called her Charlotte, or Charlie. As the Chauffeur said, Charlie was beautiful, a little angel. In the beginning she was very quiet, and kept to herself. But as the years passed, and she grew, she became angry, bitter, wild. Blaming them, her adoptive parents, for taking her away from her brother. Things got worse, and as a teenager she became uncontrollable and rebellious. They sent her to a very good private school, in the hope that it would calm her. But she fell in with the wrong crowd – began to smoke, binge-drink, take drugs. Her parents were at their wits' end, and I tried to help, by being a go-between. Somehow, she felt she could talk to me. But then, one day, I got a call – she had overdosed on drugs. Her so-called friends had vanished, abandoning her after calling the ambulance. And my brother and his wife, and I, stayed at her bedside in hospital all night. We were beside ourselves. But when my brother and his wife went out to get us some food, some drink, Charlie woke up and whispered in my ear, asking me to find her brother...*

Gaia faltered, crippled by emotion.

But the Chauffeur squeezed her arm, telling her he would continue. Though they took a minute until she was ready. When he resumed, his signs were slower, subdued, less expressive. *They eventually found me and brought me to her...*

It was a simple grave. A plain headstone engraved with a name I did not recognise. The earth smelled fresh, and I sprinkled flowers across the bed of soil. They were just dandelions that I had picked, the last one plucked from the grass next to her grave. She loved dandelions and their clocks – the little seeds, like tiny fairies, floating through the air. She used to tell me that it made her happy to watch them go free, disappearing into the sky. I like to think I made her happy in the end by bringing her her favourite little flowers. Now she is free too. He paused, and smiled sadly at Gaia. *So now you know why I am like this. Because I am an incomplete half. A child without natural parents, a twin without a sibling. A man with no name... You see, in my mind, only my natural mother knows my name, and only she can tell me it.*

Gaia shook her head at him. *We, we took you home after we brought you to Charlie's grave,* she signed firmly. *We fostered you. I am your mother, Axel is your father.*

The Chauffeur took her hand and squeezed it affectionately. *I know,* he told her. *I know now. But back then I was a teenager – angry, always angry. I took out that anger on both of you. And that is why I feel frustrated now, because when I left home, I remember, the last thing I told you was that... that... I hated you, and never wanted to see you again. That is the last thing Axel remembers of me. But... I'm so, so sorry I said that. It was my anger talking, my grief. I've been trying to tell him that. Axel. Trying to explain. But he doesn't understand. I want him to understand.*

Gaia stepped closer. *He knows,* she insisted. *He knows!*

But the Chauffeur looked at the old man half asleep in his chair, his head flopping to one side, a line of drool escaping over dry lips. *He does not,* signed the Chauffeur shaking his head. *I left it too late.*

Just then, the baby – who was nearly falling asleep – suddenly startled himself with a jolt, and began crying. Not a soft, mewling cry, but loud siren-like wails. His mother jumped up and took him from the PM's arms, rocking him to and fro, trying to calm him. But he wouldn't stop. 'I-I think he's unsettled at being somewhere new,' she told them, flustered.

Dr Kendra was startled by the crying and began looking around in agitation. He hadn't heard the sound of a baby for a long time, and the loudness of it alarmed him. He started shouting, and attempted to climb out of his wheelchair. Quickly the Chauffeur went over and tried calming him, but he wouldn't have it. He and Gaia surrounded the wheelchair, just as some of the others surrounded the baby. 'I'd better go and warm up his milk bottle,' said the mother, looking around, and then quickly thrusting the baby on the nearest person. Calista – who was still emotional after hearing the Chauffeur's story – took the child reflexively, holding him at arm's length, horrified.

Jake was amused. 'He's not radioactive, Cal,' he smiled, making wide eyes at the baby. 'Try cuddling him.'

But she just stared at the baby, and the baby, with its shock of frizzy hair like his father's, suddenly quietened as he stared back at her. The two of them took in every detail of each other's face, the infant with subdued awe, and Calista with alarm. 'What do I do!' she cried, panicked.

The baby hiccoughed, startling Calista, who almost dropped him.

The PM jumped up. 'Careful!' he cried, and gently took his son, kissing his head. But the child kept his eyes fixed on Calista. The PM grinned. 'He's totally smitten with you, Cali.'

Calista shivered, glad to have been relieved of her charge. 'I'm sorry. Never have been keen on babies.'

Jake stopped and looked at her with surprise, maybe even a hint of disappointment.

'What's wrong?' Calista asked him.

Jake looked away. 'Nothing,' he said.

But Calista couldn't help feeling that somehow she had let him down.

Meanwhile, the Chauffeur had wheeled Dr Kendra to his room, and managed to tuck him into bed, despite his agitation. The old man lay on his side, mumbling, as the Chauffeur busied himself, going around and tidying the room. Gaia had gone off to get them a little night-cap, saying that it helped Axel sleep – but the Chauffeur knew she needed it just as much to calm her own nerves.

The Chauffeur's world was completely silent, and as he put away clothes, and slipped books back onto shelves, and objects into drawers, he did not realise that Dr Kendra was mumbling at him, trying to tell him something. Eventually a missile hit the Chauffeur's shoulder, startling him – and he saw that it was a slipper, falling to the ground. He stopped, confused, and looked over at Dr Kendra – who was glaring angrily, looking directly at him. Hands poised, in front of him. The doctor glanced down at them as though they were foreign objects – moving of their own accord, like he had no control, fingers and hands coming together to make signs, forming words.

Transfixed, the Chauffeur drew closer and watched.

Not half, signed Dr Kendra, hardly understanding what was happening. *Not half!* He glanced up – but the Chauffeur shook his head, none the wiser.

Frustrated, Dr Kendra tried again. *You, not half man. You, whole man. Not half. Whole!*

Suddenly the Chauffeur worked it out, and his face melted with emotion. The doctor must have seen him tell his story in the dining room. He had been watching, and had understood!

The old man's hands were still moving. *I know,* he told the Chauffeur. *I know… you love me, love Gaia. I know you don't hate.* He glanced at his hands as they slowly formed the last words. *You. My son. Love.* He paused, looked up at him, then repeated the last sign three more times – eventually lying back from exhaustion.

The Chauffeur blinked in disbelief, then launched himself on the old man, hugging him tenderly. Decades of worry and anguish and self-torment suddenly fell away. He felt as though his heart might burst!

Gaia entered the room with a tray in hand, and was surprised to find the Chauffeur smothering her husband in a hug. She watched with bated breath as her husband's startled arms eventually relaxed and closed around the Chauffeur's shoulders, embracing him in return.

'If there's no love,

what then?'

Leonardo da Vinci

4 $3,396.5^2$

After the PM and his family had left, an uncanny silence descended on Avernus. Jemima had already finished packing, and as was her usual way of an evening, she had taken a stack of mathematics books from the BC and was reading them in the den with some of the kittens curled around her feet. Suddenly she stopped what she was doing, thought for a while, and then picked up one of the kittens and put it on her lap. Treacle hardly liked to be separated from his sister, Missy Mop, but the warmth of the fire made him drowsy, and so he curled up and promptly fell asleep. Jemima stroked his thick fur, with a thoughtful, wondrous expression – as if she had never stroked a cat before. Before long, his sister, Missy Mop, jumped up onto Jemima's lap as well, meowing loudly. She curled up next to her brother. And Jemima stroked her too.

Jake was helping Calista pack – she hadn't travelled much, and so far, all she had put in her bag was a pair of faux leather leggings, a polyester top, her make-up, a brush, hair-straightening tongs, 'Louboutain' heels, and a 'Chivenchy' quilted handbag – her usual market-bought faux designer bargains. Jake glared down at everything laid out in the suitcase on her bed. 'Babe, we're not going for a night out on the town, we're going to the Amazon.'

Calista nodded thoughtfully and then went off to return a few seconds later with some deodorant. She zipped it into her cosmetic bag. 'Anything else?' she asked.

Jake sighed with a smile, and went over to her wardrobe. 'May I?' he asked, and Calista nodded her consent. He began rummaging around and pulled out several items of light cotton clothing, sensible shoes, and a rucksack. He brought them over to the bed, took out most of the items already in the bag, and they sat down and began folding and re-packing together as they chatted excitedly about the trip.

Mei Hui was walking through the corridors on her way to find the Professor. As she passed a particular section, she stopped to look at the wall. Though the Chauffeur had scrubbed it thoroughly with bleach, faint outlines of handwriting were still visible. She remembered how Dog had sniffed the wall and then gone over to Milly, sniffing her hand too. And when they were playing 'mind game races' with the kittens that same day, she'd noticed black stains on Milly's fingertips. For a while now, Mei Hui had been feeling uneasy about Milly, sensing the beginnings of something new, something not right, brewing beneath the surface. And it bothered her. So she sought out the Professor now, to talk to him about it.

Jasmine had already informed her of his location, and she wondered why, of all places, the Professor would be there. But when she entered the pool room, she was instantly enveloped by a balmy warmth, smelled the lushness of palms, and heard the soft tinkle of the waterfall – and understood. The room imparted a serenity that soothed and calmed every sense. She discovered the Professor sitting back on one of the loungers, though it was clear he was not sleeping; a light crease on his forehead was reminiscent of lingering frustration.

'Professor,' said Mei Hui softly as she drew closer. She sat down on the lounger next to his. 'I wanted to talk to you about something that has been troubling me.'

The Professor sat up and faced her. 'Mei Hui,' he said, his voice slightly hoarse. He cleared his throat. 'Is there something wrong?'

'It is about Milly,' she told him.

The Professor nodded slowly. 'I... think I know.'

'The writing on the wall...'

'Yes. I already know. Brian came to me before, and told me about it himself. He told me that Milly used to write all over the walls of her bedroom in their house. One of the same quotes was also written in the corridor here. Except... then, she wrote normally, left to right. This was the first time he'd seen mirror writing.'

Mei Hui absorbed this. It confirmed her suspicions. 'I am very worried for her, Professor. She has also been spending a lot of time with V3 – and today I discovered cups left in the room. Almost all of them. On the sideboard, still filled with untouched tea.'

'That explains things...' said the Professor, fingering the lines of bandages on his hand.

'Do you think... mentally, she is deteriorating?' she asked hesitantly, in two minds as to whether she even wanted to know the answer. Whatever was happening to Milly could also happen to her.

The Professor fell silent for some time before answering. 'I'm not sure,' he said. 'It's possible...' He breathed deeply. 'I'm not going to sugar-coat this, Mei Hui. You deserve more than that. We saw... *you* saw first-hand the degeneration of Karl's mind in the last years of his life. And, what's happening to Milly – it may or may not be related. But, we don't know for sure at this stage, and we shouldn't, by any means, think that it's a foregone conclusion... However, I want you to know that we're doing everything we can to get this cure completed very soon. We have the best genetic experts, the best medical minds working on the cure as we speak. Dr Vassiliev especially, is the world's expert in the field. And I'm sure it won't be long now before they complete it...' The Professor did not want to tell her that, in reality, they had no idea how long it would take. Nobody knew. Karl had employed brand new experimental science, which required a steep learning curve even for their top scientists. They were navigating unknown scientific waters... He added quietly, 'It's something we hope will help Tai too.'

Mei Hui looked at him, taken aback. Being Chinese, she was fiercely pragmatic – and she was sure that nothing could help Tai's exceptional condition. Unless they miraculously came up with something that could  reverse or halt aging. An elixir of youth. But her own country's ancient history proved that such a thing was a myth: alchemists once sought the strange chemistry of sulphur, ground cinnabar, hematite, or even arsenic, as hypothetical possibilities to cure disease. But the potion was a myth. Of course, ingesting those elements would have had the opposite effect... causing severe illness, and even death.

But then Mei Hui realised that the Professor's words were, more than anything, wishful thinking and an inordinate desire to prolong and enhance life, just like the ancient alchemists. Thousands of years of advancement had not broken the collective human spirit, and desire, for perfect health or eternal life. A fountain of youth. And she could not deny the Professor one last straw to clutch. Hope. Even if it was a hope based on uncertainties. It was better, much better, than doing nothing, and standing idly by, watching Tai grow old, fade, and disappear.

Misinterpreting her silence, the Professor asked, 'Do you mind that you are not going with them to Brazil?'

Mei Hui came out of her thoughts and looked at the Professor. 'No,' she told him plainly. 'I do not mind. While Milly and Tai are... the way they are, I would like to stay here with them, to help where I can.'

The Professor nodded, glad. 'We certainly need you here!'

Just then, Jemima entered the room, hugging her books to her chest and yawning. 'Just wanted to say goodnight and goodbye to everybody,' she said sleepily, eyes half closed. 'We're leaving really early tomorrow.' She put her books down, and hugged first the Professor and then Mei Hui. Before they could say anything, she turned to leave, stopped, went back to pick up her books, and shuffled out – narrowly missing stumbling into the water.

Worried, Mei Hui jumped up and followed her, with the Professor not far behind.

She turned out to be on her way to Tai's room. When they entered, Tyaishia was perched on the bed, plaiting cornrows into her son's hair. She stopped when she saw Jemima. 'Yuh look tire, gyal,' she told her softly. Most of them were a little afraid of the woman – so they were surprised to hear her speak so kindly to Jemima. Though Jemima was the sort of person who could make friends with anyone.

Jemima hugged her. 'I'm leaving tomorrow,' she said, her voice muffled in the warm folds of her clothes. She pulled away and looked at Tai and his cornrows. 'Looking good!' she smiled, managing to hide the jarring sensation of seeing his hair streaked grey, and his face lined with wrinkles. She turned to Tyaishia. 'Will you do mine when we get back?'

Tyaishia stroked Jemima's golden tresses. 'Yuh hair's beautiful the way it is, gyal. Jus' get back safe though.' She threw a cutting look across at the

Professor standing by the door with Mei Hui. 'I don't know why yuh be sending a chil' out on a mission, Prof!' she told him sharply. 'Yuh cya see she just a baby!'

Jemima looked up at her, frowning. 'I'm not a baby, I've turned 14,' she protested. 'And anyway, I want to go. I've always dreamed of going to the Amazon.'

The Professor drew closer. 'I... I appreciate your concern, Tyaishia. I can assure you that there will be round-the-clock security to protect her. I wouldn't have anything less. But I'm afraid she's needed on the mission. Not only do we need an Ingenious child to help find the missing one, but I have a feeling they'll respond much better to her than to our men.'

Mei Hui drew closer. 'How are you Tai?'

He turned his head slightly – every movement he made was slow and painful. He smiled weakly, and looked up at her. 'I'm tired.' Even the colour of his eyes seemed lighter.

'Luk at him, him a mess!!' declared his mother. 'I don't know what yuh people did fi im in dem laboratories, but...' she caught a choke in her throat. 'But it bad, very bad!'

Mei Hui and Jemima looked at each other – realising that nobody had told her the reason why Tai was the way he was, because of what he had done for *her*. The Professor stiffened, and didn't respond – letting himself be the scapegoat. He knew that the truth would cripple her.

Mei Hui tried to calm her. 'It is nobody's fault, Tyaishia,' she said. 'It was an experiment gone wrong. There is a proverb that says, "He who blames others still has a long way to go on his journey, he who blames himself is halfway there, and he who blames no-one has arrived".' She glanced from Tyaishia to the Professor and back. 'Sometimes, when things go wrong, it is better to look inward and try our best to overcome the problem, rather than seeking blame.'

Tyaishia blinked at Mei Hui, and then looked at Tai, mumbling, 'Dem deh a *fi-ine* words,' she said, sneering. 'But dem nuh help mi son...' She stopped, faltered, and looked away. 'I... I'm sorry,' she said eventually, sniffing. She went to sit down on the bench against the wall, gripping the wood of the seat with tense hands. 'I'm just upset. Cya hardly tink straight. I know, Prof. I know yuh tryin' yuh best. I jus' feel so... 'elpless.'

They stayed in silence for some time, Tyaishia staring blankly at the bedframe, until at last her eyes lifted, and she looked at her son. 'Back den, I should never 'ave leave yuh, Tai, alone in di flat. But... but mi 'ad no money leave. Mi just 'ad enuff fi one train ticket to see mi Dad – mi tink him did dying. He *was* dying. Suh mi 'ad no choice but tuh lef yuh.'

Tai spoke out. 'You did what you had to, Ma,' he said, his voice hoarse.

The hard lines of Tyaishia's face suddenly softened. 'Yuh an angel, Tai. Always 'ave been. And mi, mi been a bad mada tuh yuh.'

'Ma!' protested Tai as strongly as he could muster.

'Mi kno' it,' she insisted. 'I want to tell yuh, want to explain...' She sighed, long and hard. 'Since yuh Dad did leave, mi been struggling wid depression, fi a lang lang time. Mi nuh making excuses, it just di plain of every... Di plain truth.' She glanced up at him, but quickly looked down again, at her feet, pressed hard on the floor. She didn't tell him that it started with postnatal depression. Just months after Tai's birth, she had struggled not only with constant sadness and lethargy, but also the guilt of being unable to bond with her baby. For many, the condition lasted months, but hers lasted for years, made worse by Tai's father leaving. She often wondered whether the depression was the cause of her problems, and the inability to commit to relationships, or whether all those break-ups made her depression worse. Perhaps it was a bit of both. But poor little Tai, innocent as he was, suffered throughout his childhood. He had been the casualty of her mental illness; he was the one who paid the price. Which made her hate herself even more. Yet despite everything, the miracle of it was that, when Tai looked at her, she always knew – *always* – that he loved her no matter what.

She looked at him now, as he looked at her, *her* pain in *his* eyes, and eventually said, 'Inna way, Tai, mi glad yuh neva did come wid mi upon di train. People dead. Lotsa dem. Mi, mi one o' di lucky ones – cos it a miracle mi alive. But somehow... mi nuh feel suh lucky.'

Jemima went to sit next to her and clung onto her arm. Tyaishia patted the girl's hand, and put on a brave face. 'It's late, young lady,' she sniffed. 'Guh t'bed now. Mi gonna miss yuh though.' They hugged again.

'I... I tink I'll get mi some fresh air,' said Tyaishia, getting up. The tension in her shoulders was tightening, and she needed to stretch.

They watched her leave. Then Jemima went over to Tai and hugged him very gently, nestling her head in the crook of his shoulder. The two stayed that way so long that the others wondered if they had fallen asleep. But then they heard a light whimpering sound, and Jemima eventually sat up, crying. Too upset to speak.

'W-what's wrong?' asked the Professor, turning his head this way and that to hear.

Tai, who was holding her hand, suddenly looked incredibly sad. He held his other hand out to Mei Hui – and the three of them linked together. Quietly Mei Hui absorbed what they were feeling, and her expression changed, her shoulders slumped. She turned to look up at the Professor, who had drifted next to her. 'Jemima has discovered something unusual,' she told him, eyes filling with tears as she spoke. 'She has discovered her… ability. Though it is a sad one, a very sad one. With her touch, Jemima can sense numbers that measure years, months… even seconds. In Tai's case, the number that comes to mind is…' she closed her eyes briefly. 'It is 3,396.5 to the power of 2.'

The Professor blinked, confused. 'I don't understand.'

Mei Hui explained. '3,396.5 to the power of 2 is the base and exponent expression of the number 11,536,212.25, Jemima's telling me.'

'Meaning…?' asked the Professor, impatient.

'That is the number of seconds Tai has left.'

The Professor fell deadly silent, blood draining from his face.

Mei Hui continued, catching a choke in her throat, her hand trembling within Tai's. 'In other words, Tai has just under four-and-a-half months to live…'

49

'The smallest feline is a masterpiece.'

Leonardo da Vinci

5 LYU-LYU

Dr Vadim Vassiliev was the only man on earth who could complete the cure that Karl König had started. But he was an exacting and stern man, and was feared by all and sundry.

He despised silly things like senseless small-talk, or forced laughter, or ridiculous jokes – especially in sobriety. Such trifles he considered puerile, and only just bearable after several stiff shots of vodka; at least it would all be forgotten in the morning. Vodka was like water to him, both because he depended on it so much, and also because he drank it copiously – always after work of course. He often thought to himself that the word for 'vodka', being a diminutive of the word 'water', was entirely apt. His excuse was that it greased the cogs of his genius scientific mind.

He did not look or behave like the archetypal 'scientist' – that is, absent-minded, wiry, glasses teetering on the end of the nose, and with a broad brainiac forehead. Instead, he was a tall, bulky man, with excellent eyesight, and a head of thick black hair that lowered his hairline onto a Neanderthal-looking forehead. Without his white lab coat one might easily mistake him for a bouncer at a night-club, and a low-class one at that – not the distinguished scientist that he was. But his work in the field of genetic therapies was world-famous. It was for this reason that Dr Fargo contacted him with a request to complete the cure for the Ingenious children. And the monetary incentive was great enough to make him drop everything immediately.

It had taken decades for Professor Wolff to discover that their genetic meddling with the Ingenious children's DNA also brought about a long-term disease, which caused rapid deterioration in their late teens, physically, mentally, and emotionally. Karl König, the first of the Ingenious children, had experienced this terrible degeneration for himself, and the last years of his life had been excruciatingly unbearable. Despite this, and having become dependent on drugs to see him through every minute of every day, at just 17 years old, Karl's genius had pushed the boundaries of medical and genetic science by coming up with an astoundingly brilliant cure. But his own illness was too far gone for it to be of any use to him.

And so, when Dr Vassiliev read the proposition sent by Dr Fargo to complete this ground-breaking therapy, it was impossible for him to refuse.

Saying goodbye to his family was not a problem. He was not close to his parents, established Muscovites who loved and frequented the glitterati socialite scene, rife with silly small-talk, constant joke-telling, and forced laughter – all the things he hated. He was worlds apart from them, despite living just a few roads away. And it was therefore easy for the doctor to leave his Mama and Deda.

But instead, he went to great pains to take care of a few very important requisites before he left Russia. Three, in fact. And he made absolutely sure that these essentials were able to be brought with him to England.

The first was a full case of 12 bottles of Beluga Noble vodka. It was of the finest quality, made from the purest Siberian artesian water and a special malt spirit – as smooth and rich as his uncle Dima. The second was his babushka's black bread, the best he ever tasted, made from rye flour and sourdough leaven; he packed a whole suitcase of loaves, yet still regretting that he could not take more.

The third necessity that he absolutely had to bring with him was the *most* precious.

When at last Dr Vassiliev arrived in England, and as he travelled to the secret location of his new home surrounded by a large security detail, he could not help but sniff the air as he went. Unlike sharp, cold Moscow air which, to him, smelled like a hangover in the morning, pancakes at lunchtime, and hookah water pipes in the evening – England smelled of cut grass, rain, and tea. He thought it most charming and quaint.

His new home in the country was stately and surrounded by landscaped gardens, rolling lawns, and a two-metre high wall. Beyond which sprawled a thick and sweeping forest immediately to the north, and a mile to the south a constantly rumbling motorway had been carved into the landscape – an arterial vein to London.

When he stepped out of the car he glanced back at the line of security vehicles that had parked behind his. He counted ten cars. Then he crouched down and gently slid the container with his most precious possession out of the back seat, carrying it with great care into the beautiful stately house.

As the doctor settled down to live in his new home, he very quickly established a precise routine. Every day, at exactly 8 a.m., he awoke to prepare and dress himself, and have breakfast, in order to be driven to the newly set-up laboratories at 8.45 a.m., just 15 minutes away. He was a demanding man, expecting nothing less than perfection – and so his work colleagues and fellow scientists stayed out of his way whenever possible, keeping unavoidable interactions to a bare minimum, with an economy of words so severe as to be almost monosyllabic. Even his security – burly silent men who never let him out of their sight – tended to stay as far back as possible. His scowling face, barked demands, and general unlikability made him an extremely unpleasant man to protect.

But, at the end of the day, as soon as the ferocious Dr Vassiliev entered his new home, perfectly aligned his shoes next to the door, took off his coat, and hung his keys on the hook, he melted instantly when he was greeted by the love of his life: a semi-longhaired Siberian molly cat. Her fluffy cream-coloured fur was smudged with grey on her face, and she had soft, copper-toned eyes. She came bounding up to him, and the doctor crouched right down to the floor to greet her. 'Lyu-Lyu! Lyubova moya!' he chanted warmly in an utterly silly voice for such a brawny man. Meowing sweetly, little Lyubova rubbed herself against his leg, leaving a smattering of fur on his trousers. But the doctor did not mind. He picked her up, so gently, as if she were a newborn baby – and gave her a cuddle as he took her into the kitchen to be fed. Softly setting her down on the table, he hurried to get her food as her meowing became increasingly louder.

And such was the endearing relationship between the man and his cat.

In the mornings, the doctor inevitably awoke to find the fluffy beauty lying sprawled around his head on the pillow, snuggling up to the warm nest of his thick black hair. And at breakfast, Lyubova jumped up on the table to wolf down her gourmet cat food, her dish placed next to the doctor's plate of toasted rye bread topped with poached eggs, sprigs of fennel, and a sprinkle of caviar – tiny glistening orange orbs, divided between his plate and the cat's. Even at bath-time they were inseparable. Lyubova would sit perched on the corner of the tub, mesmerised by the mass of heaving bubbles, trying to bat them with her paw. The man even heaped a 'crown' of foam on his head, giggling, childlike, as the cat tussled with the pile of bubbles. And in the evenings, there was nothing better for the doctor, after a long, hard day of experimentation in the lab, than to relax on the sofa and watch a good black-and-white Russian film – though not horror, as he was rather squeamish – with little Lyubova purring lightly on his lap, and a dry vodka martini, warm jam Pirozhkis, and cat treats always within reach.

And when the night air was clear and crisp, they loved sitting out on the roof garden together to watch the bright blanket of stars above – Lyubova perched on the table next to him, looking up. It was at wondrous, celestial moments like those when the doctor felt the urge to sing to Lyubova his favourite pesnya, <u>Rasul Gamzatov's</u> <u>Zhuravli</u>, Cranes – a famous Russian song about World War II, inspired by the monument to a young girl contaminated by radiation from the atomic bomb in Hiroshima, as they fled for their lives through an unceasing rain of black dust and ash. For them, an otherworldly end of days.

As Vassiliev and Lyubova watched the stars together in wide-eyed awe, the Russian imagined his baritone voice piercing through the velvet sky to reach those flickering stars, flying above them like a dance of tiny white cranes. As he sang – of fallen soldiers that, instead of being left to decay and moulder, were turned into a vast array of white cranes, gliding and flapping in an ashen mist – Vassiliev's tears mourned the souls of the soldiers that never returned, from every battle ground, of every war, through every era it seemed. And little Lyubova would listen quietly, watching the sky, and sniffing the air, as he sang to her.

•••———————————————•••

At the weekends, he and Lyubova enjoyed exploring the house grounds and gardens together, even venturing into the forest. The scientist would walk with hands clasped firmly behind his back, chatting constantly to the cat in Russian, as she scurried and pounced and ran alongside him. Being quite vocal herself, Lyubova always answered him with a stream of meows. The scientist told the cat about his experiments, taught her genetics, discussed the frustration of recent test failures, and bemoaned the fact that Dr Kendra was unable to help – for he so needed the man's unique expertise. He told Lyubova all this in between pointing out plants, scurrying animals, birds, and a variety of trees to her. The cat was his sounding board as he theorised, hypothesised, postulated, and planned, again and again, trying to complete the genetic therapy in his mind.

Dr Vassiliev's relationship with Lyubova was endearing and charming – they were inseparable.

One particular Monday morning, after a long night of thunder and lightning storms, a security guard got out of his car outside the stately house where the Russian was staying – surprised to find the skies miraculously clear and blue. He walked through the house grounds, yawning, yet still managing to admire the vivid green of the lawn, trees, and overgrowth smattered with a haze of shimmering dewdrops.

When he got to the door, he glanced at his watch, and counted the remaining seconds until it was 8.45 a.m. precisely. He knocked on the door for Dr Vassiliev and waited. Nothing. He listened intently but there was only silence. He knocked again and again. Uneasy, he eventually pressed on his walkie-talkie and urgently called for back-up. Opening the door with his spare key, he extracted the gun from his holster and went inside, holding the weapon in front of him. His colleagues soon followed close behind. Together they swept through the house, silently, skilfully, searching for the doctor in every room – finally reaching his bedroom. But the bed was still messy and unmade, and his slippers laid perfectly next to each other on the deep carpet pile.

But there was no sign of the man, or his cat.

The house was completely empty.

55

'Nature is the source of all true knowledge.
She has her own logic, her own laws,
she has no effect without cause
nor invention without necessity.'

Leonardo da Vinci

6 THE IMPORTANCE OF TREES

The great oak stood, a silent giant, on the outskirts of the land surrounding Avernus. The bark of its trunk was gnarled and mossed – edges swept into twists and knots as if carved by the wind. Branch arms extending heavenward.

The old tree, if it were conscious, and could speak, might have called itself 'Lore' – because it had lived an age, for well over a millennium, since Anglo-Saxon times. Yet most people passed by without giving it the merest thought, barely aware of its ancient existence until a sudden downpour sparked the need for shelter under its generous foliage. Knotty lesions in its wrinkled bark winked like eyes, and if they could see, they would have witnessed a history of wonders – life-altering, and death-dealing, and transformative things that notched and marked the course of time.

Its leaves swayed and rustled in a hollow wind, gently jolting its inhabitants – foraging squirrels extracting acorns from their cups, goat moths camouflaged within folds of bark, and lines of ants wending their way up and down the trunk. And despite the attack of weevils boring into the wood, and a smattering of bright red galls on the underside of leaves, the tree had survived, century after century – its roots reaching four times the area of the crown, and its branches creaking as they stretched.

The yawning cavity in its trunk, if it were a mouth that could speak, would have told of its brush with royalty – back in 1043, when Edward the Confessor happened to pass, a year after he had become king, on his way to St Peter's Abbey. He saw the young oak from his carriage and was so struck by it, that he had to stop, get out, and lie back between the tree's embracing roots. Lore offered the young king its beauty, to refresh his senses – and the man could not help but look up and admire the foliage above, spellbound by the interplay of the bluest sky and the whitest clouds scudding between the leaves.

In 1665 the great oak saw a mass exodus of wagons, carts, coaches, and people on foot – fleeing from the Plague and an overcrowded and unhygienic London, where tens of thousands had already died. The fatal error of culling cats and dogs, as suspected transmitters, made the rat population, and the fleas on their backs, thrive – prolonging the disease even more. And with the death rate skyrocketing, they soon began to dump one body after another under Lore's saddened boughs, until a place could be found, and a big enough hole could be dug, to bury them.

An influx of Irish immigrants in 1847, refugees from the Great Famine, brought a young newlywed couple to the area, on a balmy afternoon's stroll – the wife, heavy with child, needing to rest against its trunk. Puffing and panting with pains, her waters broke right there, and they stumbled off to seek a midwife. 18 months later they returned with twin toddlers in tow, laughing, and playing, and collecting the acorns that Lore dropped for them.

Almost 100 years after that, in 1944, the Luftwaffe blitzed the immediate area, and a flying doodlebug droned overhead, suddenly becoming silent very close to the great oak. Seconds later it exploded 30 feet away – and whistling shrapnel hurtled through the air, pelting Lore's foliage and bark, and engulfing it with huge puffs of acrid smoke. The explosion blasted a crater in the soil, exposing part of the tree's blackened old roots.

Still, the <u>majestic oak</u> had managed to survive through even that. And to this day, it stands tall and erect – a silent hero – slowly, quietly, breathing in carbon dioxide through its leaves, and exhaling life-giving oxygen in return. Purifying and enriching the air. Powered by the sun, it splits glucose to release energy for its own metabolism. And as a benevolent provider, the tree never refused any who came its way – birds, mice, beetles, squirrels, flies, slugs, butterflies and moths, bees and wasps, ants, woodlice, and fungi. Lore took them all in – he welcomed them, gave them food and shelter, and asked nothing in return.

And as Lore basked in early morning sun – wizened now, and ancient, and unapologetic for its towering presence – two adults and a teenager walked by the lake of Avernus, not far away. And they pointed excitedly at Lore.

'That one!' breathed Brian in admiration. 'That's Tai's tree. Before, when he walked the dogs, he came to the tree every day – and always stopped to hug it,' he grinned. 'Wonderful old thing, isn't it?'

Gaia turned to look. 'That it is!' she agreed. And they paused to take in its grandeur.

Brian pondered. 'Wonder how old it is. Must be ancient.'

'Some oaks live for hundreds and hundreds of years,' proffered Gaia. She remembered something. 'Actually, I think there's a Major Oak in Sherwood Forest – you know, Robin Hood country. It's about a thousand years old if memory serves me right.'

'Woah,' Brian said, amazed. But then he squinted at something in the tree's shadow. 'Did you see that?'

Gaia looked at him and looked at the tree. 'See what?'

'Milly, did you see it?' he asked his daughter.

Milly looked at the tree with disinterest. 'I can't see anything, Dad,' she said in a monotone.

'I bet it's the ninjas,' said Brian, sure of himself. 'The Prof said they're guarding us silently, hidden in the shadows. I bet they're there.'

Gaia looked at him with disbelief. 'Ninjas!!' she laughed. 'I don't think so! There's no-one there, Brian. If there were, Dog would've noticed and warned us by now.'

'Well, that's the point!' said Brian. 'Ninjas are supposed to be invisible, blending into the surroundings. So we'd never be able to see them, or detect them, not even Dog.'

Gaia looked doubtful and started walking toward the old oak. Brian and Milly followed her. Dog stopped, wondering where they were going, but she saw that her five kittens were trailing loosely behind them, so she ran to catch up.

Close to the tree, the ground dipped suddenly, in a pit of about three metres wide – there, the grass was punctuated by striated patches of exposed roots. The three picked their way across, and Gaia walked around the old oak, which was next to a high brick wall topped with barbed wire.

She stretched out both arms. 'No-one here, Brian,' she smiled. 'See?'

Brian shrugged. 'Well, might've been a squirrel then,' he said dismissively. But then he turned toward the trunk and suddenly hugged it, grinning like a Cheshire cat. 'This is for Tai. Hoping upon hope that he… he gets better soon!' His arm span barely reached a third of the diameter. And to their surprise, Milly followed suit, and hugged the tree next to him. She closed her eyes and breathed in the mossy scent of it. It seemed to calm her.

Brian and Gaia glanced at each other. Milly was becoming quieter and quieter by the day, a blank expression on her face now the norm. She had been spending far too much time in the comatose V3's room, sitting in the dark, whispering secretively to the unconscious form – it was unsettling, and they were more than a little concerned for her. She had become pale, and swung wildly between normality and withdrawing into herself. And so Gaia and Brian persuaded her every morning to join them on their walk with the animals.

Just then someone's phone started ringing. They all looked at each other, wondering whose it was. 'It's mine!' realised Brian, reaching inside his jacket for the mobile. 'Hey, Prof!' he said jovially. But his expression darkened as he listened. 'My goodness! Yes, okay. Yep, yep, got it,' he said, and then closed his phone. He looked at his daughter concerned. 'Apparently the Russian scientist working on the cure has… disappeared.'

'What!' gasped Gaia.

'We have to get back now,' he said, urgency rising in his voice. 'The Professor told me they're going out to investigate.'

Milly could not believe it. The cure the doctor had been working on was to stop the degenerative disease that had blighted Karl König, and now, maybe even her… It was the only hope for the Ingenious children of living past their teenage years and going on to lead normal lives – at least, as normal as one could, for child prodigies.

Oddly, despite the shock of the doctor going missing, a frisson of excitement shivered down Milly's spine. The thought of a mystery, a conundrum, was stimulating a response deep within her. She had felt trapped for some time now. Avernus – no matter how interesting, even with its extensive library – was becoming claustrophobic, repetitive, tedious. And for a genius, tedium and monotony were anathema. 'Investigate?' Milly repeated, intrigued.

Brian noticed the change in his daughter, and nodded. 'We'd better get back,' he said, and turned to call Dog to follow them back. He picked up two of the young cats, as did Gaia, and Milly picked up the rather round Pasha. And they hurried back to Avernus.

Before their walk, they had left Avernus silent and inactive – what with Jemima, Jake, Calista, and Acuzio having departed early that morning for their transatlantic flight, and everyone else fast asleep. But on re-entering, they found a hubbub of activity as the Professor shouted out instructions with urgency, buttoning up his shirt, but still wearing pyjama bottoms. The flustered Chauffeur was running here and there, fetching things to be packed, and Mei Hui went about calmly but quickly as she too prepared to leave. Tyaishia was shouting at the top of her lungs somewhere down the corridor.

Brian went up to the Professor with every intention on insisting that he and Milly go with them – wherever it was – to investigate the mysterious disappearance of the Russian. But as they both neared the frantic old man, he had already detected their footsteps.

'Is that you, Brian? Milly?' he asked, pushing the last shirt button in place.

'Yes, it's us,' said Brian. 'Prof, I really think that–'

But the Professor interrupted him. 'Please, there's no time to waste. You must pack your bags – both you and Milly. You're coming with us to… to the house where Dr Vassiliev was staying.'

'Right, right!' said Brian, pleased. He turned toward his daughter, but she had heard and was already leaving to get ready. Just before she turned, Brian had spotted a glint in her eyes. He knew that look. That spark of fascination, excitement. He hoped this meant a change for the better…

In time, Professor Wolff, with Mei Hui and Milly, Brian and Dog, boarded an army-green Puma helicopter, much larger than the one Milly had flown for the first time.

When Milly entered the new helicopter, she began to feel uneasy as the door closed behind them with a heavy thwack. They each found a seat. V2 suddenly appeared, stepping out of the cockpit with his usual breezy disposition, and Milly gulped. She found she could not look at him. It saved her from seeing the scars and marks on his face and hands – vestigial reminders of the fight for their lives, weeks ago. It was a fight that *she* stupidly led them into, she kept telling herself. Her stupidity had since plagued her, because it got V1 killed, and rendered V3 comatose.

V2 was talking to them all now, his voice a light drone, like background noise – something about remaining seated, and other flight stuff. But she wasn't able to absorb it, consumed as she was with guilt.

She felt a warm hand over hers. Her father, Brian, sitting next to her, recognised the turmoil she was going through, and looked at her with concern. 'It's gonna be all right, Mills,' he told her, in that low, warm voice that melted her. She caught her breath, found she couldn't speak.

Brian reached across, clicked in her seatbelt, and pulled the strap tighter. She was thinner, losing weight.

The engines fired up, and Milly clenched the armrests as they lifted off the ground and hurtled skyward.

It took just under two hours before they arrived at a large stately house in the country. The helicopter descended slowly onto a stone-paved forecourt, and the roar of the engines at last died down. On climbing out of the helicopter, the Professor was immediately met by the chief of security, David O'Connor, who led him into the house, engaging in urgent conversation as they walked together. The others followed them, looking up at the stunning building in admiration.

Where Avernus was brutalist in design, with dark, depressing décor, the house before them was pale grey and elegant, with the baroque architecture of tall pilasters crowned with curling acanthus leaves just below the architraves. The arch of the arcades mirrored the shape of the leaded dormer windows – and, right at the top, they could just about make out the balustrades of a roof garden, pinnacled at its centre by the dome shape of a stone cupola. Inside, light flooded into every room, and as they wandered through the hallway, a lounge, and then out into an orangery at the back, they saw that it was tastefully furnished with a mix of both original period furniture and modern but classic elements. The orangery was brimming with plants and flowers, sometimes layered in stacks, or suspended from hanging baskets, so that every corner was smothered with a riot of green, and sprinkled with flashes of colourful blooms.

The glass extension that was the orangery created a greenhouse effect, and they immediately felt several degrees warmer when they stepped in. They heard the tail-end of something the chief of security was saying to the Professor '–and this is where we believe the doctor left the house last night, sir.'

'How do you know?' the Professor asked.

'Well, it makes sense – every other door and window was locked and bolted from the inside.'

'Mmm,' absorbed the Professor. 'And you say that the outer perimeter was monitored by your men?'

'Yes. We always have shifts of ten cars parked on the road surrounding the outer wall – all within camera distance of each other. And none of them picked up any unusual activity last night. However, the road covers only about two-thirds of the periphery. Just over a third backs onto forest, but we've men patrolling that part every 40 minutes – day and night. I checked their bodycams, and can report that they completed their duties to... well, to military precision. It's all recorded. None of them saw the doctor leave, or anyone enter. We've taken every effort to keep the surrounding area secure, sir. It's like Fort Knox around here.'

'And I take it you've gone over the house thoroughly?'

'Absolutely, every inch, three times. We found nothing untoward, everything's in place, no sign of struggling, no indication that he left voluntarily – all his clothes and possessions are still scattered around, even his mobile phone left on the bedside table, charging. Nothing is missing as far as we can tell.'

'You obviously checked his phone records.'

'Yes, sir. He hardly had any UK calls – the ones he did have were exclusively from the laboratories where he was working. All his other telephone calls were from a single Russian number, which we believe to be a relative.'

'Do you know where in Russia?' asked the Professor.

O'Connor thought for a minute, finally remembering. 'Klin,' he told them, glad it was an easy one to pronounce.

'Klin?' repeated Milly, her encyclopaedic knowledge whirring into gear. 'Which one?' she asked. 'There are 15 towns in Russia named Klin.'

The expression on O'Connor's face showed that he didn't have a clue. 'I'll find out,' he told them.

The Professor continued with his questions. 'And outside, there are no footprints?'

'No, we couldn't find any. But there was a storm last night, which probably washed away any trace of them.'

'And did you get dogs in, to follow the scent?'

'I'm told we have some on standby…' he said, at the same time glancing at Dog. The man had neatly clipped brass-blond hair, and a heavily-wrinkled face hardened by an intense stare, '…but we were told first of all to wait on instructions from you, sir.' Being ex-army he was accustomed to following orders to the letter.

Brian stepped forward. 'Well, we've got Dog – so we should see if she picks anything up.' He held out his hand. 'I'm Brian Bythaway, by the way.' He loved saying that, despite his daughter's usual groans. The two shook hands.

'Pleased to meet you. I'm David O'Connor.'

The Professor answered Brian's question. 'I agree with you, Brian, about using Dog,' he said. 'But, I think we should go over the house first to see what clues we can find.'

'I can assure you that my men have checked the house thoroughly, and there's nothing to report. It appears that everything is exactly the way it was left, before the doctor and his cat disappeared.'

'Cat?' asked Mei Hui. 'There was a cat?'

O'Connor turned to her. 'Yes, apparently it was called… Lubova, I think. The doctor insisted he bring it with him from Russia.'

'That is very strange,' said Mei Hui. 'We do not know whether the doctor was abducted, or left of his own accord. If he intentionally left, it makes sense that he would take the cat with him, especially if he was so attached to it. But if he was abducted, it is unlikely the abductor also took the cat.'

'Well, it's possible it's out there in the forest somewhere, lost – he did go on long walks with the animal, because my men often saw him outside with the cat tagging along,' explained O'Connor, matter-of-fact. He motioned toward the garden door. 'There's no cat-flap, but he could've let the cat out that day.'

They looked at Dog, her bright eyes fixed on the garden through the open door. She was obviously keen to get outside.

'Well then, we need something that has both the scent of the doctor and the cat, for Dog,' said the Professor.

O'Connor nodded, and instructed one of his men, who disappeared and returned a few minutes later with a pyjama top and a folded blanket. When he handed them to the Professor, they saw that the blanket was covered with white fur. 'These were on the bed,' explained O'Connor. 'Looks like the cat slept on this one.'

'Perfect,' said the Professor. He knelt down and Dog sniffed them eagerly – she immediately turned toward the door, whining and straining at her leash.

Brian, who was holding the other end of it, exclaimed, 'We're off!' as Dog pulled him outside. They were followed by O'Connor who signalled to one of the two men standing guard in the garden to join him on the search party. Milly and Mei Hui were last in line, though the latter looked back at the Professor, who remained inside. They both knew that the forest would be difficult for him to navigate, and he would also slow them down. Instead he remained behind, both hands resting on his white cane, blank eyes staring into the distance as he listened to them go.

But the Professor did not waste time. He eventually turned and tapped his way through the room. He wanted to feel his way around the house, the furniture, the objects. Though he was blind, his other senses were heightened, and he was curious to see if there was anything O'Connor and his men had missed.

The search party was gone for hours, and in that time, the Professor made his way through the entire house – all 18 rooms. Feeling, smelling, listening, even tasting some things with a light lick of his tongue, and then spitting into a handkerchief. The last room he explored was the doctor's bedroom, and after going over all the furniture and objects, he eventually sat at the side of the bed, thoughtfully. In his mind he went over everything he had discovered.

Outside, Dog led them for hours through the forest – sniffing the ground, sniffing the air, and pulling on the leash so hard that Brian feared it would snap. It was a warm summer's day, but the dense woodland populated with ash, beech, lime, oak, and yew – ancient columns that sprang from lush clumps of fern – created a cooling canopy. The air was heavy with the scent of humus, bluebells, and wild garlic.

Their trek was slow-going. The ground was mostly solid though covered copiously with leaves and undergrowth, but as they ventured deeper into the woods they came across more and more patches of thick mud – and they could only pick themselves carefully around, to avoid slipping ankle-deep into sludge. They were eventually brought to a narrow country lane winding through the forest. Dog sniffed one particular spot, going round and round, and then sat down, panting – and they realised that the trail had come to an end.

'Looks like it's gone cold here,' said O'Connor. He told the security guard to find out where the road leads, and the man immediately got on his phone.

They made their way back through the woodland – but about two-thirds of the way, Dog began sniffing the ground excitedly. She had found another trail. Where the first one led in an easterly direction, this new trail headed north – and Dog began straining on the leash again. They let her lead them, until, after about 20 minutes, O'Connor suddenly spotted something. 'Over there!' he exclaimed, pointing. There was a clearing in the forest, and just on the far side of it, they saw movement and a flash of creamy fur. It was a cat! Dog pulled the leash out of Brian's hand and bolted after it, running across the clearing, and then disappearing into the forest.

'No!!' shouted O'Connor, annoyed. 'Why did you let go?! The cat's going to run for its life, or the dog'll tear it to shreds!' he said, eyes blazing.

'Erm, no, she won't,' Brian told him, startled by his flash of anger. 'She's got kittens. She loves cats.'

O'Connor looked at the man as though he were mad.

'Nevertheless,' said Mei Hui, 'the cat will run away from a dog it does not know. That is their nature. It will be terrified of Dog.'

'So, what else can we do...?' asked Brian. 'Leave out cat food?' He noticed that Milly looked cold, and he put an arm around her.

'Yes, we could try. But perhaps there is another way.' She turned to Milly and looked at her meaningfully.

Milly nodded slowly, guessing what Mei Hui was getting at. 'The kittens,' she said simply.

O'Connor glared at the three of them now, sure they were all completely off their rocker. He stared at his watch as a distraction to his increasing agitation, though hardly registering the time. He was beginning to wonder why children had been called upon – of all people – to investigate the very serious matter of a missing person, a Russian VIP no less. 'I think it's time we headed back,' he said, trying but failing to hide his annoyance.

'Agreed,' said Brian. He was worried about his daughter catching cold. But before they walked back toward the house, Brian whistled, long and loud. Seconds later Dog shot out into the clearing and ran across to them, her eyes sparkling with the thrill of a run. 'Good Dog!!' he exclaimed, picking out several leaves and twigs from her fur, and then patting her.

•••————————————————•••

Back at the house they removed their mud laden shoes before entering, and then padded through the rooms in their socks, in search of the others. One of the security men informed them that their bags had been placed in a bedroom each, on the first floor.

Mei Hui found her bag in a luxurious room that looked like something out of a five-star hotel. But such opulence did not impress her, and she quickly washed and changed. She was making her way along the corridor, when she spotted the Professor sitting perched at the side of the bed in the missing doctor's room, staring at nothing. In his hand was an empty shot glass.

She stuck her head inside. 'Professor? Do you have a minute?'

The old man roused from the daze he was in, and put the glass down. 'Yes, yes of course.'

Mei Hui ventured inside. 'The search today led us to a country lane about three miles northeast from here. It therefore appears that a vehicle was used to… transport the doctor.'

The Professor detected the hesitation in her voice. 'So…?'

'I was wondering.' Her eyes slid downwards briefly. 'Do you think it is possible he defected?'

He thought about this. 'I'm not ruling anything out. He may have gone on the run, as you suggest – but he may equally have been kidnapped. Project Ingenious being leaked to the news has caused a lot of public speculation – there's even been outrage in some quarters. So we need to keep an open mind, and look at all possibilities.'

'I understand.'

Just then, O'Connor entered the room. 'You asked for me, Professor?'

'Ah yes.' The Professor put down the shot glass on the bedside table and felt for the Vodka bottle. 'Can you please get the alcohol sent over to forensics straight away? I smelled and tasted it, and… something's a bit off.'

'O-kay,' he said, sure that the old man was being overly pedantic. His men after all had thoroughly checked everything. But he had to obey orders. O'Connor walked over to take the bottle, and Mei Hui stepped out of his way, watching him as he left.

She turned back to the Professor, 'Do you think it might have been tampered with?'

'I really don't know, but to me, it doesn't taste quite right… I just want to make sure we don't miss anything.'

Mei Hui nodded thoughtfully. 'There was something else I wanted to ask, Professor. Would it be possible to have the kittens brought here? Milly and I think there might be a way of using them to find the missing cat. We think we saw the cat briefly, but Dog scared it off.'

The Professor lifted an eyebrow. 'You really think the kittens can help?' he asked, surprised by this novel idea.

'It is worth trying,' said Mei Hui. 'If we can retrieve the cat, and it saw what happened to the doctor…'

'Then you might be able to discover what happened too!'

'Yes, exactly. It is what I think they call a long shot. But I believe it is worth trying. I do not have the same skills that Tai has, but I am able to discern recent events at least. If we can find it. But if we need to look further back, then Tai is the only one who can do that. Though...'

'He's too sick.' The Professor nodded slowly. 'Neither I nor Dr Fargo would recommend putting any kind of strain on the boy at the moment.'

'Yes, I agree,' said Mei Hui.

The Professor took out his mobile phone. 'Jasmine,' he called out to it.

'Yes, Professor. How can I help?' Her dulcet tones sounded tinny from the phone's speaker.

'Patch me through to V2 immediately.'

In her own sumptuous bedroom, Milly lay back on the bed after showering, wearing a fresh change of clothes. There was a ping notification on her phone, and she saw that O'Connor had made a group chat for the five of them. The message was informing them that the Klin in question was in the Moscow Oblast. Without looking it up, Milly already knew it was a town about 85 km northwest of Moscow – and that it was  the location of the composer Pyotr Ilyich Tchaikovsky's country home. She knew too that his swan song, the 6th Symphony, _Pathétique_, had been written there – a piece the composer said he loved as he had never loved any of his other musical creations. She had read once that the title of the work did not signify pity or inadequacy, as the direct English suggests – but rather, the Russian meaning conveyed impassioned emotions and feelings. Deep in thought, Milly rolled over onto her stomach and looked up the work on YouTube.

Listening to it did indeed stir up those very emotions. And she lay motionless on the bed as a low bassoon opened the first movement with haunting notes. She inhaled apprehension from them, thoughts of slow disease, sickness, and suicide. Yet within minutes the melody hinted of something else – eventually flourishing, vibrantly, with the undeniable beauty of life. Milly listened for almost an hour, so enchanted by the sonorous music, that at times she forgot to breathe, only to find herself gasping for air.

It brought tears that slipped silently down her cheeks. She knew very well why the music pained her. The symphony marked the end of Tchaikovsky's brilliant mind, and she was plagued by the possibility – or worse, the inevitability – that she might be losing hers. Added to the awful knowledge that Tai's days were literally numbered...

All of this cascaded inside of her as she listened to the stormy restlessness of the third movement, and then the sombre, funereal fourth. It churned within her mind, her chest, turning her inside out. Finally, the music came to a gentle, poignant conclusion – with the sustained bowing of celli, basses, and bassoons swaying with the exhaling-inhaling of prolonged last sighs. At last waning into a death-like silence.

Hands shaking, Milly fumbled with her phone, knowing that she needed to be pulled out of wherever she was – soon, before it dragged her into that bottomless pit.

Tremulous fingers tapped in several search words, and she scrolled through the results, and then hit play. Pushing the earphones firmly into her ears, she wiped her eyes, lay back, and listened to someone teaching and speaking Russian. She did not emerge from her room for hours.

•••———————————————•••

Mei Hui discovered, to her dismay, that night-time in the English countryside was deafeningly silent. It was about 3 a.m., and she rolled over in the large king-size bed, unable to sleep. In China, she was accustomed to hearing the constant buzzing and clicking of cicadas, or the night crickets' chirruping stridulations. They had a soporific effect, and she usually fell asleep instantly. But here, the deadly silence kept her awake.

She sat up suddenly, and huffed. Something was bugging her. Pulling on a jumper and some shoes, she scrambled around inside her rucksack and extracted a torch. Silently, she made her way out into the corridor, down the stairs, through the lounge, and eventually found herself at the external door of the orangery once again. The stiff lock opened with some difficulty, and she made sure to leave it on the latch, before stepping outside. She walked across the neatly manicured lawn, until she reached the garden gate to the forest. She stood there for a few seconds, her ear against the wood, listening intently, and when she was sure there was nothing untoward, she opened the creaky gate, and left that on the latch as well.

The small torch, in hand, shone a disconcertingly feeble beam of light – the darkness seemed to close in on her as she ventured out toward the forest. She swung the torch left and right as she walked several metres, chancing upon a large, dense bush, and positioning herself behind it. Looking at her wristwatch, she noted the time, and then switched off the torch. She did not have to wait long – just a few minutes – before she heard the crackle of radio interference, and someone talking. 'NP 1 to Falkirk, just making the rounds, and nothing to report as usual, over.'

Mei Hui peeked through a gap in the bush, and saw one of the guards dressed in a black bullet-proof vest, with something shiny, like a large badge, pinned to the front. He crunched over the leafy ground. And when he glanced casually in her direction, she quickly bobbed down, holding her breath, hoping he had not spotted her. She soon heard voices – he was talking with someone, and she peeked through again to see that he had crossed with another guard coming from the other direction. They only exchanged brief words before continuing on their way. Mei Hui noted the time and waited for the next round of guards, until she had recorded four sets of patrols.

Satisfied with her findings, and by now cold, she turned her torch on when she was sure it was safe. She began making her way back, relieved to be returning, for the forest at night scared her. But then she stopped. She had heard something in the thicket behind her, and she snapped the torch around. 'Wh-who's there?' she called out – listening hard. Silence. Her heart began to race, and she hurried back, glancing fearfully behind.

Another noise, and she stopped again, holding her breath as she listened, searching through the blackness with the weak torchlight.

A twig cracked just metres away – and Mei Hui ran with all her might, blood rushing through her ears, her breathing thunderous. She thought she could hear the sound of someone or something heavy-footed in pursuit. Fear paralysed her, so that she could not scream. Panic blinded her, making her stumble. It felt like they were nearly upon her – so close it seemed she could feel their breath on her neck.

And she gasped.

7 TUMBLING LEAVES

Flying through the garden door, Mei Hui quickly slammed it shut, and locked it behind her in one smooth but harried movement. Choking with fear, she took a slow step backward, and another, distancing herself.

Someone leaned heavily against the door from the other side.

The wood straining against the lock.

A sound of raspy breath.

The latch rattling.

And then the crackle of leaves and twigs underfoot, followed by uneven footsteps shuffling away – at last fading into the distance.

Mei Hui started breathing again, wiping the tears from her eyes. She turned around to sprint back to the house – crashing straight into David O'Connor.

'Oof!' he exclaimed, stumbling and reeling back.

I'm sorry!!' she cried. 'But... but... there was someone outside, chasing me, I had to run!'

O'Connor immediately pressed on the walkie talkie attached to the front of his gilet. 'Night patrol, are you there? This is Falkirk. What is your position? Have you spotted anyone out there, or seen anything unusual?'

A crackle of static, and a tinny voice answered. 'NP1 to Falkirk – I'm just coming up to the garden gate now, and no unusual activity to report. No sightings. Nobody out here, just me.'

They heard someone on the other side of the wall. Confident footsteps in even strides. Both Mei Hui and O'Connor followed the sound of them as he walked past, from right to left.

Mei Hui spluttered, 'Tell him... tell him there's someone there. They ran off in that direction.' She pointed straight ahead, northward into the forest. 'He has to hurry.'

O'Connor looked doubtful, and spoke into the walkie-talkie again. 'Night Patrol 2, have you seen anything?'

This time, footsteps came from left to right, coinciding with a voice on the other side of the wall that echoed in the walkie talkie. 'That's a negative, sir. I'm just about to cross with NP1, and nothing to report.'

O'Connor dropped his hand from the walkie-talkie and looked at Mei Hui, his eyes boring into her. 'I'm not sure what you think you saw, but there's no-one out there but my men. Maybe it was a fox. There's loads of them at this time of night, and–'

'It was no fox!' insisted Mei Hui, arms wrapped around herself, trying to stop herself from shaking. 'It was a *man*. I could hear him panting as he ran.'

O'Connor thought about this, and then pressed the walkie-talkie button again. 'Falkirk to NP1 and NP2 – I want you to get back-up and do a sweep of the forest. The immediate area. We may have a prowler. Do you copy, over?'

'Copy that,' came an uncertain voice. 'But... sir, it's pitch black out there. We're unlikely to see much, if anything at all.'

'Just do it!' said O'Connor losing patience. 'Over and out!' He turned back to Mei Hui. 'We've got this under control, so I'll accompany you back to the house now. The Professor has already requested triple security, so starting from tomorrow it's going to be tighter than Buckingham Palace. Meanwhile, you'll be safe inside the house and grounds. But please... don't venture out alone. That'd be asking for trouble!'

Mei Hui nodded, and O'Connor took her back.

Inside, she made sure the doors were properly bolted, and then crept upstairs, into her room, slipping under the covers of her bed. She folded her body into a ball – her mind replaying the scene over and over again. All the time wondering: who – or what – had chased her?

Before long, there was a soft knock on her door, and she peaked out from underneath the covers. Milly stepped in, took one look at Mei Hui's tear-streaked face, and – without a word – padded over and climbed onto the bed. They hugged each other, until Mei Hui finally fell asleep.

Early the next morning, the Professor and Brian immediately sought out Mei Hui, who they found in the drawing room with Milly. The two were sitting side by side on the sofa, arms linked, and leaning against each other with heads touching. Still in their pyjamas and slippers.

'There you are!' said Brian, leading the Professor inside.

They sat on the chaise opposite the girls, who calmly pulled apart.

'Is... everything okay?' asked Brian, puzzled by the way they were sitting.

'It is fine,' said Mei Hui – she had returned to perfect calm after the frightening event last night. Or so it seemed. She glanced at Milly. 'We were just... connecting,' she said. 'I cannot explain how, or why, but when we connect, Milly's headaches disappear – completely.'

The Professor sat up, listening with fascination.

Mei Hui continued. 'We discovered it when we entered Karl's mind together. Being within his subconscious for nine whole days, Milly told us that, in all that time, she did not have a single migraine. Which is why we'd been floating together in the pool every morning – in a circle, on our backs, holding hands.'

Milly looked at her father and smiled.

He grinned back at her, hugely relieved to hear that she was no longer in pain. 'Th-that's amazing!' he said.

'Yes, incredible,' mumbled the Professor almost to himself. 'It appears you all have a... restorative effect on each other.' But then he thought of something. 'Is that why you didn't want to travel with the others, Mei Hui? Because you wanted to stay back to help Milly?'

'Yes and no. I also do not take well to long flights of many hours,' she said candidly, remembering the queasy trip from China.

'I hope there are no bad effects on you?' asked Brian.

'No, I feel well,' she replied, matter of fact.

The Professor shifted forward in his seat. 'We came to find you because we heard from O'Connor what happened last night,' he said, concerned. 'Are you okay?'

Mei Hui looked away from the old man. 'I am sorry for going outside alone,' she told him. 'But I could not sleep. I had something on my mind, and... I knew how strong the security was, so I did not think there would be any danger.'

'There is most definitely danger, Mei Hui!' said the Professor, brow creasing. 'To you. To Milly. To all the Ingenious children. This infernal leak has changed everything. The public are hankering for answers to their questions. About all of you. Though, at the moment, it seems their curiosity is mild, relatively. But things can change at any time–'

'I... understand that now,' said Mei Hui, interrupting him, not wishing to prolong his anger. 'But I had my reasons, Professor. Please let me explain.'

Brian looked from her to the Professor. 'I'm sure she had very good reasons, Prof,' he echoed.

Mei Hui took advantage of the Professor's silence. 'Do you remember David O'Connor told us that his men patrol the forest section of the perimeter every 40 minutes? I needed to understand how it could be possible for someone to leave – or enter – the house from the back, without the guards seeing anything. And last night, in the forest, I measured the timing, the rate, and speed of the patrols – discovering that the guards leave the west road intersection at exactly the same time as the guards leaving the east one. They follow the line of the garden wall, and cross each other at a certain point, and then continue on their way, until they reach the opposite intersection. I timed that there is a two-minute window, on average, for someone to be able to get past the garden gate, before the next guard comes round. In fact, it was within those gaps that I myself could slip out and return undetected.' She looked at the Professor expectantly.

'I hear you,' was all he mumbled.

Brian thought of something. 'But if the doc was kidnapped, how could the abductor break in through the garden gate, which was locked from the inside? And there was no evidence of it being smashed. If they didn't use the gate, then they would've had to scale that high wall within minutes, even though it has some seriously nasty-looking security spikes. Given the gap of two minutes or so, that seems highly improbable, don't you think? They would've impaled themselves. Also, I'm told this doctor was quite a hefty man – so to forcibly take him and get him out past the guards, all without being seen, would be quite a feat.'

'You're right, Brian,' said the Professor. 'The idea of kidnapping is looking more and more unlikely. In fact, Mei Hui has an interesting theory.'

'I just want to consider all possibilities,' Mei Hui told them. 'I asked Dr Fargo about Vassiliev. And he told me that the last time they met was at a scientific conference in Moscow. However, the Kremlin stipulated that, for all Vassiliev's meetings, he had to be accompanied by authorised personnel who would report everything back to them. Even if it was just a casual appointment for drinks. Dr Fargo told me that Vassiliev was very annoyed by this paranoid treatment of him. When I did some internet research, it showed that Vassiliev had worked on a Russian project with a high level of secrecy, either level 1 or level 2 security. Level 1 comes with severe restrictions imposed by the Kremlin, including restricted international travel to a small number of countries, a maximum of five-month travel visas, and also prohibiting emigration... All this might be cause for Dr Vassiliev defecting. Which would mean that it was easy enough for him to slip out of the garden gate without detection, as I did – within that two- or three-minute gap.'

'It kind of makes sense,' said Brian thoughtfully, 'given the fact that there are no signs of struggle.'

'It also explains why he would leave his mobile phone, because it is trackable,' said Mei Hui.

'If that's true,' said the Professor, 'then it's very bad news indeed for us, because with Dr Kendra being... incapacitated, Vassiliev alone is the only one with the ability to produce the cure... I am also very alarmed that someone chased you, Mei Hui. Did you see them?'

She shook her head, and found herself shivering, though it was not from being cold. 'N-no. I-it was too dark to see clearly. But... whoever it was had heavy, uneven footsteps, similar to someone dragging their feet.'

'Could it be paparazzi?' asked Brian.

'No,' said the Professor. 'We made sure to keep this place completely confidential. The last thing we want is a media circus.'

Mei Hui closed her eyes briefly, remembering. 'That person, the sound of the way they moved and dragged their feet… I cannot be sure, but it made me think that they were not young. Their movement seemed stiff, and hindered, like an aged person who cannot easily get around.' Just the thought of it made her feel anxious.

Milly looked at her sympathetically. 'You need some tea, Mei,' she said. 'I'll go and make you some…' She got up to go to the kitchen, and her father's eyes followed her as she left.

Mei Hui suddenly remembered the innumerable quantities of teacups left untouched in V3's room, and she quickly jumped up. 'I… I think I'll go and help her,' she said, and followed her out.

The Professor fell into silence for some time.

He noticed the light whistling trill of a wren outside – somewhere low, close to the ground, perhaps hidden in a bush. Closing his eyes, he listened to the dawn chorus, thinking deeply. He was worried for the children. Danger seemed to be getting closer and closer – within touching distance. And even though they had increased the security to the house, there were really only guards, and a creaky old gate, keeping that danger out. Had he made the right decision to take them out of the fortress-like safety of Avernus? Should they return immediately? How could they then solve the disappearance of the Russian doctor if they did not venture outside? So many questions hurtled through the Professor's mind. His eyes flitting here and there, as if searching for answers.

Brian was watching the Professor. The old man's head was lowered, hands clasped so hard in his lap that his knuckles were white – ashen lips moving almost imperceptibly, in a steady stream of inaudible words. He stayed like this for some time. 'Professor?' said Brian. But he did not answer. 'Professor,' he said, louder. 'Are… are you praying?'

The old man looked up. He unclasped his hands, but they shook so much that he quickly pressed them together again. 'Praying? No, no, I'm sorry I have a habit of mumbling to myself. Thinking out loud. I… stopped praying a long time ago.'

Finally Brian found the courage to ask, 'Your family… I'm guessing you stopped praying after they died.'

The Professor sighed fitfully, and nodded. 'Yes. That is how I can understand what you went through, Brian. And what you're going through,' he said softly, still looking down.

'What were they like?' ventured Brian.

The question surprised the Professor, because it made him realise that he hadn't talked about them – *really* talked – for such a long time. He had buried their memories on the day their funeral caskets were sunk deep into the earth. He did it for self-preservation. Otherwise he was sure to go mad with grief. He thought of the way the headstones looked that day. White, cold marble. Thought of how the autumn leaves – russet-red and orange flames – had tumbled onto them, resting lightly there. Stark against the white. Until they were gradually blown away.

The Professor's lips seemed to move of their own accord, forming words, as though they had decided to resurrect the memories. Memories lain silent, and pressed down, for far too long. 'You... you really want to know about them? Chiara, and Christian?' came those unbidden words. The edges of the Professor's face softened. His sightless eyes hovered upward, glistening, as his wife, his son, appeared right there in front of him. Clear as day.

'Yes, I do,' said Brian.

'I... haven't talked about them for a while,' he admitted, his voice breaking. He stared at their smiling faces, encouraging him to go on. And so he did. 'I met Chiara in LMU – Munich University, just over 30 years ago, where I lectured in the Genetics Institute,' he said, his voice warming with affection. 'She was in my class, one of the mature students. Very clever, very bright, and... very beautiful.' He shifted awkwardly in his seat. 'At first, when she showed interest in me, I... I couldn't believe it. I wondered if it might be a "transference" kind of infatuation that students have for teachers. So I did not allow myself to reciprocate. But after she graduated, we kept in touch every Christmas – just a card here and there, brief messages, casual x's after our names. We eventually got together one year... met up for old time's sake. And that was when we fell in love.' He thought about this. '"Falling" is such a good term for it, isn't it? As light, and yet as powerful, as the irrepressible force of gravity...' he said, wistfully.

A flicker of a smile crossed his face. 'I felt like the luckiest man on earth when she accepted my marriage proposal. Even though Chiara was much younger than I – there was an 11-year age gap – she thought nothing of it, and we set the wedding for the following year. Then two years after that, a miracle happened. Christian was born...' The Professor faltered, grappling with waves of emotion. Finally he was able to speak again. 'Chiara was a perfect mother. And a perfect partner to me too, in every way. You see, I was working on research that consumed all my time. But she never once complained...

'And then, when I was asked to join Project Ingenious, which we both knew was a once-in-a-lifetime opportunity, she did not hold me back. So we moved, and... all seemed well...

'Well, you know what happened after five years, Brian. We had to break free from the project, had to steal away the children and go into hiding. Try to rebuild our lives. But it was harder than I imagined. Those years in Project Ingenious left scars, and I became a wreck. A total wreck. And so I threw myself into my work. Not genetics. After everything, I couldn't cope with working in that field, not for a long time. No, I threw myself into our family business. You see, my family own a line of retail shops that, in the hands of my uncle, was declining rapidly, eventually getting into more and more debt, losing so much money – and on the verge of bankruptcy. But when my uncle died suddenly, I inherited everything. And so I worked day and night, bringing in experts, consultants, to save the company. Save all those jobs, and livelihoods. But then...' – the Professor paused, just managing to compose himself – 'about a year-and-a-half after we left the project, I was working late in the office one evening. Undecided as to whether I should go home that night, or just sleep there. I eventually returned home at about 2 in the morning. But when I got there... I... I found fire engines surrounding the house. People watching behind barriers. But, I was too late. The flames had already been put out. The house was just a charred mess, a black shell, still smoking. And my family nowhere to be found...'

Brian reached for his hand, and the Professor gripped onto it, so hard.

He took a deep breath before continuing. 'I broke through the barriers, and ran into the house, not realising how hot it was still. But I didn't care, I was distraught, crazy with worry. I had to find them!'

He hung his head, no longer able to look his wife in the eye. 'I found them in the cupboard under the stairs,' he said, his voice low. 'Their bodies...' He sat still for some time. Eventually he forced out the words that came like fingers scratching on chalkboard. 'Th-their bodies were... on the ground, h-holding each other.' He closed his eyes. Seeing that image in his mind now, in all its horrific detail. 'That was the last thing I saw.'

He let go of Brian's hand, wiping shaky, sweaty palms on his trousers. 'When they needed me the most, I wasn't there...'

They sat silently for a while.

Eventually, Brian said, 'I'm sorry, *really* sorry...'

The Professor listened to the sound of his own breathing. Light, airy waves filtering through his lungs. Each breath pushing down those memories once more. Burying them again.

An afterthought came to the Professor. 'You know,' he said, weariness in his voice, 'that was when the Chauffeur found me. He had left home, left Axel and Gaia, and was trying to make his own way in life. Would you believe he was working as a gravedigger at the cemetery my family were buried in. He saw that I was the only one attending their funeral, and he felt sorry for me, he told me later. When he came over, he recognised me straight away as one of Axel's work colleagues. Of course, he saw that I had become blind... In a way, the Chauffeur saved me. A deaf, mute boy, saved me. You see, he insisted on helping me, and, well, you know how he can be – he's rather difficult to refuse. And so I took him in. He brought me back to where Gaia and Axel lived when he moved out, but they had already sold up – the Chauffeur told me they moved all the time, to stay safe, but he wasn't worried. He was sure they would find each other again somehow.'

'I've always wondered...' said Brian. 'Another thing I've wondered about is Avernus...'

'Avernus...' the Professor repeated slowly. 'You can imagine that, after everything, I threw myself into the family business like a man possessed, and my advisors were eventually able to save the supermarket chain from bankruptcy. But then I got to thinking more and more about the Ingenious children. I had helped engineer their DNA, but somehow, they had become part of *my* DNA... I felt duty-bound toward them. Toward keeping them safe. And so that is why I bought the industrial estate, and spent 10 years building Avernus, in the event that, one day, they might come to need it as a safe place.' He took a deep breath, frowning. He felt weary, exhausted, like a battle-scarred soldier returning from bloody fields. 'And now, stupidly, at a time when they need security the most, I've taken them out of it...'

'You can't keep them locked up forever, Prof,' Brian said quite strongly. He had learnt that from Milly. 'A certain young lady – back when she was her usual self – constantly reminded me of that. Teenagers have a real... exuberance for life. Wanting to discover, explore, widen out. They need to spread their wings, as the saying goes.'

The Professor suddenly sat up, cocking his head to one side. He'd heard something. 'Can you hear Dog whining? In the hallway...'

They both got up, and the Professor tapped his way over, with Brian beside him. They discovered Dog scratching and sniffing frantically at the front door, crying to be let out. Milly and Mei Hui soon appeared as well to see what the noise was.

Brian held onto Dog's collar and opened the door. But there was no-one there. He peered around the corners. 'What is it, Dog?' he said, puzzled. But then he realised Dog was looking up. They all followed her gaze.

The sky was a clear blue, with cotton-white clouds slowly scudding by. Squinting in the light, they at last made out a faraway dot, high up. As it neared, and got bigger, they realised it was the helicopter – the faint thak-thak-thak of its rotor blades gradually becoming deafening.

Dog grew more and more frenzied, barking and jumping with excitement as it landed. The force of the gusts of wind made them hold up protective arms, or turn away. It landed in the forecourt as before, and the door was flung open. V2 jumped out, then turned back to reach for a holdall sized carrying cage. He bent low under the rotor blades, as they ground to a slow halt, and ran toward them – followed by another agent with a second cage.

They nodded greetings as they entered the house, and went into the drawing room – placing the cages in the middle of the floor. Dog trotted behind them, and scraped at the enclosures, whining, looking around at the humans for help. V2 unlocked and opened the doors, and a young cat stuck its head out nervously, before diving straight back in. It was Pasha. Dog barked at them with happiness, her frenzied tail whipping the air. Mei Hui and Milly went over to pull out the kittens, placing them on the sofa, where Dog jumped up and began licking each of them. The young cats – although happy to see their mother – were too scared to relax.

'They look nervous,' said Brian.

'They do,' said Mei Hui. 'But they will soon get used to it.' Turning around, she spoke to Milly. 'We should get dressed to take them out.'

'Ah, this little cat experiment of yours,' said Brian. 'Let's hope it works. We don't have much else to go on.'

The girls turned to leave, but then V2 stepped forward, toward Milly. 'It's… good to see you, Milly,' he told her, before glancing uneasily at Brian and the Professor.

Milly stopped, then turned – apprehensive eyes lifting to meet his. And for the first time she took in the scars and bruises on his face, though they had faded considerably. She stared at him, blinking, helpless, like a frozen deer caught in a car's headlights.

V2 held up a hand, not wanting her to go before he said what he'd been meaning to tell her for a while. Awkward in front of the others. 'I-I just wanted to say that… it's not your fault, Milly. It couldn't be helped.'

Milly tried to let his words sink in, tried to absorb them. But she found herself turning, walking past him, and leaving.

Mei Hui smiled kindly at him. 'Thank you, V2,' she said, and turned to leave as well.

83

'It had long since come to my attention that people of accomplishment rarely sat back and let things happen to them.
They went out and happened to things.'

Leonardo da Vinci

8 TWO GIRLS, FIVE KITTENS, AND A GOOSE

Milly and Mei Hui sat alone together on the lawn of the extensive and ornate back gardens – two teenage girls with five young cats enclosed within their crossed legs. The little animals fidgeted with insatiable curiosity, craning necks to look up at the flowing clouds, sniffing the air, paws batting at aphids, round eyes drawn to the star-like purple clematis climbing up the trellis behind them.

'Are you ready?' asked Mei Hui.

Milly returned her stare, and nodded.

They had been shown numerous photos and videos of Lyubova from Dr Vassiliev's phone, and each time Milly blinked they flickered through her thoughts like the images in a spinning zoetrope, coming to life in her mind. She extended an index finger and lightly tapped the top of each cat's head, implanting those images like plump, molten seeds. The last head she tapped was Olly's – the grey striped cat whose inflated bravado belied his timidity. The curve of Milly's finger lingered on his head, and in that touch she sensed the physiology of him, a symphony of biological processes, the quickened drumbeat of his heart, blood coursing through a network of veins, the rush of adrenaline, and cascading neuronal signals flashing through his brain.

One by one, each cat stopped what they were doing and began looking around. They scrambled out and jumped lithely onto the neatly cut lawn – first Treacle, followed by his never faraway sister, Missy Mop, then Max, Pasha, and lastly Olly. The girls got up, carefully stepped over them, and led the way across the lawn, through the gate, and out into the forest. The young cats trailed behind them, meowing, and looking around with curiosity.

Behind them followed O'Connor and two of his men, hands never far from their holsters – keeping their distance, yet staying close by.

The warmer days after the storm had baked and tightened the soil so that it was easier to walk through the forest, and both Milly and Mei Hui retraced their steps to the place where they had caught a glimpse of the missing cat. They remembered the way faultlessly, remembered the look of every branch of every tree, the shape of a yew, the patterns of bark on a beech, the citrus-resin scent of a fir – each leading them like a map to where they wanted to go. Every now and then they stopped to look back at the cats – nimbly dodging shrubs and jumping over clumps of mud, as they followed.

At last they reached the spot where they had seen a flash of fur, and they walked across the clearing, parting the bushes in the exact place where Dog had disappeared. The thicket was dense, slowing them down as they squeezed through packed bushes and trees, at last reaching a more secluded part of the forest, deeper than they had ever been. Following yet another path, they at last came to a trail.

The cats soon overtook the girls, and started leading the way, bright eyes sparkling with adventure. Suddenly the cats stopped, necks craning, ears flicking forward, noticing something ahead. Following their gaze, the girls saw a cat in the distance. It froze for a second, before turning and scampering away. The young cats chased after it, as did the girls and the men behind – running for some time, until they at last reached a broad, leafy clearing. Several stacks of large flat overlapping boulders dotted the area, covered in blooms of yellow-green lichen – on top of them were heaps of fallen branches, twigs, and leaves.

The cat scurried toward the safety of the boulders. And as the girls neared, they saw that, sheltering in the gaps between each rocky shelf, was a colony of feral cats – in a riot of cream, brown, white, and grey. They spat and hissed, inching deeper into their dark hiding places. The cat they had chased jumped up in great leaps onto the boulders, and then climbing into the branches of a tree. It turned, and sat – watching them smugly in the knowledge that it was unreachable.

Wary of the strangers, the feral cats kept beady eyes fixed on them.

Meanwhile, the girls hung back and watched as Olly, Max, Treacle, Missy Mop, and Pasha advanced toward the colony, meowing blithely. Max reached the boulders first, standing out with his black tuxedo-like markings. He stopped close to a striped grey-and-white cat, and they sniffed each other cautiously, and exchanged meows. Behind him, the other kittens fanned out, with Pasha bouncing cheerfully in their wake, eager to make new friends.

O'Connor and his men watched in amazement as the kittens systematically made their way to each of the wild cats, sniffing, meowing, searching. Some of the feral cats reciprocated with curiosity, some with friendliness, while others hissed and ran off. The tiger-like Olly jumped up with ease onto the branch where the first cat was, and they sniffed each other with affected disinterest. Olly sat back on his haunches, side by side with the cat, delicately sniffing the bark, then casually scratching claws into the wood as if passing time.

At last the young cats – having sifted through every single one of the wild ones – eventually returned to the girls, meowing all the while. The girls and men backed away slowly until they reached the other side of the thicket, out of sight of the colony. Mei Hui bent down and picked up Treacle, kissing him, and whispering into his ear. She hugged him for a while, closing her eyes, absorbing and soaking in his thoughts. They waited patiently as she did this with each cat. In time, she put down the last cat and looked at Milly and the men with disappointment. 'The cat, Lyubova, is not there,' she told them, matter-of-fact.

O'Connor frowned with disbelief. 'How can you know that?!'

'I… just know,' said Mei Hui, reluctant to explain. She turned to Milly. 'We should go back.'

O'Connor exploded. 'What on earth are you talking about, girl! Do you expect us to believe that you can "communicate" with cats? You're crazy! *This* is crazy!! I can't believe I'm baby-sitting two girls and five cats on a completely wild goose chase. This is all just silly games and make-believe – wasting my time!!' He threw up his arms in despair.

Calmly, Mei Hui reached out and touched O'Connor's hand briefly. When skin touched skin, she took in the briefest sense of him – discerning that while, on the whole, he was a good man, his circumstances, his life, his upbringing – maybe even his DNA – gave him a temper that was easily ignited. She looked over his face. His red, bulging eyes, cheeks crazed with fine thread-veins, a stubble of silver grey on his jaw. And she remembered the simple truth, that rage is not without reason. Yet she did not want to excuse him. Instead she said, 'We have a wise saying, David O'Connor – a Chinese proverb, of which you may take note. It is: "If you are patient in one moment of anger, you will escape a hundred days of sorrow".'

The men behind sniggered, and O'Connor shot them a warning glance. He gritted his teeth, trying hard to keep calm. 'I think we had better return to the house,' he said, seething.

'Agreed,' said Mei Hui, and she looked to see that all the kittens had returned. They had – either sitting patiently at their feet, or playing with leaves, and Pasha was even lying down, rolling in the dirt. But Mei Hui discovered an addition. It was hiding behind Milly's legs, having followed the kittens when they left. Milly stooped down to greet it. 'Hey there, little fellow,' she said softly, so as not to scare it. A small tortoise-shell kitten – its dirty matted fur a mishmash of black, beige, and ginger, and perhaps no older than five months – sat looking at Pasha with mild interest. Milly took some treats out of her pocket and gave it some, which it wolfed down hungrily. She treated the other cats too for a job well done.

9 AN IMPOSSIBLE MEMORY

An exasperated call from Dr Fargo to the Professor resulted in Tai and his mother also being transported to the house by V2. Tyaishia had been going out of her mind being locked away in "hell's dungeon" as she called it – and she in turn, was driving everyone else crazy with her unhappiness.

Tai was glad to be reunited with the girls, as well as Dog and the kittens. And every day he was wheeled out in his wheelchair to enjoy the house grounds and gardens – drawing comfort from the fresh air, and warming sun. The boy was clearly happiest when he was surrounded by nature, and within a matter of days he became a little brighter, though still ravaged by the infirmities of old age. In the evenings, they watched concerts, operas, documentaries, and films together in the beautiful drawing room, with its elegant décor of intricate mouldings, a honey-coloured parquet floor, and 19th century paintings – all bathed in the subdued light of a Venetian chandelier. There was even an antique grand piano which Tai was able to play briefly, on his good days – though arthritic stiffness in his hands confounded his best efforts.

Tyaishia physically relaxed, and became less shouty. Deciding, instead, to take it upon herself to mother everyone. Just as well, because for some unknown reason the housekeeper had stopped her daily visits to the house. And so every day they enjoyed curried chicken with coco bread, or grilled snapper, rice and peas, or cod and ackee, all mopped up with the fluffiest, tastiest dumplings. She also decided to organise everyone to death, making sure that the girls kept up with their schooling, and they looked after the animals 'proper', and also ensured that no 'chaka chaka' mess was left in any of the rooms. Or else!

The Professor told the team of doctors working on the cure to continue with their work, despite the missing Dr Vassiliev. He hoped upon the remote possibility that they might, by some miracle, complete it without him.

And every evening Brian left out a bowl of fresh cat food on the patio, on the off-chance that the cat, if it had strayed, might be enticed to come back. But each morning he found the food left untouched.

One afternoon, just after they had eaten lunch together, O'Connor came in holding the mobile phone that Dr Vassiliev left behind. 'There was another missed call from someone in Russia, from that place that you were asking about the other day,' he said, looking at Milly. 'Klin.' He showed her the phone.

Milly's eyes lit up, and she pulled out her own mobile and keyed in the number.

'But what if it's the Russian mafia or something!' exclaimed Brian, looking around, ever protective of his daughter.

Milly, too deep in thought to register his concern, listened as the steady clicks gave way to a ringing tone. Someone picked up, and Milly began speaking in fluent Russian. A heated exchange followed – with Milly trying to calm down the person at the other end of the line. Eventually they were able to have a proper conversation, with Milly both asking and answering questions. After about 25 minutes she eventually hung up.

O'Connor raised an eyebrow. 'You speak fluent Russian?'

'Along with 23 other languages,' she said, matter-of-fact. 'I collect them. After you told us about the telephone calls from Klin, I started to learn it.'

'And?' asked Brian.

'They weren't the Russian mafia, Dad,' she said, resisting the urge to roll her eyes. 'It was Dr Vassiliev's grandmother. She's out of her mind with worry. She said that after someone reported that he was missing, no-one's been able to answer any of her questions. I told her we were doing everything we can to find him. Then she asked about his cat.'

'Why would she ask about the cat?' asked O'Connor.

'She said that the cat is "lyubov' vsey yego zhizni" – in other words, the love of his life. She told me that he would never go anywhere without her, and he would never leave her behind.'

'So it's likely the doctor took her with him, if he's done a runner,' said the Professor.

'It's possible,' Milly replied. 'Though, I noticed earlier, the cat carrier is still here…'

They turned to follow her gaze, and lo and behold, they saw the cat basket nestled, hidden, between a couple of pots of overflowing plants.

•••———————————————————•••

They were acutely aware of time passing.

Each day was special because it was a day with Tai. Every little smile, every piece he played feebly on the piano, and every softly-spoken word, was treasured even more.

Dog sensed that something was not right, and apart from needing to tend to the young cats from time to time, she barely left the boy's side. Her bright eyes watched his every move, when he went to the bathroom, or was taken outside. She fetched for him, picked stuff up for him, threw things away, and if he stumbled she immediately barked a warning. Even in the darkness of night, with no-one else around, Dog knew when Tai wept quietly in a corner of his bed – and she would jump up, whining, and nudging his hand with her snout, making him pet her. Somehow it worked, because each stroke of her fur seemed to unload a little of his angst. And each time Dog licked his hand, or his cheek, it lessened his anxieties.

Tai spent a lot of time thinking. That was pretty much all he could do for himself nowadays. He realised that his depression was an angular one, with sharp corners and slippery slopes. Just when he thought he was reaching a plateau, he would come to an acute angle that either stabbed him painfully, or made him slip into unknown emotional depths. The depth of feeling, the intensity of thoughts, was like nothing he had experienced before. Each hour, minute, second was a corner or a slope – and he never knew where each one would take him next.

But as with most things, the boy bore it with taciturn stoicism.

That was, after all, all he could do.

Before long, 12 days had already passed, with no news of the missing scientist, no word yet from Jake, Cal, and Jemima in Brazil, and still waiting for the results of the forensic testing of the vodka shot glass.

One lazy Friday afternoon, when the temperature was much cooler, and the sky overcast with grey clouds, they decided to bring in catering for once, to give Tyaishia a well-deserved break and a special treat for all her hard work – they picnicked together in the orangery, from luxurious hampers delivered straight from Harrods. Eating finger sandwiches of oak smoked salmon, cream cheese and cucumber, and Wiltshire ham. Scones with clotted cream and strawberries, dolloped with artisan jam. There were pastel-coloured pastries, and light but chewy macarons – all washed down with elegant flutes of sparkling champagne, or elderflower cordial. Distracted by the conversation and delicious food and drink, no-one noticed Dog get up from lying next to Tai's feet. She walked over to the closed garden door, her tail wagging, and sat down, looking directly outside.

There was a light plink of water on the roof above them, followed by another, then another, until it turned into a melodic pitter-patter of rainfall. Brian looked through the glass to check the weather, and noticed Dog staring fixedly outside. 'Don't like the rain, girl?' he called out to her, and she glanced at him, but soon turned back to stare through the glass door. Suddenly Brian stopped, and quickly hushed everyone quiet. They all turned round to see what he was looking at.

On the other side of the garden door was a shock of white fur, sitting and peering inside at Dog – the two animals practically nose to nose. The sides of its little mouth stretching into inaudible meows. Dog's breath was fogging up the glass, but they knew immediately who it was. 'Lyubova!' gasped Milly.

'Don't move!' Brian said in a low voice. 'We might scare it away. I'm going to go over slowly to open the door. Tyaishia, can you get a bowl of cat food please? And everyone else, just keep very still. Okay?'

They complied without a word, and both Brian and Tyaishia got up as quietly as they could, the former making his way to the garden door, and the latter disappearing into the kitchen.

As Brian opened the door and Dog padded backward, they immediately heard the cat's weak, raspy meows – she was losing her voice. She was clearly a stunning cat, despite the damp, matted fur, and dirt-stained paws – and her right flank was much grubbier than the other. She walked in hesitantly, looking up at them, perturbed by the strangers invading her house. But after several steps, she wobbled, lost balance and fell on her side. Scrambling up, she continued looking around and meowing for her doctor.

'I think we'll need a vet, Prof,' said Brian, concerned. 'She keeps falling over.'

The girls followed her as she made her way through the house, room by room – wandering, falling, and getting up again. Searching continually. But the doctor was nowhere to be found. And she finally circled back to the orangery, dismissing the food that Tyaishia put down for her, instead looking at each of the humans. She singled out Tai, and, with some effort, jumped up onto his lap.

Above them a rhythm of rain pelted down on the glass.

The cat looked at the boy and meowed at him in earnest.

Carefully, steadily, Tai extended a hand to stroke her shivering wet fur. And the boy watched the haze of colours that glowed around her – a blend of purple-red distress and alarm, mingled with deep blue tinges of sadness. A broken heart, and lost hope. The love of her life, nowhere to be found.

Tai stroked her tenderly, burying chalky fingers into thick fur. And he closed his eyes. Calmly absorbing the cat's thoughts for several long minutes – the patter of rain resonating in his ears. But his serene face gradually knotted into one of puzzlement, then disbelief, then horror. His eyes flashed open as his hand snapped back, trembling. He looked wildly around at the others. 'I-in the cat's mind, I saw… a burning house,' he said, his voice a gravelly whisper. 'Flames everywhere, black smoke.' He stopped for a moment, looking visibly sick. 'I saw a woman. In her arms a boy, about… about 12 or 13 years old.'

The Professor froze, blood rushing from his face. He got up, stepped forward, as if in a trance.

Tai continued. 'But they are crouched inside the house, under the stairs, right in the middle of the flames. Swallowed up by fire. They are screaming, terrified...'

The Professor stumbled, his legs giving way beneath him.

'...burning!'

And all of a sudden the Professor's body folded in on itself, eyes rolling back. The whole world spun into a dizzying vortex within his head.

A vortex of flames, and smoke, and rain, and blackness.

Losing consciousness, he fell to the ground.

10 DRIP DRIP DRIP

Distant voices.

'Professor! Professor!!'

Pain throbbing in his hip.

A dreamy stasis.

Wraithlike figures floating.

The edges of reality quivering and hardening.

And he groaned. Found himself on the cold stone floor. Dog's hot tongue rough against his skin. Someone was holding his hand – Tai. And the Professor realised he could see. People hunched over him, others running around in agitated commotion.

'Here drink this.'

His head lifted from a cushion of fabric. A glass pressed against his lips and tepid water dripping down his throat. The rush of air over his tongue.

'Prof! Are you okay? Prof!!' came Brian's voice, the faintest whiff of wine and cucumber on his breath. 'We've called a doctor. Just... hang on.'

At last the Professor came to, in the dim light of a quiet room – discerning someone close-by. 'Wh-who's there?'

'Oh thank goodness,' someone breathed, leaning forward. The creak of upholstery springs. 'You gave us a bit of a fright there, Prof.'

'Brian. W-what happened? Where am I?' The old man struggled to sit up, and Brian leant over to prop up some pillows behind him.

'You fainted,' he said, sitting back down. 'You're in your room now.'

The old man closed his eyes and remembered. 'The cat!'

'Yes the cat,' said Brian in a hushed toned. 'It's... unfathomable. What Tai saw... he described *exactly* what you told me. About how your family died.'

It was all flooding back now, and the Professor felt queasy. He flopped back against the pillow. 'How? How is it possible?'

'It's not. It defies logic… It's a random cat, belonging to a bloke who lived in Russia!' He thought about it for a moment. 'How on earth could it have seen that fire?! I'm pretty sure the cat didn't even exist back then, because it looks young still.'

There was a moment of silence before the Professor said, 'The children would be able to tell us.' His voice was distant, uncertain, as if he had disconnected from reality. As if unsure of whether he was still in the throes of a nightmare.

'Yes, and they will, but all in good time, Prof. We've called for a vet who's on his way right now. Poor little thing's obviously been through a lot. And you should rest. So like I said, in good time.'

But the Professor barely registered what was being said. He was still in shock.

•••———————————————————•••

Tyaishia found Lyubova feebly wandering around the house, and she suddenly grabbed her, and brought her – running – into the drawing room. She set her down on the coffee table, where a stout man was waiting. He had mousy hair and a round face, reminiscent of the gazing cherubs in Raphael's painting of <u>The Sistine Madonna</u>. He sat down, speaking directly to the cat in friendly tones. 'Hello!' he said, beaming down at her. 'Aren't you a beautiful little lady! Now, let's have a look at you.' He examined her gently, feeling  for any broken bones, wounds, foreign objects, checking her paws – eventually shining a light into her ears and peering in. He asked Tyaishia to hold the cat down, while he took her temperature. Noting the reading, he put away the thermometer, then snapped off his rubber gloves. Tyaishia and Mei Hui, both standing on the other side of the coffee table, waited patiently for his verdict.

'Looks like the little bunny's had a really rough time!' he said, gently bending back one of the cat's paws. 'Can you see her paw pads? They're really scratched up and bleeding. And the pattern of wear and tear, with the front claws being really sharp, and, here, the back claws worn right down to the nail beds – all this suggests that the cat's been walking for a long, long time. You see, the back legs are used for propulsion, and the front claws for scratching. So the poor possum's been walking for days.' Released at last, Lyubova jumped onto the divan and started licking herself down. Mei Hui sat next to her and stroked her.

The man straightened up and brushed back his tousle of light brown hair, which seemed too fine for a man. 'Now, as to why she keeps falling down: there's some nasty discharge from the right ear, which looks like a deep ear infection. Together with the random imbalance that you mentioned, it's likely she has vestibular disease. Now there are two types, one more serious than the other, and only imaging will be able to tell which one it is. But as a start, I'm going to prescribe a course of antibiotics, both locally as eardrops, and orally. I'll also leave you with some steroids, anti-nausea and anti-vertigo medication. They'll help the cat maintain balance, and regain appetite. And please give it a simple diet of chicken and rice for now.' The man flashed a sympathetic smile, then rummaged inside his battered leather Gladstone case to extract the medicine. He clicked out a biro and started scribbling instructions, eventually leaving the paper, medication, and his card on the table in a little pile. 'So we'll see if little chicken improves in about a week to 10 days. But if she gets worse, call me, and we'll take the next step of sending her off to imaging, okay?'

When the vet left, Tyaishia and Mei Hui sat down together, trying to decipher his scrawled instructions. Eventually Mei Hui said, 'It is good that the vet has helped Lyubova, but there is one thing I do not understand. Why did he refer to her as a possum, a chicken, and a bunny?'

Tyaishia slapped her thigh and guffawed with laughter. 'Not good if a vet can't wuk out which animal it is!'

Mei Hui giggled.

'Dem's just ways of talkin' 'bout something wid affection, though.'

'Ah,' said Mei Hui. 'Terms of endearment?'

Tyaishia nodded. 'That's it! They're just cutesy yuh know? In Jamaica, a wife could call 'er husband "Daddy", or the husband might call 'er "Mumz". I know, makes no sense! When Tai was likkle, mi used to call 'im "Pumpkin"...' She trailed off, suddenly overcome with sadness.

Mei Hui changed the subject quickly and turned to look for the cat, but she had already disappeared up the stairs. 'I wonder what Lyubova went through! I would like to try and find out what happened to her.'

Tyaishia stirred. 'Wouldn't we all, sweets,' she said softly. 'Wouldn't we all...'

When night fell, and silence descended on the house as everybody retreated to their rooms, a washed and cleaned Lyubova was still wondering whether her doctor was ever going to come back home. She was beside herself, hardly knowing what to do. But like most animals, she found herself drawn to Tai, and quietly padded into his bedroom. The room was dim, with slithers of moonlight permeating through the arched windows, sketching hazy silver outlines. She went up to the bed and stretched up on her hind legs, peaking over the top. There was a heap of other cats and a large dog lying on and around the boy. She meowed at them, and Dog looked at her with mild interest, while one or two of the other cats lifted sleepy heads to see who it was. The others slept on.

Lyubova gauged the height, wriggled her bottom, and jumped up onto the bed with some effort – she searched for a place to rest, though almost everywhere was already taken. The boy himself was deep in sleep, and so she sidled on top of the pillow, the last remaining space, and began kneading the plump softness of it, before settling down. She curled her body around his head, hugging it, in the same way she used to hug her doctor every night. It was a warm place, epitomising, to her, home and safety and protection. She sensed this from Tai too, as she at last drifted off to sleep. Her broken heart pining.

Throughout the night, Tai slept more peacefully than he had in a long time. He did not realise it, but as the soft warm fur of the cat's belly rose and fell against his head, a slow and steady trickle of memories seeped into his subconscious. A drip-drip-drip of images – at first vague and indistinct, but then crystallising into clearer pictures – gradually formed a reel of memories that unrolled subtly within his mind. Memories of what had happened since that stormy night two weeks ago. When it had rained all night, and bolts of lightning whipped across the sky in empyrean flashes – thunder crashing and booming in the distance.

99

'Why does the eye see a thing more clearly in dreams than the imagination when awake.'

Leonardo da Vinci

11 THE STORM

The night of the storm, it seemed to Lyubova as if the whole world was exploding.

She hid underneath the bed, cowering and trembling with fear. Dr Vassiliev's head suddenly appeared behind her, as he stooped down on the floor and spoke reassuringly, telling her that it was all right, and she shouldn't be frightened. He reached underneath the bed and tugged her, though she dug her claws into the thick carpet and meowed in protest. But he pried her out, and deposited her on the pillow where she liked to sleep. When he lay down himself, she cowered behind his head, at times peaking fearfully over the top of it, at the window.

She sniffed the doctor's face and mouth with interest, the whiff of alcohol on his breath. It was a smell that she was familiar with, for he drank it every night – but tonight it smelled different, slightly off.

The doctor fell asleep straight away. She did not like this, because she needed him to stay awake, to protect her from the monstrous storm outside. And so she meowed at him, but in vain.

Lyubova too must have fallen asleep, because she found herself waking to a constant ringing noise. It was not the normal sound of the glowing thing that rang on his bedside table, but a muffled ringing, hidden somewhere. The doctor snuffled and stirred, eventually rolling over to search for the source of the ringing – he started opening and slamming drawers, agitated and sleepy. Eventually he pulled out something from the bottom drawer – another glowing thing. He looked at it for some time, as though he did not understand it, did not know what it was. He pressed it cautiously to his ear and lay back against his pillow, listening to someone's voice, eyes closed. After some time, he snapped the glowing thing shut, leant over and reached inside the same drawer, pulling out a small black object. Again, he stared at it for a while, then put it on the bed, next to the glowing thing. The object was about the size of a bee – round, flat, and rubbery. Lyubova resisted the urge to jump on it and bat it with her paw; the storm outside was too frightening for such playfulness.

Surprisingly, the doctor got out of bed and began dressing. Lyubova glanced at the window – with the curtains undrawn, she could see that, outside, the night was still thick with blackness. That meant it was time to sleep, not go out. She glared at the doctor and meowed, telling him so. But he continued dressing, putting on his going-out coat, then stashing the glowing thing in his pocket, and pressing the black bee in his ear. He left the room, and her, without a word.

Lyubova watched him disappear through the door in disbelief. She quickly jumped down and followed him.

The doctor went downstairs, feet a flurry on the steps as he ran. He walked straight to the back, to the garden door, and he stooped down to pull on his boots. They were his walking boots still caked in mud – dried clumps and flakes scattering on the floor. The glowing thing in his pocket rang again, and he touched the bee-shaped thing in his ear, before opening the door.

Once again, he left her without acknowledgement, pulling the hood over his head, and hunching from the rain, before disappearing into the howling, windswept storm.

Sitting as close to the open door as she dared, she stared out, watching him go – anxious pupils dilating like tiny black expanding universes. She was sure the storm would eat him alive, so she called out to him, telling him to come back. But her pathetic meows were drowned out by the rain.

Lyubova hardly knew what to do. She was frightened of the storm, but if she stayed inside, she would still be afraid without him. In a split second she made a decision.

Bounding down the garden steps, she chased after him. The rain pelted against her back – fat, cold, water bombs, soaking through her fur in seconds. But still she followed him down the garden.

She found him waiting at the gate. He had stopped. Dead still, like a bent, silent tree. He stayed like that for a while, unmoving, and she meowed at him as loud as she could, shouting at him, telling him they needed to go back. But he ignored her. And then he suddenly opened the garden gate, and walked purposefully outside. Little Lyubova had no choice but to follow him.

The faintly glowing forest was a different beast at night.

In the bright light of day it was a lush, green place of wonder and adventure. But in the dark it terrified her. Yet still she bounded after the doctor, rushing to keep up with him. Scared that she would be left behind. He walked for an age, without stopping, not even noticing she was following. She was confused, felt like she was drowning with so much rain, paws heavy with mud, shivering from the cold, wondering where he was going, water flooding her ears and eyes. Everything made her jump. Twigs underfoot, the flutter of a stray leaf, claps of thunder overhead, shots of lightning – all conspiring to terrify her. Yet the doctor still walked on and on. And she wondered when this awful nightmare would end.

There was something in the distance. A light just visible between the trees and the downpour. It was a car, its eyes shooting out beams of light. Next to it stood a coated figure – so dark it looked like a shadow. The shadow opened the back door, before walking round and getting into the driver's seat, movements slow and stiff. The doctor climbed in without a word, and Lyubova just managed to dart inside before he closed the door. She wanted to shake herself down, but the belly of the car began to roar and quake, and all she could do was cower underneath the doctor's legs as the car lurched forward. The side window had been left open just a crack, and now and then, whenever she dared, she sniffed the air that flowed inside. She was still afraid, but at least she was with her doctor – though he just sat still, staring straight ahead in a daze like he was asleep with open eyes.

They travelled for hours, and Lyubova shivered under his legs, both from the damp and nausea. Soon the car became warmer and she started dozing off, but the car jolted her awake again and again. As the night gradually passed, so did the storm, and by the time the car began slowing to a stop, the light of dawn soaked through the clear air, birds singing brightly.

When the car ground to a halt, Dr Vassiliev opened the door and climbed out, again without even a word to her, or a glance. Lyubova quietly jumped down and trailed behind her doctor. He in turn was following the shadow into a run-down house. But the shadow turned and spotted her, and began stamping feet and waving wild arms like a madman – shooing her off. Lyubova arched her back, fanned her tail, and hissed, before running away. She sheltered behind a tall, smelly wheelie bin, and watched with a sinking feeling as her doctor disappeared into the house – flies buzzing distractedly around her head.

In the same way that Lyubova often scanned the garden for birds, the shadow stopped to look slowly, deliberately, all around, before quietly closing the door.

12 THE HOUSE OF SHADOW

Lyubova stared at the house for a long time, not knowing what to do. The dread in her gut made her feel physically ill, and so she crouched down, sphinx-like, and waited. Her pupils narrowing into thin ellipses as she watched. The house was clad in dark roughly-hewn stone, with a similar colour roof, three floors from the ground. Giant trees plump with foliage surrounded it, casting shade, so that the building seemed to repel light. Fitting that the shadow lived in such a place.

She looked around – but apart from the house and its yard and outhouses, there was nothing else except greenery, and no signs of other human life. They were completely remote. Her ears twisted forward, funnelling sound from the house – doors opening and shutting, single footsteps, a raspy cough, other unknown noises.

Night soon fell, and she had no choice but to find shelter in the bough of a tree, catching sleep only here and there – the raucous calls of wild animals and birds constantly waking her.

The next day she felt brave enough to go closer to the house, inspecting it, sniffing it, and searching for a way to get in. But despite pacing around it several times, she found nothing.

Once, the front door opened, and the shadow walked out purposefully, toward one of the smaller outhouses. She watched from afar as he went inside, and clattered around. He finally appeared again holding a thick metal strip, narrower one end, and an edge lined with a sharp row of teeth. When the shadow disappeared inside his dark house, there came prolonged rhythmic ratchety sounds, then something dropped with a dull thud. Sharp, loud banging noises made Lyubova jump – pounding again and again.

Days turned into weeks, and Lyubova survived on drinking from puddles of rainwater and catching field mice, of which there were many. Sometimes she was even able to pounce on a bird, or two, or three. Her fur began to matt, the lustre in her eyes dulled, and even her whiskers seemed to droop from despondency. Yet still, every day she walked slowly around the house, trying to find a way in.

In time, her keen eyes spotted something on the top floor.

She got up, whiskers twitching as she crept over to the house, one paw at a time, her belly low against the ground. She reached the porch, and her tail flicked nervously as she surveyed the height and gauged the distance. Powerful thigh muscles sprang her up onto the wall, so that her body hugged the vertical corner – with sharp nails digging into the crevices of the hewn stonework, her back legs pushed her upward so that in just a few nimble leaps she reached the sloped porch roof.

Silently she padded up to the highest point, her tail balancing her steady as she walked along the gable to the vertical fascia of the first floor. Ears twisting round 180 degrees and back, she listened keenly, assured that no-one inside the house was nearby. Again, she leapt up, but this time straight onto the ledge of a second-floor window. She walked nimbly along it without looking through the glass, trusting her senses that there was nobody there. Despite aching paws, she still jumped over the top of the window, and clawed her way to a juliet balcony on the third floor. She slipped through the bars with ease.

But there was yet one last hurdle.

Jumping up onto the thin handrail, her paws wobbled slightly, tail flicking, as she regained her balance. And then she poised. Without a second thought she leapt off the balcony – nothing but a gaping drop beneath. Her body stretched like an uncoiled spring, front paws reaching forward, until she landed with a thud on the ledge of the loft window – a jump of nearly two metres.

Glancing at the ground 10 metres down, she saw that a fall would have meant the unthinkable. But she did not dwell on this, instead she turned round to check out the gap at the top of the window – thankfully, it was wide enough. She jumped up and slipped through it with ease, snaking down the other side onto a bureau. But in doing so she knocked over a picture frame, and it dropped to the floor, smashing. Lyubova jumped with fright.

There came a distant sound of movement from the other side of the door on the far wall. Footsteps on stairs, climbing, getting louder. The thud of awkward running. The handle turned, and the door flung open. Shadow stepped in and looked slowly around, before walking over to the window. It bent down with a grunt, and picked up the broken frame – clinking shards of broken glass on top of its shattered surface.

Hiding underneath the bed, Lyubova watched the shadow's shoes, just a few feet away from her. She listened as it huffed, closed the window shut, and then turned around – at last, leaving the room the way it came. Shuffling steps winding slowly downward.

Lyubova waited several minutes before crawling out. She padded toward the door, looking up at the walls as she went.

She had never seen a room like this – pictures of all sizes, and in vivid colours, covering every inch of space. On the floor, stacks of them leaning against furniture, or on chairs piled in precarious bundles. And though she could not understand what they were, somehow, they awed her.

She reached the closed door and stood in front of it, looking up at the handle. This one was easy – in theory. But it took her several jumps before she managed to flick down the lever, finally releasing the catch – and she pawed the door open, her body curling through the gap.

In the dim light of the landing her eyes dilated, and she saw again pictures hanging on the walls, covering every inch. Lyubova ran silently down the stairs, and she poked her head through the doorway of each room that she came across, before walking inside, warily looking around and examining objects – searching for her doctor. Slowly she made her way through the house. Not a single room was without a clutter of pictures.

One room in particular held her attention. There was a musty smell about it that spoke of stagnant air, cobwebs, loused wood and furnishings of a bygone era. It seemed even dimmer than the other rooms, and so she wandered cautiously inside, not noticing the large painting leaning against the wall, even though she walked up to the base of its gilded rococo frame, and sniffed the wood. Just then, outside, clouds shifted and parted, and powdery rays of light penetrated the window and suffused the room's air, spotlighting motes of floating dust. The room brightened, the painting illuminated, and that's when Lyubova saw the fullness of the image before her. Hissing, spine arching with fear, she inched backward as anxious eyes darted over its awful glory. Flames of orange, red, and yellow. Coal-black smoke. The charred remains of a burning house. At its centre a woman and a boy, crouched on the floor – the woman with terrified eyes, the boy burying his face into her chest. Melting, like Dali's pendulous motifs, into each other.

Lyubova's skin tingled with alarm. Fire leapt out at her from the canvas, singeing her fur. The stench of it seemed to fill her nostrils. Cloying smoke in her throat. She crept further back, whiskers quivering nervously. Eventually peeling her eyes away, she quickly turned and fled.

With a pounding heart and jangled nerves, she pushed on with her search, making her way through the next room, and then the next. Until there was left just one... and she hoped upon hope that her doctor would at last be there. But she knew there would also be the shadow.

Standing before the entrance now, in the dim corridor, Lyubova lifted her nose to the wedge of light bursting through the crack of the door left ajar. The air plumed with warmth, and it smelled as if the doctor was close. So close. Surely he must be there. Her ears twitched at the sound of someone talking, mumbling. Their voice, rough and guttural. She pushed the door open with her flank and barged inside, meowing loudly for her doctor.

Shadow looked up from across the room, dropping the knife on the table with a clang. A chair scraped back loudly as it stood up.

Lyubova walked casually in, picking her way over bits of wood strewn over the floor. She jumped up onto a chair and then the table, which wobbled slightly as she landed. Looking all around, her heart sank as she discovered her doctor was nowhere to be seen.

Lyubova found herself face to face with the shadow.

She stared up at it, as it stared down at her.

And then she casually sat down, and started licking her paws, because they ached.

Gradually shadow inched sideways, away from her, and slipped behind as Lyubova continued grooming. Every hair of her back tingled, as she sensed his movements though he was out of view. There came a click of a latch, the rustle of material, and when shadow suddenly pounced on her, she jumped away in a blink of an eye, yowling and scrambling. The shadow had a sack in its hands – and Lyubova crashed from one place to another, shrieking as she jumped around to avoid the fabric that swept above her. Her lithe movements dodged the shadow's clumsy ones, again and again. Wood, nails, brushes flying all over. A triangle-shaped frame clattered to the floor. Her paws slipped on pungent oil seeping from a fallen bottle. As she leapt, and jumped, and scrambled, Lyubova tried to calculate a way to escape, but there seemed no way out – the door was shut, windows closed.

In all the chaos, she inadvertently jumped on the source of the heat in the room, a large metal box lit up with the same flames she had seen in the painting. Her paws burnt with a sizzle, and she yowled with pain. Jumping off reflexively, her head knocked against the inglenook mantel – and she collapsed on the floor in a heap.

The shadow stopped for a few seconds, then picked its way over to her. Wood cracking underfoot. Worn shoes, that smelled of old leather, came so close they nearly touched her nose.

Lyubova's eyes slid closed, and she passed out.

Consciousness came and went in nauseous waves.

Blackness with pinprick light seeping through coarse sackcloth.

Thrown callously onto a soft surface.

The thwunk of a car door.

Hessian fibres tickling her nose.

The stench of mould.

In time, Lyubova found herself coming to, inside a sack, within the car, recognising the same mechanical thrum of the machine's belly, the light breeze from a window stuck slightly open. The jostle of motion.

They travelled for some time, though nowhere near as long as the other night. And before she knew it the car had stopped, the door opened, and the sack with her inside was dragged out, onto the springy damp of grass.

Lyubova twisted round so that she was back on her paws, crouched low within the hessian – every sense sharpened, ready for the attack.

But shadow's footsteps retreated and returned to the car, and the iron beast roared to life. Wheels shlopping through mud, its purring engine gradually vanishing into the distance.

Lyubova dared not move for some time. But in the end, desperation forced her to take action. The sack was tied firmly closed, but she twisted round until she spied a small frayed hole with blades of grass poking through. She systematically scratched at it, even though her paws throbbed with pain. Scratching and biting and clawing and tearing. Until at last the hessian frayed and she was able to crawl out – kicking off the sack with her back paws.

She looked around, looked up at the rich blue of the sky, the sun drenching her in warmth. Blinking through the buttery light. She paused to breathe in the soft pure air... grasping where she was in the world... diaphanous gusts sifting through her fur...

As she stayed statue-still, the iron-rich haemoglobin in the blood coursing through her brain aligned with, and gave her a sense of, the geomagnetic fields around her – fields that sprang from the great molten core below, deep, deep within the belly of the earth under her paws, whirling and cascading up and around her. A stream of charged particles vanished into the sun, looped round, and flowed back again. Lyubova absorbed all this, like a sixth sense. She delicately sniffed the air, and then turned to face away from the brilliant orb in the sky, purposefully running off in a south-westerly direction across the field.

She had not found her doctor in the house of shadow, so there was nothing left but to return to the place where they were staying before. In the hope that by now he must surely be finding his way back to her there, just as she was finding her way back to him.

••• ———————————————————— •••

She walked for miles.

Across fields, and roads, and through towns. Her paws were cracked and raw. Each step punishing her with stabs of pain. An empty belly growling relentlessly. She had stopped meowing a long time ago; silence her only companion.

When night fell, she forced herself to find shelter. Walking casually into people's gardens, she often found a garden table or chair on which she could rest and curl up to sleep, shivering from the cold. And she soon discovered that if she peered through their clear glass doors, humans would notice, and make kindly, soothing noises. They often laid out a dish of food or milk, and she rubbed herself gratefully against their legs, purring feebly, before wolfing down the food, or lapping the milk. And if she felt particularly weak, she would stay with them a few hours longer, enjoying being stroked and fussed over as she rightly deserved.

Lyubova knew foxes came at night. Their otherworldly howling and barking terrified her. And so, because the foxes shunned them, she learnt to stay as close to the humans as possible, taking sanctuary in the relative safety of their walled gardens.

She continued walking for days and days.

By now her ear was beginning to ache. It felt sticky inside, and throbbed hot and cold, making her dizzy.

On the sixth day of her travels, the nausea was so strong that she lost her balance and kept falling over. The ear itched to distraction, and she would rub her ear flap against the rough surface of tree bark to alleviate it. But it only seemed to get worse.

By day 11, Lyubova was feeling incredibly weak. She could only walk a few shaky metres before falling on her side, struggling to get up onto uncertain feet – only to fall over again. But still she kept on, her will unbreakable.

After nearly two weeks, Lyubova at last found herself peeking through the tall iron gate of the house. She looked at the building for some time, weary to the extreme – wondering if she was dreaming, hardly believing she was there. Eyes fixed on the house for fear it might disappear, she stepped between the cast iron pickets, and shuffled ever closer at a snail's pace. Finally she made it to the back of the house. The garden was a welcome sight, the familiar purple clematis running up the walls, the solidity and shine of the back door that embodied security and protection. She stood staring through the glass for some time, seeing unfamiliar figures inside, hearing dull noises. She meowed constantly, but they did not notice her.

Rain began pelting down on her back – and she was so weak, her skin so sensitive, that each drop seemed to whip and scourge her. Still she meowed and meowed despite a sore throat. And at last a large black dog came walking over to the other side of the glass and sat right in front of her, staring back.

Then one of the humans noticed her too, and opened the door.

At last, at last!!

Lyubova walked shakily inside.

13 PUZZLE PIECES

When Tai awoke the next morning, he sat up in bed with a heart that felt like lead. He wiped the tears from his eyes, and turned to face the sleeping cat. <u>Lyubova</u> was snuffling lightly on the pillow next to his. He scooped her into his arms and cradled her, lightly kissing the top of her head several times.

The cat opened sleepy eyes, luminous circles of copper flecked with gold, disappointed to find that it was not her doctor. Still, she basked in the adoration, closing her eyes to revel in it.

Tai's mother came in shortly after, pleased to find her son sitting up. But when she saw his tear-streaked face, she drew closer, concerned. 'What is it, Tai?' she asked anxiously.

'I know what happened... to the cat, to Dr Vassiliev,' he told her. His voice sounded even huskier than before. 'You need to call the others.'

Tyaishia's eyes widened as she absorbed this, and then she turned and ran out into the hall, shouting madly at the top of her lungs. 'Everybody wake up! Wake up!!' She banged several times on each of the bedroom doors, and after a few minutes, they gradually emerged one by one. Tyaishia shimmied them all into Tai's room. 'Quick, quick! Get in wi Tai. Him knows what 'appened!!'

A very tired Milly padded to the other side of Tai's bed and just curled up on it, with her father coming to sit next to her. Mei Hui sat down on the chair next to the bed, looking from the cat, to him, anxiously. She knew what he must have done. 'I hope that you did not drain yourself, Tai,' she said. 'You must conserve your energy.'

'I'm okay,' he replied, his eyes softening at her concern. 'It happened while I was sleeping, when the cat came next to me. It was like a dream, so I didn't feel a thing.'

The Professor tapped his way into the room, wrapped in a navy dressing gown, hair a silvery-grey mess. 'What's going on?' he asked.

'The cat slept on my bed last night...' said Tai, releasing Lyubova from his arms. She jumped across to the window ledge, and sat on it, her tail wrapping around herself, looking regal as she peered through the pane. 'I found out what happened to her... to the doctor.' He threw a glance at his mother, and absorbed the colours of the aura surrounding her. Fascination and disbelief. 'This is what I was telling you about, Ma. You gotta believe it.'

Tyaishia nodded, holding her tongue, and urged him to go on.

Tai closed his eyes briefly, and remembered. 'The night of the storm, the doctor drank from the bottle in his bedside table, like he always does every night. But this time it was drugged with something – the cat smelt it on his breath, a smell she didn't recognise. Later, in the middle of the night, a phone started ringing. Not his own mobile phone, which he kept on top of the bedside table – but it was a phone he found in the bottom drawer. I think that was the first time he'd seen it, because he looked at it strange, like he'd never seen it before. He answered it and listened for long, but didn't say anything.

'When he put the phone down, he took something else out of the same drawer – an earbud. And then he got dressed to go out, and put the earbud in his ear, and the phone in his pocket. He answered another call just as he was leaving through the back door. Lyubova followed him out, and watched as he stopped at the garden gate. He waited for a bit, then suddenly rushed out of the gate and into the forest. I think the person on the phone was giving him directions. The doctor walked through the forest in the dark and the rain for a long time...

'In the end he got to a road where there was a car waiting, and a shadowy person standing next to it. The doctor got in at the back, and Lyubova jumped in before the door closed. She hid underneath the doctor's legs, but he never even looked at her. They drove until morning light... I'm not sure how long it took. But they stopped at a house – a dark grey house, next to some tall trees, in the middle of nowhere. And they went inside. It took a long time before Lyubova found a way of getting in – through a window left open on the top floor. Inside, there were lots and lots of paintings, everywhere. On the floor, piled on furniture, all over the walls.' Tai looked at the Professor. 'The memory I saw before, of a burning house – that was actually a massive picture that Lyubova saw there too. It scared her.'

The Professor sat down on a nearby chair, trembling hands squeezing tight the top of his walking stick.

Tai continued. 'She couldn't find the doctor anywhere in the house. But in the last room, there was a man. The shadowy man. He was talking to himself... There were bits of wood on the floor – and on the table, four pieces of wood nailed together in a square. He'd cut them with a saw. He was also cutting out a thick white cloth on the table. I think he was making another picture, a painting, because there was one of those triangle-shaped picture-stands as well...'

'An easel?' asked Milly.

'Yes, an easel. And there were loads of brushes and different coloured paints, all on the side. A jar of yellow stuff spilled over when she ran from him. She kept slipping on it, and it was really smelly...'

'Maybe that was linseed oil,' murmured the Professor, almost to himself. 'It's used for oil paintings.'

'Yes, maybe,' said Tai. He looked across at the cat, who was still gazing outside. 'Lyubova burnt her paws on a metal box with fire inside, and accidentally knocked herself out. She was put inside a sack and dumped somewhere by the man. She clawed her way out, and managed to find her way back here, though it took long.' Tai suddenly thought of something. 'I also saw the way the doctor treated the cat, before. He loved her very much. I know that he would never abandon Lyubova on purpose, or ignore her...'

'Just like the Russian grandma said,' said Brian.

Mei Hui nodded. 'It looks like he was drugged and kidnapped against his will.'

'Yes,' said Tai. 'The way he was acting was like he'd been... hypnotised. He just did everything the man told him.'

Brian was fascinated. 'So, what did the kidnapper look like then?'

Tai frowned. 'I could not see. He wore a cap, a tatty old brown cap, so his eyes were in shadow, and a grey beard covered most of his face. And he moved like an old man, with a bent back.'

Mei Hui stiffened. 'It might be the same person who chased me.' She turned to Tai. 'You said there were lots of paintings. Did you see what they were of? Was there a signature on them?'

Tai closed his eyes and flicked through the cat's memories in his mind. 'She only really looked at one painting properly, the one of the burning house...' Tai brought that memory to mind, and homed in on the picture, examining it. 'There *was* a signature!' he exclaimed. In his mind he zoomed into the scrawled handwriting, tracing the flow of lines of each brush-stroke. He snapped his eyes open. 'F. Jaffrey!'

Quickly, the Professor pulled out his mobile. 'Jasmine, do a search for paintings by F. Jaffrey.'

'Good morning, Professor,' said Jasmine, cordially. 'F. Jaffrey was a famous 19th century painter...'

'No, no,' interrupted the Professor. 'Someone more recent, who's living now. Are there any living artists by the name of F. Jaffrey?'

'Negative, Professor,' replied Jasmine. 'There are no known records of contemporary painters by the name of F. Jaffrey.'

'Perhaps he painted under a... what're they called again?' asked Brian, annoyed at himself for forgetting the word.

'A pseudonym,' said Milly.

'But even if he painted under a pseudonym,' said the Professor, 'the name should be recorded somewhere.'

'Unless he painted only for himself, and never exhibited or put up anything for sale,' proffered Brian. 'Sounds like he might be a very private person, living in the middle of nowhere and all.'

'It is very strange,' said Mei Hui, deep in thought, 'that there is also a 19th century painter by the same name. I wonder if there is a connection?'

'That's a good question, Mei Hui,' said the Professor. 'But one thing is certain. We need to get to this man, and the painting, as soon as possible. It's possible that the doctor is still locked up somewhere there too, somewhere that was not obvious to the cat.'

Brian turned to Tai. 'Can you describe what the house looked like?'

Tai thought about this. 'Yes,' he said, though he realised there was a better way.

'Good,' said the Professor. 'Will you also be able to explain the route the cat walked to get back?'

Tai nodded slowly. 'But the man drove for a bit before dumping her. That's the missing part.'

'Well, at least we'll be a bit closer to finding him,' said Brian. He got up. 'I'll get a laptop, and we can work out the route together.'

'Good,' remarked the Professor. 'I'll also ask O'Connor if we've got the lab results yet for the vodka. And he'll need to look into the missing housekeeper too. I don't think they thought much of it when she stopped coming – but now we know someone spiked the vodka that night, and planted those things in the bedside cabinet, she is looking more and more suspicious.'

'And I will do some research on F. Jaffrey of the 19th century, as well as male F. Jaffreys today to see if there is a link,' offered Mei Hui. 'Milly, do you want to come and help me?'

Milly by now was nestled next to Tai, her head resting on his shoulder. Contact with him was alleviating the first twinges of a headache that had started almost as soon as she woke up – but in the short time she was with Tai, her head was almost clear. She sat up, nodding. ''Kay,' she said, stretching and yawning. Brian offered her his hand, she took it, and he pulled her up. He kissed the top of her head. 'You sure you're okay, pigeon?'

Mei Hui glanced at Tyaishia and they exchanged a smile.

Milly nodded up at her father. 'Yep, I'm okay.'

'I'll get on wid cooking breakfast,' said Tyaishia. Perhaps that was the most important task. 'Yuh genius kids can't be doing much geniusin' widout some good food in yuh,' she said, winking at Mei Hui.

As the humans were talking, Lyubova sat silently on the windowsill, looking outside. Her tail thumping wistfully against the magnolia-painted wood as she scanned the garden. Despite the room being filled with people, she felt lonely.

Something was meowing feebly on the floor just below. And she peered over and saw the tortoise-shell kitten looking up at her, crying for attention. All the other cats had gone with Dog downstairs for food and water, but she had been left behind. The kitten was trying to find a way up to her, and eventually scrambled onto a chair, then a cabinet, and lastly jumped up onto the windowsill. The little creature padded over to Lyubova, meowing scratchily, and then crouched down next to her – eyes suddenly magnetised to birds flitting across the landscape, from tree to tree. Lyubova felt suddenly protective, and she nestled closer, licking the kitten's ear briefly, and then settled down to watch the birds too. Both cats' heads moved in unison, left and right, like spectators at a tennis match.

•••———————————————•••

After an hour, the Professor returned to Tai's room, and discovered that everyone else was there too. 'I found out about the vodka,' he told them. 'Just as we suspected, it was spiked with something called Rohypnol – a benzodiazepine, which is used as a tranquilliser for sedation and insomnia. Commonly referred to as a "roofie", it's also used by nefarious people to drug unsuspecting victims to take advantage of them, because under its influence they're highly suggestible. Afterwards, people who are given the drug don't even remember what happened to them.'

'Yeah, I've heard of it on the news!' said Brian, who was sitting next to Tai with a laptop. 'And it makes sense that it was given to the doctor. It explains why he did everything he was told, without question. And also why he left the cat behind too. Oh, by the way, Tai and I have been tracing the cat's route, and discovered the location where she was dumped. Would you believe it's about 150 miles north-east from here! Beggars belief she was able to find her way back!' He looked down at the map on the screen. 'Thing is, we don't know where the man drove from to leave her there. Though from Tai's description of the house being remote, in the middle of nowhere, and surrounded by really big trees, after studying the map, I think Northumberland fits. There are lots of woods and forests there, you see. I read too that loads of monumental trees can be found there.'

The Professor nodded slowly. 'Good. Good work.' He pulled out his phone again. 'Jasmine, get V2 to come here immediately will you.'

'I've sent him a priority message, Professor,' she said.

Both Milly and Mei Hui were sitting cross-legged on the floor together, huddled around a tablet. Mei Hui stood up and perched on Tai's bed. 'We have also discovered something,' she said. 'There is an ongoing exhibition of F. Jaffrey's work at the National Portrait Gallery, in London. It has remained there for decades, due to its popularity. If it is all right, Professor, Milly and I would like to go see it. To look at the paintings.'

The Professor thought about this. As usual, his over-protective nature tugged at him. But he knew he could no longer keep them hostage to his own fear and insecurity. He sighed. 'If you will agree to the usual security provided by V2, then yes, you may go, see what you can discover. If that's also fine with you, Brian?'

Milly shot her father a wary look. 'Is… that okay, Dad?'

Brian eventually nodded. 'Yeah, okay. I trust V2 and his men. They'll keep you safe.' He remembered how the agents valiantly fought off Penny Thompson's cohorts. He was also greatly encouraged to see Milly excited about something…

Milly got up, linked arms with Mei Hui, and made to leave. But V2 strode in purposefully, blocking their way. He nodded at the girls, and then turned to the Professor. 'You wanted me?'

'Ah, V2. Yes, two things. First you need to round up some of your best security to accompany Milly and Mei Hui on a trip to London. The National Portrait Gallery to be precise. They want to view an exhibition there today. And secondly, we need to get some agents to search for a particular house. I'm afraid all we've got to go on is a description, and a rough location, somewhere near Northumberland we believe.'

'O-kay,' said V2. 'We can definitely get some of our men to trawl satellite images, with Jasmine's help. We'd need the best description of it you can give.'

Tai piped up. 'I've thought of a better way…' He held his hand out to Milly, and she went over to take hold of it. Then Milly turned to V2 and, hesitantly, held out her other hand to him. 'Will you give me your hand please?'

Puzzled, he extended his hand and Milly grasped it, closing her eyes.

Suddenly, V2 pulled away, as if he'd just received an electric shock. He blinked several times as an image appeared inexplicably in his mind – of a three-story dilapidated house, clad in grey stonework, and nestled amongst a copse of tall trees swaying gently in the breeze. He shook his head, but the image was still there, clear as day. 'I... I can see it, in my mind!' he said bewildered. 'H-how is that even possible?'

The Professor, cocking his head to hear, guessed what had happened. 'That, V2, is confidential I'm afraid. And will remain that way, do you understand?'

V2 composed himself, and nodded, remembering it was not his place to question. 'Yes, sir,' he said firmly. He gulped, and turned to Milly. 'I... I'll get a sketch drawn up for the team. Erm, thanks. When are you planning on leaving for London?'

Mei Hui answered him. 'We can be ready very quickly. In T-minus 30 minutes.'

Brian grinned. 'Mei, you've been watching too many American cop shows.'

She smiled. 'They are... interesting. But also the British ones are good too. Especially Sherlock!'

'A Study in Pink!' Milly chimed in. 'That's my favourite.' The girls circumnavigated around V2, and walked out together, chattering about their favourite parts of the show.

14 GREAT MINDS

Just over two hours later, and the two girls were walking through the short forecourt of the National Portrait Gallery, toward the impressive pedimented entrance and glass doors. They took in the Renaissance style architecture, the three busts of the founders on the wall, and the coat of arms above the door – before stepping through the entrance, into the hallowed silence of the museum's inner sanctum. There was a faint smell of wood-wax in the air, and echoes of hushed chatting from scattered onlookers.

A greeter swooped upon them almost immediately – a pretty young woman with a tangle of ginger hair, and horn-rimmed glasses. She seemed to have a permanent smile on her face. 'Hello! And welcome to the National Portrait Gallery. How are you doing today?'

'Fine, thank you,' said Mei Hui courteously, bowing her head with respect.

'Wonderful,' beamed the greeter. 'Would you like tickets for an exhibition, or are you happy to roam the galleries by yourselves?'

The girls looked at each other, and Milly said, 'Erm, we just want to see the Jaffrey room please.'

'Amazing choice!' she said, ecstatic. She indicated toward the shop. 'We have a guidebook for that particular floor if you want–'

'Actually,' interrupted Milly. 'We're fine to just go and see it ourselves.' She had already speed-read and memorised a guide as they travelled.

'That's not a problem at all,' the greeter said as she darted a look at the clock on the wall. 'If you hurry, you'll be able to listen to a tour on 19th century art, which will visit the Jaffrey room as one of the stops.'

'Thanks,' said Mei Hui thoughtfully, 'that would be good.'

'Fantastic! Let me just get you a map, so you can find your way...' she said, holding up a finger.

'Oh no need!' said Milly. 'We know how to get there. First floor, room 30.'

'Great, yes, correct. You're very fortunate, because today's tour guide, Mrs Parry-Johansson, is a specialist in <u>late Victorian oil paintings</u>, with particular expertise on Jaffrey's work. She's actually retiring at the end of the month, so these will be her last tours. It'll be the end of an era when she goes…'

'I would very much like to meet her, thank you,' said Mei Hui, before being pulled away by Milly who had grabbed her arm, eager to see the paintings. By the time they reached room 30, the tour guide was already there speaking to a small group of 12, and was just about to leave.

'Oh no, have you finished here already?' said Mei Hui, disappointed.

Mrs Parry-Johansson looked sympathetically at her. Her hair, now snow white, was no longer in a beehive, but cropped short to frame a delicate jawline. She still wore a twinset and pearls. 'I'm so sorry, yes. I've just finished my talk for this room. We're moving on to room 31 if you'd like to join us?'

'We're only interested in Jaffrey's work really,' Milly explained, almost apologetically.

'Well, I'm doing the tour every afternoon this week,' she shouted out to them, already heading out of the door.

Milly raised a hand. 'Thank you, but we won't be able to come back…' She said this in vain, because the guide had already disappeared round the corner, with the group trailing behind her. Milly turned to Mei Hui who had already worked out how the paintings were ordered – by year and date – and was walking over to the earliest, on the far side of the door. Milly joined her, and they systematically went to each of the paintings together, studying them, reading their labels. They admired the rich density of colour, muted fusion of tones, and the fluidity of brush-strokes. They absorbed too the different subjects for each painting: some single figures looking sternly into the distance, other sitters were couples, or entire families – there was even a portrait of a dog. All exquisitely rendered.

The girls lingered in the room for almost two hours as they examined closely the finer details of each picture, or stepped back several paces to admire it as a whole. Behind them came other visitors entering, hovering, and disappearing.

'All these paintings,' remarked Milly – eyes jumping from the portrait of a young black dandy, smug in a stiff high-collar and cravat, to the next picture of a pale maid with startling green eyes, wearing a bodiced dress and a sheer bonnet – 'it's like a painted Facebook.' She peered admiringly at the exquisite detail on the maid's glazed eyes. 'This one looks as if she's about to burst into tears.'

Mei Hui came next to her and looked too. But then she felt a tap on her shoulder. They turned to find that the tour guide had returned. 'I've finished my tour, and very glad to see that you're still here,' she told them, smiling kindly. 'Jaffrey is one of my favourite artists, so I'm always happy to find others who have a keen interest in him too.' She looked at them both, trying to discern their ages. 'Are you studying his work for college?'

'No,' said Mei Hui honestly. 'We just think his work is very... interesting.'

The guide nodded. 'That it is! In fact, it's one of the reasons why I've become so fascinated by him – you see, F. Jaffrey was a pseudonym, and the man's real name is still a mystery to this day. We know very little about him, except for just a handful of things mentioned in letters written by people who'd commissioned him for portraits.'

'That is a shame,' remarked Mei Hui, wondering if they had travelled all that way for nothing.

The guide waved toward one of the largest paintings in the room, opposite a window, where it received the most natural light. 'Take the portrait of Lord and Lady Masterson for example, the largest and most elaborate work we have of his. Lady Molly wrote letters to her niece, Mrs Elisabeth Bailey, purporting that they had never had to sit for the artist. Not even once. She wrote that the artist had sent them instructions for their first meeting, saying that they should wear the clothes they wanted to be painted in, and had to position themselves in the desired setting and arrangement, ready for when he arrived. Lady Molly also mentioned in the letter that the artist came to their house late one winter's evening, keeping his coat and his hood on at all times, so that they never actually saw his face. He asked if they had any special requests, they discussed how they would like to be painted, then he drank some port – and that was it! No sittings at all. So we're led to believe that he was able to paint this entire picture to every last detail from memory!'

Milly and Mei Hui looked at each other in amazement and barely suppressed excitement, immediately gravitating toward the portrait in question. It was huge, elaborate, and beautiful, and their eyes swept across it in silent awe.

'That's extraordinary,' said Milly, mumbling to herself – her mind already whirring with possibilities.

Mei Hui, being short in stature, drew closer and tiptoed to take a better look. Then she remembered something, and turned toward the guide. 'I wonder if I may ask... you mentioned that the mystery around F. Jaffrey was *one* of the reasons why you became so fascinated with his work. What were the other reasons?'

'Top marks for noticing!' she smiled. 'Well, there are many – apart, of course, from his wonderful artistry. A very coincidental reason was because, right at the beginning of my career here at the NPG, a certain young man kept visiting the room – and he made quite an impression on me. He was probably a little younger than yourselves when I first met him.' She smiled with fondness as she remembered. 'At first he came with a shiny polaroid camera hung around his neck – and like you, he was only interested in this artist, and these paintings. Never went to any of the other rooms as far as I was aware. I think I counted that he visited 14 times, if memory serves me right – all within the space of around...' she placed a thoughtful finger on her chin, '...about four or five years. He was enthralled with every single painting, kept taking pictures of them – so many pictures. Then one day, he stopped bringing his camera. Instead he brought a pad and pencil, and would sit on the floor, cross-legged in front of each painting, sketching away for ages...' The guide's expression turned to one of wonder. 'His drawings! They were... unique. Inspired. Masterful! And over time, we built up a little friendship, he and I, what with his numerous visits. And I have to say that the style of the child's artwork bore more than a little resemblance to Jaffrey's sketches, underdrawings, and even the imprimatura – which is the first stain of colour. I know, because we had started studying the maestro's work in depth, even taking x-rays of the paintings.' She swept a hand around the room. 'Jaffrey had a very unique, very particular style, which I'm told is exceptionally difficult and almost impossible to imitate. And yet the boy mimicked that style... to perfection. In fact, I probably wouldn't be able to tell the difference between the boy's drawings and Jaffrey's.' Her eyes glazed over as she remembered something. 'All those decades ago, I used to watch with fascination as the boy sketched, and the odd thing was... he hardly looked up at the original paintings themselves. Yet, what he drew were near-perfect replicas, with exact proportions and dimensions.'

'Could it be–' started Milly, at the same time as the guide said, 'I did wonder whether the boy might have been a descendent...' – which was exactly Milly's thought too. The girls looked pointedly at each other.

'You... you think the boy was a relative of F. Jaffrey?' asked Mei Hui, her excitement mounting.

The guide seemed to come out of a daydream. 'Sorry, yes, that's what I meant.' She beamed. 'Since then, I've done my damnedest to find out everything I could about the great F. Jaffrey, most of all to discover who he really was, and whether he had any children, relatives, etc. But sadly, despite all my connections, I came up with absolutely nothing...' She shrugged her shoulders in resignation. 'C'est la vie! Anyway, I hope that answers your question. It's all thanks to a certain young man sparking my increased interest in Jaffrey. Sadly, in time, the boy stopped coming. I think... I think the last time he came was in 1972, when he must've been around 18 or so.' She sighed wistfully. 'I've since entertained the idea that I might have befriended a long lost descendent of a master painter. Himself a budding artist.' She smiled. 'A girl can dream!'

'That is interesting!' nodded Mei Hui. 'Thank you very much for confiding in us, Mrs Parry-Johansson.'

The guide looked impressed. 'I see someone's told you my name?'

'Yes, the greeter at the entrance,' said Milly. 'She told us you were an expert on Jaffrey.'

'Ah! It's not an easy name to remember – believe me, I've been called all sorts. Parry-Johnson, Parry-Hansom, Perry-Janson.' She rolled her eyes. 'So again, top marks for getting it right.' She thought about something. 'Funny thing was, it just came back to me now... that boy remembered my name the first time too. Great minds, eh!'

Mei Hui looked at her quizzically. 'Great minds...?'

'You know, the expression. Great minds think alike.'

'Ah, I understand!' said Mei Hui. She felt Milly's hand creep into the crook of her arm, tugging her sleeve, and she quietly absorbed Milly's thoughts. Mei Hui glanced at her and raised an eyebrow, before turning back to Parry-Johansson. 'I hope you don't mind if we ask one more thing,' said Mei Hui, courteous as ever. 'You mentioned that Jaffrey visited the Mastersons on a late winter's evening, when it must have been dark. Yet their portrait is painted showing bright daylight.'

The guide nodded in appreciation. 'My goodness, you girls are very astute. Youngsters these days, so clever! You're absolutely right. I've thought about that, and I imagine it was something the Mastersons requested, and so Jaffrey must have used a bit of artistic licence. That is, if we're to believe the whole "memorising" thing.'

'I believe it!' said Milly, a surreptitious smile creeping across her face. Mei Hui frowned at her, worried that she might give them away. Heedless, Milly turned to the guide. 'I've seen a YouTube video of someone with autism who was able to draw entire city landscapes, all from memory – with every detail of every single building.'

'Yes, yes, you're right,' said the guide. 'I think I know who you're talking about. That young chap... Stephen something-or-other. I'm not denying that there are artistic savants out there. But are you saying you think Jaffrey had autism?'

'No, not necessarily,' Milly replied. 'Just that it's possible to draw from memory.'

'I see. Well, in that Stephen's case, we're talking about line drawings – though it's true his photographic memory is amazing. But with paintings like these, that's a whole different ballgame. I'm sure I don't have to tell you that apart from memorising every single object, their positioning and detail, you would also need to remember textures, colours, shade, light. Which makes it very difficult to believe that something like this,' she waved toward the prodigious Masterson portrait, 'could have been done just from memory.' She shrugged. 'But who knows? I suppose that's part of the fascination with Jaffrey. The air of mystery, and the hype over his methods.'

There was a pause, before Milly ventured with one last question. 'I... don't suppose you know the name of the boy who kept visiting?' she asked, hopeful.

The guide smiled. 'Yes, of course I do! I remember his name very well, not only because we built up a little friendship, but also because he was the son of a billionaire, and always had two bodyguards accompanying him everywhere he went. You don't forget someone like that in a jiffy...'

The girls stared at her, expectant.

'Ah yes, the boy's name! It was Jeremy Fitzsimmons.

Milly tightened her hold on Mei Hui's arm. They were both very excited, though Mei Hui's cool demeanour betrayed nothing.

'Well, I must say,' said Parry-Johansson, 'it's most refreshing indeed to find girls like yourselves so interested in art. I hope you continue – there is much we can learn from it.'

'It's fascinating,' said Milly, with genuine interest, her gaze already returning to the pale maid. She let go of Mei Hui's arm and drew closer. 'I was just looking at the detail on this one. Her eyes are beautiful. So magnetic.'

'Yes!' agreed the guide. 'It's a very simple painting, yet the eyes are incredibly expressive – a light shine on her lower eyelid makes her look as if she's just about to cry.' They all crowded round and peered closer. 'And the hands,' continued the guide. 'Hands are so very difficult to get right – but Jaffrey mastered them to perfection. Look how delicate the fingers are, the translucency of skin colour, one hand subtly caressing the other...'

'As if she's consoling herself,' said Milly.

'Exactly,' smiled the guide. 'A simple but poignant picture, don't you think?'

Milly took out her mobile, and took several photos, even zooming into the eyes.

'Well, I must be going,' said the guide, glancing at her watch. 'I have another tour soon. But it was lovely to meet you.'

The girls thanked her profusely – she had no idea how useful she'd been. They said their farewells and the woman left.

After that, Milly and Mei Hui were anxious to get back to the Professor to tell him what they had learnt. But first, Milly wanted to take photos of the other portraits, and on the way out, she dived into the shop to buy herself an A5 sketch pad and some graphite pencils. The shop had a handful of customers milling around, taking their time browsing through souvenirs, and Mei Hui noticed in particular an old gentleman in a Burberry trench, with a tweed cap, and glasses, stooping over a stack of poster prints. She walked up to him and tapped his shoulder, but oddly he refused to respond. In the end, Mei Hui leaned in and said, 'Excuse me, V2.'

The man's head dropped, before he turned around reluctantly. He straightened up and looked at her, slightly annoyed. 'You're giving me away, Mei!' he said, looking around cautiously.

'I apologise,' she said, also checking that no-one was listening. 'But we need to get back to the Professor straight away, we've discovered some very interesting information.'

'I know,' he said. He couldn't help a half-smile, as he scratched underneath the itchy wig. 'One of the agents overheard your discussion with the tour guide, and communicated it to me straight away.'

It was Mei Hui's turn to be surprised. 'They heard us?'

'Yes, they were posing as visitors. There was never a time when you were completely alone. Anyway, it seems very likely that this Jeremy Fitzsimmons could be our painter guy – if he was 18 in 1972, that'd make him about 67 years old, which fits the description from Tai. So I immediately informed the Professor.' V2 looked furtively this way and that, before continuing. 'The Prof also got Jasmine to do a search on Jeremy Fitzsimmonses in the narrowed-down area, and she came up with someone with that name, so we have an address!'

Mei Hui raised an eyebrow, she was impressed. 'That is very good! Do you know if his house matches Tai's image?'

'Of course we checked, and it did!' said V2, a nondescript look on his face; he was awestruck, astonished, and a little fearful all at the same time of Milly's ability, having experienced it himself. The image floated up in his mind now, but he quickly blinked it away. 'Anyway, we've already sent a stealth squad over. I'm hoping we'll find the doctor there.' He paused before he left. 'Good work, Mei Hui. Very good work.'

15 THE ART OF IN-JUTSU

The ninjas moved liked silent spectres gliding through the forest.

Their every step in split-toed tabi boots made not a sound against the undergrowth; the fabric of their black shinobi shōzoku didn't even rustle against the wind. There was no laboured breathing as they ran from tree to tree, surrounding the grey house nestled between a verge of dense forest, and a copse of black poplars so tall they tickled the sky.

In the blink of an eye the shadowy figures had darted out from the trees, slipping behind the two outhouses, and in another blink, they were pressing themselves against the walls of the main house, where Jeremy Fitzsimmons lived, careful not to clang the curved katana swords on their backs against the stonework. They stood there for as long as they dared, melting into the grey – masters of the time-old art of in-jutsu: stealing in without being seen. Ears pressed against the wall, they listened. And in a few minutes, they had sensed that there was one person moving around in the house, on the east side, in a medium-sized ground-floor room. They heard the crackle of a stove burning wood, food hissing in a fry-pan, and heavy feet repositioning on dusty cobbled flooring. There was also a second person, deep below, perhaps in a basement – the faint sound of feet pacing back and forth.

Two ninjas had already moved silently to each of the two entrances, and one had closed in on the window of the room in question – a bare kitchen-cum-utility room. A sixth ninja remained pressed against the fourth outside wall, waiting.

A crow flew overhead – an ominous black cut-out against a sea of blue. It squawked and cawed shrilly, and in that instant a loud cracking sound marked the ninjas kicking in the front door, followed in a fraction of a second by the bang of the back-door caving in. By the time the ninjas flew into the kitchen, surrounded the target, and slid katana from their sheaths, the old man had only just whirled round at the sound of the broken doors, cap dropping from his head to the ground. He found himself caged in a criss-cross of glinting swords.

At the sight of the man's face, agent V6 caught his breath, nearly breaking the ninja code of silence. The others slid eyes toward him, sensing his momentary loss of control – but he quickly righted himself, planting feet firmly on the floor, and re-gripping the sword tightly in his fists.

The old man raised protective hands above his head, shying away from them, like a bat shunning light. But his face was clear. A hideous, awful chaos of lumps and pock-marks, whiskers sprouting between dense folds of skin – a bulbous engorgement on one cheek, and a pigmented blotch spattered across a wrinkled forehead. He dared to turn his face briefly, glancing, frightened, at the razor-sharp blades. Heavy arms quivered, as he shrank back, pressing himself into the wall.

He closed his eyes, and turned away. Squirming from the shine of the swords. Trembling with fear.

16 THE PROFESSOR'S JEKYLL AND HYDE

By day, Professor Harald Wolff was the picture of calm, composure, and polished civility. But by night, as he slept, his mind betrayed him, and he turned into the wreck that he really was. Sleep was the divide between a hopeless dichotomy: the man *before* the death of his wife and son, and the man after. Not quite the extreme of Jekyll and Hyde, yet there was an undeniable similitude in that both versions existed within him, at once. He simply managed to keep the bitter, desperate, grief-stricken Harald Wolff hidden from view...

But when night descended, his 'other' self cruelly came out to play, tormenting him as he dreamt.

It was then that he saw it, again and again. Nesting, hapless, within the bleak crevices of a dark, cavernous night. That one, singular image seared into his memory. Seared into him. Mingled with acrid fumes of smoke, dense black columns rising from the ashes. Waves of stifling heat that branded his flesh. Choking, coughing, stumbling. Finding them at last, with a gasp of horror. Disbelief – *No, no, please no!! Not this. That can't be them!* – blinking through the haze. Dropping to his knees. An otherworldly howling ripping right through his body. *His* howling. Renting him in two. That one last image, before he lost his sight. Before he lost consciousness. Two blackened corpses lying amidst the charred wreckage. Disintegrating.

But it was daylight, and the image was coming to him even now, in his waking hours. In the form of a painting. And he questioned himself – was he dreaming still, was he awake, or hallucinating? – questioning his sanity. But the sick feeling in the pit of his stomach, and a voice, calling him, told him it was real.

'...Professor!' repeated V2, worried. 'Are you okay?'

The Professor closed his eyes. Listened to the soft inhalations of his own breathing – a series of sighs, in and out – and forced his mind to come out of that image. Come back to the here and now. 'I... I'm fine, I think,' he managed to say, throat dry. He patted the table for the glass of water he'd left there, and took a few gulps. It was tepid by now. 'I'm sorry,' he said, dabbing at his mouth with a handkerchief. 'Please... go on.'

V2 was uncertain. He noticed that the old man's hand, as he wiped his mouth, was trembling. His face, pale and withered. 'Are you sure, Professor? If you want to take a break–'

'I said I'm fine, V2,' a stony edge in his voice. 'Again, continue...'

V2 looked at him, tried to remember where he got to, and then resumed giving his report. 'Erm, well... as I was saying, the old man is being kept in a secure location for now. Meanwhile, about the paintings – we've arranged for someone to catalogue and archive them, and I wanted to know what we should do with... with the one of the burning house. Clearly that has a... personal connection.' He shifted awkwardly, chair squeaking. 'Should that be put in storage with the others?'

'I don't want it moved...' insisted the Professor '...yet. In fact, I don't want anything in the house touched. I need to see it all myself first. Especially that picture.'

'See, sir?' V2 asked, baffled.

'Milly,' was all the Professor said in response. V2's stunned silence gave him pause for thought. The Professor had been tormented, ever since becoming aware of the existence of the painting. And now, it was possible to see it for himself. But should he? He kept swinging wildly between adamant resolve, and uncertainty. But apart from overcoming his own fears, seeing it would mean calling upon Milly, and her abilities, and she was already unstable in every way... Also, he wondered what else they might find looking through the paintings. What other horrors... He was so torn!

'I'll arrange it then,' said V2 hesitantly, breaking through his thoughts. 'Is first thing tomorrow afternoon okay for you, sir? After the interview with Dr Vassiliev?'

The Professor paused, and found himself nodding. And just like that, it was happening.

17 WINDOWS OF THE SOUL

The Professor didn't come down for dinner that evening.

Milly and Mei Hui were bursting with questions about Jeremy Fitzsimmons and Dr Vassiliev, even seeking out V2 to try and extract information, but they soon learnt he had rushed out after his private meeting with the Professor, and still had not returned. In the end, they resigned to going to bed with their questions unanswered, only to bump into the Professor as he was shuffling down the corridor, looking lost.

'Professor!' said Mei Hui, surprised. He was wearing his bedgown, tied haphazardly. 'Do you need help?'

He was without his cane, an extended hand feeling his way along the walls. He looked confused, turning his head this way and that. 'I... I don't recognise Avernus...'

Worried, Milly stepped forward, taking his arm gently, and turning him back round toward his room. 'We're not in Avernus,' she told him. 'We're in the country house.' She led him inside his room, and sat him on the bed. 'I think you need to rest.'

'Or something to eat?' asked Mei Hui.

He shook his head. 'No, no, I'm fine.' He lay back, and closed his eyes. 'I'm fine,' he repeated, trying to convince himself. His eyes sprang open again, 'I remember now... I was going to get some water.'

Mei Hui went to fetch some, returning before long with a couple of bottles. 'Here you are,' she said, handing him one. 'I've also put a bottle on your bedside table, for later.'

He drank the water in great gulps, gasping for air afterwards. 'Thanks,' he breathed.

Mei Hui took the bottle from him, put the cap back on, and placed it next to the other one. Then tucked in his bedcovers neatly, force of habit from when she cared for the children – at the same time raising an eyebrow at Milly, who was on the other side of the bed. Eventually Mei Hui said, 'Actually, Professor, we wanted to ask you about Jeremy Fitzsimmons, and the doctor. Did… everything go all right?'

'Erm, yes, it did. Thankfully they recovered Dr Vassiliev, who was unharmed, if a little shaky. And Fitzsimmons was taken to a secure location for now… Tomorrow we're arranging for Avernus to be evacuated, so we can hold him there while we… interrogate him.'

'Do you know his motive for kidnapping the doctor?' asked Mei Hui. 'And what did he look like? Did you find out about his background? And what about the painting…?' she asked, bursting with curiosity. She thought about the teenage boy described by Parry-Johansson, the boy he once was, and his obsession with Jaffrey's art – and was itching to learn more about him.

The Professor blinked, startled by all the questions. 'You have many questions, Mei Hui, but… you'll have to be patient. He'll be interrogated soon. The important thing is that we have Dr Vassiliev back, who will be able to continue work on the cure. But you shouldn't worry about the other details. Both of you. These matters are best left to the professionals, the agents, who are trained to uncover as much information as possible.' He sat back against the headboard. 'Now, if you don't mind. I'm very tired…'

'Of course,' said Mei Hui, though she was disappointed.

'Oh by the way,' said the Professor, trying to sound casual. 'We'll need to look around Jeremy Fitzsimmons' house tomorrow, and… I would like you to accompany me. To help me see…'

Even the equable Mei Hui was surprised by this. She saw that Milly too mirrored her astonishment. 'A-are you sure, Professor?' asked Milly. 'That painting will be there.'

The Professor faltered for a split second, before recovering. 'Yes.'

They stared at him in disbelief. 'Well… if you're sure…' started Mei Hui.

'I'm sure,' said the Professor, not quite as convincingly as he had hoped. He turned his head away, eyelids lowering. 'It… it's been a long day. So if you don't mind, I'll see you in the morning.'

'Okay…' muttered Milly.

'Goodnight, Professor,' said Mei Hui.

But the Professor knew very well, as he listened to them leave the room, that it wasn't going to be a good night for him at all...

Later, in her own bedroom, Milly found she could not sleep. The subdued light of a single shaded lamp etched the outlines of furniture in platinum grey, giving her room the tone of a sombre charcoal drawing. Milly lay in her pyjamas on her bed, swiping casually through the photos on her mobile. She was browsing the pictures she'd taken of F. Jaffrey's paintings at the National Portrait Gallery.

At last she settled on one particular portrait. An unusual choice of a middle-aged man who was far from being blessed with good looks, had thinning black hair, and was sitting stiffly in a damask armchair. His head was turned slightly away, and his eyes seemed vague and unfocussed, as though glancing only in afterthought at the painter. The harsh light of the chiaroscuro style created a black background, with a single light source shining on a softly-glowing face that was half in shadow – merging him with the darkness. Milly stared at the portrait for some time, wondering why she was choosing that particular picture; something about it made her feel uncomfortable. There were no obvious reasons why. Both his expression and body language were neutral, and there was nothing else in the painting to give anything away. But the more she stared, the stronger became her visceral aversion. Not to the artwork, for that was, true to Jaffrey's usual form, magnificent. She was repelled by the sitter himself.

Ignoring her misgivings, Milly turned her phone sideways, zoomed into the one visible eye, and pinched outward so that it enlarged to fill the screen. She leaned the phone against the pillow, sat up cross-legged, and reached for the sketchpad and pencil, resting the pad – already folded onto a blank page – on her knee. The pencil was heavily-chewed at the top with her own teeth-marks.

Her slow hand worked its way clumsily across the page, at first sketching simple outlines of the oval eye, the iris, a perfectly circular pupil, an eyelid, a flutter of lashes, and the strong arch of a thick brow. Then she went back over it and filled in more detail – the radial lines through the iris, a catch-light over the pupil, a lower lid, thickening lashes.

Lastly, shading to define dark and light, adding depth, dimension, then blending and smudging to smoothen. She worked with a frown, deep in concentration. When she made a mistake, she rubbed it out with a huff, and re-touched. At last, she held the pad in front of her, tilting her head this way and that. But she was not happy with it. The drawing was crude and coarse, and lacked the finesse and natural talent of Jaffrey's artistry. She ground her teeth and ripped out the page, crumpling it into a ball, before throwing it into the bin. It bounced off an overflowing mound of screwed-up paper – sketches of lips, noses, ears, and hands, all rejected. She flung herself face-down on the bed, arms covering her head, growling into the pillow.

Rolling onto her side, she simmered and stewed as she stared with frustration at the image on her phone. It lay next to her pillow, like a macabre third eye. Noticing something, she suddenly sat up, grabbed the phone, and zoomed in as much as she could. But it was too dark, and so she quickly swiped and tapped the screen to adjust brightness and contrast – and then went back to staring at it. Her mouth suddenly dropped open with disbelief, absorbing what she was seeing. She switched screens, did a fervent Google search about the portrait and the sitter, and then speed-read through several pages. She stopped to think for several seconds, eyes roaming distractedly over her room, as if the answers were somewhere there. Turning back to the phone, she swiped through the photos again, to another portrait, zooming into the eyes, then another, and another – until she had studied every single painting.

The first pangs of migraine began gnawing into her skull, and her stomach churned with nausea. She winced – bad timing, she thought. Yet she stared at her phone, trying hard to concentrate through the pain… It was beginning to make sense to Milly why the man in the painting made her so uncomfortable. She caught her breath and slid off the bed, clenching the phone in a sweaty palm – at the same time, she asked Jasmine to tell Mei Hui to meet her in Tai's room, urgently. She pushed feet into slippers and shuffled there herself, deep in thought. When she knocked lightly and pushed the door open, Tai was propped up against a pillow, watching something on his phone. He looked up at her. He seemed to be getting older by the day.

She sat on the bed next to him without a word, putting her feet up.

'What's wrong?' he asked.

Just then, Mei Hui arrived, baffled by the sudden call. 'Is everything okay?'

'Lock the door,' Milly said in a low voice.

Mei Hui complied without a word, and Milly reached out a hand to her. She went over, sat opposite them on the bed, and took both of their hands so that they formed a circle. Tai closed his eyes and bowed his head, as if in silent prayer, and the girls did the same.

An electric energy sizzled between them, passing through their fingertips with a light tingle – their skin, their very being, fusing and deliquescing into a whole. Gradually, their minds joined, and Milly breathed deeply as the sharp edges of the migraine began to dissipate, her shoulders loosening, head clearing.

Now that she was relaxed, she recalled a memory.

Suddenly, the three of them found themselves within the Jaffrey room at the National Portrait Gallery. The ubiquitous fragrance of floor polish hung in the air, and the hushed chatter of onlookers echoed behind them. Instead of just Milly and Mei Hui, Tai stood next to them now – looking fresh-faced and young. Milly was patting the beanie hat that now appeared on her head, happy to have it back.

They were standing in front of that same chiaroscuro portrait of the man she disliked. The portrait shimmered, like a mirage, and then began extruding from the wall, expanding and growing until it reached full ceiling height. At the same time, the three of them floated slowly up into the air as it grew. They stopped and hovered when they reached the subject's eye.

Look at that, Milly told them without moving her lips. *Look at the eye.*

The dark ellipse of the iris had enlarged so that it was as big as their heads, and they hovered closer to examine it. They saw the bright shine of the light source – and within that there was a reflection, a mirror image, of the room in which the man sat, like an inverted negative of a photo. But there was no painter, no artist standing in front of him. Instead, they saw the sordid silhouettes of two figures. One, a terrified woman bending backwards, falling to the floor, and the other, a man standing over her. His hand raised in the air, mid-swing. Gripping a knife pointed downward at his victim.

Mei Hui gasped, eyes wide, and turned to look at both Milly and Tai.

I was trying to sketch the eye, Milly explained to them in her mind. *I wanted to learn Jaffrey's art. And that's when I saw it.* She nodded at the image. They inspected it for some time in stunned silence.

Mei Hui turned to her. *'That's incredible! The level of detail too, expertly painted within such a small space. But... their faces are not clear. It could mean one of two things. Either the man, the subject, had* observed *the murder of that woman by someone else. Or the man himself was the murderer. How do we know which one?*

Well, I Googled him, said Milly, turning around. They were still floating mid-air, and when both Tai and Mei Hui turned too, a giant image of her phone appeared, just as the portrait shrank back into the wall. The phone showed a webpage.

This article gives some info,' continued Milly. The screen scrolled upward by itself, and stopped at several highlighted sentences. *The man in question, the sitter, was called Hugh Charles – he was arrested in August 1878, and later tried for murdering his wife. But he was let off on a technicality. The following year, he commissioned the very expensive F. Jaffrey to paint his portrait, even though he had previously been declared bankrupt. When the police looked into where the money came from, they discovered that just a few months before his wife died, Hugh Charles had taken out a £5,000 life insurance policy against her. A fortune at that time. He was later re-tried, found guilty, and executed for her murder. So I think... I think the reason the portrait made me feel so uncomfortable was because, somehow, Jaffrey knew his secret, and painted him in a way that made him... creepy.'* She said all this with wide, round eyes.

Mei Hui nodded thoughtfully. *Yes, I agree. It is artfully done. There is an air of evilness about the man.*

But how could Jaffrey have known! breathed Milly. *He saw it like he was there. He painted it in the man's eyes. Don't you think it's–*

Too close to home, finished Mei Hui. There was silence, and suddenly unsure of her English, she asked, *Is that the right expression?*

Perfectly right, said Milly. *Too right in fact! You know, since I learnt from the Prof why we're so... intelligent, I've been reading about the kind of genetic engineering they must've done to graft the so-called genius genes into our DNA. The method I imagine they used was endonuclease-mediated gene targeting, knocking in novel transgenic material into particular segments of the host's DNA...*

Mei Hui and Tai exchanged a look, none the wiser.

In every-day language, explained Milly, *it means they got the genius genes from a* third *source – separate and distinct from our parents' DNA. So instead of having DNA from two people, we have the DNA of* three *people in us!*

Mei Hui tilted her head, grappling with understanding. *I don't think... that is... good,* she said slowly. *Ethically... morally... it seems–*

Shady! It was Milly's turn to finish Mei Hui's sentence. *And physically, that might be why Karl, in the end, got very sick. Because of the genetic mutation of the novel DNA. His body was rejecting the transgenic genius genes. I don't think human bodies, or any kind of bodies, were meant for that kind of messing around.*

They were playing God, said Tai simply.

They all thought about this. Mei Hui looked pale. *I feel... somehow... violated.* Her body, her entire being, her whole life, was an awful experiment. She felt like a genetical Frankenstein's monster. A new, sapient creature, sewn together from parts of others. No-one had stopped to think of, or were too short-sighted to even bother with, the consequences...

The museum fell away from around them, like a theatre backdrop collapsing to the ground with a whoosh – and they opened their eyes to find themselves sitting on Tai's bed again. Mei Hui's eyes brimmed, damp.

Milly hooked arms with her.

'They were acting under orders, don't forget,' said Tai quietly. 'The Professor and Dr Kendra. The lives of their families were threatened. In the end, that is why they got us all out from the project... Mei Hui, you know the Professor is good, don't you?'

Mei Hui nodded emphatically, wiping her eyes.

'Don't forget,' said Tai. 'They're trying their best to find a cure for us...' His voice had a tranquil, reassuring quality. It calmed them.

Milly found herself examining Tai's face – his wrinkled, centenarian face. Despite his own condition, and the fact that he just had a few months left to live, *he* was reassuring *them*. She felt her heart breaking all over again.

'You're right as always, Tai,' said Mei Hui. She thought of something. 'I would like to get your opinion,' she said, looking at them both. 'If the genius genes they put in us came from a third person, who do you think that is?' She wanted to see if the others confirmed her suspicions.

'Isn't it obvious?' said Milly, looking at them both. 'It must be Jeremy Fitzsimmons.

18 THE MOST BEAUTIFUL IMAGINARY BUTTERCUP

The Professor had spent nearly a decade and much of his profits from the family business, a national chain of supermarkets, building Avernus – driven by an inordinate obsession that hinged on nothing more than a vague possibility. A possibility that it *might* become useful as a safe house for the lost Ingenious children. And while his foresight could not be faulted, the question of his balance of mind could. He had lost his wife and son in an awful fire, and throwing himself into such a huge and ambitious project that took up his every waking hour, sapped all his brainpower, and drained his bank account, was all he could do to stop going insane from grief. A lamentable obsession; an almost superhuman drive that both kept him alive and wore him down. He had not been able to protect his own family, so instead he would do everything – *everything* – in his power to make a safe place for the Ingenious children, or so he convinced himself. But even though the security for the most part relied on the maze of tunnels surrounding the entrances, the Professor soon learnt from the near-fatal mistake of bringing the disturbed Karl König into Avernus, that safety did not necessarily depend on the thickness of walls...

And now, a decade later, after all the blood and sweat of building it, Jeremy Fitzsimmons was being brought into Avernus – making it nothing more than a glorified dungeon.

Everybody was immediately told to evacuate, for 'safety' reasons, though it was not divulged what exactly the threat was.

But Mrs Gaia Kendra, wife of Dr Kendra – one of the geneticists who had worked on Project Ingenious right from the start, some 18 years ago – was used to moving. Ever since they had sabotaged the project because of the flagrant disrespect their superiors had shown for the sanctity of human life, they had been on the run, changing identities, and moving house time and time again. They had set free the Ingenious children, and themselves – yet somehow, they never felt completely liberated. Despite being incognito, they were always looking over their shoulder, and wondering if the creators of the project would ever catch up somehow, and find them. Wanting to claim what they thought was theirs. The children.

And because of all this, moving had become part of the norm. So when Gaia heard about this change of events, she just sighed, and pulled out a suitcase from under the bed – sneezing from the dust. She looked at her husband, Dr Kendra, rocking back and forth in his chair as he listened quietly to *The Archers* on the radio. His eyesight by now was failing, and while he could not read, or watch programmes, at least he could listen. He was far from being the brilliant scientist he once was. No longer were his thoughts occupied by nuclear and mitochondrial DNA mutations, gametes, or spindle transfer of mtDNA – but with a mind now ravaged by dementia, his only concerns these days were about the unsatisfactory amount of baked beans on his toast, or not enough sugar in his tea, or his favourite: complaining about the constant and irritating blow of the aircon. He chatted to himself or to Gaia about things that had occurred decades ago, as if they had only just happened – and he mentioned 'recent' conversations, in great detail, with people who had long since died. As if his mind had been reset to 40 years in the past without him even realising.

Gaia packed resignedly, humming slightly out of tune an old Melina Mercouri song, in time with the rhythmic creak of her husband's rocking chair.

After a while, the Chauffeur came in, greeted Gaia cheerily, and then stood in front of Dr Kendra, smiling with affection and waving a silent hello. He no longer expected a response or even recognition these days. The frequency of the doctor's moments of lucidity were noticeably reducing in ever decreasing circles – and when there was cognizance, it only lasted a few wonderful seconds. But the last time had been weeks ago, and they were beginning to lose hope that he might come back to them, however fleetingly. It was also worrying that he still had not divulged the whereabouts of the last missing Ingenious child, not even inadvertently through his constant mindless babbling. And without that knowledge, the child was lost to them. All they seemed to get was a stream of rambling discontent, or blankness in his eyes, or thin lines of drool running from a gaping mouth.

Though perhaps there was still hope…

When the Chauffeur stooped down to wave hello right in front of his face, so that he couldn't be missed, Dr Kendra looked up at him and smiled briefly, before reaching up and mussing his hair – in the same way that he used to do years ago when the Chauffeur was a teenager. The Chauffeur clapped his hands together with delight. He quickly waved at Gaia to catch her attention, and told her with frenzied signs what had just happened.

Gaia smiled and walked over, resting a hand on the Chauffeur's shoulder. 'You're in fine spirits today, Xeli!' she told her husband, smiling.

The old man made a funny snorting laugh, then took his wife's hand, and kissed it tenderly – leaving a glob of dribbled saliva.

'Eugh, Xeli!!' laughed Gaia, wiping her hand on her trousers. The Chauffeur couldn't help gurgling with amusement.

Dr Kendra's eyes still sparkled with rare cognition as he looked over his wife's rosy-cheeked face, as if seeing the woman he had fallen in love with for the first time. 'You… you look beautiful,' he mumbled.

Gaia smiled, slightly abashed. 'Thank you, my dear.'

The doctor leant across the side of his chair, searching all around – and then, very delicately, picked up something imaginary from the sideboard. He held it out to Gaia, pinched between his index finger and thumb.

Puzzled, Gaia glanced from the empty hand to her husband. 'What's this?'

'A <u>buttercup</u>,' he croaked, with a smidgen of embarrassment. 'For you.'

Touched, she rested a hand against her cheek, and plucked the invisible flower from the doctor's fingers. 'It… it's beautiful!' she told him, her heart melting.

But the all too familiar creak from the rocker feet signalled the inevitable. A return, once more, to dementia. The doctor's eyes gradually glazed over as he began swinging back and forth yet again.

The Chauffeur and Gaia exchanged a saddened glance. Gaia tucked the imaginary buttercup in her hair, signing with her other hand. 'How do I look?'

Lovely! the Chauffeur signed back to her with a wistful smile.

•••————————————————————•••

Professor Wolff had given them strict instructions to be out of Avernus by 9 a.m. But it was already just after 10.30 a.m., and they were still there. There had been complications with transporting V3 – a rather intricate and involved operation, as she was still on life support – and the gurney on which she lay was only just being trundled out of Avernus from the garage entrance, into the waiting helicopter.

Dr Kendra too, having returned to senility, had become crotchety and bad-tempered, and was not cooperating at all, prolonging their departure. But at last Gaia and the doctor climbed into the back of the steel grey FX4 taxi cab, waiting for the Chauffeur, who had just run back into the garage to fetch something that Gaia had forgotten.

Gaia stuck her head out of the car window on hearing the loud thak-thak of an engine above them, at first thinking that the helicopter with V3 was returning for whatever reason. But she soon saw that the shape of this helicopter was slightly different, with a pointed nose, sleeker lines, and a body painted a deeper shade of green. She thought nothing of it, and went back to reading her mobile phone to catch up on the news – not noticing that her husband had opened his door and climbed out, until it was too late. 'Xeli, get back in!' she shouted out at him, ducking down to see through the door. But her voice was drowned out by the roar of the helicopter, and so she unbuckled herself to go after him, grumbling under her breath.

The helicopter landed, and the door slid open with a clunk. Though it was still noisy as the momentum of the rotor blades only just began to slow. Five ninja agents, fully masked, jumped out, followed by their prisoner, who was mostly out of view behind them. All that was visible was the man's chained feet shuffling slowly forward, as they led him toward the entrance.

Dr Kendra drew closer, hidden from behind the corner of the garage. Gaia reached him and was tugging at his arm quietly, coaxing him back to the car, not wanting to be seen by the agents. She knew they weren't supposed to be there. But as the agents parted, and the prisoner looked up, Dr Kendra suddenly gasped with fright as the man's hideous face came into view. 'It... it's him!' he said, backing away, eyes wild with fear. He twisted his arm out of Gaia's grip and ran. Fleeing in blind terror away from the helicopter, away from that awful man.

Gaia ran after him, but her husband was slim and fast, and he darted around several corners, looking this way and that, before darting off in another direction. Gaia puffed frantically after him, vaguely aware of heavy footsteps behind her. They ran for what seemed like ages, though it was barely 10 minutes before they reached the outskirts of the industrial estate – marked by an empty ring-road devoid of traffic. Still, Gaia saw the road and panicked. She struggled to catch her breath, reaching out her hand to him. Trying to call his name. 'Stop, Xeli...' she gasped, breathless. Perhaps he had heard her even though it was barely a croak, because her husband faltered on the road, turned, and saw his wife struggling to reach him. His face softened when he saw her, and he opened his mouth to say something. But a deafening claxon horn drowned him out. A huge truck loomed out of nowhere, hurtling toward them. A screaming screech of tyres breaking. The reek of burnt rubber. And the colossus swerved left, toward Gaia, and then twisted far right, to avoid the old man. The cabin whooshed behind Kendra at frightening speed, bounced against the concrete road barrier, finally crashing, and coming to a halt. But the rear of the trailer was still moving, having lost control. It verged inward... struck the doctor so that he twisted into the air... his body hurtling metres high... tumbling with a dull thud on the tarmac. Gaia screamed, choked, stumbled and fell. She scraped herself off the ground and ran to her husband, throwing herself down at his side. She could barely breathe, eyes watering so much she could hardly see. There was just a broken heap where her husband should have been.

Something moved. His head lifting to see her, a hand stretching for hers. Gaia sobbed as she took it. It was warm and sticky with blood.

He smiled at her, fleetingly. His grey eyes like slithers of cut diamond against smears of red and black. Blinking up at her distraught face, he reached tremulously for her ear. 'The buttercup...' he said, his voice raspy and thin from a crushed larynx. He glanced at the imaginary flower tucked in her hair. It was so delicate, glossed radiantly yellow. He looked over his wife's face. 'It's... lovely... on you...' he wheezed with great effort, his face lined with regret.

The Chauffeur collapsed on the ground next to Gaia, wide eyes sweeping over the doctor's broken body, mortified. He howled with anguish – thick, muffled, bellowing cries. His hands hovering over the old man, searching for some discernible part to hold on to. To grasp. To keep him from being snatched by death's groping claws.

But the doctor's eyes were already sliding slowly and gracefully closed, as though he were imagining something lovely. At the same time, his hand went limp within Gaia's.

She screamed his name, red-faced, calling him back to her.

But it was no use.

19 BURNING QUESTIONS

Professor Wolff had idolised Dr Axel Kendra since the publication of his mind-blowing research paper on Next Generation DNA Sequencing, whilst doing his own MSc on Genetic Manipulation and Molecular Cell Biology, in Oxford. Kendra's superlative findings on the possible applications of unlocking the abundant data held within genetic strands, were not only ground-breaking and pioneering, but extraordinarily insightful. And after reading the paper, six times no less, a young Harald Wolff knew then and there that he wanted to work in gene therapy.

But now, Dr Kendra was gone. And the Professor felt as though he had once again been plunged into the depths of a cataclysmic event – like a total solar eclipse that left him in the darkest umbra. Overcast, seemingly in perpetuum. He wondered how much more grief he could take. The all too familiar ache in his chest made him feel physically ill.

And worse still was Gaia's own listlessness, as reported by Brian. She wandered around the country house, in total silence, a vacant expression on her face, not quite knowing what to do with herself. Refusing company, she went instead on long rambling walks alone. And even the Chauffeur, who was also beside himself, could not penetrate the invisible barrier within which she immured herself.

Everybody grieves in different ways, the Professor told the Chauffeur quietly. Some are more vocal, and cry, or become angry. Some need to talk. Others become introspective and just want to be left alone. She is the last type, and we have to be patient and let her grieve in her own way, he said.

The Chauffeur found this hard to understand. Despite being mute, he was much more vocal with his emotions. It was entirely possible to tell exactly what the silent man was thinking purely from his facial expressions and body language, he was so expressive. But though he wanted with all his heart to help her, to grieve with her, he accepted what the Professor said. So the Chauffeur left Gaia alone, only every now and again bringing her a cup of tea, leaving it next to where she was sitting, or a slice of cake, or a freshly-picked flower from the garden. He would place a gentle hand on her shoulder, before leaving without signing a word.

Dr Vassiliev's hands never shook – ever. Until now. The coffee cup and saucer rattled as he picked it off the state-of-the art machine, coffee sloshing everywhere. Swearing under his breath, he quickly put down the cup on the counter, grabbed several serviettes, and wiped the brown liquid from his hands, his trousers – still shaking. He leaned against the counter, head lowered, and took quick breaths, trying to calm himself. He thought he was okay, after being rescued from weeks of captivity. But his body betrayed him. He continued breathing deeply. In and out. When he heard someone open the door behind him, he turned to find the Professor being led into the interview room.

'Kherry!' said Vassiliev. He picked up the cup and saucer again, holding one hand with the other to stop the trembling, relieved to be able to put it down on the table. He hugged the Professor, then cupped the old man's face with both hands and tenderly kissed each cheek. 'My dear tovarisch, Kherry!' he exclaimed. 'It is good to see you. I... I want to thank you, and your men with mask, black clothing, kung-fu fighting – so cool, very cool! I thank you all for rescuing me from that living nightmare!' He patted the Professor's back vigorously for good measure, and sat down at the table, squeezing his hands between his legs.

It was a simple birch table, surrounded by minimalist chairs with tubular steel legs, reminiscent of old school stacking chairs. And the Professor sat next to him, while V2 positioned himself by the door.

'I'm so, so sorry that you went through such a horrible ordeal, Vadim. I can only imagine how traumatised you must be...'

Vassiliev nodded slowly, staring into his coffee cup. He was gasping, really needed to drink it. 'Yes, was trauma,' he said quietly, gulping. 'That man... his face... believe me, I'm having many nightmares.'

'They told me about his... appearance. You must have been terrified!

But do you have any idea why this man abducted you? Was there something he wanted from you?'

The doctor's expression switched to one of bewilderment. 'I have not a clue, Kherry. I do not know who is he, or what he wanted from me. In fact, he did not speak much.' He thought about it, and corrected himself. 'I tell lie. He did not speak *at all*. Not one word. I tell him, I tell him why you keep me here? I shout, I cry, I beg him!' The doctor lifted his hands emphatically, face reddening. 'Why?! I ask. But he just look down, say nothing.' Vassiliev shook his head, baffled.

He decided to try for the coffee, gripping the cup with both hands – it wasn't too hot – and he managed to get it to his mouth without spilling any more. He took great big slurps, wishing it had a dash of vodka in it. He clattered the cup back on the saucer, deep in thought. 'That man. He just come and go, bring food, bring drink. Simple things, beans and bread, or kind of goulash, water, coffee – like that. Three times every day he bring me food...' He paused. 'I many times stay quiet to hear, to listen. Try understand, where I am? What he doing? But I hear nothing! Not even television, music on radio, people speaking. Just hear sometimes when he walk, come down stairs. Once I hear banging, and sawing – but mostly nothing. As I say, even man himself, not speak.' The doctor closed an imaginary zip over his mouth. He blinked at the Professor and sighed. 'You know why, dear Kherry? Why he take me?'

The Professor had already suspected the reason. 'My only guess is that it has something to do with... with your work for us. The gene therapy. The children.'

Vassiliev nodded thoughtfully. 'Yes, perhaps, the children. How are they? How are their symptoms?'

'Stable for the most part. Milly was withdrawing into herself and started exhibiting some... strange behaviour. But it's up and down. At the moment, she seems fine.'

'That is good.'

'The man who kept you, did he try to communicate with you in any other way at all?'

'No.'

'And... did he threaten you?'

The doctor shook his head. 'No, no threats. He say nothing, do nothing to make me think he want to hurt or kill me. Just his face scary, you know? I'm glad you cannot see his face, Kherry…' he said as an afterthought.

Then he stopped for a moment. 'But… one thing strange, *very* strange,' he said with a faraway look on his face. 'First time he come to basement, and I see him, you know, really see him – he hold out his hand to me, like so.' The doctor extended his hand and rested it on the table, as if offering a handshake, but with splayed fingers – he gently put the Professor's hand onto his, so that he could feel the shape of it. Thankfully he'd stopped shaking. 'Like this, see. When he do, I move away, no touch. No like. And then second time he come to basement, he do again. Again, I refuse. But third time, he grab me! Like this.' The doctor moved his splayed hand onto the Professor's wrist, gripping it. 'Every time he come down, do same. After third day, I know, I must give him my hand, or no food, no drink. Do you understand, Kherry? Very strange thing.'

The Professor blinked – his heart suddenly racing. He thought of the children, and their need to touch in order for their abilities to manifest. And he wondered… At last he spoke quietly. 'I'm sorry, I-I don't know what to say…' He was thrown, and faltered momentarily, but managed to compose himself with an awkward cough. He desperately needed to change the subject.

But the doctor himself changed it. 'Now, all is good,' he slapped his leg vigorously, as if trying to slap away his anxiety. 'And I am ready to go back to work. I realise something important in scary man house. I realise not just one thing, but many thing, to help with gene therapy. And I think I have solved, in my head. Is very good. Very good! You see, for many weeks our experiments *not* working, keep going wrong, keep messing up. Drive me mad! But in scary man house, I think of solution.' He tapped his temple with a finger, a knowing look on his face. 'Somehow, it just come in my head. Maybe I needed quiet, and many time, to think. But now, I am sure I have solution – at last!!' He raised his hands in a eureka moment. 'So you see, I must go to work, Kherry, to test, to experiment. To help children. You let me go back to laboratories, okay?'

The Professor blinked, at first with disbelief, then delight, and finally deep relief at such amazing news. 'Yes, yes, that's fantastic, Vadim! We will get you back to work soon.' He paused to settle his excited nerves. And then he remembered. 'But first...' he said, turning round and motioning to V2, standing by the door. 'We brought you something. I'm sure you will be pleased to see her, with her little friend. They've become quite inseparable.'

V2 opened the door, and fetched a carrier from the corridor. Doctor Vassiliev's eyes widened like saucers. 'Is it...?'

V2 placed it on the table in front of the doctor, who immediately stood, his face lighting up. An alarmed meowing emanating from the carrier answered the doctor's question. But then he realised that there were two distinct cat voices, and he quickly unzipped the cover. A little tortoise-shell kitten stood up on hind legs and poked her head out cautiously, and the doctor clapped his hands with delight. Then Lyubova also peaked out and looked around – and when she saw who was waiting for her, she meowed even louder. Dr Vassiliev picked her up tenderly and cradled her in his arms, hugging her so gently, near to tears. 'Oh my Lyu-Lyu, Lyubova moya,' he murmured several times, in between kissing the top of her head. 'My little Lyu-Lyu!'

The Professor just had to tell her amazing story. 'I'm not sure if you were aware, Vadim. But this incredible cat stowed away in the car that took you – and she even searched for you in the scary man's house.'

'What!' exclaimed the doctor, looking down at his baby with disbelief.

'She was caught and then dumped in the countryside somewhere. And somehow – though don't ask me how – she managed to find her way over 150 miles, back to the house. She was quite poorly at first, but she's improved greatly.'

'What!!' repeated the doctor, with wide eyes. He hugged the cat again, rocking her to and fro. 'Oh my poor, amazing, wonderful Lyu-Lyu.'

The Professor smiled. 'You can say that again!'

Lyubova curled up, snug, in her doctor's arms, legs sticking up from the crook of his arm, her head pressed against his chest. Bright copper eyes gazed lovingly up at him, and she extended a paw, resting it softly on his chin – as if checking that he were real. As if wondering whether this was a dream...

•••———————————————————•••

After they had driven Dr Vassiliev, Lyubova, and her little kitten friend, to a new, different house close to the laboratories, V2 drove the Professor back to the country house where they themselves were staying. But before they got out of the car, the Professor put a hand on V2's shoulder. 'Please, do not tell a soul about what Dr Vassiliev said today. Especially not the children. Do you understand?'

V2 had learnt his lesson by now: never wonder why, never ask questions. 'Yes, of course, Professor.'

The old man grunted, opened the car door, and climbed out – feeling slightly dizzy as he filled his lungs with the fresh, pure country air. His head swimming with questions that he was sure only Axel Kendra had the answers to. So many questions... But there was no way to ask him now. Like opening a door to reveal only a hard brick wall, he had come to an abrupt impasse. And he was never going to be able to get those answers.

His muscles literally ached with the grief of losing first his family, then his dear friend – Herculean emotions so strong, it was as if they had been made solid, balled into fists, delivering sucker punch blow after blow. And as he lay, metaphorically, on the floor, one last after-thought delivered the final kick. It was impossible now to find the lost Ingenious child...

The frustration, and the warped, misshapen irony of it all, simmered inside of him as he quietly tapped his way back to the house.

20 A PITIFUL SELF-PORTRAIT

When the Professor walked silently into Jeremy Fitzsimmons' house, the sense of foreboding was palpable. An overpowering smell of turpentine and damp hit him, followed by nebulous layers of beeswax, linseed oil, walnuts, and the sweet pungency of geraniums.

Milly's hand crept into his, and he quickly clasped it – needing desperately both the comfort of human touch, and to be able to see. But her hand wriggled uncomfortably, and, realising he was clenching too hard, he loosened his grip. Dry eyes blinked several times as he adjusted to the sensory overload. Awed, breathless, by the miracle of sight – though from a slightly shifted perspective, from Milly's view. Muted tones of light and shade, hazes of colour, vague shapes hardening – all bloomed before him. Seeing silenced him. His heart thudding from the wonder of it. And as they moved quietly through the dark house – it was still shadowy, even with the curtains pulled right back – he absorbed everything with awe. Behind them trailed Mei Hui, and together they traversed the rooms, one by one.

The experience was surreal. Dream-like. It seemed to him as if he were a wandering, lost ghost, floating through the halls, and haunting a house that was not his. Before him came the faces of its inhabitants, through a thousand portraits, hanging on every inch of wall-space. Unlike him, they were real, solid people. His eyes locked onto each of theirs in a stare-out. Inevitably they won, as he glided on, to the next, and then the next.

They came to the darkest room of all. And when the light was switched on, someone gasped at the portrait that greeted them, though it was not the one they were expecting. It covered nearly the entire wall, and unusually, there was nothing else in the room. No other pictures, no furniture, no carpet or rug. There was just that one portrait.

Their footsteps were dampened drum-beats on the wooden floor, as they drew closer.

It was a painting of a young woman with long, ash-coloured hair that tumbled in beguiling curls around slim shoulders. Near her head was the flash of an azure <u>dragonfly</u>, suspended in the air. The woman herself was larger than life, standing on a mossed boulder at the edge of a stream, dipping a foot into the shimmering water, ivory toes creating lustrous swirls and ripples. Her clothes, long diaphanous layers of white, were so sheer that the hazy form of her slim body could be seen against the light. She seemed unaware of the hidden onlooker, the artist, stealing a glance from behind a bush. Her face was downcast, with jade eyes caught in the gleam of a setting sun, burnished against silk-smooth skin. She was beautiful. A paragon of virtue. Almost too exquisite to be true.

Yet, as they pored over it with silent amazement, they somehow knew how special she was. Venerated and adored. Encased in double-thick layers of scumbled brush-strokes, her image seemed to extrude, like she was stepping out of the canvas, into real life.

Entranced, Milly's hand was drawn to it – the tips of her fingers gliding over the hard, puckered paint. But her hand flicked back, cradled by the other, like she'd had an electric shock. She stepped back. 'I don't like it,' she said, grimacing. 'She seems... too real.'

'But, it is so beautiful,' Mei Hui remarked, her eyes irresistibly drawn back to the picture.

Milly tugged on the Professor's hand. 'Let's go,' she insisted.

As they left the room, they made sure to turn off the lights – perhaps for the same reason that Fitzsimmons left it in the dark: mere mortals were not worthy of its loveliness.

They continued wandering room to room in Fitzsimmons' large, shadowy house. And eventually they came to the one. Before the Professor even set eyes on it, he knew. He knew it was there. And he gasped.

Time and the world collapsed away, as he stood in front of the painting propped against the wall. It stole his breath. He looked upon his Chiara, his Christian, engulfed in a brimstone inferno. The likeness of their portrayal was unmistakeable despite the twisted terror on their faces. Her mouth opened in a hollow scream. The boy's eyes squeezed shut.

Mei Hui came to the Professor's other side, and gripped his arm and hand firmly, bringing him back. His heart racing so much that he thought it might erupt from his chest. He forced himself to breathe. Forced himself to keep staring, until it mounted and mounted, and became too much to bear. At last, he tugged Milly's hand, and she tore her eyes away, looking anxiously at him instead. Catching her breath.

He saw himself then, as Milly saw him: heaving shoulders, dropped head, and tears that he hadn't even realised were there, trickling from his chin.

A still, a snapshot.

The picture of a lone, pitiful, broken old man...

His own pathetic portrait added to the myriad paintings they had just passed.

•••———————————————•••

For nearly the entire ride home, the Professor was lost in a riot of thoughts, still smarting from the painting, raw nerves on edge. In time, somehow, inexplicably, the mayhem in his mind distilled to a simple and unexpected realisation that, of all things, he was missing Calista deeply. Pondering and musing over why, kept for now the horror of that painting out of his mind... He knew she loved her 'Gramps' more than anything when he was alive, and as she had sheltered in Avernus all those months ago, their relationship grew in a similar way. The Professor thought about her particular kind of natural genius, a jarring clash with unashamed superficiality, and emotions so bluntly expressed. He needed her now, needed her outspokenness.

It had been weeks since she and her party had left for Brazil. And after a patchy phone call from her about seven days ago, where she told him of a lead they were following, which meant heading out very close to uncharted jungle, that was the last he'd heard. Before she rang off, she had told him in her cheery cockney accent, 'Miss you, Prof!' And instead of coughing out an awkward 'Erm, thanks, me too' reply – he had given her only a dismissive goodbye. Which he regretted now. Very much.

If she were here with him, right now, she would have intuited his state of emotional turmoil, and leaned into him, resting her head lightly on his shoulder. Nothing overly emotional, just a simple touch of affection to show that she understood, and was there for him. But for the entire ride home, he stayed on his side of the car, head turned toward the window, passively aware of the flicker of light behind closed eyelids – while the girls rode on the seat opposite, huddled together on the other side.

They were gifted empaths, but they couldn't guess for one second that he desperately needed reassurance.

It wasn't until V2 announced they had nearly reached the country house, that Mei Hui mustered the courage to speak. 'Excuse me, Professor.' She sat up, her cotton trousers sliding softly against the leather upholstery. 'Milly and I have been thinking... We would like to see this Jeremy Fitzsimmons. We can try talking to him, but if that fails, we would just need one touch to be able to find out–'

'No!' interrupted the Professor, more forcefully than he meant. 'Absolutely not.'

Milly shuffled forward. 'Why not?'

The Professor tried to calm himself. Quite apart from the way the man looked physically, if his own suspicions were correct, Fitzsimmons would be the last person he'd want them to meet. Besides, he didn't yet know what the man's mental state of mind was like. 'Just... no,' he told them firmly. 'In fact, I don't want you to go anywhere near Jeremy Fitzsimmons. Do you understand?' It was more command than question, and clearly, as he turned back to the window, the end of the conversation as far as he was concerned.

The girls retreated, holding their cards close to their chest; they did not yet want to show their hand. It was neither the time nor the place to ask about their genetic make-up, and whether Jeremy Fitzsimmons was the one from whom the genius genes had been taken. Especially after everything the Professor had been through...

When the car rolled into the front driveway, Milly saw her father, Brian, coming out of the front door to greet them – and after the car was parked, eager to get out of the cloying atmosphere, she flung the door open and went over to hug him, without a word.

He melted and hugged her back. 'Everything all right, Midge?'

Milly glanced back at the Professor who was pulling out his cane, and shook her head slightly. He was within earshot, so Brian just nodded. Then she realised. 'Midge?! Where did that come from?'

'Well, you don't seem to like it when I call you "Pigeon", so I thought I'd give "Midge" a try...' He looked at her expectantly, waiting for the challenge.

'Dad, a midge is a blood-sucking fly!'

'Oh. Well, it *sounds* cute. What else can I call you then?'

'Er, how about my real name. Milly, Mills, Melody?'

Brian was pleased to see his daughter back to her normal self, though he wondered how long it would last. He parried back with, 'But I rather like the blood-sucking little fly nickname!'

Milly sighed. 'Fine! But only if you don't call me that in public.'

'What do you mean by "in public"? Are we in public now?'

The Professor listened to their ongoing banter as they disappeared inside the house. Yes, he missed Calista more than he wanted to admit. He was worried about her, worried about them all – and the lack of communication from the entire party, including the agents who were travelling with them, didn't help.

As he began tapping his way up to the house by himself, a hand on his arm stopped him. He paused, and felt a set of arms envelop him in a sudden hug. Mei Hui clung onto him, burying her face into his arm. She was so upset for him. Had been ever since he forced himself to see that horrific painting. And even though the Professor's body language told her that he wanted to be left alone, she couldn't help herself. She clung onto him for dear life, and wanted to tell him how sad she was for him, and that she was so very sorry.

She didn't need to say a word though, because her gentle sobs told him everything.

21 IMPULSE

Harald Wolff rarely did anything on impulse. But today was a terrible exception.

Since Jeremy Fitzsimmons' capture, the Professor had been in a quandary about the upcoming interviews that the agents were to have with him. On the one hand, he knew that agents D1 and D2 were specially trained and highly-skilled to be able to retrieve as much information as possible – but on the other, he desperately needed to know about that painting for himself, and what hand Fitzsimmons had had in the burning of his house! Had he killed the Professor's family in cold blood? Or was he an accessory, aiding and abetting the perpetrator? Or did he just stand by, watching, as the two people the Professor loved most in the world burnt to death?... His blood boiled the more he thought about it. His heart raced. And though, with steely grit, he allowed the passage of night to distil and clarify his thoughts, he still knew that he must speak to Jeremy Fitzsimmons in person. Face to face. Even if it was the last thing he did.

And so he called D1, and told her. He was going to Avernus this afternoon, and he wanted an interview with the man himself. She vehemently opposed his decision, and warned him of the dangers, the consequences. But the Professor told her in no uncertain terms that he was going ahead whether she liked it or not.

He was on his way now, to see Jeremy Fitzsimmons. He had told D1 that the prisoner's hands must be left untied, and that the interview should be just the two of them – alone.

'Hello, Professor.' Jasmine's beautiful voice greeted him as he entered Avernus, the solitary sound of his cane tapping sharply against the walls. He paused and straightened. He'd missed her – even though she was readily available on his mobile, it wasn't quite the same as the high-fidelity speakers here that gave her voice such depth of tone, it was as though she were a real person standing right in front of him. 'Hello, Jasmine. It... it's good to be back.' He continued tapping down the corridor. 'Can you tell me where the prisoner is being held.'

'He is in room 12, Professor.'

The old man stiffened, keenly aware that the agents had inadvertently chosen the same room that Karl König had been kept in. The room where he died. If he were a superstitious man, it would have been the worst kind of omen. But as he walked, he told himself, again and again, that he didn't believe in superstition...

The two agents standing guard outside the room moved apart when he arrived, and one of them held his key card to a silver RFID reader on the wall. The door clicked, and he held it open – but the Professor did not move. 'Sir?' said one of the guards. 'The door's open...'

The Professor roused, pulled himself together, and tapped his way inside. But just a few steps in, he heard the door being firmly shut and locked behind him.

He tried to discern where the table might be. Where the man was. But there was only silence.

His skin tingled with apprehension.

The hairs on his neck prickled.

And he willed himself to move, with all his might.

He heard a squeak of a chair – about three metres ahead, and 30 degrees left – and he froze.

A fly buzzed past his face. He felt the flutter of wings against his cheek.

Whispers of air-conditioning somewhere high up.

The Professor's feet moved forward of their own accord, toward the noise.

The cautious tapping of his cane reverberated starkly in the near-bare room. The cane hit something. A chair. And he reached out a hand, pulled it back, and sat down.

Sluggish eyelids bobbed up and down as he listened.

Still nothing.

'Are... are you there?' the Professor asked. He could almost imagine the soundwaves of his words floating through the air, fanning out in undulating ripples. Dampening against the shape of the man sitting opposite him.

He thought of the man's hideous face as it had been described to him by V2. Cold eyes boring through him.

Silence.

'Can you... can you tell me your name?' the Professor asked.

Again, nothing.

The Professor sat quietly for some time, his head static, blind eyes fluttering downward in spirals.

He waited, listening intently. But he couldn't hear a thing. For a moment, he wondered whether the man was even there. Yet the chair had creaked. He had definitely heard it.... or had he?

Minutes passed. And at last the Professor decided to ask outright. 'D-did you paint that picture... of my house?!'

He waited, but there was no reply.

Patience wearing thin, anger suddenly flared inside of him. 'Were you *there* when it happened?!' he asked, hand tightening around the top of the cane, white knuckles straining against stretched skin.

'Why won't you say anything!!' he seethed, angrily hammering the cane against the floor.

He closed his eyes. Tried to calm himself. Taking deep breaths.

He decided to change tack. 'In your house... there's a large painting of my wife, my son. Burning. How did you come to paint it?'

No reply.

'Please...' he said, almost begging. 'I need to know. Don't you understand h-how it felt to discover that painting? Can't you see I need answers!!'

The Professor listened intently, but there was not one sound. In the end, he leant resignedly against the chair, lapsing into silence.

He sprang open the face of his wristwatch, and impatient fingers pawed at the clock hands, then gradually stilled.

It was turning into a long waiting game, a silent battle of steely determination.

Hours passed with not a single sound from the man.

And though the Professor turned his head this way and that, to hear, eyelids half closed with concentration, he wondered how anyone could stay so still, so completely silent, for such a long time?

The pins and needles in the hand holding the cane forced the Professor to swivel round and take the stick with his other hand. At the same time, his resolve cracked, and he felt himself succumbing to resignation and futility. He had waited hours, for nothing. Lowering his head in unspoken defeat, he at last gave in. He might as well leave.

Just as he was about to push himself up, he stopped in his tracks. Something came to him. A thought, an impulse.

His heart pounded at the idea of it, and he slowly turned back to sit squarely at the table – leaning his cane against it.

Blood rushed through his ears, deafeningly.

He wiped a sweaty hand on the fabric of his trousers.

Dug fingernails into his legs, mustering courage.

Eventually, he placed his right hand on the table, and inched it tremulously forward. Fingers splayed in a reaching motion.

And he waited.

It was unnerving... the feeling of the unknown. Like thrusting a hand inside the Bocca della Verità, the Roman stone 'mouth of truth', not knowing what was lurking inside... hidden behind layers of dusty cobwebs.

There was a whoosh of air – and he flinched.

A bristly hand clamped his.

Long, bony fingers curling tightly.

Coarse nails digging in.

A vice-like grip, squeezing, with almost inhuman strength.

The Professor wrestled to breathe, gasping.

Fearful eyes blinked with desperation.

But as his eyelids descended, as if in a drugged stupor, silently snapping shut, he found himself cocooned in a dark and misty place. A Cimmerian world.

And he panicked!

There was a faint stench of something lingering in the air.

Above him, around him, and underneath, there came out of nowhere a deep-blue midnight sky... completely devoid of stars... soundlessly sombre... and hushed with gossamer breaths of smoke...

22 A STARLESS MIDNIGHT SKY

'I hate you!!!' screamed the boy, his red face contorted with anger.

Chiara Wolff stood resolute before her 12-year-old son in the kitchen of their home, hardly believing the force of his anger. 'You... you don't mean that... If Papa heard you speak like that to me, he'd be so, so angry!'

Christian glared at her, his face eclipsing with darkness. 'I don't care! He's never here anyway – always working. He doesn't care about me. He only cares about his dumb work.'

'That's enough, Christian! Your father loves you very much. I-it's just a difficult time for him right now. Thousands of jobs are at stake. People's livelihoods. He's trying his best to save them, save the company.'

'I. Don't. Care!!'

For the second time, Chiara held out her hand to him. 'Please, just hand it over. You know the rules. No games before bed.'

The boy stepped back and folded his arms, tightening his grip around the Game Boy.

'Christian!'

He cocked his head, a quizzical look on his face, and sniffed the air. 'What... what's that smell?'

Chiara sighed. 'I can't smell anything – my nose is still blocked after the cold. But stop trying to change the subject! Just be a good boy will you. Give me the Game Boy, and I promise I won't tell Papa about your outburst tonight.'

'No!' he said defiantly, and turned away.

'That's it!' she seethed. Lunging forward, she wrangled the Game Boy from his hand, and turned it off without thinking, putting an end to that infernal tinkling music.

'No!!!' screamed Christian, staring at her. 'It wasn't saved!! It took me ages to get to that level, and you've ruined it!' Blind with rage he looked around, grabbed an opened tin of chopped tomatoes left on the table, and hurled it at her.

Chiara stepped away, but it hit her forehead, narrowly missing her eye. She cried out. The tin fell near the back door, exploding in a messy splodge of red across the pristine white floor.

But the boy had already disappeared, feet stomping on the stairs as he retreated to his room, fuming.

Chiara fingered her forehead, not sure whether the red on her hand was blood or tomato. She tore off a reel of paper towels, dabbed at her head, and then ran out to the hall – shouting up from the bottom of the stairs. 'Christian, *please*!! Come down. We... we can talk.'

There was a bang as he kicked his door shut.

Chiara heaved a deep sigh, feeling tears well up. A spark of pain splintered her forehead, and she checked the paper towel and saw that it was blood. 'Great,' she mumbled to herself. She shouted out, 'You cut my forehead, Christian – I'm bleeding!'

Silence.

She walked back to the kitchen, pulled out the first-aid kit from a drawer, and with shaky hands fiddled with the antiseptic, dabbing haphazardly at roughly where the cut was. She managed to extract a plaster and stick it on – batting away an annoying housefly that buzzed very close to her ear. But before she could put the kit away, she stopped, hunching over the worktop, head dropping, shoulders heaving – succumbing to tears. She shook her head, mumbling, 'I can't do this... I can't do this anymore...' Then she heard something. Outside. And she looked up, squinting through the window to try and see past the glaring reflections.

Jeremy Fitzsimmons had been watching silently on the other side of the kitchen window, hidden in the dark of night. Though he had not been there long, he was already frozen, and he scowled from the cold. A battered old cap mantled his face in shadow. There was a faint smell of something in the air, but he ignored it, distracted as he was by what was going on inside. He saw the boy hug something to his chest. His hair was lighter than he'd imagined, and though he had the same intense, dark eyes of his father, he looked more like his mother. Fitzsimmons studied her now with increasing interest. Her ash blonde hair, tumbling over slim shoulders, reminded him of someone he knew decades ago. Someone very special to him. And though they were not very much alike, when he looked upon Chiara Wolff, somehow he saw his Georgina…

Peering keenly through the window, he watched the boy's tantrum, saw him grab something and throw it weakly at his mother, heard it clang on the floor. Then the boy ran off. The mother dabbed at her forehead with some paper towels, and when she disappeared into the hallway, Fitzsimmons strained to hear what was being said. When she returned unexpectedly, he quickly slipped back into the shadows, and then watched as she cleaned her wound. After a while, she crouched over the worktop, shoulders shaking. Crying.

As he observed her with quiet fascination, it suddenly dawned on him what that smell was. Irked, he stepped back to look over the wall of the house, not realising that he had drifted partially into view just as she looked through the window. Seconds later, the door suddenly opened, and a bright light shone directly into his face! It was her, holding a torch in her hand. She screamed at the awful sight of him – a pathetic, gurgling scream – then swung something at his head with the brute force of pure terror. He ducked, and the object clanged heavily against pipework nestled between the door jamb and the vertical fascia, cracking the old, rusted pipe. The gas that he had smelled earlier suddenly became much stronger. A cast-iron griddle pan clattered heavily on the ground. The door was slammed shut and bolted.

Fitzsimmons regained his balance, and threw himself against the door, banging on it furiously with a clenched fist. Bang! Bang! Bang!!! Each sound elicited faint screams from inside. The gas had become so overpowering that he covered his nose and mouth with a sleeve, while at the same time kicking and throwing himself against the door.

A neighbour's light switched on, just as the door cracked and gave way against his shoulder. It swung wide open, and he ran inside – only to slip on something wet and lumpy on the floor. His head smashed against the jamb, and he fell to the ground on his back with a thud. Stunned eyes rolled back, just as he lost consciousness.

Chiara screamed as she swung the griddle pan in a blind panic. She missed, hitting the wall instead, and she dropped the pan on the ground with a clang. Scrambling inside the house, her flustered hands fumbled with the lock. Then she ran to the corridor.

Christian was just treading quietly down the stairs. His eyes glistening red. 'I... I'm sorry I hurt you, Mama,' he cried, lips trembling.

'Christian!' she gasped, looking over her shoulder.

Bang! Bang! Bang!!!

Christian jolted his head toward the noise. 'Wh-who's that?!' He took in his mother's wild eyes, the cut above her eyebrow, drips of blood.

She looked up the stairs, then along the corridor, stricken with fear, trying to decide. 'Please, Christian,' she hissed, distracted. 'Just... just do as I say.'

Bang! Bang!!!

Christian's round eyes glanced from the back door to his agitated mother. 'What's happening?...' he whimpered, scared.

Chiara looked around in desperation, then took a gamble and opened the small under-stairs cupboard. She bundled Christian around, pushing him inside – he fell down and scraped his knees, crying out.

'Shhh! Please, just get in,' she hissed.

Bang! Bang! Bang!

The boy hobbled inside, and Chiara followed him, twisting round and pulling the door shut. There was no internal lock, so she held onto the door handle with both hands, wedging her feet against the wall for leverage.

It was pitch black, and he was scared of the dark.

Christian sniffled and cried. Small fingers exploring the graze on his knee – welts, torn skin, and sticky blood. 'Ow...' he whimpered. It really hurt.

'Be quiet!' whispered Chiara again.

And then the banging stopped.

They waited – one minute, two, three. It seemed like an eternity.

'I think they're gone, Mama,' whispered the boy, hands latched around her arm.

Chiara listened a while longer. 'It... it might be a trick, to draw us out. Just wait.'

'But I'm scared!' He screwed up his nose, wondering what that rotten egg stench was. It burnt his eyes, so he rubbed them. He suddenly felt overwhelmingly sleepy.

Chiara's hands were bristling with pins and needles, but she dared not let go. 'Just... wait,' she whispered – not understanding why her words were slurred. And though she was tense, her muscles began relaxing of their own accord, little by little. She didn't register that consciousness was seeping away from her, didn't realise her eyes were sliding shut. She slumped against the wall.

The slight movement woke Christian. 'Mama?' He jostled her shoulder, trying to get her attention. But she didn't move. He tried again. 'Mama, what's wrong?' He felt so tired, confused, desperate to see. He leant over and reached for the corded light switch...

A deafening explosion!

Head surging with pain, Jeremy Fitzsimmons groaned as he roused to the ear-piercing wail of fire engines. Gradually regaining consciousness, he became aware of something hot and crackling and dancing with light. Waves of fire lapping at his feet. The heat, so tremendous that it felt solid, like molten blades, searing and nicking his skin. Red-yellow-orange flames rose up like monsters, growling and roaring, as they engulfed the kitchen, spitting molten sparks that popped and jumped onto him. He scrambled up and ran out, throwing himself on the grass – rolling this way and that, batting at his smoking clothes. In time, he wobbled onto uncertain feet, relieved to find that he could stand. He looked back at the inferno, acrid fumes rising from his clothes. There was a wild look in his eyes, yet he dithered, didn't know what to do. He looked around, panicked, searching for something. But then there came a commotion in the neighbour's garden. Firemen rushing out. And he ran away. To the bottom of the garden. Jumping into the bushes.

Looking back, he realised that they hadn't seen him. They were fixated on the fire, unreeling metres of hose – shouting to each other, and releasing onto the inferno arcs of spraying water. A shower of glistening crystals raining down.

He watched them anxiously, hyperventilating. Heedless of the stinging patchwork of burns on his skin. He stayed there for as long as it took them to put the fire out, nearly two hours. And though the flames had gone, it was still so incredibly hot that he could feel the heat even from the end of the garden.

Time passed, and he found he could not move. Mesmerised by the whiff of the possibility of death. Needing to know if they had escaped, or burnt alive. Then he heard a commotion. Someone shouting. Crashing noises. And he realised that somebody was running around inside. Yelling, frantically calling, searching. Then there came a long silence. A silence so thunderous that it squeezed the breath from his chest. He flinched when it was shattered by hysterical screaming and wailing, choked with horror, grief, anguish.

He froze in the bushes. His blood curdling. Heart exploding from his ribcage. They hadn't made it, and he felt like something had been torn away from him. Felt like he had failed Georgina all over again. He struggled to breathe, and fell to his knees, groaning so deeply that his whole body spasmed and arced with torment.

Yet he couldn't help lift his head... as those primal screams echoed dully in the night. Couldn't help but trace, with bloodshot eyes, the dense columns of black smoke winding their way upward... evanescing, tenderly, into the excruciating blue of a starless midnight sky.

23 THE DAISY

'To be honest, I'm not sure it was a good idea. You know, to go and see that painting of his wife and son,' said Brian. The Professor had disappeared for two whole days, and with V2 gone as well, he, Tyaishia and the children were talking about him with undertones of worry. But Brian always tried to be realistic. 'I'm guessing he's probably taking some alone time, to get over the shock of it...' He and Tyaishia were in the kitchen peeling a small mountain of potatoes.

Tyaishia chimed in. 'If sup'm 'appened to 'im, mi tink they would've told us by now, isn't it?'

'Mmm,' said Brian distractedly, trying to gouge out a particularly deep black spot.

Milly and Mei Hui had only just returned from taking Tai to the garden, as part of their morning routine to get some fresh air before lunch. They had pushed him in the wheelchair to the end of the path, and after reaching a row of young weeping birch trees, the girls helped him onto his feet so that he could slide his hands over the silky paper-white bark, turn his face upward, and blink under the swaying shade and dappled light. The trees certainly didn't have the presence of the great oak that he was so fond of, by the lake of Avernus – but he was still happy to be surrounded by nature. He doddered slowly through the garden, hanging onto Milly's arm, trailing pale fingers through the fragrant jasmine that wound its way along the pergola, and then the potted myrtle, lavender, and raised beds of rosemary, basil, and tarragon – stopping now and then to breathe in the heady scents that lingered on his hand. Even so, he soon became exhausted and returned to the wheelchair. The girls helped lower him into it, his legs shaking from fatigue. They always finished their walks by picking a selection of wild flowers and leaves for his mother. Tai took his time choosing, then pointed out to them the pink and red campion, yellow cowslips, the last of the bluebells, a few glossy buttercups, and a mix of primroses.

Tyaishia had taken to pressing flowers within a large and heavy antique Bible she'd stolen from the house library. If she had remembered that one of the 10 commandments was 'Thou shalt not steal', she might have chosen to buy herself one instead. But she was becoming fond of the old book and its wise aphorisms – reading verses randomly, and marking favourite passages with a blossom. The girls deposited on the worktop a tumble of flowers, their morning's pickings – and a delighted Tyaishia stopped to inspect them. But then she paused briefly, and turned away to wipe off a furtive tear. Wondering whether, one day, she would be looking at those very pressings with a broken heart, after Tai was gone...

Brian noticed, placed a gentle hand on her arm, and then quickly changed the subject, talking jovially about cracking on with lunch. He rummaged in the fridge and pulled out a wedge of cheese and some cream. 'I fancy some cheesy potatoes, Taish!' he told her, depositing them on the worktop. 'What's that posh way of saying it again? Dolphin... Dolphinoise?'

'Right, right,' sniffed Tyaishia, swiping at her eyes. She looked for a suitable knife from the cutlery drawer. 'We can fry up some corn fritters too.'

Milly, who was sorting out the flowers, looked up. 'It's Dauphinoise, Dad!'

'Yeah, that's what I meant,' he told her. 'I wonder if the Professor'll be back in time – he's partial to Dolphinoise.'

Milly sighed.

Mei Hui drew closer. 'I hope we hear from the others soon,' she said. They knew she was referring to Jemima, Calista, and Jake. 'It is worrying...'

'I'm sure they're okay,' said Brian, trying to keep upbeat. To him, there was no point in thinking the worst, unless there was solid reason for it. 'No news is good news!' he said brightly. 'Actually, if I remember correctly, when they went to find you in China, Mei, I was told they were gone for months. I think they just like to travel – probably having a whale of a time doing a bit of sightseeing while they're at it! Especially since someone else is picking up the bill,' he winked at her.

Mei Hui raised an eyebrow. To the Chinese, winking was a rather vulgar gesture, along with whistling, and pointing chopsticks at people, or worse still, stabbing food with them. But she was getting used to the English ways, and was in fact learning to embrace them. She smiled at Brian's gesture – a smooth blink of an eye, with a naturally light grin. She had never winked at anyone before, but wisely refrained from trying, knowing it would probably look more like a demented squint or a tic.

She quietly observed Tyaishia and Brian who were chatting away amiably. Mei Hui knew from her connection with Tai that his mother had not always had such an affable and good nature. True, she had suffered from years of post-natal depression, and then struggled with feelings of rejection when Tai's father left. But it was an almost miraculous change. It seemed too good to be true... Mei Hui suddenly realised that the change in her personality came *after* Tai had revived her from the coma, and she wondered if there might be a connection. Her eyes drifted over to Tai, who was resting on the side sofa. His head tilting forward slightly as he began to doze. He seemed so fragile, so docile. Yet he was the most powerful of all of them. Didn't even know his own abilities. Didn't know the full extent of what actually he was able to do. And she wondered whether they would ever find out...

Her own ability was simple enough. The clear and indescribably perfect sense of someone's integrity. Whether they were good or bad, genuine or fake. She knew straight away that the woman she had asked to look after the children, Yin, was inherently a good person. Even though she had made mistakes, and faltered momentarily with indiscretion, she knew they were wrongs that came out of desperation and loneliness. But when she had touched Yin's hand, her own energy – a kind of latent kinetic power – passed through sizzling fingertips to Yin, and flowed right into her and then back again, with hardly any impedance. In this way, Mei Hui sensed that Yin's soul was undeniably pure.

She closed her eyes fleetingly, trying to discover the purity of her own soul, her own thoughts. Since learning of Jeremy Fitzsimmons, she and Milly had been eager to discover more about the man that might be the progenitor of their genius. But was it so important? Couldn't they just be happy with the status quo, and leave the man alone? Especially since the Professor was adamant that he didn't want them to go anywhere near him...

She had been mulling over this for a while. And a single meaningful glance from Milly – who was casually leafing through Tyaishia's flower pressings – gave her the answer she was seeking. Mei Hui went to sit next to her, and they looked through the flowers together, shoulder to shoulder. That contact, that balmy warmth of body heat, was the conduit through which they affirmed to each other that inexorable need to see Jeremy Fitzsimmons for themselves. A tacit, wordless understanding. And now, with the Professor's mysterious disappearance, there was nothing to stop them. They resolved to go and see Jeremy Fitzsimmons that very day.

They managed to convince the Chauffeur to drive them.

Milly and Mei Hui told him that they were worried for the Professor – which was true – and wanted to go back to Avernus to discover what had happened to him. The Chauffeur was initially reluctant, vaguely divining, in the Professor's absence, that he would not have wanted that. Not least because Dr Kendra had just died there. But at the same time the Chauffeur was aching to do something useful. Aching to get on the road, and fly along the motorway behind the wheel of the FX4, leaving behind all his pain... So in the end he agreed.

Milly told Tyaishia and Brian that they were taking Tai for a drive with the Chauffeur, and not to worry if they were back late...

The Chauffeur dropped them off at Avernus. Normally he would have waited in the car for them, but knew he'd probably go out of his mind, left alone – so he intended to distract himself with picking up various bits and bobs in town. He told them to send him a message when they were done.

They watched the silver FX4 speed off and disappear around a corner, before turning and wheeling Tai into the garage entrance, waiting with silent expectation as they descended in the car lift. It was eerily quiet when they entered the maze-like corridors, and they hoped that their security access for Avernus had not changed, because none of them had any clue about how to program Jasmine the way Calista and Jake did. The door opened for them without a problem. 'Hello, Tai, Mei Hui, and Milly,' came Jasmine's pleasant voice.

'Hello, Jasmine,' said Milly. 'Is the Professor here?'

'Professor Wolff is not in Avernus.'

'And what about Jeremy Fitzsimmons,' chimed in Mei Hui. 'Which room is he in?'

'He is in room 12.'

Milly asked her, 'Can you tell us who is in Avernus, and where they are?'

'There are currently eight people in Avernus, besides Jeremy Fitzsimmons. Mitchell Erickson and Sam Khan are at the entrance of room 12, Linda Beresford, Lauren Swanson, Noah Sterling, and William Tipper are in the kitchen, Daniel Fu is walking west along corridor d9, Suzie Green is walking south along corridor a12.'

Milly gulped. 'That's a lot of people,' she mumbled. She extracted some earpieces, and gave one to Mei Hui, one to Tai, and put the last one in her own ear. 'Right. Please speak to us only through our earpieces from now on, okay?'

'Affirmative,' said Jasmine, switching to the correct channel.

Milly continued with her instructions. 'We're going to visit Jeremy Fitzsimmons, Jasmine. And as we go, I want you to tell us exactly where the eight people are at any given moment. So you need to lay out Avernus onto a grid map. The top of the map should be true north, making the bottom south. The x and y axes should be equivalent to the actual latitude and longitude coordinates, respectively. Then abbreviate each of those six people by... by...' Milly went suddenly blank, and looked at Mei Hui for inspiration.

'By their initials,' Mei Hui answered her.

'Yes, by their initials,' repeated Milly. 'And let me know their coordinates, expressed as minutes and seconds only, as they move. Do you understand, Jasmine?'

'Affirmative, Milly. I understand.'

'Right, show me that map on my mobile.'

'The map of Avernus as you described it has been transmitted to your mobile.'

Milly took out her phone and looked at the image for several seconds

– memorising every millimetre. She put her mobile away in her pocket. 'Lastly, Jasmine, I'm guessing Jeremy Fitzsimmons' room is being monitored?'

'It is, Milly.'

'As we go through the corridors, and when we get to room 12, I want you to loop the camera footage so that nobody can see us on the CCTV recordings. Okay?'

'That will be done, Milly.'

Mei Hui added, 'And silence all our phones until further notice!'

'Your phones are silenced, Mei Hui.'

Mei Hui glanced at Milly, noticing pink flushes on her cheeks. 'Are you okay?' she asked.

Milly nodded as they walked down the dimly-lit corridors until they reached the outer wall of the main hub of Avernus. Thankfully, the security code had not changed, and they were able to let themselves in.

'Ready?' asked Milly.

'Ready,' repeated Mei Hui, wondering how Milly would hold up under pressure. She placed a hand on Tai's shoulder, and he nodded his understanding. He had to stay completely quiet.

Milly tapped in the access code, the door sprang open, and they wheeled Tai into the glowing light.

What followed was a long, silent dance, as the girls and Tai chasséd through corridors on their way to room 12. Their teacher from the Rambert Dance Company would have been proud of the poise and grace in their natural movements. And so, the three of them were easily able to avoid Daniel Fu and Suzie Green – the former on his way to bathroom 5, and the latter heading to the BC. Jasmine was informing the children through their earpieces, rattling off a series of continuously changing coordinates. Coordinates told with such speed, that anyone else would have been completely dumbfounded. But Milly listened attentively, her brow creased with single-minded focus, as they moved like ballet dancers – floating along corridors in smooth glissades, avoiding Daniel Fu's footsteps reverberating at the far end, then quickly pirouetting to switch direction, before Suzie Green rounded the corner. They ciseaux-leapt into an empty room, as two people, Sam Khan and Mitchell Erickson, came their way. Waiting still and silent behind doors, or around corners, poised, in fourth-open position.

Before long, they found that they were just a few turnings away from room 12 and Jeremy Fitzsimmons – breathless, with the end in sight. But suddenly, Jasmine's voice detonated in their ears with a dizzying plethora of coordinates reeled off at top speed. Every one of the eight security staff were on the move, all at once! Their paths criss-crossing through Avernus in random scattershot directions. Milly ground her teeth, sweat dripping from her face, as she increased to allegro tempo, leading them into rooms, waiting, then out again, further along corridors, and diving back in. She held her nerve admirably.

Just two more corridors to go, and as they swept past a line of doors, Milly spotted something at the side of her eye. It was small and shrivelled on the floor, discarded outside room 23. She gave it the merest glance – a dried-up daisy, flattened and dirty – then suddenly stopped in her tracks.

Mei Hui glared at her, puzzled, looking fretfully up and down the corridor. She didn't have Milly's lightning-speed computational skills, and she could not discern where the security people were in relation to their position – but she knew they were all still on the move. 'Milly?!' she whispered, on edge.

Milly tore her gaze from the daisy, and looked up at Mei Hui, eyes wide with mortification. She recognised that flower. And at last remembered. Remembered that she had made daisy-chains for V3, crowning her tousled white hair with stacks of them, as she slept. Milly had watched her for days and days. Watched the bruises on the agent's face turn from red, to purple-blue, and finally yellow-green – like shifting aurora borealis skin tattoos. But how?! How could she have forgotten V3? She was supposed to have a photographic memory, learning by heart entire books, even whole languages, within days... Milly caught a choke in her throat. Felt like she was fragmenting. Suddenly confused.

Someone's footsteps echoed at the end of the corridor, and Mei Hui quickly opened a nearby door, heaved Tai inside, and pulled Milly behind her. Closing the door, just in time. They stood in the pitch black, listening nervously as the footsteps drew closer... clomped right outside... but then passed and began to fade. Mei Hui sighed with relief as the patter eventually disappeared. Then she heard the sniffling sobs of someone crying.

Milly's disembodied voice floated up through the dark. 'H-how could I have forgotten?' she sniffed, almost to herself. 'I-I don't know what's happening to me... I don't understand. I feel like I'm... fading.'

For once, Mei Hui was at a loss for words. Her mind buzzing. She blinked stiffly in the darkness – hemmed in by two overwhelming problems. On one side, the danger of being caught by the security men. And on the other, Milly having a breakdown. Mei Hui forced her mind to calm. Tried to think.

In the end, it was Tai who spoke up. 'It's okay, Milly,' was all he said. The gravelly voice of an old man, scarcely a whisper.

Milly silently absorbed those simple words, as if they held a power over her. She repeated them, convincing herself. 'It's okay...'

Mei Hui began breathing again. She joined in. 'Yes, it is okay, Milly. We are here with you. But... we need to get to Jeremy Fitzsimmons, now. It is just two corridors away. Can you help us do that?'

After several seconds, Milly gave a shaky nod, and grappled to tame her emotions. She took a deep breath, and galvanised herself into action. She opened the door and stepped out, while, at the same time, Mei Hui swivelled Tai's wheelchair round, pushing him into the corridor.

They barged straight into a passing security guard.

William Tipper stopped in his tracks, amazed to see two girls and a frail old man in a wheelchair.

Tai immediately flicked out his hand, and grabbed his arm.

Their eyes locked onto each other's, magnetised.

Then, after several seconds, Tai let go – his wrinkled hand falling, limp, on his lap.

William Tipper straightened, turned back in the direction he was going, and continued walking. As though nothing had happened.

When he was out of earshot, Mei Hui placed a gentle hand on Tai's shoulder. 'Are you okay?' she asked.

'Yes,' was all he said.

Milly and Mei Hui glanced at each other; they knew what he must have done. He must have erased the memory of them, the sight of them, from that man's mind – as easily as wiping dry chalk from a blackboard.

Milly gulped. In their ears, Jasmine was still rattling off a multitude of initials and coordinates, and she focused her mind. Absorbing the locations of each person. Then, glancing back in the direction William Tipper had gone, she turned in the opposite direction, and beckoned for them to follow. At the end of the corridor, they waited, listened, making sure it was clear before turning sharp left.

They walked halfway down that corridor, stopping at a junction – the very last corner – and they paused. Mei Hui touched Milly's arm, and in turn, Milly touched Tai's shoulder, forming a chain. Empathically, they coordinated their next move. Then, all at once, they rushed toward the two men standing guard outside room 12, and in one seamless movement, the girls took hold of one of Tai's hands, and with the other they grabbed the arm of a startled guard.

The men froze, their eyes drifting away from the children, staring instead straight ahead, as if in a trance. One of them took out a key card and held it to the card-reader, and the door clicked open.

The guards stepped back and resumed their positions at the side of the door. Their minds having been temporarily dulled and rendered senseless – like a telephone switched to mute.

At last, Milly and Mei Hui pushed Tai tentatively inside the soundless room.

24 INTERLUDE

As they walked quietly into room 12, Mei Hui's mind buzzed with a thousand thoughts. So wrapped up was she in the mystery of Jeremy Fitzsimmons that her mind clouded out anything else. She saw within that mystery only what *she* hoped for.

She thought of how dearly she loved her mother and father. Yet there was no getting away from the fact that they were simple people, who were content to live a simple life. And so she wondered whether this Jeremy Fitzsimmons might be on her same level… might understand her way of thinking… And if she were completely honest, she half hoped for a kind of father figure. One that she could relate to. But then, as they walked into the room, one last thought came to her – far, far too late. She suddenly wondered, with almost childlike naivety, why there was so much security guarding a single old man…

When Milly entered the room, on the other hand, she felt numb – still in shock from discovering the vast sinkhole in her memory. The thought of it made her queasy, because she knew it was just the beginning. The beginning of the end of an exceptional mind. Like a sparkler that all too quickly fizzes with brilliance, only to dampen to nothing. And so she followed Mei Hui into the room, trembling. Listening quietly to the voice inside her head. 'Be careful,' her mother whispered. 'Be careful, my love.' And Milly stiffened.

Tai, instead, remained silent as they wheeled him inside.

He fixed eyes on the shadowy figure in front of them, searching for his colours. But he found, to his puzzlement, that there were none…

And as the three children thought of all these things, and stole silently into the room, nothing could have prepared them for what they were about to find.

Their moment of reflection was perhaps just a fleeting interlude. The lull of calm before a blazing storm.

25 BROKEN TEARS

Jeremy Fitzsimmons was sitting oddly on the edge of a bed, against the light, so that his form was virtually a silhouette.

The children could not see his face as they drew closer without a word – they were only able to make out the form of him: slumped shoulders, a head bowed as though in shame, arms hung limply by his side – like a marionette with cut strings. As they drew closer they saw his long, matted beard, a thin body, with a back arched in a slump, barely filling the simple clothes he wore – a layer of crumpled, grey linen.

For some reason that even they did not understand, Mei Hui and Milly hung back and only watched, as Tai slowly pushed his wheelchair forward, going right up to him. When the man at last lifted his head, and looked at Tai, and then at the girls, they saw the full horror of his grotesque face. The girls gasped. Wanted to turn away, yet found, inexplicably, that they could not.

Tai sat, unmoving, in front of the man. They stared at each other, face to face. The boy's eyes roaming over every sordid detail. Incongruous bulges, patches of whiskered and mottled skin, crudely cut hair tumbling grey around his ears – and Tai felt his heart breaking. He pulled his sweater sleeve over his hand, reached forward, and wiped the tears that brimmed in Jeremy Fitzsimmons' eyes.

The old man flinched, but then stilled. He allowed the boy to touch his face, though it unsettled him. But in the space of a gasp, the man lashed his hand upward and grabbed Tai's wrist – clenching it crudely in a vice-like grip.

Tai cried out, and the girls rushed forward. Milly grappled with his hands, while Mei Hui pulled and tugged at Tai's arm, trying to wrench it free.

But with a sudden flick, the man grabbed Milly's wrist too, and she cried out in fear – a thin, gurgling sound. Mei Hui grasped Milly's arm as well and tried to wrench her away.

But the circle was closed.

The old man released a silent energy that snaked and hissed through them. Tai slumped unconscious in his wheelchair – followed by Milly and Mei Hui, dropping to the floor in a heap, emitting the faintest of sighs.

Jeremy Fitzsimmons kept holding firmly onto Milly's wrist with his right hand, and Tai's with his left. Wrists that seemed thin and brittle as twigs. He stooped down, close, and slowly looked them over. Glassy grey eyes flashing with determined intent. He explored every inch of Mei Hui's pale, smooth face, Milly's forehead creased with intensity even in sleep, and Tai's wrinkled skin and grey hair. Sniffing the air, sniffing them, like a primal animal scrutinising its prey.

The old man closed his mismatched eyes – one eyelid drooping lower than the other. And slowly, unashamedly, he breathed them in.

'If the painter wishes to see beauties that charm him,
it lies in his power to create them,
and if he wishes to see monstrosities that are
frightful, ridiculous, or truly pitiable,
he is lord and god thereof.'

Leonardo da Vinci

26 THE MEMORY COLLECTOR

1879. Jeremy Fitzsimmons the 1st had told his wife Cyrena that she and the twins should sup without him that evening, for he would be working late on a painting. A painting that disturbed him to the core.

He glowered with silent concentration as he put the finishing touches to it. His hair speckled both with flecks of paint and a profusion of grey strands. He set down his palette and knife, absentmindedly wiping hands on an apron stained with a riot of discordant colours, itself reminiscent of an abstract painting. Taking several steps back, he tilted his head, and for a long time he stared at his work, immobile, fingers tugging at his beard in contemplation.

He scowled even more. He was never quite satisfied. Unable to let go, because he demanded perfection from himself, as well as something else that he just couldn't put his finger on. He wanted... no, *needed*, to capture the subject's being. Their very essence. And as such, the portrait before him was lacking...

Fitzsimmons' eyes darted over the image, from point to point. There, the mouth, a delicate line tracing a hint of absentminded concentration, and there, wisps of hair that merged into the blackness of the background. The hands, and crooked fingers, were perfect. The pallid skin, cheeks stained with red, were true, as well.

He drew closer, and inspected the painted eyes. Those hateful eyes. Blank, like the man's blank soul...

And that was when he realised what was missing.

Urgently, he looked over the sideboard filled with jars of paint, rags, bottles of oil, and brushes – searching through for the finest sable brush. Ah, there it was. The one with the wide handle, for steadiness, and the tip tapering to a hair's breadth.

Closing his eyes, he breathed in the memory... That time he visited the subject of the painting. Hugh Charles. He remembered the door opening. The man greeting him. Small, hard eyes in a long face. A wattle of loose flesh hanging below his chin. Hugh Charles' extended hand, and Fitzsimmons' lingered handshake, his own fingers draped over the man's. The feel of cold, waxy flesh. Fitzsimmons stiffened from visceral fear as the man's memories flooded his mind – sludges of mire muddying clear waters. And he gasped, as he found himself shaking hands with a murderer. Absorbing his gruesome, bloody, macabre memories.

Fitzsimmons opened his eyes, and found himself back in his studio, and suddenly doubled over, dry-heaving from the thought of that awful moment. At last he straightened, composed himself. And in time came back to his senses, though pale with a veneer of sweat.

He quickly turned to the sideboard, sweeping up the palette with a trembling but frenzied hand. He busied himself with mixing and loading the board with smears of colour. Black, mostly black, with some lead white, a dab of viridian, cadmium yellow, and just a touch of vermilion, for the tip of that savage knife. He took the laboratory magnifying lens and set it on a stand in front of the canvas at exactly the right height, then went to fetch the open-wick globe kerosene lamp, so that there was no flicker – slipping it onto the wall hook slightly above and to the side of the canvas.

He rolled up his shirt sleeves, and carefully dabbed the sable brush with a lick of colour. Pressing the leather end of a Mahl stick against the canvas, he rested the side of his hand on the stick, and peered into the magnifying glass – a Cyclops eye louring through the convex lens. But his hand betrayed him. It trembled from the thought of what he was painting. He closed his eyes, shook it out, and leant in again. This time it was perfectly steady.

Fitzsimmons took his time. Such fine precision required it. He blocked in the shapes with thin colour: the negative space, light source, and the silhouetted figures. When that was dry, he started on the detail. The woman tipping backward, and that sickening man, Hugh Charles, one hand clamped around her neck, and the other held high in the air, holding a knife already drenched in her blood and gore.

It did not take him long to complete, just over an hour. And he at last pushed aside the magnifier, his head dizzy-light from concentration. He stepped back to look at the painting. Without the benefit of magnification, the miniature figures disappeared in the sheen of the eye glaze, and he breathed easy. At last that awful image burdening his conscience for months was purged from him. The eye detail was itself a grisaille impression in its own right, defiled with a hint of colour. A painting hidden within a painting. Simple, in its beautiful complexity.

Tired yet relieved, Jeremy Fitzsimmons cleaned and washed his brushes, tidied the studio, hung up his apron, and carefully reached for the kerosene lamp, taking it out with him. He did not usually secure his studio, but this time he made sure to turn the brass key firmly inside the barrel of the door lock, placing the key in his waistcoat pocket.

He wound his way down the stairs – and as he went, he found, to his relief, that the queasiness and aching head had dissipated. The weight of his steps was much lighter than it had been when he climbed up to the studio six hours earlier.

He thought about the telephone call he'd made to the police station just after his visit to Hugh Charles' house. He had asked to speak to the officer investigating the death of Penelope Charles, the man's wife, and he was put through to Inspector Madden. Fitzsimmons informed him straight away about Hugh Charles commissioning a self-portrait – also hinting, in passing, of the likelihood that he was being paid with the ill-gotten money from his dead wife's insurance policy... This was news to the inspector, and he immediately sent officers to arrest the man, for a second time. The resulting trial ended with the unanimous decision of his guilt – justice at last! And the man was sent to the gallows in just two days, and hanged to the raucous cheering and levity from the crowds. Yet even then, Jeremy Fitzsimmons had not felt as light as he did now, after completing the painting.

He had known of the cathartic effects of his work for a long time. But this particular painting helped him to understand even more the nature of his unusual... ability. When he touched people, when he absorbed their memories, he somehow absorbed a lifetime's worth of thoughts and images. And though it had not affected him much in the beginning, in time, and after years of collecting such memories, his mind, his body, was beginning to strain from the onerous accumulation. Weary bones creaked from the burden.

And now he realised that painting was the only way to cleanse himself. It purified his mind, wholly, from those imaginings, particularly the ones from Hugh Charles…

Fitzsimmons no longer shuddered when he thought of it now, guessing it was because that savage perturbation was no longer part of him, released instead, and locked into, the canvas.

He knew that this night, for once, he would sleep easy.

When Fitzsimmons visited the water closet before going down for supper, he stopped to inspect his face in the mirror, lingering, scrutinising, in the same manner that he surveyed his portraits. Though most of his face was covered by bulges, hair, and whiskers, his pale skin was still noticeable, evidence of the fact that he spent far too many hours indoors.

In the dim light, with fatigued, half-closed eyes, he could almost imagine himself having a normal visage. He sighed. Fanciful thinking. Still, he had come to terms with his appearance. And though it had never occurred to him before, he did wonder whether it was perhaps impolitic to believe that everything good in his life hadn't come without a price. A Faustian bargain. And if his facial deformity was indeed the price he was paying for all the presently enjoyed good fortune, health, happiness, and safety of his precious family, then he would gladly take on the disfigurement again and again.

But his perfect, blighted life could not be so easily expounded. Nor was it to last.

17 years later, Jeremy Fitzsimmons the 1st died of the consumption. And he left behind him a desperately grieving widow, and a son and a daughter: twins, William and Fidelia.

Fidelia herself mothered twins, and William married late in life, fathering three children in his sixties, two boys and a girl.

Of his sons, one was childless, and the other sired four strapping boys, as if making up for the lack of his brother. But only one of those siblings chanced upon a good life: one later died in war, another died of smallpox, and a third died after an unfortunate accident with a hatchet, when the ensuing gangrene took hold. That left just the second-born alive.

The surviving son did not marry, but an illicit liaison with a 'lady of the night' produced a bastard son, discovered by the father only several years after his birth. And that son, in turn, fathered Jeremy Fitzsimmons the 3rd on 8th September 1952.

By this time, five generations on, it became discomfiting, perturbing, and entirely clear to each successive family that there was no getting away from the affliction. That every male, at some point in their lives, would be blighted by facial disfigurement. It always started as a mole on the face. And no amount of surgery, or medicine, or even a desperate attempt at psychic healing, could rid them of the slow-growing deformity.

And though it was also accompanied by the most unusual and alarming mind abilities, which manifested in both minor and major ways from generation to generation, still, their condition was invariably looked upon with pathos.

The Fitzsimmons curse was passed from generation to generation, and there was absolutely nothing they could do about it.

187

'Obstacles cannot crush me;
every obstacle yields to stern resolve.'

Leonardo da Vinci

27 LIMBO

After entering the room where Jeremy Fitzsimmons was being held, deep in the heart of Avernus, Tai, Milly, and Mei Hui found themselves pressed flat on the ground by an invisible force. Their movements restricted.

When they opened their eyes, they could not make sense of their surroundings… Where they were. Above and around was just blackness. The ground underneath them seemed like a sheet of glass – hard, smooth, and mildly warm, at body temperature. It glowed with soft, vague colours.

Milly was crying, flat on her back, unable to move.

A stunned and silent Mei Hui grappled with being squashed, face-down.

And Tai, appearing as his usual 15-year-old self, was trying to push himself up onto his knees, teeth clenched, and shaking from immense exertion. But he failed, and fell on his side, grunting with frustration. They were spaced several metres apart, sprawled out flat, against a colossal globe-like structure, like flies on honeyed paper.

Mei Hui's cheek was pressed hard against the ground, but she managed to say, 'Wh-where are we? What is this place?' She put all her efforts into moving her arms, patting the surface around her with explorative fingers, feeling, touching, gliding. But something needle-like pierced her skin. 'Aiee!' she cried. 'I-I've cut my finger!' She gritted her teeth and wrenched her hand up and around, so she could see it. There was a splinter wedged in the round of her fingertip. With great exertion she managed to pull it out, sucked a drop of blood clean, and spat.

'You okay, Mei?' Tai called out to her.

'I am fine. It was a splinter.' She puffed as she heaved her hand closer, to inspect it. 'Glass,' she discovered, flicking it away. 'It is a glass splinter. Be careful!'

Tai patted the ground around him. 'It's smooth here.'

'But there are jagged parts, like flintstone,' said Mei Hui. She struggled to push herself sideways, shimmying along on her stomach, trying to understand what they were lying on.

Milly floundered as she heaved herself round, panting, and managed to roll onto her stomach. 'What's happened?! Why can't we move?'

They tried their hardest to pull themselves up from the ground. Grunting and shouting, heaving and yelling – all in their minds – while their physical bodies lay inert and unconscious at Fitzsimmons' poised feet, on the floor of his prison cell. But it was no use. They were trapped.

Tai eventually gave up, and lay defeated on his side – trying to make sense of it. Then he realised. 'I think... I think we've jumped into Jeremy Fitzsimmons' mind,' said Tai, closing his eyes. 'Though I sense... mixed feelings. He's curious about us, but at the same time, he's wary. That's why he's glued us down.'

He remembered that when they were in Karl König's mind, there was a bad tang in his mouth, as if he were tasting sickness itself. But here, in Fitzsimmons' mind, there came the sensation of iron or silica – like smooth, warm glass sliding against every inch of his skin. As if they had been swallowed whole by a crystal anaconda, entombed and helpless within its sinewy gullet. It was at once viscous, solid, and slimy. And he shivered from the stomach-churning sensations.

'It is no use,' said Mei Hui, giving up.

'So...' cried Milly, desperate, 'there's no way out?! We're just stuck in this... this limbo?'

'Yes,' said Tai. 'All the time he's holding us, we're gonna be trapped.'

They lapsed into silence for a long time, and Milly's sobs eventually petered out. She had struggled onto her side, an ear pressed flat against the glass, when she suddenly realised something. 'C-can you hear that?'

Tai shifted and pressed the side of his head against the ground too, and listened. 'Yes, it sounds like... beating. A heartbeat!'

They listened – it was almost imperceptible, like the faintest of pulses. Though with every gentle boom-boom, they discerned the glass-like form quivering and trembling, as though alive.

Milly struggled to flip onto her front, and then pressed curved hands against the opaque surface, peering through. 'I can see things moving inside. Shapes. Images. I think… I think they're people, things, places. But it's all foggy. Impossible to see clearly.'

Mei Hui swivelled round to the splintered edge nearby, and followed the line of it. 'The glass appears to have long markings all over. Like… veins, though they are not veins. More like…' She paused to think. 'More like cracks or fissures.' She squinted an eye, and lined it up with the chink in the crevice, careful to avoid the rough edges. 'I can see through!' she breathed. 'Only just. It's a really thin crack.'

Both Tai and Milly followed suit, searching for the nearest fracture, then looking inside. 'Yes, I can see as well!' said Milly, squinting against it.

'Me too,' chimed Tai. 'There's a boy, sitting on his father's knee. I think that's him, Fitzsimmons, when he was little…'

'I can see a woman,' said Milly. Then she gasped. 'It's that woman we saw in the painting at his house! You know, the one in the dark room, by itself.'

Mei Hui went quiet for some time, eventually saying, 'And I am seeing flames. Big flames!' Jeremy Fitzsimmons' painting of the Professor's burning house immediately came to mind. And the possibility that the man had something to do with it became more real in their bleak entrapment. She gulped. What had they done by coming here?… Had she really been so wrapped up in the romantic notion of finding a father figure, that she completely overlooked the possibility of danger? She felt sick. Tried to think what his intentions might be. But it was impossible to understand him. She could not even detect whether he is good, or bad. Impossible to penetrate through the thick structure they were lying on… through the thick wall of glass. 'It's like… a glass heart,' she murmured, almost to herself. That was it. 'A glass heart that has been shattered into a thousand pieces…'

'Oh my goodness, yes,' said Milly, thoughtfully. 'A kind of physical representation of it. They say the heart is the centre of a person's thoughts, their emotions. But he must've put up a barrier, so that we can't get inside. Hang on. That must mean that, just like we guessed, he has–'

'…Abilities, like ours,' finished Tai softly. 'Mentally, he is trying to keep us at arm's length, but at the same time, he doesn't want to let us go…'

'But why?' asked Milly.

'I don't know,' Tai said, flummoxed.

Milly thought of something. 'So, why the cracks?'

Tai shook his head, equally baffled.

'I am just guessing, but it looks broken, doesn't it?' said Mei Hui. 'Metaphorically speaking. Something has happened to him in the past that has affected him. It has caused his heart to fracture, to shatter.' She thought about the Chinese proverb, 'A clear conscience is the greatest armour.' She wondered whether something was troubling his conscience, making him unhinged, causing chinks in his armour. And now, she felt an overwhelming compulsion to find out. 'We are trapped here – for how long, we do not know. While we are here, we should try to discover what we can. By looking inside. Even though we can only see the briefest glimpses.'

'Until he breaks the connection,' said Tai. 'Until he lets go.'

'Which could be at any moment,' Milly said. 'I gotta say, if he is the person they got the genius genes from, I want to know how it all happened…'

A flutter of red flames through the crack caught Mei Hui's eye. 'And I would like to know if he started the fire at the Professor's house.'

Tai craned his neck to see them – he could make out Mei Hui in her entirety, but just the top half of Milly. 'Here we go again…' he mumbled, resigning himself to the inevitable.

They wasted not a second more. Each of them returned to the hairline fissure directly underneath them, and they lined up an eye as best they could, squinting, and peering inside. Connected as they were, they absorbed their own fear, trepidation, and insatiable curiosity – as they delved nervously into Jeremy Fitzsimmons' heart.

PART 2

28 THE HEART OF SHATTERED GLASS

'......lights are low
He sings this song and away they go
Horsey, horsey don't you stop
Just let your feet go clippity clop,
Your tail goes swish and your wheels go round,
Giddy up, we're homeward bound.'

Little toddler, Jeremy, was perched on his father's knee, being bounced up and down to raucous squeals of laughter. In time, he collapsed, slumping in his father's arms, giggling hysterically. He was a handsome child, with flawless, alabaster skin, and a mop of brass-blond hair curling around his ears. He yawned, and reached up, as he so often did, burying inquisitive fingers in his father's tickly ginger beard. Droopy eyes poring over that warm, familiar, deformed face. 'Wuv you, Dadda,' crooned young Jeremy. With chubby fingers buried in his father's beard, he absentmindedly explored every lump and bump of his father's jaw – vaguely knowing that he would grow up to be just like him, and look just like him. Which was everything he ever wanted. To be like his Dad.

'Love you too, Jem,' his father, Maxwell, responded. 'But it's time for bed now,' he said, bracing himself.

'No!!' shouted the child. 'Wanna stay. Not tired!' He began sucking his thumb defiantly, in loud squelchy clicks.

But the child was small enough to be carried, and so his father kissed the top of his head, and simply lifted him up and walked out of the lounge, through the hall, up the sweeping, curved staircase, and into the first bedroom of the east wing. In a house where no expense was spared, the boy's room was unusually bare, almost austere. The child preferred it that way, always kicked up a fuss when they tried to bring things in. He took out unwanted items straight away, leaving them in the hallway, to gather dust. There was already a heap of discarded books, toys, games, left outside on the plush carpet.

The child was gently lowered into bed, and a blanket tucked around him. He lay back, knowing better than to fight it. 'Storwy?' he asked, hopeful.

Max sighed. He was exhausted. 'Well… just a short one then.'

The boy's eyes lit up, 'Capsen! I want Capsen, Dadda!' he insisted.

His father smiled. 'You mean, Prince Caspian?' It was a recently published book that he'd been given as a present.

Little Jem nodded with excitement. 'Apple twee,' he begged. And then he remembered the special word. 'Pweeeeaaaase!' He held out his left hand with his little finger sticking out – and his father responded by hooking his little finger around it. The boy closed his eyes, lips carving a soft smile across his face as he saw in his mind the image that his father showed him, bright as day. It was the illustration in the book of the tall, old apple tree, heavy with golden fruit, within the mossed walls of a secret garden. He pored over it. The delight on the faces of the children in the illustration was mirrored by his. He shifted sideways to make space on the bed, his father put his feet up whilst stifling a yawn, and they both lay back, eyes closed, fingers hooked. He was far too tired to speak. Instead, he recounted the chapter from memory directly into his son's mind. 'Once there were four children whose names were Peter, Susan, Edmund, and Lucy, and……'

……Four-year-old Jem Fitzsimmons sat cross-legged on the floor, in front of a painting that was propped against the wall, in the hallway. The picture was twice as tall as he was, standing. His mother, somewhere behind him, was deep in conversation with her sister. 'No, Barb, no. I think it deserves a more open space. It's lost here. No-one will appreciate it. They'll just walk by without giving it a second thought.'

'It's gonna get walked past wherever it is, to be fair. Anyway, it blends in really well here, and the colours match the décor.'

Young Jem, not really listening to them, was eating a hard-boiled egg from his hand, biting into it like an apple. He ate as he examined the artwork, mesmerised by the hardness of the shadows, the softness of light.

'Will you look at him!' hissed Barbara to Anne, taking her sister to the side. 'How can you let him eat like that? Out of his hand, like a wild child?!'

Anne breathed a withered sigh. 'Barb, he's four. He has a love-hate relationship with food. And if I don't let him eat like that, he won't eat at all. Is it really so bad?'

'But why would you allow it!'

'That's just him. He needs to *feel* the food in his hands.' His mother stopped there. She would rather not tell her sister the whole story, that the boy *lived* by touch. He could not understand a thing without handling it first. He explored the world through his fingertips. 'Just... just be grateful, okay! He's healthy, he's happy... I think. Maybe a tad too quiet, but he's okay.'

Jeremy polished off the egg, licked his hand clean, and then reached out to touch the painting.

'Jeremy, no!' his mother cried. 'You've got eggy hands, and that's a very precious family heirloom. Your great, great...' Anne paused, unsure of how many 'greats' there were. '...One of your ancestors painted it. It's very special. You shouldn't touch it, okay?'

He glanced back at his mother and blinked. A constellation of freckles smattered across his nose and cheeks. 'Ever?' he said in a high-pitched squeak, upset.

She didn't like denying him, and already felt herself caving. 'Well... maybe when your hands are super, super clean. And dry!'

Inspired, the boy jumped up and ran off to wash his hands.

Barbara stood with her arms crossed, glaring at her sister. Anne looked down. 'I'm doing my best, Barb. Like I said, we should be grateful, 'cos it's only a matter of time before he changes, and... and...' She glanced away, overcome.

Barbara softened, and touched her arm. 'You never know. It might not happen...'

'That's what I keep telling myself,' she said, catching a choke in her throat.

Jem came flying back down the corridor, and jumped right in front of his mother – holding squeaky clean hands up to her face. Anne couldn't help but smile. She clasped his hands in hers, and kissed each one; they smelled of eucalyptus soap. 'Go on then,' she grinned, ruffling his hair as he turned away.

'Cool!' he said, and went back to the painting, standing in front of it. He pretended he was the painter, his hand the brush, and he closed his eyes, trailing his fingers along the lines of the impasto brush strokes. Swirling along every contour. Imagining in his mind's eye its creation.

Anne melted with a smile. As they watched him, she said under her breath, 'I wouldn't have you any other way, Jem Fitzsimmons.' She sighed. 'Just, don't change, or, or......'

......Tap. Tap-tap. Tap. Tap.

The fly bounced randomly against the window pane, trying to get out.

Nine-year-old Jem stared at it, distracted.

'Jem!' said his father. 'Concentrate.' They were sitting at the large dining room table, with an array of books spread out in front of them. There was no writing paper, no pens. 'Have you been listening to a word I've said?'

Jeremy looked at him and nodded – unconvincingly.

His father narrowed his eyes, and scratched between the whiskers on his cheek. They were constantly itchy. 'Okay, let's see then. Edward the Confessor. When did he die?'

Jem looked at him with blank eyes. 'You... didn't say?'

'I did! I just told you.' Max sighed. 'He died on 5 January 1066. And almost a hundred years later, they canonised him, or in other words, they made him a saint. Two years after that, his body was transferred to a specially-made shrine in the heart of Westminster Abbey, where he lies to this day. He was the last but one, the penultimate, of the Anglo-Saxon kings of England. Now, can you remember anything that he was known for?...'

The boy screwed up his face trying to think. 'Er... smallpox?'

His father blinked at him in disbelief, resisting the urge to groan. 'No,' he said, as calmly as he could muster. 'Maybe you're thinking of a different Edward. Edward Jenner, from our science lessons, perhaps? He invented the *vaccine* for smallpox. Edward the *Confessor* was known for being deeply religious... Jem! You must concentrate, history is so important. We can learn so much from it.'

Jem huffed, fingering the edges of the nearest book. 'I hate history!!' He flipped several pages. 'Look, no pictures! It's *soooo* boring.'

His father took the book, and turned to a page with a <u>simple line drawing of the king</u>. He pointed at it with his index finger. 'There! There's one there.'

Jem folded his arms on the table, and rested his chin on top – glaring at the picture. 'There's no perspective, no depth, no colour. Boring!'

'Well, I can see your art lessons are sinking in... But the king wasn't boring at all. His life was fascinating, as the book goes on to show. For example, he was very pious, living quite a humble life despite being king. He was also the first to believe that his royal touch had the power to heal, and so flocks of people queued to see him. His successors also believed they had this miraculous touch, for many hundreds of years. They thought it was conferred upon them by God. Even Shakespeare mentioned the ceremony of the royal touch in "Macbeth", when he said,

"Tis called the Evil:
A most miraculous work in this good King,
Which often, since my here-remain in England
I have seen him do. How he solicits heaven
Himself best knows: but strangely-visited people,
All swollen and ulcerous, pitiful to the eye,
The mere despair of surgery, he cures
Hanging a golden stamp about their necks,
Put on with holy prayers: and 'tis spoken
To the succeeding royalty he leaves
The healing benediction."

Maxwell had remembered the quote word-for-word. 'Now, the hanging gold stamp put about their necks was actually a gold coin called the "Angel", so-called because the coin depicts Archangel Michael slaying a dragon – a scene from the Bible book of Revelation. So, when the patient was healed, they were given an "Angel" threaded on a ribbon which was hung about their neck, supposedly to ward off any further disease. So you see, Jem, it's quite fascinating!"

But Jem's expression – eyelids half closed, as he continued fingering the pages – was of complete disinterest.

His father sat back in his chair, deflated. He had known for a while that Jem didn't have the academic genius that he and his own father had. Still, for years, he kept trying to draw it out from him. Working hard to teach him to be more studious, to love learning. Be more like *him*. But he was beginning to give up hope... Maybe it was time to accept defeat. His son was never going to have *that* kind of genius.

Tap-tap. Tap. Tap-tap.

The boy turned to look at the fly bouncing against the window, and then turned back, large eyes imploring his father.

Max sighed. 'Go on then.'

Jeremy sprang up, noisily scraping back the chair, and ran over to the fly that was bashing itself against the glass. He slid the top pane down fully, but despite the boy's wafting arms, the fly kept hovering around the lower pane. 'Dumb fly,' he mumbled. The fly suddenly buzzed loudly and jumped onto his nose. Jeremy looked down at it. 'Eurgh!' he cried. He was just about to brush it away, when the fly jumped off and landed on his index finger instead. Slowly, Jeremy brought his finger nearer, to see it close-up – cross-eyed. It was resting, and cleaning itself, twitching veined wings that looked like crinkled slices of glass in the light. With his other finger, Jeremy began stroking those delicate wings, perfectly steady. The fly stopped, and hopped round to face him – it seemed to be staring right up at him. And then it flew off with a zizz, disappearing through the open window.

Jem ran over to his father, excited. 'Did you see that, Dad?! The fly... i-it let me stroke him!' He jumped up and down on the spot, balling his fists with excitement. 'It was so coo–……'

'……then you dial in the focus, here.'

Max was hunched over a shiny new Polaroid SX-70 on the coffee table, with Jeremy sitting on the floor next to him. 'This is the light meter, here. And you can change exposure with the compensation dial, right here.' He pointed to the black and white dial. 'Then just press the red button to take the picture. Got it?'

14-year-old Jeremy still wasn't quite sure, but he nodded anyway.

'Don't worry, Jem. We can practise a few times. You'll get the hang of it.' He snapped the gadget closed, and hung it around his son's neck. 'Ready to take your first photos?'

'Yes,' said Jeremy, so excited to have his very own camera. He looked around the room, at the paintings on the wall. 'Can we do the pictures?' His voice had not yet broken, though it was a little deeper, huskier.

'Sure, yes, we can do the pictures.' He got up. 'Where do you want to start?'

Jeremy shrugged. 'You choose.'

'All right then.' He waved across at a random painting. 'Let's start there.'

They shuffled over to the picture in slippered feet – it depicted a stampede of magnificent black horses, throwing up plumes of dust as they ran. Jeremy saw the artist's familiar signature in the bottom corner, and he turned to his father. 'I've been meaning to ask, Dad. Who exactly was F. Jaffrey, and how come we've got so many of his paintings?'

'I… I thought you knew, son?'

'Bits and bobs. I know that he's a relative, and he had a photographic memory, like us – but that's all. Mum doesn't know. She said to ask you.'

'Oh, okay, well… F. Jaffrey was a pseudonym used by–'

'What's a "pseudonym"?' asked Jeremy.

'It's a name used by artists or writers to conceal their true identity. And your forefather, Jeremy Fitzsimmons the 1st – a not-too-distant relative, I think about four or five generations back – used it for all his paintings.

Actually, he was the first known Fitzsimmons to have been born with...' he waved an awkward hand at his face, 'with this.' His eyes slid sideways to study Jeremy's expression. He seemed okay, and so he continued. 'He was a master artist who painted a lot, and was in great demand – or so the story goes. His paintings were mostly commissioned portraits, but he also did animalier, like this one, as well as landscapes. Over time, I've been buying the paintings back gradually, whenever I've been able to locate them. Working through a proxy, I've offered at least double the market value, which most sellers agree on quite quickly. We needed to be discreet, so we've always told the seller *never* to tell anyone about the sale – if they valued their life! But that's just between you and me.' He winked, and held a finger to his lips.

Jeremy's jaw dropped.

Max broke out into a smile. 'I'm joking!' he said, laughing at the expression on his son's face. 'Sorry, I've been reading too many stories about the Kray brothers in the news! No, no, we just made really good *monetary* offers that they couldn't refuse, sometimes even rising to three or four times the market value when they weren't budging. Money's not the issue. I just want to reclaim all his work – bring it back into the family.'

'Oh, okay,' said Jeremy, relieved, absentmindedly fingering the camera.

Max thought of something. 'You know, I think you have an artistic streak, Jem. You should try painting, see how you get on with it.' He looked at the Polaroid. 'But first things first – the camera! Do you want to try taking some pictures yourself first, and then......'

......Jeremy soon got used to the Polaroid, and built up a small library of photobooks with all the pictures he had taken of anything he fancied. Paintings, flowers, leaves, a swish of gathered curtains, a Schreiber brass handle. And he captured people's faces too, snapping his father as he dozed after dinner, as well as his mother chatting for hours on the phone, twirling the corkscrew cord around a finger, and bouncing a foot up and down as she talked. He loved the feel of the pictures in his hands, the weight of them. They were the only things he allowed in his bedroom –

that and the small wardrobe of his clothes. Images that he could see, and fabrics that he could touch.

He had been lying on his bed, sorting and arranging photos, then sticking them in the book with self-adhesive photo corners. He preferred that type, to the other photobooks where the images were trapped behind plastic film – he didn't like anything sticking on the photo.

Yawning, he caught his own reflection in the full-length mirror on the wall. He stopped to stare at the young man looking back him. His own pallid skin, a mess of thick, brassy hair. Then he looked at a photo of his father. And he wondered if he would really change to become like him. No-one had ever told him it would happen. But whenever he inadvertently touched his father, he just knew. He somehow knew the entire history of the man, without a single word being spoken.

His heart skipped a beat.

He remembered idolising his father when he was small. Remembered wanting so much to be like him, look like him. But now, just the thought of his own face transforming and swelling into whiskery bulges, made him sick...

He closed his eyes, took a moment to let the anxiety subside – and then reached for the SX-70. He weighed it up and down in one hand. It felt like it had two pictures left, and he checked his guess against the counter. He was right. He adjusted settings and dials, then turned the camera around, at himself, held it at arm's length, and pressed the red button. The picture emerged, and he waved it in the air, wondering if it really helped the drying time, or not. Turning the photo round, he saw a deadpan face looking straight ahead, just above the camera lens. An okay-looking boy, with distant, slightly droopy eyes, and a well-defined bone structure. He stared at the photograph for some time, before leafing through the photo book. He decided the picture deserved a page of its own.

As he lined it up, he wondered how many more pictures he might be taking of his face the way it was now......

'......and so I said, I said, "Move over, love, before you fall over!!"'

Barbara giggled after her little anecdote, comically batting the air over her plate. There was a peel of raucous laughter.

They were having an anniversary lunch for Jeremy's parents, with aunty Barbara, uncle Danny, and their two children, John and Pamela. They were sitting around one end of the large 18-seater dining table; most of it was left empty. Jeremy was eyeballing his cousins, who were a few years younger than him, at 10 and 11 respectively. They in turn were staring with revulsion at his father, in between cupping hands around the other's ear, frantically whispering.

Both annoyed at their rudeness, and offended for his father, Jeremy was just about to tell them off, when their mother, Barbara, noticed – and lightly slapped her daughter's shoulder. Pamela jumped, straightened up, and went back to eating her food.

A young maid rushed into the room, bringing the plates for their starter. When she looked up, and saw Max's face, she suddenly screamed and dropped the tray. It clattered and smashed on the floor.

They turned to find her, frozen, hands over her face in horror at the sight of him.

Anne quickly got up, and stood in front of her husband, blocking him from view. Through the doorway came another, older maid – her mother, Estelle, red-faced and apologetic. 'I'm so sorry, Ma'am!! Really, really sorry, sir!'

Anne frowned. 'What's going on? Where's Angela?'

Estelle bundled her daughter out of the room, and Anne followed them into the kitchen. 'Angela rang in sick,' she explained, flustered. 'And I... I needed help to do the lunch at short notice. So I asked my daughter, Gemma. I did explain to her... I did tell her about Sir Max. B-but I don't think she understood properly. I'm sorry, Ma'am!'

Anne sighed. She went to pour a glass of water, and returned, saying to the distraught girl, 'Sit down, dear, take a deep breath for goodness' sake! Here, have some water.'

Gemma looked up at her, then took the water, her hands shaking.

'It's just his face,' Anne told her. 'A *different* kind of face – but he's a good man, with a good heart. And he will treat you a hundred times better than any other employer. Now, take a moment. But get over it. You've that mess to clear, and the starters to serve. Followed by lunch, then the cheese tray, and finally coffee. So lots to do!...'

Estelle flew past her, grabbed the dustpan and brush, and went to sweep up the broken china.

When Anne returned to the others in the dining room, she was greeted by a wall of silence – broken only by the siblings chortling. Anne flashed them a steely look, and they immediately shut up. She sat down, gently patting her husband's hand.

Max had an awkward expression on his face. 'So...' he said, brows furrowed, 'I'm hoping my £2,000 bottle of brandy wasn't smashed, because that'd really be a disaster.' He winked at Jeremy, and they all smiled with relief. Tension, at last, discharged.

Anne rolled her eyes. 'You think he's joking?! If anything happened to that brandy, I'm a dead woman...'

Max squeezed her hand comfortingly and kissed it. 'You know that's not true, my dear.'

'Oh it's true,' said Anne. 'It's definitely tr–......'

'......No touching!' said the woman in a plaid skirt and beehive hair-do. She stepped forward, holding her hand out and looking nervously around to see if anyone in the gallery noticed. But the milling crowds were too absorbed.

14-year-old Jeremy snatched his hand back, at the same time breaking his gaze from the portrait of Lord and Lady Masterson.

The woman glanced at the bodyguards standing several metres away, and remembered who she was speaking to, the son of a billionaire. 'Please,' she said politely. She straightened her skirt, and cleared her throat, before drawing closer to the painting, and pointing toward the old woman. 'It's interesting to note that the subject, here, Lady Masterson, mentioned a rather fascinating detail in a letter written to her niece, purporting that they had never needed to sit for the artist – at all. According to her, he just arrived at their house, agreed his terms with them, drank some port, and then left – all within half an hour or so. So *apparently*, from that brief encounter, the man was able to paint this entire portrait from memory, with Lady Masterson affirming that the artist's depiction was perfect and accurate in every way, even to minute detail.' The guide laughed and circled a pointed finger around her temple. 'The woman was obviously a sandwich short of a picnic!' she said, rolling her eyes.

The boy looked away from the picture and glared at her, deadpan. 'What do you mean? Why is that funny?' he asked, fingering the shiny camera hanging from his neck.

'The old girl was obviously crazy,' she explained.

'Why?'

'Because no-one can paint an entire portrait like that. Just from memory.'

'Why not?'

'Just... because. Because it's impossible.'

The boy fell into thoughtful silence, then turned again to the masterpiece in front of him. He took several steps back and opened his new Polaroid SX-70 – he enjoyed unfolding it, almost as much as he enjoyed taking the pictures. It made him feel like Sean Connery from the latest James Bond movie, bestowed with a new gadget by Q. Looking through the viewfinder, he dialled in the focus, adjusted the exposure, and then pressed the red shutter button. After a while, a picture reeled out from the front, and the boy picked it out, careful not to the touch the still-damp chemicals. He began fanning it in the air as the tour guide continued with a light cough.

She tried to remember where she'd got to, and then continued her discourse. When she mentioned that the majority of F. Jaffrey's works were missing, Jeremy had to check every muscle in his face, to stop himself from grinning. He knew exactly where those 'missing' pictures were. He had grown up with them, at home, in Oakley Hall – his father's growing collection.

As Jeremy listened quietly to the guide's discourse, he began to admire her passion for art. It was infectious. She was certainly very knowledgeable, technically, and she loved Jaffrey's artistry almost as much as he did. But when she suggested they continue the tour in other rooms, to discuss other painters' work, he realised there must have been a mistake. He was not interested in anybody else, he explained, just Jaffrey.

But she looked flustered, and began to falter – for a reason he did not understand. Instinctively, he held out his hand to her, to find out why, offering a handshake. And in that touch, he realised that she thought she'd made a mistake, done something wrong, to make him leave so early. 'Don't worry,' he told her. 'You haven't done anything wrong, Ms Parry-Johansson.' Although she hadn't ever told him her name.

'Oh, thank goodness!' she said, relieved. She smiled kindly. 'Well, it was nice to meet you. I hope you'll come back to the NPG sometime.'

She did not realise the effect her love for art had on him. 'I'll definitely be coming again,' he told her. 'Nice to meet you t–......'

......Young Jeremy often wandered about Oakley Hall, staring for ages at the paintings. Apart from his family of course, to him, those pictures were the most interesting, most fascinating, most beautiful things in it. It was not just the artistry. It was the message, the emotion, the sentiment they conveyed. And it seemed that each painting held a secret, and somehow, only by breezing the round of his fingertips gently across the surface of them, could they begin to speak to him.

As he wandered around, like a visitor at a gallery, he thought about all the things Mrs Parry-Johansson had told him. And he began to look at the paintings in a different light, began to see things in them that he had missed before. He trailed his hands across the artwork, feeling and absorbing each picture's whispered impartations. And he suddenly bristled from the flinty aloofness of a sitter's gaze, raised an eyebrow at the unspoken passion between two lovers standing side by side, he felt at peace from the tranquillity of a babbling brook, and was thrilled by the magnificence of crashing waves. By the time he had walked the length of the corridor, he was breathless, his heart pounding in his chest, as if he had just returned from a tumultuous journey of experiences.

He remembered then what his father had told him... that he had an artistic streak, and he should learn to paint. His finger lightly traced the last portrait, and he wondered if he might dare hope that such a gift could also be his. After all, his father, brilliant as he was, had no artistic inclination whatsoever. Nor did anyone else in the family.

If he were truthful with himself, to be able to paint as beautifully as F. Jaffrey, was closer to his heart than he realised. The more he thought about it, the more the desire kindled within him. Flaring, incandescent. And he knew that he could not go a moment longer without at least trying.

He turned around, and went back the way he came – to his bedroom, to change into going-out clothes. It was time to make a visit to the art shop......

......When Jeremy turned 19, he took to going on long walks in the country by himself – the battered old Polaroid strapped around his neck. His family's extensive land, deep within the Oxfordshire countryside, was beautiful in summer, and he took his time, feeling his way through the fields – touching crackled tree bark, or stroking the peach-fuzzed leaves of lamb's ear plants. Or he just lay back in an isolated meadow, chewing on a wheat stem and burying fingers into the thick carpet of dewy grass that soaked his clothes, his skin, as he watched the ever-changing cloudscapes. Sometimes he walked by the river that meandered lazily through meadows and wooded vales. He ambled along its banks, listening to the water's calming susurrations, dazzled by the dance of light on its surface. He stooped down to sift fingers across its flow, disturbing his own reflection. He understood now why the beauty of rivers and countryside was so often captured by painters.

The water gradually petered out into a stream that was narrow but rocky and murky. It was when he was stooping down, framing a shot of the river's haunting reflection of the trees, that he was startled by the sound of light laughter. Staying low, he parted a clump of bellflower stems to see a lone, barefooted girl, tip-toeing into the water. She wore cut-off dungarees, and a tatty blue t-shirt. Tumbling tendrils of ash-coloured hair around slim shoulders. Her eyes, caught in the light of the setting sun, were like burnished orbs of jade against silk-smooth skin.

A dragonfly flitted close to his ear. Startled, he ducked away from it – then watched as it flashed in azure streaks through the air, toward the girl.

She too dodged away as it hovered close to her head, before rattling and flitting off elsewhere. Its departure left a look of spellbound wistfulness on her face – as though she had just been enchanted by a tiny fairy.

Jeremy found himself slowly standing up.

And she saw him.

For a few seconds they stared at each other, gauging how to react.

'Hey!' she called out to him eventually.

Jeremy nodded acknowledgement, wordless.

She noticed the camera around his neck and smiled. 'You wanna take a photo of me?'

He couldn't help but mirror her smile, and nodded without thinking.

'How do you want me?'

He blinked at her.

'How should I pose for the picture?' she explained.

'Oh!' He shook his head from indecision. 'Um, just do whatever you were doing before.' He lifted the camera in his hands. He only had one film left – and he kicked himself for not bringing a spare film-pack. He had to get it right.

The girl thought for a moment, tiptoed to the edge of the boulder, and then dipped a foot into the water. She giggled with the same light laughter he'd heard moments before. 'It's cold!' she gasped, looking down.

Jeremy took the picture, and it reeled out with a whirring sound. He gripped it carefully as he walked toward her. The boulder she was standing on was nearly halfway across the stream, so he was just able to reach over and hand it to her.

She stretched forward on the edge of the rock and wobbled, nearly losing her balance – but managed to steady herself. 'Phew!' she smiled, relieved, and took the picture from him.

'It just takes a few minutes to develop,' he told her. 'Careful. Don't touch the wet chemicals.'

She waved it in the air, impatient, and he smiled. 'What's so funny?'

she asked.

He shook his head. 'Nothing. Just... I do the same. Every time.'

'It's taking forever, even if it is just a few minutes!' She flapped it harder – but it suddenly flew out of her hand, right into the water. They stared in astonishment as it tumbled downstream, and then, after glancing briefly at each other, the girl ran after it. Jeremy immediately followed. But the river conspired against them, throwing bushes and trees in their way, twisting and turning, as they chased the picture in a mad dash. The girl's side of the river was not as crowded as his, and she flew ahead of him, giggling and shrieking with the excitement of the chase. Jeremy couldn't help but steal thrilled glances at her as he navigated the river bends. Her hair, flowing behind her in golden rivulets. They eventually came to a point where the banks suddenly rose steeply, and the stream disappeared under a bridge. They stopped, and could only watch helplessly as the photograph disappeared from view.

Jeremy bent over, gripping his legs, catching his breath – and the girl plonked herself down on a verge of grass, exhausted. 'I'm... sorry... it's lost!' she breathed, gasping for air.

When Jeremy recovered, he walked over, crossing the small bridge. He sat on the grass next to her.

She rolled her eyes. 'I'm so clumsy!'

'Don't worry,' said Jeremy, daring to glance at her. She was beautiful. Red blooming on her cheeks. 'I don't have any more film on me, though. That was the last one.' He began picking at the grass for no particular reason.

She copied him, and started making a little mound of grass on her lap, wriggling her dirt-stained toes. She thought for a moment and raised an eyebrow – somehow everything she did was elegant, even that small movement. 'So... what were you taking pictures of?'

He fumbled inside his camera bag, pulled out a stack of photos, and handed them to her. She went through them. A hawthorn. A bee gathering nectar. A cloudscape. The glimmering light on the stream's surface. Each successive picture seemed to delight her even more. 'Wow, wow, wow!! These are amazing!' she said. 'You've got such a good eye.'

'Thanks – and as you can see, no peeping-tom pictures of strange girls…'

She laughed – light and bubbly, like the stream. 'Just thought I'd check.' She stopped to look at him, really look at him. 'You know, you remind me of someone – but I can't put my finger on it… I'm guessing you live around here?'

He nodded. 'I'm a true Oxonian I'm afraid – born and bred.'

'I love it, love the accent, the people. I'm up from London myself, visiting my Nan.' She pointed a thumb over her shoulder. 'She's having her afternoon nap, so I'm just… hanging by myself.'

'How long are you here for?'

'Two weeks. Two *whole* weeks!' she crinkled her nose.

'Don't you like it here?'

'It's just… well, I don't really know anyone – apart from Nan.'

'Ah, okay. I can fix that.' Jeremy wiped his hand on his trousers, and extended it. 'My name is Jeremy Fitzsimmons. Pleased to meet you!'

She shook his hand courteously. 'Nice to meet you too, Jeremy. I'm Georgina Whyte, with a "y".'

'Hello, Georgina Whyte. And there you go, you know *me* now!'

She looked at his hands. There were smatterings of dark red under his nails. 'Either you've been painting something red, or you've just murdered someone and are rubbish at hiding the evidence. I'm kinda hoping it's the first one…?'

He held up his hands. 'Guilty as charged!'

She looked at him.

'Guilty of painting, that is,' he said, laughing at the worried look on her face. He started scraping out the paint with a fingernail.

They lapsed into silence for some time. She turned to gaze at the stream for a while, and then lifted her face up to the warmth of the sun, closing her eyes, and humming.

Jeremy listened quietly. 'I know that song from somewhere.'

'Course you do, everyone knows it! It's the Beatles' latest – *Let It Be.* Me and Paul McCartney – such a heart-throb! – are an item you know.'

Jeremy was confused. 'Um, didn't he marry what's-her-name recently? Linda Eastman.'

'Shush! Don't say such things. You're breaking the illusion!'

'Ah, a fantasist, that explains everything...' Jeremy leant back on his elbows.

'What d'you mean?!' she said, throwing grass at him.

'Nothing!' he said, smiling cryptically. He turned away and sneezed. 'Ugh, hay fever!

'Oh no, I didn't know you suffered – sorry!' She swept the grass from his shoulder.

'Don't worry, I'll be fine once I get indoors.' He brushed himself down.

She suddenly stopped. 'That's it! You look a bit like Paul McCartney – has anyone ever told you?'

'Not at all!'

She looked him over. 'A blond, slightly taller, slightly more upper-class version of Paul McCartney.'

Jeremy laughed. 'If that's supposed to be a compliment – thank you, I think! So I kind of look like him, but I don't look like him?'

'Exactly,' she said, picking off a blade of grass from his hair. 'Something about the eyes... and you've got a cute little dimple too.'

Jeremy stopped, and cupped the side of his face with a hand.

'Don't look so worried!' she said. 'It's just a teeny-tiny thing – you can hardly see it. It's cute is all I'm saying!'

Jeremy suddenly got up, turned aside, and dusted himself down. He felt red hot, as if the spot on his face was burning into him. 'I-I'd better go. My parents, they'll be wondering where I am.'

Georgina looked up at him, disappointed. 'You don't wanna hang out?'

He paused, undecided. Eventually he said, 'Tomorrow okay? I'll bring loads more film-packs.'

She beamed. 'And I'll bring some sandwiches, to thank you.'

'Fab. We can meet at the same place then. Is 12 ok–......'

......It wasn't long before the two fell hopelessly in love. Hopeless, because it was an inevitability that was impossible to fight. Georgina adored Jeremy's laid-back charm, and the way he treated her – like a lady. Like an art dealer handling a precious Ming vase with the utmost care and delicacy. And on Jeremy's side, apart from Georgina's astounding beauty, he loved the way she teased him, but at the same time cared about his opinion, and always listened respectfully to everything he said. It was also endearing to see how attentively she looked after her grandmother, who lived in a small, thatched cottage, not far from the stream where they first met. She invited him back for afternoon tea, the day before she had to return to London.

'Georgie told me you remind her of Paul McCartney,' said the old lady, Viola, who was small but perfectly manicured. Her make-up was immaculate, her clothing well-kept and tasteful. 'But I can't see it myself. Maybe something about the eyes, but you're definitely much more handsome,' she smiled kindly. 'She also tells me you're from around these parts?'

Georgina poured tea from the bone china teapot into a dainty cup, and handed it to him. 'I'm not sure about that, but thank you!' he said. 'Yes, I live about two-three miles from here. Not far. I often come walking down this way, following the flow of the river.'

'Two or three miles upriver, you say? So you live in Oakley Mead, the town?'

'Not quite. Just a little bit further out.'

She thought for a while. 'The only other place around that way is Oakley Hall. Do you... do you live there?' her eyes widened just a touch.

'Yes,' said Jeremy absentmindedly, picking a custard cream from a selection offered by Georgina.

Viola nearly choked on her tea. She started coughing, and Georgina patted her back gently.

'Nan, are you okay?'

The old lady dabbed a handkerchief around her mouth, and squeezed her granddaughter's hand. 'I'm fine thank you, dear.' She turned back to the boy. 'So... you're a Fitzsimmons?' She quickly took another sip of tea, to calm her nerves.

'I am.'

'That is just... amazing! Your family's lived there for many centuries – I know, because my family have always wondered about the... eccentricities of yours.'

'Nan!' Georgina threw her a look of disbelief.

Jeremy blinked at her. 'Eccentricities?' he said, brushing off biscuit crumbs from his trousers.

'There have been many rumours about your family. For example, it's always been thought that the artist, F. Jaffrey, was really a Fitzsimmons...'

Now it was Jeremy's turn to nearly choke on his tea. 'Really? I... I don't know what to say.'

'One of your forefathers, Jeremy Fitzsimmons, who I understand now was your namesake, was a very mysterious man. He went about in a hooded cloak – spotted here and there riding by on his horse, or in a barouche. No-one actually saw what he looked like. And of course, the painter, F. Jaffrey, was known for turning up at people's houses in a hooded cloak too. Another thing, the initials are the same, but the other way around. All coincidences, but we country folk do like to talk...'

Georgina looked apologetically at him. 'I'm sorry, Jeremy.' She turned to her grandmother. 'Nan! I don't know what's got into you.'

Viola put down her teacup. 'Forgive me!' she said, looking apologetic. 'I hope I haven't offended you. But I've wondered about who lives in that great big house since... since forever!'

They lapsed into silence, broken by the awkward crunch of biscuits, and the tinkle of a spoon mixing tea.

But Viola wasn't done. She couldn't help saying, 'Though... if your forefather *was* the painter, and you don't of course have to tell me, I only wanted to say that I'm in awe and admiration of his work, and his astounding talent. He had such a beautiful way. An exceptional skill. And mere mortals like me can only look upon people like him and his consummate artistry with nothing short of reverence and veneration. I think I've always wondered about your forefather, because... because I've always wanted it to be true.' She thought for a moment. 'Let me put it this way. Having such a renowned artist live nearby is far, far more exciting than the highlight of my year – the recent marrow-growing competition. Which is about as thrilling as it gets around here!'

Jeremy couldn't help but laugh. 'I wish it were true too,' he told her, flicking his eyes downward without giving anything away. 'But I have to say that the marrow-growing competition was pretty spectacular this year!' he grinned.

Viola clinked her empty teacup onto its saucer. 'You know, since I was young, I've always dreamt of being immortalised in a painting.'

Jeremy considered that word thoughtfully. 'Immortalised,' he said. 'I like that. What a fabulous way of looking at it.'

Georgina suddenly got excited. 'I've always wanted to be painted too, Nan! That's another thing we have in common.'

'So... what are the other things you two have in common then?' asked Jeremy, looking from one to the other.

The two women stopped to think, and Georgina raised an eyebrow. 'Where to start. Well, we're both terrified of flying...'

'Oh, and we can't stand the latest poncho craze...' said Viola.

'And we're heartbroken that the Beatles have disbanded!'

Jeremy laughed. 'Okay. At least I know never to take you on a plane, wearing a poncho, singing sad Beatles songs.'

Georgina giggled.

Eventually, Jeremy said, 'But seriously, about my forefather. I can't say whether he was the great F. Jaffrey or not, but... I've taken up painting myself. A few years ago. And though I'm still learning, and not very good, I would love to paint you both sometime. Together.'

Viola gasped, cupping hands around her mouth. 'To be painted... th-that would be a dream come true. And I'm sure you're much better than you're letting on, dear.' She looked at her granddaughter with excitement.

Georgina threw her arms around Jeremy. 'Thank you, thank you, Jeremy!' But then drew away. 'Only... I'm leaving tomorrow.' She looked at her grandmother, then back at him, disappointed.

'Don't worry,' said Jeremy. 'I can take some photos of both of you, here, now, in front of the window,' he turned to the old lady. 'With your permission, of course. And I can work from those. Would that be okay?' Of course he knew that, really, he didn't need any photos.

Viola clasped her hands together. 'That would be more than okay, dear. It would be wonderf–'......

......Jeremy was both ecstatic with the thrill of being in love, and at the same time, sick with the worry of what might become of him, physically. And though he clung on to the possibility, however remote, that this thing he dreaded might never happen, it still overshadowed him, like a grey cloud constantly above his head, just out of sight. Always threatening rain.

'There is no greater love than one that can overlook the physical, and see only the goodness and purity of heart,' his mother told him. 'To me, that is the test of true love.'

Jeremy watched her face as she said this. It was like she had a light inside her, making her glow. She still loved his father so much, even now, after decades of marriage. And Jeremy allowed himself a smidgen of hope......

'......Hey Georgie,' came Jeremy's subdued voice over the telephone.

She knew immediately from his tone something was wrong. 'Baby, what is it? Talk to me.' He never usually called at this time. She glanced over her shoulder, down the hallway, worried her parents might complain about being on the phone so late at night.

There was a deep sigh, a long silence. But he was too choked to speak.

'Jeremy...?'

He managed to pull himself together. 'I... Can you just... talk to me?' he asked, his voice cracking. He couldn't tell her what was wrong.

'Jem, you know if there's anything I'm good at, it's talking non-stop!'

Jeremy managed to laugh.

'I love hearing the sound of your laughter!' she said.

Somehow he could hear the smile in her voice, and it warmed him.

Another silence.

Georgina stopped to think – then took a deep breath, priming herself. 'Well...' she said, 'Mummy and I want to see the Rolling Stones concert in Sweden this year – so we're being *extra* nice to Daddy, hoping he'll let us go. Business hasn't been great – but it's the Rolling Stones for goodness' sake! In Sweden! We simply must go. And Mick Jagger is just amazing, such a performer – and his hair is to die for. I think Mummy's got a bit of a crush on him, but that's between you and me. And did you know Jagger bought a manor house in Hampshire? Can you believe it?! We're practically neighbours. Well, not really, but you know what I mean…'

In this way, Georgina wittered on, while Jeremy sat in his hallway, slumped on the floor next to the telephone stand. Leaning sideways against the full-length hall mirror – the cold glass pressing against his cheek. He avoided the reflection of his face.

He listened to her quietly. He loved her so much it ached.

……Georgina was unable to wait the full three months before her next scheduled visit to see her grandmother. She was dying to see Jeremy, and his painting, so much so, that after just three weeks she booked an advance train ticket for the following week. Jeremy met her at the station, and she released herself from the carriage, clad in a belted, baby-blue dress, and her hair a soft tangle of sunlight. When she saw Jeremy she flew into his arms. 'My goodness, I've missed you so much Jeremy Fitzsimmons!' she breathed into his neck. She drew apart quickly, her face creased with concern. 'But what's happened to your face?'

There was a white square dressing covering his left cheek. He looked down at her suitcase, and took it from her. 'Let's sit down for a mo, Georgie.' He pulled it through the station and into the cafeteria, where they found an empty table and seats. 'I… I had to have some facial surgery while you were away,' he told her, forcing himself to look her straight in the eye. But he quickly looked away again. 'That spot. They thought it might be… cancerous – so they decided it was best to have surgery.' It was only half a lie, and he justified it by telling himself that it was to protect her.

Georgina took his hand, and held it firmly in both of hers. 'My poor baby! I can't imagine what you went through! Does it hurt? Did they manage to get it out completely?'

'It doesn't hurt too much anymore; it's been 10 days already, and it's healing well. They managed to take it all out – in fact, they cut out about two centimetres.'

'But i-it was only a tiny spot.'

'They took out a margin of about half a centimetre all round as well, just to be sure it was out completely. So I'm going to have quite a boast-worthy scar.' He smiled, trying to make light of it.

'Oh Jeremy, that doesn't matter, so long as you're okay. I'll still love you – scar or not.'

He stopped. 'Hang on a minute. What did you just say?'

'Scar or not...'

'Not that. The bit before.'

'I'll still love you,' she smiled. 'There, I said it! I... I missed you so, so much, that I just knew. I was doing homework one afternoon – you know, boring old stuff, biology or chemistry, or whatever – and I just couldn't concentrate, thinking about you. That's when I realised. Right there and then.'

Jeremy beamed. 'You... you don't know how happy that makes me!'

'I mean it,' said Georgina. 'And... even if – God forbid! – the cancer comes back, I'll help you through it. We're in this together, okay?'

That was exactly what Jeremy hoped to hear, and his heart burst with relief and happiness. He blinked at her, absorbing every detail of her face. Her expression was softened by a sincerity that was practically her signature expression – slanted eyebrows, eyes sparkling with emotion – and he melted. 'I... I feel the same! It was like, every minute of every day you were in my thoughts. Moments kept coming back to me of our time together, replayed over and over. And with each memory, I couldn't help feeling like I was falling for you. So you see, that's why I'm so happy. You... you're just too good to be true, Georgina Whyte.'

She smiled. 'I may be that, but... I'm also dying of thirst. Will you buy me a drink, Jeremy?' she smiled at him with those imploring eyes. 'That train ticket cost me my entire week's allowance. And Dad's been strict with money because America's recession hit his company pretty hard.' She picked up the menu card from the table, looking it over. 'He thinks it's just a matter of time before Heath takes us into recession too, then we'll really be in a pickle.' She tapped the menu with a finger. 'I'll have this if you don't mind. Good old bangers and mash. I'm famished! Are you going to eat with me?'

'I already had lunch at home, but I'll have a snack.'

They waved for the waitress, who took their order, and when they were left alone again, they instinctively drew closer.

'I'm dying to see Oakley Hall,' she told him with barely suppressed excitement. 'Is it really big? Do you get lost in endless rooms?'

Jeremy took the paper napkin from the table, absentmindedly sliding fingers over its scalloped edges. 'Not really. It's not that grand. I mean, it's quite big – but not enough to get lost in.'

'Nan's romantic notions about your family have infected me, I'm afraid. I can't wait to meet them! Did you tell them about me?'

Jeremy felt suddenly wary. 'I... did.' He flashed a brief smile. 'Dad's away on business most of the time, but I suppose you could meet Mum sometime. She's quite old-fashioned you know, about dating. She likes introductions, and to do things the old way, with chaperones and stuff.'

'Tell me about it! My parents are the same – so much for the free love they're touting all the time!'

'But... I kind of agree, don't you?' he ventured. 'I mean, with Mum. The free love of the last decade made it cheap... disposable... casual. The *art* of love – I mean, real, proper love, not just sleeping with partners that are here one minute, then gone the next – *real* love deserves so much more. If you want the genuine thing, if you want it to last, you have to invest in it.'

Georgina looked at him with a wry smile. 'Invest? I'm sorry – are we talking about love, or economics?'

'What I mean is that you need to invest time, care, and attention on the person you love, to make it more... more...'

'Meaningful?'

'Yes, that's the word.' Jeremy smiled, slightly abashed.

'I couldn't agree with you more, Jeremy... Ooh, yum!!'

The waitress had arrived with their food, setting down dishes and drinks on the table.

Georgina laid out the napkin on her lap, and took up the cutlery. 'This looks delic–......'

......The picture was set very carefully on Viola's chintz divan in her sitting room – a beguiling cloth draped loosely over the top. It was bigger than they had expected, a good one-and-a-half metres tall, and Viola was already wondering where she would find the wall space to hang it. That is, if the boy's artwork was not a complete disaster... For weeks she had worried that it would turn out to be an abstract of the kind that made them look like hideous monsters. In Viola's mind, there was art, and then there was art. Both she and Georgina were standing in front of the painting, clinging onto each other with nervous apprehension – with a slightly embarrassed Jeremy standing aside, his fingers pinching the muslin.

'Jeremy, we're having kittens! Please just put us out of our misery!' pleaded Georgina.

Jeremy took a deep breath, and pulled off the fabric.

For several seconds, the two women froze into statues – the only movement was from their eyes, poring over the canvas. Viola made a kind of throaty sound. In time, she prized her eyes away from the picture, roaming instead over the real table and window next to it, where the picture was set. Then she looked at Jeremy, and back at the painting. Blinking and processing what she was seeing. 'I... I can't believe it!' she gasped. Tears welled up, glistening momentarily, before flowing down her cheeks. 'I really can't believe it,' she repeated, dumbfounded. It was not just the beauty of the painting itself – the finesse of their forms, in pretty, muted shades, the captured expression of wistfulness on her exquisitely rendered face as she scooped up a cup and saucer with elegant fingers, and Georgina's glance of attentive concern toward her, as they sat at the table in front of the window, and outside, in the distance, a gilded stream, hazy from the setting sun – no, it was not just perfect artistry, it was that he had captured the very essence of a grandmother's relationship with her granddaughter, the quintessential English afternoon tea, and the serenity and peacefulness that embodied it. And then she gasped, raising trembling fingers to her mouth, as she realised only then something revelatory. She realised that the artwork was in exactly the same style as

F. Jaffrey's. It was unmistakeable. And her dreamy fantasy about the Fitzsimmons family, and the connection with F. Jaffrey, must now, almost certainly, be true.

She blinked at the young man, who was standing awkwardly with a cloth draped in his hands, still looking embarrassed. She knew that by revealing the painting to them, he had also bared his soul – it was before them now, exposed, and naked. As though he had just uncovered who he really was.

When Viola looked at him, she saw not Jeremy Fitzsimmons the 3rd. She saw F. Jaffrey. And when she looked at his painting, she saw Jaffrey's work. *At last*, she thought to herself. *At last!*

There were no spoken words. Words would have tarnished the sublimity of the moment. There was just her and F. Jaffrey's progeny standing before them, uncertain, a little gawky – and in some inimitable way, imbued with the same resplendent talent of his predecessor......

......Jeremy felt sick.

16 months had passed since they first met, and both he and Georgina had begun talking seriously about getting engaged, yet he had been putting her off meeting his parents, again and again, especially his father, Maxwell. But he could not keep the family secret from her any longer. So they at last set a date that everyone agreed upon, for a family get-together.

And now, Jeremy had to have a serious talk with her.

'Will you sit down?' he asked.

Georgina was pacing anxiously up and down the back-garden patio of Oakley Hall, wringing her hands. 'But what if they don't like me?! What if they take one look at me, and just... just hate me?'

Jeremy got up from his chair, and stopped her in her tracks, holding her arms. 'They are going to love you!' he said. 'How can they not? You're beautiful, kind, thoughtful!' He led her over to the wrought iron table and chairs, and scraped back a seat for her. 'But...' he sighed '...there's something I need to tell you. About Dad.'

She sat down without taking her eyes off him.

Jeremy took a seat and sat right in front of her, their knees touching. He took her hands in both of his. 'It's just that he has this... condition.'

Georgina gasped. 'He's not ill is he?!'

'No, no. He's perfectly fine, that is, health-wise. But the condition, it makes him *look* very different.'

She stared at him, confounded. 'Is he... handicapped? If he is, that kind of thing doesn't bother me at all. I'm only sorry that–'

'That's not it, Georgie. It's his face. It's kind of... scary.'

'Scary...?'

'Yes, the condition made his face change when he was about 22 I think, and it gradually got worse, until it became what he looks like today. That's why he doesn't show himself in public anymore, since the change. So he keeps himself to himself.'

'Oh no!' said Georgina, concerned. 'Poor thing. That sounds awful!'

'But apart from that, he's a really good father – and my parents are still very much in love. They're the best! So... so when you see him, it'll be a bit of a shock at first, or even the first few times. But please remember, he's my Dad, and he's a really good man. If you just get to know him, and look past his physical appearance, I'm sure you two will get on fabulously!'

'Oh, Jeremy! You know that looks don't matter to me!' She tenderly cupped his left cheek with her hand, lingering there. Eyes fixed directly onto his. He was still incredibly handsome, despite... everything. 'In fact, I kind of love him already, because he's your Dad. And he made you. So he must be a wonderful man, no matter what he looks like. I-I thought you would know that about me by now.'

'I do. But I only wanted to prepare you. It can be... quite a bombshell. Just remember, I'll be by your side the whole time. So don't let go of my hand, okay?'

'Don't worry, I'll be holding onto you for dear life! But I can't help thinking that you're putting too much into it. I've got a feeling we're all going to get on like a house on fire!' Georgina softened, and she sat back in her chair.

Jeremy wasn't quite so relaxed. 'I hope so,' he said. 'I really hope so.'

There came the sound of movement inside, and so they got up and went in, holding hands.

The dining table was being set to perfection by the two maids. Georgina looked at them oddly, her family didn't have the kind of wealth that could afford live-in domestic staff. They only had a cleaner that came twice a week, so she wasn't quite used to being waited on.

'Estelle, are my parents around?'

The middle-aged maid peeled her eyes off Georgina; strangers in the house were rare. 'They went up to get dressed about... half an hour ago, Master Jeremy. So they'll be down soon. Would you or your... young lady, like something to drink?' She smiled timidly. Jeremy looked at Georgina.

'Peach Schnapps and lemonade?' Georgina asked, uncertain as to whether she meant just tea.

Estelle nodded. She could see that the girl needed something to calm her nerves, and she would most definitely need it.

'A Strongbow for me, thanks,' said Jeremy.

As the maid left to get the drinks, she crossed with Jeremy's mother, Anne, entering the room. Her auburn hair was now cut to a neat shoulder-length bob, and she was dressed elegantly in a pale pink satin blouse and matching floaty skirt. As soon as she saw Georgina, she went over to her with open arms and embraced her. The girl smelled of orange blossom. 'Georgina! It's lovely to meet you at last. Jem's told us so much about you.' They parted, and she looked at her appreciatively. 'Now I understand why he's so smitten.'

Georgina herself was dazzled. The woman was beautiful, and she looked from her to Jeremy, blushing. 'I feel the same about him, Mrs Fitzsimmons,' she said shyly. 'Really!'

'You must call me Anne,' she insisted. 'Let's sit down.' They went over to the divan, and Estelle appeared and placed their drinks on the walnut coffee table. 'Anything for you, Ma'am?' asked Estelle.

'Bring a bottle of Penfolds 1971 Grange, will you? Plus extra glasses – Barbara and her husband will be coming soon.'

Estelle nodded and floated off.

Georgina took a quick sip of her drink, it was the best Schnapps she had ever tasted.

'So,' said Anne, smoothing down her skirt and adjusting a pearl earring. 'Jeremy's told us a few things, but I'd love to hear from you what you've been up to.'

'Well, I've just graduated from Imperial College with biochemistry and physiology degrees. I'd like to work in pharmacology someday, but I'm still not sure which kind of job yet.'

'Ah, beauty *and* brains, I see,' said Anne, beaming with approval. 'And did you go straight through, or take a gap year?'

'I took a few months to work with Relief International in America. My father has business dealings there, and he knows someone who knows someone else, who got me intern work within the charity. They help bring food, education, and medical supplies to underprivileged people all over the world.'

'Well, I must say that it's lovely to meet a young person who really cares. That's very commendable! What kind of work were you doing there?'

'Mostly administration. Nothing amazing. Lots of database entry, sending telexes, and making back-ups on floppies. That sort of thing. And most important, keeping everyone's teas and coffees topped up! But it felt good to know I was making a difference, no matter how small.'

Estelle returned with the wine and glasses. After clinking them onto the table, and pouring some out, she said, 'Sir Max is coming down shortly, Ma'am.' Before she turned to leave, Georgina thought she saw a look of alarm in the maid's eyes – but she was so flustered about making a good impression, that she didn't think more of it.

Anne stared meaningfully at Jeremy.

'I've explained about father,' was all he told her.

His mother nodded with approval. She turned back to Georgina, blinking several times to try to contain her own apprehension. She took a deep but steady breath. 'I've been married to Jeremy's father for 27 years now. And yet, somehow, all that time seems to have passed in the blink of an eye. It's like we were only married yesterday!' she smiled. 'Marrying Max was the best thing to happen to me.' She glanced lovingly at Jeremy. 'Especially because this young man came along a few years later. Jeremy has the same decency, kindness, and understated brilliance of his father, you know – and in that way, he very much takes after him. I'm sure you'll be able to appreciate his father's wonderful qualities, if you just give him a chance...'

Georgina looked at her, slightly puzzled, not really understanding what she meant about giving him a chance.

There came the sound of footsteps from the sweeping, curved staircase.

'Ah, he's coming!' said Anne.

Each step reverberated in the hallway.

'His ears must be burning!' she laughed nervously.

The footsteps were drawing closer. And it was as though the room itself inhaled and held its breath. Hushed to silence. Georgina felt Jeremy's hand squeezing her own, it was unusually tight, and she clung on to it as he'd instructed.

They all turned to watch as Maxwell Fitzsimmons entered the room.

When Georgina saw him, she gasped and suddenly tensed. Every muscle in her body went rigid with shock.

Max walked closer. He was smiling amiably, yet there was a hint of something else about his expression. Uneasiness.

He stooped to give his wife a kiss on her cheek from behind.

'Ah, there you are my love,' said Anne warmly to her husband. But her words fell on deaf ears.

Georgina began to hyperventilate – her entire chest heaving and trembling so fast.

'Georgie?' said Jeremy.

She was still staring at Max, a terrified expression on her face.

Jeremy spun round, kneeling on the floor in front of her, still holding onto her hand. 'Look at me, Georgie,' he said firmly, urgently. 'Breathe!'

Georgina tore her eyes away and fixed them onto Jeremy. And she saw in all its sordid glory the pitted patina of scars that had almost obliterated his entire left cheek, as if she were seeing them for the first time.

Since they met, Jeremy had had four operations on his face. Each one extracting a wider area of flesh.

Her head spun and reeled. At the same time, words from before resonated in her mind.

'F. Jaffrey went about in a hooded cloak; no-one actually saw what he looked like.'

'Maxwell's face changed when he was 22.'
'It gradually got worse, until it became what he looks like today.'
'Jeremy takes after his father, you know.'

And the full meaning of those words snapped together in her head like perfectly aligned puzzle pieces. And she finally began to understand.

The same thing was happening to Jeremy. He was 23, and that… hideous face was going to become his.

She wrenched her hand from Jeremy's, shaking her head with disbelief. She could not look at him. Could not look at his parents. Turning away, a strange gurgling sound erupted in her throat. It was a scream, fighting to get out. But she wouldn't let it, *couldn't* let it.

She backed away, still shaking her head.

Shoulders hunched with fear, disbelief, horror.

Hands held out in front of her. Cringing, crooked fingers, not wanting anyone to come close.

'Georgie!' cried Jeremy, as he watched her run out of the room. 'Georgie!!' He started to run after her, but his father grabbed his arm. Jeremy turned toward him, a wild look in his eyes, unable to grasp what was happening.

'I'm sorry, son,' said Max, pale with concern. His eyes said it all.

Jeremy pulled away, and ran after her……

……He could no longer paint. For day, weeks, months.

Eventually his mother packed up his materials, unused canvases, tubes of colour, bottles of liquid, his sketchbooks – all coated in thick layers of dust that gathered like grey hoar frost. Her heart breaking for him. Before she wrapped the last item, the canvas of an unfinished painting, she stared at it for some time. Eventually she sighed, and reached for the wrapping-paper.

Jeremy had hardly talked since that day, internalising all his grief, and mostly keeping himself locked away. Georgina would not answer his calls; her grandmother did not open the door to him. And none of his family could penetrate the wall of silence that he hid behind, despite trying everything.

In the end, and as a last resort, Maxwell called upon his own father, Isaiah Fitzsimmons. Jeremy hadn't seen him since he was a toddler, because the man was practically a recluse himself. He arrived at Oakley Hall late one night, going straight to bed in a guest room. Despite that, he still woke early the next morning to breakfast with Max and Anne.

Max went to fetch his son from his room, knocking on the bedroom door, and eventually letting himself in.

Jeremy was still in bed – and he groaned, and rolled away, turning his back on his father.

Max sat on the edge of the bed. 'Son,' he said, placing a hand on his shoulder. But Jeremy shrugged it off, and moved away. 'Jem, please. Grandpa Isaiah flew in all the way from Chile to see you. Won't you get dressed and come down. He's waiting for you downstairs, in the morning room. He's really looking forward to seeing you.'

Silence.

'He booked a chartered plane, son. Went to a lot of trouble to come here...'

'I don't want to see anyone!' came Jeremy's muffled voice from under the covers. Max sighed, waited for several minutes more, then got up and quietly left.

Five minutes later there came another knock on the door. They let themselves in, and sat on the chair opposite the bed, and just waited.

Eventually Jeremy huffed, turned around, and said, 'I told you, I don't want–'

Isaiah Fitzsimmons shifted uncomfortably in the chair. 'It... it's good to see you, Jeremy.'

Jeremy blinked, rubbed the sleep from his eyes, and sat up.

The old man's facial hair was white as snow, and though his features had mellowed with age, his face was still malformed, misshapen.

Jeremy stared at him. 'Grandpa!'

'Jeremy, I'm so, so sorry about what happened,' he said, shaking his head with regret. 'Really.'

They looked at each other for some time, the space between them static with unspoken words.

Eventually Isaiah said, 'You know, me and Max were fortunate. My dear Gracie was worth her weight in gold. She completed me. Stayed by my side all our married life. Sadly, she passed away nine years ago, and, well, it'll never be the same without her... But on the other hand, my father had a similar experience to you. His first love couldn't take it, and... she broke his heart. In fact, he didn't think he was going to have any children at all, until quite late in life when he discovered a... well, an illegitimate son.'

Fully awake now, Jeremy leaned against the wall and hugged his legs.

'I'm telling you all this, not to rub it in, Jeremy. Only... only to let you know that, sometimes, it's just the luck of the draw. That's all. I don't know this young lady of yours. I'm told you'd been seeing each other for a while – so I'm sure she loved you. But we can't hold it against her if... if she can't handle it.'

Jeremy stirred, awkward. 'I'm sorry about grandma... I didn't know.'

'Of course you didn't. You were just a kid when we last saw you. It's our fault that we weren't around much when you were growing up, which I'm sorry about...' He looked fixedly at the ground. And they lapsed into silence.

Jeremy scratched his cheek. The whiskers were growing back over the scars, and though he wanted to scratch them even more, he forced himself not to. He clamped his hands between his bent legs, staring again at his grandfather's face. Jeremy had desperately clung onto thin straws of hope that it might not happen – relying, doggedly, on surgery as a solution. But now, looking at his father's father – it hit him. And his heart sunk into even deeper despair. 'I-it's inevitable, isn't it?' said Jeremy quietly, numb with realisation.

Isaiah was puzzled, but then soon understood. He nodded. 'Yes, I'm afraid so. Even with all the modern medical methods these days, we can't get away from it. It's never skipped a generation, never skipped a Fitzsimmons male.'

Jeremy closed his eyes and groaned, burying his face into the duvet. Isaiah got up, stumbling a little from stiffness. He sat on the bed and put his arm around the boy's shoulders.

'It's okay to cry, Jeremy.' His voice was as soft and warm as a wool blanket on a bleak winter's night.

For nearly an hour, they sat there, Jeremy's muffled sobs the only sound in the room.

It was perhaps just as well that Georgina had left him, for he vowed then and there never to have children of his own. He would never, *ever* want to pass onto them the awful legacy, locked and concealed inside of him, like a hidden beast, straining wildly at the leash.....

......Months turned to years, and years turned to decades.

In time, Jeremy's parents died naturally – first Anne of old age, and then Max, from a broken heart. They left everything to Jeremy, their only child.

He became a recluse, got rid of all the staff, and completely shunned people in general. Leading a simple life, he kept to just a few rooms in Oakley Hall, the warmest, or the coolest, depending on the time of year. Not long after he had lost Georgina, the internalisation of grief was followed soon after by a gradual transformation. And as the deformity slowly devoured Jeremy's face, lump by lump, whisker by whisker, in turn it shifted the balance of words, so that he barely spoke. There was, after all, no-one to talk to. He only emitted soft grunts, or groans, or unintelligible mumblings as he went around the house, alone.

But he still felt, and still thought.

And though he remained mostly speechless, voluntarily, there was no way to switch off the rampant thoughts and ponderings and imaginings of his mind. It was all he could do to keep them under control. Surrounded by a world of silence, made the inner noise of his cogitations that much more amplified – deafening even. Disembodied voices that conspired to drive him mad......

......When Jeremy turned 47, he became preoccupied with counting down to Y2K – the world was preparing itself for the millennial bug, and the possibility of breakdowns in technology and computers unable to function with a date beyond 2000. Organisations invested billions trying to pre-empt disasters by re-programming technology and replacing machinery. And the world collectively held its breath, as the midnight clock struck 12:00. Yet seconds, minutes, hours ticked by without catastrophe, and everyone soon resumed their activities. Life continued. There were however scattered mishaps that were yet to be discovered in the ensuing months, some major, others minor. From a man being hit with an extortionate bill for renting a film for 100 years, to an increase in Down's Syndrome babies due to hospital computer systems incorrectly registering the birth dates of their mothers.

Jeremy had already sold his father's businesses, and was sick with worry that the resulting billions, which he transferred to savings accounts spread around in private offshore banks, might lose their value. The millennial bug made him realise that stockpiling money in bank accounts wasn't as safe as he had initially thought. He lived off the ample and healthy interest, shored up by a stable economy – for now. But that could all change overnight. And a nagging voice in the back of his mind told him that when he died, what use was there for such vast savings anyway?

Meanwhile, Jeremy watched the news with interest, his only link to the outside world. He was particularly fascinated to hear about James Watson, one of the scientists who discovered the double-helix structure of DNA. He keenly followed Watson's project to map each of the 30,000 genes in the human genome. It was the world's largest collaborative biological project, with an international team of researchers. When it was completed in 2003, it sparked a genomic revolution. All with the goal of preventing, diagnosing, and treating human disease. The Guardian newspaper ran a series of articles on this. One of them mentioned a particular scientist in the UK who was becoming renowned for his work in genetics, Dr Axel Kendra. In the article, the doctor claimed that their discoveries would advance genetic therapies and treatments through gene editing. And they would soon be working on revising, removing, and even replacing mutated or diseased genes from DNA strands.

Jeremy read the newspaper article with rapt interest. He had to stop several times to re-read sentences – and when he finished, he went right back to the beginning to read the article again, his heart pounding. He caught his breath. Though he could not fully understand everything that was being said, instinctively he knew. Knew that this might at last be the unexpected answer to the Fitzsimmons curse. And he mused on whether he might dare allow himself a glimmer of hope......

......The foxes scampered through the gardens unexpectedly. Two of them. Gekkering, and barking, and screaming in the night, as they fought with invaders that dared enter their territory.

At first Jeremy spent hours observing them from afar with mild fascination. And then he started to leave out unwanted leftovers for them – and watched as they wolfed it down. When he saw them sniffing around the grounds, the very next day he began emptying the shed of all the gardening equipment, piling the contents into a disused room instead, intending to make a shelter for them. But he soon discovered that they were already digging a den underneath the shed – and were slipping silently in and out from the side.

In time, in mid-March, the garden became very quiet. And when Jeremy crept over to the shed one day, kneeling down and shining a torch inside the gap, he saw to his surprise a litter of flame-coloured pups – two were sleeping, one was blindly following the scent of milk, while two were already suckling from their mother. The vixen was lying on her side, squinting and blinking in the white light. After that, Jeremy made sure to leave out even more food for them – and there were rare sitings of the larger male, with its long snout and bushy tail, toing and froing as it provisioned its family with the scraps.

But by April, Jeremy began to notice that the parent foxes were constantly scratching, and their matted fur was rubbing off in large patches, their eyes sticky and crusted. He quickly set a simple trap – a baited cage with a spring-loaded door – and left it out for the male. It came at night, and gulped down each piece of meat left in a trail, until it stopped at the cage door, sniffing the rusted metal with suspicion. It crouched low, bobbing its head up and down as it inspected the unknown contraption. Eventually it pounced on the food inside – and the door instantly dropped down, trapping it. Quickly Jeremy rushed over to the den, reached inside with a gloved hand, and pulled out the vixen. She bayed and barked and writhed in protest. But he managed to hold her at arm's length, until she stilled – the two of them stooping low on the ground. Her black, glossy eyes fixed on his. Both watching the other's every move. Jeremy had not come face to face or touched another living thing in years. And as the vixen crouched, stock-still, his free hand moved slowly closer. She didn't even flinch when his fingers sunk into the fur at the back of her neck.

He closed his eyes, and breathed slowly.

Something happened. He could not comprehend what it was – only that he felt overwhelmed with a sudden understanding. It tingled like pins and needles over his entire body. And as he and the vixen breathed in unison – slowly exhaling, gently inhaling – Jeremy suddenly knew what it meant to exist as a fox. To live nocturnally, its natural habitat swallowed up by buildings, pavements, towns – needing to adapt to survive, rummaging through rubbish, becoming outcasts, anathema – their own brothers, sisters, parents, children mowed down by speeding traffic, or poisoned, or torn to shreds through territorial battles. Battles to the death. Jeremy absorbed too the vixen's primal instincts, to protect her pups – all five of them. Absorbed how intimately she knew each one, their unique body scent, the odour of their scats, their habits, the way they slept, every sound they made, from their low barks calling for her, to high-pitched playful yips. Stunned, Jeremy began to comprehend the feelings that only a mother or a father can have for their children. A carnal, animal will to feed, nurture, defend.

His head swam with a thousand sensations as he slowly picked himself up, lifting the fox from the ground with him, bearing her weight. Steadily he walked over to the cage, still holding her at arm's length – and carefully put her inside, with her mate. He went back to the den, and gently pulled out each of the pups, placing them in a cardboard box lined with an old curtain. He took them inside the house.

He immediately sent emails – marked urgent – to the local emergency vets to come and get the trapped parents, and two hours later, they came in through the side entrance that he left open, and took the caged animals away.

Jeremy sat at the kitchen table, eyes peeking over the top of the box.

The pups were five weeks old, and no longer blind and deaf. Their fur was sandy-grey, deepening to a rich orange on their backs. Stick-like legs were dark, almost black, and the bush of their tails was tipped with a splotch of cream fur. When his hand delved inside the box, the pups veered away, or snapped at him, or screeched in a high-pitched *ack-ack-ack!*

Frustrated, Jeremy wondered what he could do. He thought of their mother, the vixen. Thought of everything he had just absorbed from her – her primal instincts, her knowledge, her fierce protectiveness. And the more he dwelled on her thoughts, the more she filled him. When his hand ventured inside the box again, like a father reaching to his babies, they no longer shrank from him.

Instead, the pups quietened, scrambled closer, and started licking his fingers. He picked one up by the scruff of its neck and set it on his lap. It sprang up on its hind legs, jumped up, and licked his chin. It barked at him, then twisted round and round, until it curled into a ball, and settled down. Jeremy stroked its rough red fur, as it snuffled, sleepy eyes closing. He sat quietly for some time, amazed at the transformation of their behaviour. Stroking the pup, deep in thought......

'......H-hello?' said Axel Kendra, uncertainly. Gulping. A flicker of doubt in his eyes.

The inside of the room seemed darker even than night.

There was just a triangle of light from the corridor, straining weakly to penetrate the black interior. From the doorway, Kendra stepped closer, reluctant to cross the divide. To enter the gloaming. 'H-hello?'

'I'm here,' came Jeremy's voice from within. It had been a long time since he'd last heard the sound of his own voice form coherent words. They tumbled out surprisingly smoothly, like drizzles of slick, black oil.

'I... I can't see you,' said Kendra. 'Should I turn on the light?'

There was a pause.

'If you want.'

Kendra tried to remember the words from their email exchanges. Something about his appearance... and he hesitated.

'The switch. It's on your left,' said Jeremy.

Kendra patted the wall, feeling for it. The light came on, though it was dim. Perhaps just as well.

The two men stared at each other.

Jeremy was sitting in a brown Eames lounge chair, his lower arms hanging over the armrests. The swell of facial hair, bulges, whiskers exposed only the skin around his eyes – puckered and pale like rice-paper.

Kendra struggled with great effort to control his outward reaction. 'I s-see,' was all he said.

'It's hereditary.' Jeremy's voice sounded clinical, like a doctor talking about somebody else, not himself. 'Every single male in the Fitzsimmons family had the condition. For me, the change came when I was 23. But my father, I'm told, changed earlier. I am the last in line. And I vowed never to have children...' The end of the sentence hung, broken and jarring, in the air. '...Until now.'

Kendra began to understand the connection with his work, with genetics. He looked around the large room. It was bare, save for broken glass on the floor by a smashed arch-top window – and above, cobwebs that hung like ripped muslin from the ceiling. Yet despite the emptiness, the air was ripe with the must of bygone days.

Jeremy followed Kendra's eyes. 'I like to live simply, here, in Oakley Hall,' he told him. 'My mind is already over-charged with a thousand thoughts, processing thousands of images, feeling a thousand sensations. So the less clutter there is, the better.'

Kendra nodded his understanding. 'I've been meaning to ask. Your desire for children... is it because you want someone to leave your fortune to?'

'My wealth? That does not concern me as much as... another kind of legacy. One that is far, far more valuable than money, or this house, or the land. But the only way you will be able to understand, Dr Kendra, is if I *show* you.' He held out his left hand, fingers curling open. 'Please. Come closer.'

Kendra's every sense bristled; his chest braiding tight with fear. A gut reaction to run, run far away from this place, from this horrific man, swelled in him. Yet his legs had a mind of their own. Against his will, they drew him closer. And his arm reached out, unbidden.

Jeremy clamped his hand around Kendra's wrist. 'Now I will show you.'

As if zapped with an electric shock, Kendra gasped, stunned. His eyes closed momentarily, and he saw in his mind a blizzard of swirling images. His own childhood, running, laughing, playing, his teenage years, a see-saw of self-doubt and over-confidence, meeting Gaia, their wedding, trying for children, her tears of frustration, his brilliant father reduced to a vegetable, deep, deep grief and depression, his work, the science of genetics, the unfolding of tightly-packed DNA strands from chromosomes, interlocking nucleotides spiralling and cascading ribbon-like, and the wealth of information locked within them, tumbling into a world of possibilities, and at last – the here and now. Jeremy Fitzsimmons sitting before him. Kendra's horror at seeing his face for the first time. Raw, knife-sharp fear.

Kendra wrenched his arm away with all his might, and stumbled back, rubbing his wrist where there was left a red imprint – a palm and splayed fingers. Smarting from the burn and sizzle of every nerve in his body. 'W-what just happened??!!'

'I read you,' said Jeremy, calmly. 'And played it back in your mind. Your entire life condensed to mere seconds.'

Kendra rubbed his sore wrist. 'But... how?!!'

'That is why *you* are here, Dr Kendra, to find out. The answer must be locked within my DNA. You see, every Fitzsimmons male had some kind of ability. Each was different. From artistic talent, to genius intelligence, to... to what I've just demonstrated. I do not pretend to understand it. However, any naturally-born male child will inherit some aspect of it, along with this... inescapable defect.' He motioned toward his face. 'It is the unfortunate joker in the pack. Perhaps nature's way of balancing out the brilliance, with the grotesque. This is why I need you to unlock from me the secret of this ability, with the joker removed...'

After the shock of what had just happened, Kendra's mind was beginning to return and make sense of this astounding revelation. This extraordinary ability! His scientific mind whirred with possibilities. He knew that the ongoing human genome project was unlocking every single DNA trait, but this amazing thing... perhaps a genetic mutation... left him speechless. If he could locate the gene, or genes, that had the code for these traits... then they could be harnessed and transferred – in vitro – to embryos... Kendra coughed, at last finding his voice. 'I-I think I can help you,' he said, tremulous. 'But... I'll need funding.'

'Money is no issue.'

'A-and I'll need to speak to someone – a good friend, a politician, high up in government. I need to discuss the plausibility of it all, the ethical implications, and getting it sanctioned, because of all the... risks.'

'I trust you, Dr Kendra, to get this done. Now that science and technology have advanced sufficiently to make it possible, I realise that I would like more than anything to have successors, a continuation to the Fitzsimmons family line. To inherit my... unique legacy.'

'I understand,' said Kendra, eager even now to get things started. 'I need to arrange everything. It will take time. But... I will be in touch as soon as I can.'

'Thank you,' said Jeremy.

Dr Kendra nodded, already backing out of the room.

Jeremy listened to the man retreat – hurrying, nervous steps, padding down the corridor, into the hallway. Heard the sound of the front door opening and closing behind him. 'Thank you...' Fitzsimmons murmured to the empty room.

He got up, and went through several rooms, reaching the kitchen back door. The night seemed even darker than usual. He turned on the garden lights, and went to fetch a large bowl from the fridge – taking it outside into the garden. Sitting down at the edge of the patio, he put the food on the grass at his feet. The foxes poured out from the shadows. Not just the five pups that were almost adults now, but their parents too, who had been cured of their mange, and returned. Jeremy picked up the smallest one, stroked her, kissed her, and then put her down to eat with the others. He watched them all with satisfaction – a sense of elation edging into him, like shards of piercing glass, lancing a decades-long inner tension. Silently, he petted the wild animals as they guzzled their food beside him......

......The downy filaments of the dandelion clock rose lightly on a puff of breath.

Transfixed, the eyes of the five-month-old toddler followed them, raising its little arm in the air, opening and closing its little hand repeatedly. When they disappeared from view, the baby turned back to Jeremy, and bounced up and down on his knee, wanting more. Jeremy picked another clock, and counted each time he blew on it until the tiny seeds detached – drifting skyward. 'It's five o'clock!' announced Jeremy to the baby, eyes wide.

The baby was the first child born to Project Ingenious, who they called the Alpha. He reached up to sink explorative fingers in Jeremy's beard, burying them deep within, and then suddenly tugging hard.

'Ow!' cried Jeremy, gently pulling baby's hand away.

Alpha latched onto Jeremy's finger instead, and brought it to his mouth, chomping it between toothless gums as his bright eyes roamed over Jeremy's face.

For once, Jeremy did not feel tense from being so keenly observed. He sat the baby on his knee and bumped him up and down in the same way his father used to do with him. Alpha giggled. And the words of a nursery rhyme came to Jeremy's mind. He sang it to the baby as he bounced him.

'Farmer Grey's got a one-horse shay
He takes to town on market day
travelling home while the lights are low
He sings this song and away they go
Horsey, horsey don't you stop
Just let your feet go clippity clop...'

Baby gurgled with laughter. The moment – an innocent child playing with a hideous man – was surreal.

Kendra sat opposite them, on a garden chair, watching with rapt approval. 'He likes you!' he remarked, delighted. 'He's a very particular baby, very fussy. So you're quite privileged!'

Tired by now, the child lay back in the crook of Jeremy's arm, still sucking on his finger.

'But he is pale,' remarked Jeremy, looking him over. 'And skinny. Is he all right?'

'Yes, we've been monitoring him closely, with all the usual tests. He's perfectly healthy... but the nurses are having a hard time getting him to drink from the bottle at the moment. We're not sure why. As you know, he was rejected by his natural mother, so that might have something to do with it. But we've started him on solids recently, so we're hoping that will improve weight gain.'

Jeremy nodded slowly as he listened. 'Good. Very good. And any news on further babies?'

Kendra visibly stiffened. 'I'm afraid not. We think that maybe Alpha's birth was an incredibly lucky first attempt, because subsequent babies have not been... forthcoming. Even though we've kept to exactly the same method as we used for the Alpha.'

'That is... unfortunate.'

Kendra paused. 'It's just that... there's a high ratio of miscarriages, and malformed foetuses. The cost to human life–'

'You will keep trying!!' snapped Jeremy. Baby, who was falling asleep, was jolted suddenly awake. His lips quivered, and he burst into tears. Jeremy stood up and rocked him to and fro, himself agitated, yet trying to calm the baby. But Alpha cried even more.

Kendra went over to take him from Jeremy. He put him over his shoulder and patted his back soothingly. 'There, there.' And the baby soon calmed down as he sucked noisily on his thumb.

Jeremy turned away, grappling to control himself. 'I've sunk millions into the project,' he said eventually. 'And I don't care what it takes! But you *will* keep trying.' His eyebrows knitted together into a single, black underline, emphasising his anger. Hands balling into tight fists.

Kendra was silenced. The baby felt soft and warm against his shoulder. He didn't know what abilities the infant might have been born with, but he was conscious of remaining calm, for everyone's sake. 'I hear you,' he said eventually, in a low tone loaded with apprehension. He tamped down his rising disquietude. 'We'll keep trying……'

……Four years later, Kendra turned up at Oakley Hall on one of his usual updating visits. He was jumpy and ashen-faced, but before knocking on the door, he paused, took a deep breath, and calmed himself.

When Jeremy opened the door, Kendra smiled breezily, saying, 'Good morning!' But it was just a pretence.

Jeremy let him in. 'You're in good spirits.' He took him through the house, and straight out the back, where there was a garden table, with an empty plate and a tall glass half-filled with a milky-brown drink. One of the garden chairs had a crumpled newspaper lying on it. It was a balmy spring day, with slow-drifting ivory clouds in a turquoise sky. Tiny midges stippled the air with black dots.

The two men sat down.

Jeremy smoothed out the newspaper on his lap and folded it neatly, laying it aside. 'I trust you have good news?'

Kendra blinked. 'Erm, yes, good news in that baby Omega is doing well.'

'I'm glad. *How* well?'

'For just a month old, Omega's showing very promising signs. Like all the other babies, they start off very quiet, hardly crying – I imagine because they're silently absorbing everything. But they soon develop excellent motor skills, hand-eye coordination, and in due course, incredible communication skills too. So, good news... in the sense that we have four girls and three boys – all healthy and developing above and beyond the norm.'

Jeremy hardly missed a thing. 'In the sense that...?'

The optimism in Kendra's face faded. 'I've told you many, many times, Jeremy. There have been hundreds, if not thousands, of deaths.' He battled to keep his emotions in check. 'M-mostly at embryonic stage, but many foetuses too, and unexpected abortions, with some infants dying during or after birth. Even... even some mothers have died from sudden haemorrhages whilst giving birth. Two of them.' The last words echoed starkly in his mind. Vibrant lives reduced to a statistic, a number. He thought of Kara Winters, the latest casualty. He had had a soft spot for her. She was a beautiful, good-natured young lady. But now, each time he thought of her, he saw only her grey-tinged corpse lying cold on a slab, being covered by a hollow white sheet.

Jeremy disappeared inside the house, and came back with a tall brown drink. 'Here,' he said. 'It's coffee with a dash of dark rum – early I know, but you look as if you could use it.'

When Kendra took it, his fingers brushed lightly with Jeremy's, and he bristled from the jolt of an electric shock. Though he was not inclined, he sipped it for Jeremy's sake, wiping off a moustache of froth before placing the glass on the garden table......

......Four days later, Jeremy was sitting in the same garden chair, with the foxes dotted around him on the grass, or on loungers, each of them bright balls of orange, curled up and fast asleep after being fed.

A beep on his Blackberry heralded an incoming message. He was inclined to ignore it, but then thought better, and stirred, reaching into his pocket for the phone. He scrolled through to the Inbox, read several lines of the message, and suddenly doubled over. The Blackberry dropped onto the grass, its screen still lit with the end of the message: '...laboratories have burnt down entirely. No sign of survivors. No signs of life.' Waves of nausea and pain jarred his senses, clouding his mind. Intermittent bursts of agonising despair, numbness, disbelief.

The tail-end of a thought came to him. The last time Kendra came, he was conscious that something was amiss. When their hands touched lightly, a spark of electricity jumped between them. And only now did he understand fully what it meant. He had felt Kendra's uneasiness, masked by an air of nonchalance – and he realised that, even then, the man had been hiding something.

Jeremy fell to the ground, and cried out, again and again.

A gust of cold wind, as if from nowhere, slapped his face with spots of rain. Overhead, storm clouds were brewing.

Alarmed, the foxes jumped up and gambolled around him, wondering at the man's strange behaviour. Some sniffed him, sensing his pain – and others paced wildly around the chair.

As Jeremy succumbed to sobs of grief, the foxes joined him – breaking out in a hysterical cacophony of frightening, otherworldly screams......

......The BBC News from the old television set droned on in the background as Jeremy wrapped each of the paintings in brown paper and stacked them carefully into crates. The pain of losing all seven children from the project silenced him once again, rendering him mute.

And to make matters worse, he had sunk all his money, and more, into the project, and was forced to sell Oakley Hall to pay off the debts. Adding the heartache of losing his family home to the chasm of despair.

There was a large roll of something wrapped in brown paper, waiting to be packed. It was left casually on the old dining table pockmarked with crumbling termite holes. He drew closer to it, hesitant, knowing exactly what it was. The unfinished painting. He unpicked the binding and tugged back the paper, to reveal sketched tresses of billowing hair. He traced the tips of his fingers along the zephyr-tossed, swirling tendrils, before closing his eyes and turning his head away. Quickly, he pressed down the wrapping paper over the roll. Reaching for the sellotape, he tore off a piece with his teeth – and stuck it firmly down......

......He had been searching for Axel Kendra and Harald Wolff for months, but with no results. It was as if they had disappeared into thin air. They must have changed their names, and relocated. But after some time, Jeremy discovered that Wolff's family owned a business, and when the owner had died, he'd left everything to his closest relative, who he knew was the Professor. Jeremy looked up the address of Madeley's headquarters, and began staking out the office building in a hired car with darkened windows. Before long, Professor Wolff turned up – getting out of a black taxi cab that had pulled up kerbside. The man stood outside for quite some time, looking up at the tall building. Eventually, he went inside.

Wolff came regularly after that, almost every day – and it was easy enough for Jeremy to follow him, to discover where he lived. He soon found out that he had a wife called Chiara, and a son, Christian.

Jeremy went to their house in the evening, in the thick of winter, when darkness descended early. He knew Wolff was still at the office, and so he sneaked into the garden and watched the wife and child inside the house, quietly and patiently waiting for a time when they might leave, so that he could break in, and see what he might discover about his children. He watched patiently for hours, growing numb from the cold, and saw when the boy had a tantrum, the mother arguing with her querulous son.

The breeze changed direction, and Jeremy was suddenly distracted by the whiff of noxious gas. He stepped back to see where it might be coming from, only to kick a stone, sending it skittling across the paving slabs. Before he knew it, the wife had thrown the door open and swung a heavy skillet at him. She narrowly missed and hit the side of the door instead, breaking the leaking gas pipe nestled against the door jamb. Things went badly wrong after that. A spark ignited the gas, and the fire that exploded seemed to engulf the entire house in a matter of minutes. Hiding in the bushes, Jeremy doubled over, unable to breathe.

In the end, all he could do was limp back to his car, the stench of smoke in his nostrils, and the skin of his legs smarting from burns.

Sleep had never come easily to him. But now, it was even worse. Whenever he closed his eyes, it opened up a realm of Stygian black spirits, perpetual flames as red as blood, and a slithering, seeping river, black as death......

......12 years later, withered dry by age, and leading a solitary, lonely life, Jeremy was listening to the BBC News in the old stone house nestled between a verge of forest and a small copse of tall black poplars. He had stored all the paintings there. The pictures lined every inch of wall, were stacked on every surface, wedged into every space. He was eating a simple meal on the table he'd made himself – a crude hammering together of bits of wood. It was not quite square, and one leg was wedged with a folded page of newspaper, to stop it from rocking. He could have made the table perfectly, but he had lost the zest for life, and the will to right it.

Breaking news suddenly flashed up in red letters on the screen, and a stern-looking man with sallow skin began speaking urgently. The newsreader touched his earpiece, listening for a few moments, before turning back to the camera.

'We've just had breaking news about the seven Oxford students, all of whom were studying Genetics when they came down with the same sudden onset cancer. They all died within days of contracting the disease. Dr Peter Davids, the cancer expert who was consulted by the scientific council formed to investigate the disease, has now stepped forward saying that there are striking similarities with – and therefore, he believes, a connection between – what he alleges is a secret government project, code-named "Project Ingenious". Dr Davids claims that the project was formed to create babies genetically engineered with a genius gene. Seven in total...'

The spoon dropped from Jeremy's hand, clanking onto the bowl – a chip of broken-off porcelain skittered across the table. He scrambled for a stub of pencil, and a piece of paper. On it he wrote, 'DR PETER DAVIDS' – going over the letters several times to make them solid......

'......Wait. Wait. Wait.' His voice was low, raspy, and monotonous; cold words with no soul. The patter of rain beat down on his long grey raincoat. 'Now, open the garden door and come out!' Jeremy was standing behind a tree, peering out cautiously from behind it, and speaking into a wireless headset hidden underneath the hood. The guards had just disappeared from view, and he had waited until they were out of earshot, before directing Dr Vassiliev. The doctor strode out purposefully, feet sinking into damp, springy leaves, his eyes glazed from the vodka the housekeeper had spiked. 'Now follow me,' said Jeremy, already turning away, and glancing back only now and then to check the doctor was within sight. They walked for miles in silence, two lone dark figures. Jeremy at last reached a solitary car parked on the road – a tarmac path gashing the forest. The doctor had fallen behind, and he waited by the car, looking this way and that, nervously. At last the man appeared, and Jeremy opened the back door for him to climb in, and then got into the driver's seat, stiff with rheumatism aggravated by the damp and cold.

The following day, late at night, Jeremy left the still drugged Vassiliev securely locked in the basement, and drove the two-hour journey back to the country house. He knew they would investigate the doctor's disappearance, and – like a murderer returning to the scene of the crime – he itched with curiosity to discover what, if anything, they might have found. When he drove casually along the road that passed the front of the house, he saw that it was surrounded by a much heavier security detail, which made him wonder... He parked the car a safe distance away, more or less at the same spot where he'd parked the night before, and walked back silently through the forest. It was a much drier night, the terrain easier to navigate, yet he stumped his foot on the woody root of an old tree, hidden underneath mulch and leaves. It was all he could do to stop himself from crying out, and he bit his tongue, smarting from the pain. He hobbled on, until he reached the back of the house – and stood several metres back to watch it silently.

When the young Chinese girl slipped quietly out of the garden gate, he had to blink several times to make sure he wasn't seeing things. He knew instantly who she was.

The faint light of the moon bathed her in silver, so that her skin glowed like porcelain. Silky hair hung loosely above her shoulders, and she looked around nervously. She turned on her torch, and he stepped back, hiding behind a tree. She too positioned herself behind a large bush, and watched the night guards come and go, for some time. Checking her watch each time.

Jeremy looked on from afar, his heart thudding from being so close. Within a stone's throw. Revelling at the sight of *his* progeny. But unlike him, her brilliance would never be marred by his awful defect...

He wondered what he could do. He yearned, ached to know more about her – and a sudden impulse came to him. He could take her now. Between patrols, he could sneak up to her, clamp his hand over her mouth, and drag her with him. But he leant against the bark of the tree, paralysed by indecision.

He saw that she was getting ready to leave, and his heart leapt as he leant forward, not wanting her to go. His coat brushed the tree, and she must have heard, because she turned around, shining the torch in his direction, calling out, 'Wh-who's there?'

Jeremy stepped back, a twig cracked, and the girl ran – flying back to the house. He went after her, limping, his foot still painful. She pushed open the garden gate, stepped inside, frantically locking it behind her. But there was no further sound of footsteps, and as Jeremy pressed his ear against the door, the wood creaking, he caught his breath, knowing she was just on the other side. He desperately wanted to say something. Tell her who he was. Surely she wouldn't be frightened if it was just his voice. If he just spoke to her softly.

But he heard the sound of someone approaching. And he ran off, hobbling, in the dark......

'......Why you keep me here!!!' shouted a muffled Russian voice from the basement.

Jeremy stopped. Now that the drugs had worn off, the doctor was shouting constantly. He ground his teeth, irritated, which he instantly regretted as it sparked off a throb of pain from an infected root. Jeremy was very tempted to spike the man's drink again, just to shut him up – with the same stuff he had paid the housekeeper to put in his vodka bottle. But then he realised that he needed the man's mind to be as clear as possible.

He continued pacing around the kitchen, rubbing his jaw, which only added to the tension. In the end, he just decided to do it.

He took the tray of food, and went through what looked like a cupboard door – but instead it opened to reveal steps leading down to the basement. The air was noticeably chill as he descended. There was another door at the bottom, bolted and locked, and at the side, a ledge and a small sash window with safety glass criss-crossed with black mesh. Jeremy rested the side of the tray on the ledge, pushed up the bottom pane, and then attempted again to slide the tray through; the doctor had already smashed the first two trays to the ground. But it was over 24 hours since his capture, and he guessed that pure hunger would make him accept this third tray.

Hesitantly, the doctor drew closer and reached for the food – and in the blink of an eye, Jeremy grabbed his wrist, holding it with a vice-like grip. Vassiliev's eyes rolled back as electricity sparked through nerves and sinews, eventually sizzling through his brain. Jeremy closed his eyes and teased out the doctor's memories. He saw white laboratories filled with shiny equipment. Technicians, researchers, scientists, working with DNA sequencers, a mass spectrometer, a flow cytometer, and large, powerful microscopes. He listened to Vassiliev's explosive temper, shouting at the other workers after so many experiments, failure after failure. Confounded and exasperated expressions on all their faces. He saw equations and notes scrawled out on four whiteboards hugging the wall. Names written in careful blue lettering at the top of each whiteboard. Milly Bythaway. Tai Jones. Mei Hui Li. Jemima Jenkins. And Jeremy's heart skipped a beat. They must be four of the children! *His* children.

He let go of Vassiliev, and both men stumbled back – Vassiliev rubbed his sore wrist, retreating to skulk in a corner, and Jeremy remained leaning, stunned, against the wall next to the stairs.

Over the next few days he quietly reflected on everything he saw in Vassiliev's mind. Pored over the charts, notes, and experiments – went over every word that was said with his colleagues. He was slow, and it took him a while – but eventually it dawned on him. The children were dying, and they were doing everything they could to save them. Vassiliev muttered constantly about Dr Kendra. He needed information that only the doctor could provide. But the old man's mind was lost to Alzheimer's, and now – frustratingly – there was no way of finding what they needed. They had reached a dead end.

And then Jeremy remembered, from years back, what he himself had seen inside Kendra's mind. Their first meeting, when he had absorbed the man's entire life and played it back to him, to show him what he could do… And he thought of an experiment of his own.

The next time Jeremy went down to Vassiliev, he held out his hand.

Wearily, tentatively, the doctor extended his arm, knowing that he must do this in order to survive. And though he did not realise it, Jeremy opened the doctor's mind, and began to feed him – piecemeal – everything that he had learnt from Dr Kendra. The pure science of decades of research, mapping the human genome, discoveries in genetic engineering, and advancing gene therapies. The methods used to create the Project Ingenious children, their make-up, the defect, the mutation, and ultimately the reason for the degradation of their bodies, their minds.

After days and weeks of it, Vassiliev became accustomed to this strange ritual. And a shift in the doctor's thoughts toward him, by degrees, brought about a kind of Stockholm syndrome, where food and sustenance and life itself became synonymous with his captor. The clasping of hands became revelatory and meaningful. And in time it turned into a kind of addiction – each touch a measured, drug-like dose. Though the doctor had no idea the medical breakthrough that came to him was by no means his own.

Yet at the same time, Jeremy also made an unusual discovery of his own. In imparting Kendra's knowledge to Vassiliev, it had a reciprocal effect on him. Each time his hand loosened from the doctor's wrist, it felt as if a weight had been lifted from his shoulders. The pain of inner turmoil lessened, even the pain from his sore tooth. Tentatively he ground his teeth together, to test that it was really true. Nothing. No pain, no ache.

He took a while to process this. And for the first time in decades, he felt suddenly light.

But then, out of nowhere, there came an unexpected itch, a faint prickle in the back of his mind. As he walked down the stairs from his bedroom, his fingers tumbling over the rough, dry canvases of the paintings on the walls, the itch blustered, like a spark to dry kindling – inflaming to a smouldering desire. And by the time he reached the bottom, there was only one thing he could do to extinguish the thing burning in his bones......

......It had been nearly five decades since Jeremy had put down his paintbrush. The portrait of Georgina and her grandmother was his last complete work. And though he had marvelled at his newfound skill back then, the ensuing depression and despondency that plagued him when Georgina left, brought an abrupt end to the creativity that was only just beginning to bud. Until now.

He rummaged around the garden shed to find the saw that would shape the wood for the frame. He took his mitre box too, to align the perfect angles for sawing the wood. Adding 45-degree pieces of wood to each corner to keep the frame square. He unrolled the unfinished painting from its brown wrapping paper – eyes shying away from his sketched outlines as he stretched and stapled it around the frame's edges. Finally, he propped it against the wall, satisfied.

Readying the room he would display it in, he then prepared the paints, the brushes, and the linseed oil, laying them all out neatly.

He dared himself to face it now. Holding his breath, he turned and stared at it. The lightly sketched outlines of his previous handiwork, now decades old. Dizzy with an adrenaline-rush, he closed his eyes. Saw the image of that first sight of her. Sparkling with crystal clarity, frozen in time. His mind scoured over every detail, right down to the shade and slant of each blade of grass. The pattern of light on the water. The dragonfly zipping close-by. Each wisped curl of her hair.

Shaky hands took up the paintbrush, and he at last began to paint.

Working in a frenzy both day and night, it took him nearly a week. Only pausing to prepare food for himself and the Russian, catching just a few hours' sleep. Even his dreams were filled with the feverish flourish of brush against canvas. He could not stop until he had emptied the image from his mind, laying it out in an image of softly glowing hues.

And when at last it was finished, he put down his palette, his brush, and stood back, spent, haggard, and exhausted, to see it in its entirety.

His skin prickled. His thudding heart ached. He saw her standing before him now, gloriously beautiful, as though she was really there, as though the canvas was a portal to another time, another place, and he was peering – voyeuristically – inside. He thought he might expire, both holding his breath, yet struggling to breathe. But he was still there, still heaving with emotion, silent for an eternity, as he watched her.

And once again, he felt a lightness inside, a cathartic weightlessness that stunned him. As though years of pain and regret had simply fallen away. For such a long time he thought that he had let Georgina down, could have done something differently, explained better, could've made her understand. But why hadn't he seen it before, when it was so clear? Why did he realise only now, after all this time?

That it wasn't him...

It was *her*.

He caught stutters of breath in his chest and wiped the tears from his eyes. Backing out of the room, he turned off the light, and quietly closed the door......

......Armed with the knowledge that painting brought about such catharsis, he knew now that there was at least one other painting he must get out of him. Must purge from his mind. The Professor's burning house. That too had tormented him. He had always wondered: if he had never gone there, would the fire still have happened? He needed to know. He must know. And, again, the next day, he set about painting that too.

After many days when it was completed, he stared at the resulting painting in all its awful glory for what seemed like hours. But this time, the answer was not so clear, like looking through glass fogged with condensation. Horrified eyes wandered across the flames and the warped, melting faces, examining every inch of the image – but still, no straightforward answer came to him. No relief. The gas pipe was already cracked, but even if he hadn't been there, would it have broken of its own accord? A slammed door, someone bumping into it, vibrations through the building... Or was that just a line of reasoning to appease his conscience and excuse himself...? He couldn't be sure. Hated not knowing. Still felt just as plagued that he had done wrong.

And so, breathless, he picked up the fine-tip paintbrush to finish it off with his signature – but his hand shook uncontrollably. He gripped his arm with his hand, desperately trying to steady himself. But it was no use. Putting his own name would be like an admission of guilt – signing an invisible dotted line, guilty as charged. He should have left it blank, but he did not know what came over him when he found himself leaning forward, writing, 'F. Jaffrey' – telling himself that that would be his pseudonym too.

Turning away, he could not bear to see the image a moment longer. Instead, with pain aching in his chest, he banished it to a room he hardly used, and propped it against the wall on the floor. Couldn't even bring himself to hang it……

250

'Art is never finished,

only abandoned.'

Leonardo da Vinci

29 DAZE

The Chauffeur burst into the room, and saw the three children crumpled on the floor in a heap, with Jeremy stooping over them, like a dark raven. He ran over and wrenched the man's hands from the children's arms, flinging him against the bed with a thwomp.

Several others burst into the room, and pinned Jeremy Fitzsimmons down, extracting handcuffs and clicking them around his wrists. A trickle of blood appeared on his forehead, where his head had knocked against the wall – it seeped into his eyes, turning his vision red.

The children stirred. First Milly, and then the others – and the Chauffeur sighed with relief. He helped the girls stand up on shaky legs, and Tai was pulled into his wheelchair by one of the men.

Milly rubbed her head. 'H-how long have we been out?' she murmured, groggy.

One of the security personnel, Sam Khan, with dark skin and hair that seemed too white for his age, answered. 'From what we can tell, and what the Chauffeur told us, you've been here for about 50 minutes.' The children blinked at each other with disbelief – it had seemed like a lifetime.

'H-how did you know to come and get us?' asked a woozy Mei Hui, clinging on to the Chauffeur's arm.

The Chauffeur read her lips, and simply pointed up toward the ceiling. 'Jasmine,' he mouthed, making a throaty sound.

Sam Khan explained. 'Jasmine's sensors detected an alarming rise in your heartbeat and temperature, and alerted the Chauffeur. We didn't see a thing because you'd looped our CCTV... Though I gotta say, that's one smart computer!'

Just as they were leaving the room, hobbling and exhausted, Milly briefly looked back at Jeremy Fitzsimmons. He was sitting, crumpled, looking pathetic, on the edge of the bed. He was crying... though she couldn't understand why. And she felt sorry for him.

They were brought to the den, where all three were generally fussed over and given something to drink. Milly mumbled something about Professor Wolff being sure to blow a fuse when he finds out what they had done. Sam Khan and Linda Beresford glanced at each other and were about to say something when – to their surprise – Dr Fargo rushed in, looking very concerned. He began checking each of the children over. 'Dear oh dear,' he repeated again and again. 'You did get yourselves into a sorry state... But, thankfully – and amazingly – you're all okay!'

Milly was baffled. 'How come you're here?' she asked.

Dr Fargo looked at her oddly. 'You... don't know about the Professor?'

Their blank looks gave him the answer.

Dr Fargo explained. 'Two days ago, the Professor came with V2, insisting that he wanted to see Fitzsimmons, alone, and with the cameras off. And under no circumstances should they be disturbed. The Professor disappeared inside the room for hours, with V2 waiting outside. After quite some time, V2 disobeyed the Professor's orders and went in to find him slumped on the table. When V2 rushed over, Fitzsimmons grabbed his arm, and he blanked out as well.'

Milly looked suddenly frightened.

Dr Fargo continued. 'Both of them went into a state of shock. We rushed them to the hospital, and after they were looked over, it was decided to keep them in intensive care... In time, V2 recovered, and though the Professor was still unconscious, he was showing healthy signs of brain activity, so we thought it best to transfer them to Avernus, where it's safer. That's why I'm here now, because we've just installed and set up all the medical equipment.'

The children looked at each other. 'They're here?' repeated Milly.

Dr Fargo nodded. 'I think you had better see for yourselves. Are you feeling up to it?'

'Yes, we're fine,' Milly said, eager to see the Professor and V2.

They were led out of the room and down several corridors, with Khan pushing Tai's wheelchair. 'While they were in the hospital,' said Dr Fargo as they walked, 'I'd been checking on them several times a day. They were in a kind of catatonic state, like I said, as if they'd been shocked. Thankfully, last night, V2 came around, which is very good news indeed. But the Professor... he still hasn't woken up yet.' He opened the door, and they went inside.

There were two beds, and both of them contained a sleeping form. One of them stirred from the noise of people entering. V2 turned and opened sluggish eyes. Milly couldn't help herself, and ran over to him, giving him a hug. 'Hey,' he said, hugging her back. 'Don't look so worried, I'm okay... I think.' He glanced at Dr Fargo for confirmation.

'That you are,' he said. He went over to double-check his vital signs on the monitor. 'You're doing very well. I'd recommend another day of bed-rest though, but after that, I'd be happy to discharge you.'

The Chauffeur went over to the Professor's unconscious form, and took his hand. Tai wheeled himself over, and touched the Professor's arm.

'Be careful, Tai,' said Mei Hui, worried. 'Don't do whatever you did to your mother...'

'I won't,' he said, glancing at her. He was looking incredibly tired, with dark shadows around sunken eyes. He stared at the Professor's face. The old man looked at peace as he slept, like a baby, with not a care in the world. Very different from how he was just a few days ago – his nerves constantly on edge.

Suddenly the Professor stirred, and sucked in a deep breath.

'Tai!' cried Mei Hui, grabbing the handles of his wheelchair and pulling him away.

But he had already let go of the Professor's arm. 'I... I didn't do anything.' His wrinkled face creased even more.

Dr Fargo went over to the Professor. 'I think he's coming around...'

Mei Hui put a hand on Tai's shoulder, telling him, 'I'm sorry,' she breathed. 'I did not want you to get worse. You... you have to conserve your energy, your strength.'

Tai smiled at her. 'Yes, Mum.'

The Professor sat up, confused. 'W-what happened? Where am I?' His voice was hoarse and croaky. He cleared his throat. Focused his mind. He soon began to recognise the 'feel' of Avernus around him, the smell and echo of it.

'You're back in Avernus, Harry,' said Dr Fargo gently. 'And thank goodness you're okay! How are you feeling?'

He thought for a moment. 'Weak, and a little groggy, but fine.'

'Excellent!' beamed Dr Fargo. He drew closer to shine his pen torch into each of the Professor's eyes. 'Just look ahead for me,' he mumbled as he examined them. 'Pupillary reflexes are fine... nothing untoward,' he said, also casting his eyes over the monitor. 'Vitals are good too.'

The Chauffeur was very happy to see the old man recovered, and patted his back, making soft gurgling noises in his throat.

V2, who had swung his legs out, was sitting on the edge of the bed facing the Professor. 'Prof. What happened to you in there... with Fitzsimmons?' He glanced at Dr Fargo, then back at the Professor. 'Do you remember?'

Dr Fargo was giving the Professor a much-needed drink, and after gulping it down, he gasped to catch his breath, wiping his mouth with the back of his hand. At last the Professor spoke. 'That man...' he said in a hushed, awed tone '...he can take you into his mind. He can make you see things... Things that happened to him.'

Both Milly and Mei Hui looked at each other.

The Professor continued. 'He showed me the night of the fire at my house. And I saw what happened. He... he was there.' His face reddened with anger, and sinewy fists clenched the bedsheet.

Milly couldn't help pipe up, 'But he didn't mean it to happen!'

Everyone turned to look at her.

The Professor blinked. 'H-how do you know?' The tension in the air thickened.

Mei Hui spoke up for her. 'We needed to find out more about him. And so we snuck into his room, and... connected with him.'

The Professor closed his eyes briefly. 'That is exactly what I didn't want you to do! That man is *extremely* dangerous...'

'He's our father!!' cried Milly, unable to control the avalanche of emotions barraging through her, making her pulse race. 'Our genetic father!'

They were silent for some time.

The Professor absorbed this with numb stupefaction. Their genetic father… It was something he had suspected for a while, a nagging feeling that he could not verify. During Project Ingenious, Dr Kendra was the one that provided the genetic material, the genius genes, for grafting into the DNA of each test-tube baby. But he himself had been so involved with the intricacies of the splicing process, pressured by the powers above to produce more healthy babies, that he did not stop to question where those genes came from. Only now, after all this time, and far too late – after Dr Kendra was gone – did he realise the significance. Especially to the children. The all-important provenance of those genes… Finally, he found his voice. 'H-how can you be so sure it's him? That he's the one the genes were taken from?'

'Because we saw his life,' said Milly at the same time as Mei Hui said, 'He has the same abilities as us.'

Mei Hui looked at Milly, and then the Professor. 'We saw his entire life, Professor. He has been blighted with what they call the Fitzsimmons curse – one that every male in their family inherits, along with their genius. We also saw what he could do. He has… amazing abilities.'

'He can do a kind of mental download!' said Milly, remembering the time Fitzsimmons had absorbed Dr Kendra's mind, and all his scientific knowledge. 'And, he's also able to upload those same memories into others. It… it's amazing! That's how Dr Vassiliev was able to come up with the final piece of the puzzle for the cure for us. It was because Jeremy discovered what was missing, and then fed it into Vassiliev's mind all the time that he was trapped in his house.' There came an unexpected frisson of excitement as she thought about the completion of the cure. After everything, there was hope for them. And for her.

'Jeremy?' repeated the Professor quietly, recognising the tinge of affection in Milly's voice. 'You're on first-name terms? Milly, you don't know what you're getting involved with. He could be extremely dangerous. He knocked me out, V2 as well, with just his mind!'

They turned to Mei Hui.

'Mei?' asked Milly, 'How did you feel about him?'

Mei Hui tilted her head and looked confused. 'I… I am not sure. He is not black or white, good or bad. It is not so clear to me. I cannot understand why I am unable to tell…' She was puzzled. She had never before come across someone she could not read. 'His powers must be very strong,' she said thoughtfully.

Then Tai remembered something. 'When we went into his room… I couldn't see any colours around him. That's never happened before. It's like… he has no feelings.'

They thought about this for some time, until V2 shifted forward on the bed. 'If he has such strong powers, why did he let you read his mind? Why didn't he just stop?'

'I think because he sees us as his offspring,' said Milly simply. 'He funded Project Ingenious right from the start because he wanted Dr Kendra to produce children without the faulty gene that disfigures him. And then, when he found out that the laboratories had burnt down, he started searching for us. He searched for years. And now that he's found us, I suppose he wanted us to see the real him, beyond his… appearance. He's really happy he found us.'

Mei Hui remembered something. 'Yes, I sensed that too, while we were connected with him. There was a kind of… triumph. It was overpowering. But…' she faltered. 'Strangely, toward the end, I also detected grief, mourning, sorrow. It was as if he had just discovered someone had died.'

Milly visibly stiffened, realising something. 'Is it possible that, all the time we were reading his mind…'

'He's been reading yours,' finished the Professor, his voice grim. He closed his eyes. That was the very thing he feared. The man's unknown powers and abilities, and what he might do to the children. What he might already have done.

Milly stifled a gasp, tears brimming. They dripped down hot cheeks, and over her lips, salting one single word. 'Karl,' she said tremulous, realising now why Fitzsimmons was crying when they left. 'He found out about Karl, from us. That we…' She stopped. She was going to say that they had killed him. That they'd pushed him over the edge, and twisted his mind so much, that he committed suicide. But the stabbing pain in her heart stopped her. Instead, she said, lightheaded with disbelief, 'While we were discovering his life, he was absorbing ours…'

Eventually V2 said, solemnly, 'So he knows everything.' He thought about this. 'I kind of hate to say this, but… I'm worried about this mental upload thing… If he could do it to Dr Vassiliev, might he have done it to you?'

They all thought about this, particularly the Professor.

'It *is* possible,' said Mei Hui, stunned that, if it were true, they had been so easily duped. Despite their genius intelligence, they still possessed a child-like faith in human nature.

There was a noise, the squeak of rubber on the floor. And they turned to find Tai trying to get up from the wheelchair. His stick-like arms were shaking as he gripped the armrests to push himself up.

Mei Hui rushed to grab him, support him. But when Tai looked at her, and her ruby red cheeks, he felt his legs buckling beneath him. And as he collapsed, time changed gears, shifting to slow – and he watched as beads of his own sweat fell in a glistening shower around him. Blackness seeped into his vision. When his body thudded onto the floor, sharp pains spasmed through him. The grit of dust between clenched teeth. In his mind, the echo of a thought…

He lay twisted and crooked on the floor. Blinking slowly as everyone rushed towards him in a snow-storm flurry. His hands, arthritic and knobbly, shook uncontrollably. Skin pale and delicate as rice-paper. A scrawny chest rose and fell – rasping and wheezing – battling for breath. And all the while, that thought tumbled through his mind again and again.

What…

White hair shivering. Lips trembling.

Have we…

Eyelids shuddering closed.

Done.

258

259

PART 3

'Though human ingenuity may make various inventions, which by the help of various machines answering the same end, it will never devise any inventions more beautiful, nor more simple, nor more to the purpose than Nature does; because in her inventions nothing is wanting, and nothing is superfluous.'

Leonardo da Vinci

30 THE FLOATING SKY ISLAND

Some have described it as the largest, most savage natural battlefield on earth – an explosion of greenery, water, and wildlife, all vying in a truculent, interminable fight to survive; eating and being eaten, ebbing and flowing, living and dying. The essence of life in a pulsing, palpitating, throbbing, breathing kingdom of green. Many an explorer losing their battle without anyone knowing of their bloody fight to the death. Never returning – absorbed, silently, within the understorey, and slowly sinking into the red, acidic soil...

Yet the young and slight Saffie Morales, still just a teenager, walked into the dense, dark foliage of the Amazon – alone – with just a woven, palm-fibre rucksack on her back, a machete on her hip, a bow and arrow, and a water flask and pan. Walking as casually as if she were going for an afternoon stroll. Her long, black hair was scraped into a high ponytail, swishing across dark shoulders that were already glistening with sweat from the heat. She turned around before disappearing completely, waving a light-hearted hand at her parents who were standing at the water's edge, watching her go. She did not call out her usual farewell to them, 'Nos vemos!' It would never be heard above the din of the howler monkeys, the tonk-calls of bare-throated bellbirds, and the pheasant-like curassow and their alarming whistles. The click and buzz of cicadas too, was omnipresent; insects that never seemed to sleep.

As she watched her daughter vanish, Saffie's mother was hugging, so tight, the leather-bound notebook she had left in their charge, as if it were part of her daughter.

'She will be fine, mi amor,' said father to mother.

'I know,' she sighed, not one flicker of worry in her eyes. There was a withered surety in her voice that came from years of doubt proven wrong.

'I know.'

Father hobbled back to the riverboat, wincing from the pain in his leg. It had never been right since a run-in, years ago, with a pig-like peccary attacking him to protect its young, although he had only been passing by. The couple climbed into the riverboat, and she placed the precious book in her bag, the soft leather already hot and melting from just a few minutes in the burgeoning heat of the sun, even though it was not yet seven in the morning. He steered the boat around with ease – the stench of petrol and the loud puk-puk-puk of the engine fading into the distance.

Saffie walked for hours through the undergrowth. Where the morning sun had blinded her, layers of jungle canopy plunged her in muted shade, with oblique blades of glinting sunlight stabbing through at intervals. The braided, rubber-soled huaraches on her feet were well-worn; her preferred closed sandals for long treks in the jungle. Despite the heat, she wore heavy, full-length trousers to protect her legs from the deadly Lachesis viper's bite – aptly named after one of the three sisters of fate from Greek mythology, who measured the thread of life with her rod. One bite from such a venomous viper, and the thread would be cut short. The leather straps of Saffie's rucksack were sown with pads stuffed with alpaca wool, to protect her shoulders from the constant rubbing.

She cupped hands behind her, below the weight of the rucksack, and gently hugged it. 'Only two days' journey, Sabu.' The rucksack made a light noise – a cross between a sawing sound and a purr. 'Just hold on, niño. Hold on,' she told it. Her voice, though warm, was tinted with worry.

Despite her stature and slim physique, Saffie was strong and relentless. Only stopping intermittently to sip water, sometimes wiping off copious amounts of sweat, or taking her machete to hack through thick bush and coiling liana. Now and then she checked her position on the GPS device strapped to her arm, constantly correcting her direction. She was fuelled by a dogged will that only the precarious teeter of life and death hanging in the balance could engender. It fired her to keep going.

As she went, she thought about the events of the past days. And pangs of pain tore through her chest. The load of the creature in the rucksack a heavy reminder of the burden bearing down on her soul. She remembered how the curandero, the tribal healer who looked to nature for remedies, the jungle being his living medicine chest, had travelled for hours by plane and boat to arrive at their animal sanctuary one late evening. A tearful reunion, not only because they hadn't seen each other for years, but because Sabu's parents had just died. Their beautiful, limp bodies still warm under the tarpaulin. He was too late to save them, and instead, he and Saffie cried together – a topographical map of wrinkles on his sun-dried skin, squinching as they sobbed. 'Their spirit is at last free,' he whispered in a voice that was like coarsely ground cocoa, treacly rich yet rough.

'But the cub...' sniffed Saffie, wiping her eyes. She took his hand and led him inside. 'He is suffering with the same ailment, Eligio.'

The old man hunched over the little bundle sleeping fitfully in a corner of the bare room, nestled amongst layers of cheesecloth. Its eyes sticky with infection.

'As you know,' said Saffie, 'both my parents are vets, trained in western medicine – and nothing they have tried works.' She spoke in hushed tones, wary of death hovering close-by, not wanting to give it reason to descend closer. 'I've also applied the ancient ways of the Amazon you taught me. Certain roots, leaves, bark, and tree sap that I spent days collecting. But that too has failed.' Her lips quivered as she glanced at the cub, little Sabu, just over two months old. His flank tremulous with scant breath.

Eligio couldn't help checking. 'You harvested Uña de Gato to boost immunity...?' It was a plant with curled thorns like cat claws.

'Yes.'

'Sangre de Grado...' Dragon's blood – the red, blood-like sap of a flowering tree.

'Yes, I did.'

'Tawari bark... Lapacho for infection...?'

'Those too. I've tried everything. *Everything.*' Her eyes pleading for help.

The curandero sighed, deep in thought, and turned back to little Sabu, gently stroking his soft fur – he was so hot. And just then, in his mind, like the Aru jungle mist that appears seemingly out of nowhere, a song came to him. He began to sing it in a low, warbling voice that somehow pervaded the entire room. Lyrics that the trees and plants and flowers taught him. A melody that came from the wind and the rustle of leaves. It was a healing song, and he sang it for hours, invoking the forces of nature for help. But still, in the end, the cub was unchanged.

Finally, the old man sat back on his haunches, disturbed, troubled. 'I understand now...' he said quietly. 'It is a new disease. One that is foreign to the Amazonas, one that I have never before come across.'

Saffie heard the hoarseness in his voice. She disappeared for a while, and returned with her mother, who bore a cup of coca tea. They greeted each other with affection, entwining arms, and wordless in the face of death. He took the tea and slurped its bitter sweetness, the yellow-green liquid immediately soothing his throat, calming him.

Saffie sat down next to the curandero, and dripped droplets of water into the side of the cub's mouth, intermittently fanning him to lower his temperature.

The old man thought for a long time. 'There is one last thing,' he told Saffie eventually, wondering if he might regret telling her this. 'I would not mention a remedy so dangerous, but... only because Sabu is the last of his kind, and we must try everything in our power to save him...'

Saffie quickly turned to him, expectant with hope. 'Tell me. I will do anything.'

'It will require traversing very close to the wilds of virgin jungle, unmapped territory that we know very little about – in Anavilhanas, deep in the heart of the Amazonas. It is a good two days' hike from the nearest river-drop, and the terrain is savage. Only someone with your... oneness with nature, will be able to survive such a journey. But you must go alone. If you bring others, others that have a spirit not like yours, who are not at one with Mother Earth, it will aggravate and inflame savage animals, provoking attack. And the jungle will swallow whole even you. You might not come out alive,' he warned, sombre.

Saffie looked desperately at the cub. 'I will do it.'

The healer searched her face for any hint of doubt, and, satisfied, he continued. 'There is a tepui, a table-top mountain, nestled within the arms of the Rio Negro, where it divides in two. In the morning mists it appears as a floating island in the sky. A place that has been forgotten by time. It is a special place, where wild animals lounge in a paradise of sandy white beaches, clear waters rife with fish, plants and trees heavy with sweet fruit. Once inhabited a thousand years ago, there are only ruins of their dwellings today. As you know, Mother Earth, has provided healing flora for sicknesses. Including diseases that have not yet been discovered. She is generous and ripe with beneficence, and she knew we would need the medicine before even illness entered the world. You must climb atop the tepui, and there, search for a special medicinal flower. It is a flower with pollen so yellow that it burnishes gold in the low sun of evenfall. Descendants of nomadic tribesmen, fleeing the brutality of the barons of the fiebre del caucho, the rubber boom, discovered the place just a hundred years ago, and that is how I know about it – from local tribesmen, the isolados, who dare only whisper about it from generation to generation.'

'But... but... how can you be sure this flower, and the floating island, actually exists? If no-one has been there since?'

Eligio briefly closed his leathery eyelids and sighed deeply, remembering. 'When my Núria was diagnosed with cancer just three years ago, and after months of battling with it, I set out for this place myself, leaving my dear wife in the care of her sister. I followed a tributary that led me to the Rio Negro. But I was too hasty... climbed the wrong tepui, the first one I found, over-eager and desperate. Being old, I was half dead from exhaustion with only a day's food and water left in my satchel by the time I reached the top. I searched and searched, but the flower was nowhere to be found. And then, as Grandfather Sun rose to its zenith, its piercing light divided the mist and showed me an adjacent tepui further downstream. From afar I saw on its back a mass of lustrous yellow. The healing flowers. I... I'm sure of it. I was so close, yet I knew with a heavy heart that I could go no further if I wanted to return alive. Though I was tempted to try. It was a devastating mistake...' The curandero blinked, finding himself back in the room. Back with the ailing cub. 'But with your ways, Saffie, and your strength of youth, you will be able to find it. I know it.'

Saffie squeezed his arm. 'If you are sure this is what I need, what Sabu needs, then I will go.'

The medicine man nodded. 'We must hurry. I will draw you a map.'

The jungle was the girl's chacra, her food garden. And as Saffie hacked her way through the undergrowth, she collected and picked things she would need, here and there. Things that the curandero had pointed out to her when she was under his tutelage for many months. He knew the jungle like no other, and revered its ways. And to reward his respect, the jungle in turn gave him its offerings. Though Eligio taught her that if there was something she did not recognise, she should leave it alone, no matter how enticing it looked, for it could well be poisonous. They were to take only what they knew, and only what they needed there and then, not hoarding the fruit and berries – which would easily spoil in the humidity, but also attract the unwanted attention of insects, snakes, birds, or worse...

So as Saffie trampled through the understorey, she gathered the things she could use. With the tip of the machete, she cut off mushrooms that clung to wood like brown limp leaves, placing them in a pouch. Walking on, she was nearly hit on the head by something falling, and saw that it was a cacao fruit, bulbous and fragrantly ripe, which was quickly scooped up and taken with her. The bright yellow-orange flowers of the Matico plant called to her, and she went over to pick, not the flowers, but the sage-like leaves.

Further along, she was glad to chance upon a dead Chonta palm surrounded by the faint smell of rot, and she hacked at the spiked bark to reveal crumbling wood stuffed with fat, wriggling beetle larvae – creamy globs as large as dates. She brushed off the ants and picked out twenty or so grubs, placing them carefully in her bag. Later, a laurel tree was plucked of its shiny green bay leaves. And later still, on finding a clump of tall, green bamboo, she jostled each stem to discern the movement of water inside, then bent one onto the ground, and hacked a nick into a section – capturing the trickle of liquid in her bottle. She did this to several sections, until the flask was filled with the clear, sweet water that the bamboo had filtered naturally.

When daylight began to fade, she started searching for four firm, strong trees in a rough square configuration. Overhead, thunder rumbled and lightning cracked in blinding flashes. The canopy swayed and bent as one, bowing to the wind, churning both warm and cold eddies around her. She found four Poui trees, about two metres apart, surrounded by thick bushes of undergrowth that would act as windbreakers. Hacking away large sections of loose bark from a nearby tree trunk, she arranged the pieces on the ground in a stable pile – then carefully took off her backpack, and set it on top, loosening the cords to reveal Sabu. His small body lay nestled inside – and he blinked slowly, barely conscious, his black fur clumped and damp from sweat. Saffie crouched down and kissed the top of his head, and he growled weakly.

She took him several metres away, and set him on the ground where he half walked and half stumbled in a daze. Saffie watched intently, urging him, 'Please, please, please...' Finally he squatted down weakly, before at last urinating. 'Yes!' said Saffie, as the little cub shook himself down, before flopping to the ground. She picked him up and hugged him, saying, 'Good boy, Sabu. Good baby,' before laying him back on the bark stack.

Needing to work fast before the dark of nightfall, she hacked off branches from two of the Poui trees, and hooked the tubular hammock onto the stumps. Then she went around collecting concertina palm fronds as large as her, and wove them in between the intersecting branches of the four trees, lashing them together with young vines to create a sloping, layered roof.

For the fire, she collected larger logs, split them, and shaved off the dry inner wood into ribbons – piling them into an upturned bark tray, with progressively thicker pieces of chopped wood. Two y-shaped twigs were wound into the dirt on either side of the stack.

She then took three long, thin young branches – full of sap so they wouldn't burn in the heat – and lashed them together over the fire to make a tripod, and a piece of cord was hung from the apex, with the other end fastened to a twig. On it, she hooked the aluminium pan, filled with bamboo water. She tossed in three Matico leaves together with some dried herbs she had brought from home.

She lit the kindling with the waterproof matches her father had given her, blowing gently to help it take. When the fire flared up, she stood back and watched it for several seconds, hypnotised. The dance of orange reflected in her eyes. She never tired of admiring the beauty of the flame, and hearing the comforting crackle and pop of burning wood.

Next, she took a stout twig to skewer the writhing chontacuro grubs between the mushrooms. She balanced the stick on the y-shaped rods, over the fire, turning it now and then as the food sizzled and hissed in the heat.

She had left aside several grubs for Sabu, and while her food was cooking, Saffie carefully scooped him up onto her lap. He stirred, sleepy with sickness, his mouth slightly open, revealing a pink tongue lolling between two long incisors. Saffie talked soothingly to him as she slow-drizzled some water into his mouth, careful not to choke him. Then, she bit off one end of a live larva and squeezed the cream onto his tongue, drip by drip. Little Sabu was barely aware of what was happening, but a swallowing reflex helped the protein-rich ooze go down. After four grubs, he turned away, weakly licking his mouth clean – and Saffie was satisfied that he'd eaten and drunk enough. Carefully she took him over to the hammock, and zipped the mosquito-resistant netting around him.

By now, her own food was ready, and the chontacuro grubs had browned nicely – so she drizzled water over her hands to wash them, then took one of the skewers, blowing it cool. She bit off each of the grubs, chewing the leathery skin that tasted of mild sweet bacon, with its black domed head crunching between her teeth. The mushrooms were a wonderful earthy, crispy complement – the food so rich that two skewers were enough to fill her. Dessert was sucking the white flesh of the cacao fruit, mango-sweet with a slightly sour aftertaste, spitting out the beans onto the ground, like pellets.

When the fire had died down to glowing orange embers, Saffie threw bunches of bay leaves on top, and the grey smoke – thick with pungent oils – wafted into the air: a repellent to keep Sabu insect-free.

When the Matico tea had cooled, she drizzled some into the restless cub's mouth, and before long, he went quiet, his body loosening, as he fell into a deep sleep.

Saffie hooked her rucksack onto a branch, making sure that nothing was left on the ground, where trails of leaf-cutter ants would tear anything in their path to shreds. Taking out her small notepad and pencil, she slipped them into her pocket, and then climbed into the hammock with Sabu, nestling him against her stomach. He was still burning up.

As she stroked him, she sang quietly. Not quite the improvised songs that Eligio crooned, but melodies her mother had taught her. But it wasn't long before she could sing no more. Tears coursing down her cheeks as she thought of the cub, so close to death. His parents lying cold and immobile, life snatched so cruelly from them. 'I'm so sorry, Sabu,' she whispered. 'So, so sorry...' She wanted to say much more, to bare her soul, but rain started to fall, drops as large as marbles. Thunder rumbled, and electricity discharged overhead in whip-cracking bolts. The palm-leaf covering protected them for the most part, but plinks of water still dripped through. And as the smoke swirled around them, as the rain poured down, and lightning bolts exploded, the raging elements whipped up her own feelings of remorse. She kissed his hot, damp fur. 'Sleep,' she whispered, her own eyes drooping with exhaustion. 'Sleep, mi amor.'

As Saffie herself drifted into slumber, the nagging thought that she had pushed down all day now floated to the surface. She wondered whether this whole trip was una búsqueda inútil – a futile, wild goose chase. The possibility rumbled inconsolably through her dreams.

The next morning, it was not the loud cry of the howler monkeys that woke Saffie, though their screams could be heard for miles around. There was something crawling on her trousers – the lightest sensation of tiny feet making their way up her leg.

She looked down and saw the matt black body of a scorpion, about 10 cm long. Its thick carapace rolled at one end into a raised segmented tail with a pointed stinger, and at the other, were large claws that pincered as it scurried along. It was so fast that, before she even blinked, it had reached her hip, and stopped, cautious, at the edge of black fur, where Sabu was lying against her. The cub juddered from the chills, which alarmed the scorpion, and its eight legs manoeuvred into an attack stance, at the same time uncoiling and straightening its tail. The hook-shaped stinger quivered and glistened with a drop of venom at its tip – poised to inject a lethal dose into Sabu's unsuspecting flesh.

Quick as a flash, Saffie's hand swooped in and pinched one of the chunky metasomas of its tail, between her thumb and index finger, careful not to touch the stinger. She held it up, and the scorpion dangled helplessly, peddling its legs in the air.

Her hand swooped swiftly upward and stopped in front of wide eyes, long eyelashes batting as she inspected it with keen interest. 'Woah! Tityus obscurus – the famed Amazonian black scorpion… What a beauty!' she said, whistling with appreciation. She jostled onto an elbow to take a better look. It was the first time she'd seen one in real life. 'And you look like a female, nicely fattened, maybe ready to moult. Or…' a thought suddenly occurred to her, '…maybe even ready to give birth!' Her eyes widened. 'That would be so cool!' She turned her hand this way and that as she inspected it. 'Love the way you guys carry your babies on your back, until their little exoskeletons harden. Except… it's not nice that you eat your offspring when there's no food. Not nice at all.' The scorpion dangled, stock still, as Saffie scolded it.

Looking around at the netting of her hammock, she saw that they were completely enclosed. 'Now how on earth did you manage to get in?' she wondered. She did not know that it had dropped from an overhanging branch onto the netting, and used its sharp pincers to nip a hole just big enough to slip through. It remained immobile, quietened and fearful of the thunder, until morning came, and the storm passed… Hunger animating it to search for its next victim – a cicada, a worm, a centipede, or even a bird.

Manoeuvring around, Saffie opened the netting and slipped out, careful not to drop the scorpion on Sabu, for its deadly venom would kill him in an instant. She found a broken log on the ground several metres away, and stooped down to allow it to scamper underneath. Returning to Sabu, she gently took him outside the camp, placing him on the ground, where he paced around on wobbly legs, and relieved himself. But he soon collapsed in a heap from lack of strength. Scooping him up, she sat down, and put him on her lap. 'I've got you, niño,' she said, smattering his head with kisses. In between each one, she told him, 'Just hold on.' 'We're almost there.' 'I'm not going to let you down.'

She reached for the last of the cold Matico tea, and drip-fed it into his mouth. He licked it up weakly. 'It's good for you, Sabu,' she said softly. 'It will help lower your fever and relieve the pain.' Soon, his head began drifting down, and he was fast asleep again.

Saffie set about clearing the little camp – and after she pressed down the hammock into her rucksack, she placed the drowsy cub on top of the wodge of netting, then gathered the water bottle and small pan, hooking them onto the bottom of the rucksack. She slipped her invaluable machete into the holder at her hip, and set the bow and arrow crossways over an arm.

But then, something made her stop in her tracks, and she stood still – closing her eyes, and lifting her face to the sky. A ray of light cast over her face through a gap in the canopy. Eyebrows creasing into a frown. She remained still for several minutes, trying to understand what she was feeling. Concentrating, absorbing. And then it dawned on her, and she opened her pretty eyes, wide. 'Longing!' she said triumphantly. Quickly she scrabbled for the little notebook and pencil in her back pocket, noting down the time, the date, and the sensation. She was both pleased and puzzled by what she'd just experienced, but there was no time to ponder over it now. She put the notebook away, checked the GPS, and at last set off. As she walked, she munched on guarana seeds to stimulate energy and sharpen her senses. And along the way, the jungle offered her a sweet lemon here, wild berries there, and tufts of edible fern.

Just after midday, she emerged from the canopy, blinking in the bright, hot sun. Her eyes followed the rolling slope she was on, and took in the murky brown waters of the river down below, snaking through the Anavilhanas. She traced the course of the water's flow, to find a mesa looming in the distance. Saffie's heart skipped a beat, and she half walked half slid down the slope that was crazed with a tangle of tree roots, to reach the water's edge. The tepui seemed so close, yet as she traversed the landscape, it took her many more hours scrambling over spurs that abutted the sides of the river valley.

At last she arrived at the base of the mountain – but she remembered the curandero's words, not to be hasty. It was the second mesa she was to look for her, and so she continued following the river.

There came the sudden rustle of foliage from the jungle above her, and Saffie froze. It was not the wildlife she was scared of. Far more savage were illegal gold miners and loggers, slashing and burning their way through the forest. And drug traffickers, los narcos, setting up makeshift factories to produce coca paste, the base ingredient for cocaine. They would rather kill intruders than risk the possibility of their factory location being informed to the police. Saffie had to be extremely careful never to stumble upon them or their territory, for she knew it would mean a fight to the death.

As she turned toward the noise, her hands reached swiftly for her bow and arrow, and at the same time she side-stepped to hide behind a boulder.

A dark man appeared, completely naked except for a circlet of bright yellow toucan feathers across his forehead, an armband of red feathers, and a string of necklaces adorning his chest. His skin was oily brown, his hair black and pudding-bowl shaped. He could be 20 years old, or 40 – someone thrown from a distant primitive past, into the present. He had not drawn his bow and arrows, they were slung casually over his shoulder. Small, narrow eyes searched for her beyond the rim of the boulder – and when he spoke, his language was a close relative of Portuguese. 'Is that you, daughter of Mother Earth?' he shouted out.

Saffie did not reply, did not reveal herself.

'We have been tracking you. If I had wanted to harm you, you would be dead a long time ago.' After more rustling, an adolescent girl stepped out from behind him – and the two glanced at each other briefly. She too was naked, though was not wearing any flamboyant feathers like her companion, but she carried in her arms a chubby baby, perched upright. The girl craned her neck to see who he was talking to.

The young man shouted out, 'This is my sister, and my baby brother. We mean you no harm.'

At last, Saffie stepped out, though her bow, nocked with an arrow, was still poised in her hands, pointing downwards. 'Who are you? What do you want with me?' she asked. Her Portuguese was good but not perfect; she had never taken much to languages.

'We were out walking and searching for toucans, to add more feathers to my collection…'

Saffie nearly smiled at such an indulgent past-time. And she knew that, this deep into the jungle, they must be members of the isolados – isolated tribes that preferred to keep themselves away from civilisation.

He was still speaking, '...and then I spied you earlier today with a baby jaguar. Is... is it really true, that you have a black jaguar? I thought they had been wiped out completely six seasons ago, after their habitat was destroyed.'

Saffie heard the earnestness in his voice. The indigenous people had a healthy respect for the jungle and its inhabitants, replanting what they cut down, and only killing when there was a need. Even when they hunted for feathers, they blow-darted the birds with a natural poison called timbó, which was so mild it only stunned them while they were plucked of select colourful and flamboyant feathers – the birds quickly recovering afterward and fluttering away. Saffie put down her bow, and drew closer. 'I also thought the black jaguar was extinct.'

'The spotted jaguar is declining as well – when we go on nocturnal forages, there are hardly any sightings. It won't be long before they too are extinct...'

Saffie shook her head with deep regret.

'We are from the Mapui tribe,' the man told her. 'Have you heard of us?'

She looked up at him. 'No. I haven't. How many of you are there?'

'We are as a large group of white-lipped peccary.'

Saffie thought about this. A squadron of wild peccary could range anywhere from around 20 to 300, so she was still none the wiser. Such isolados never needed to learn to count beyond the fingers on their hands; mathematics was irrelevant to them in the jungle.

'Do you want to come meet our chieftain? I think he would like to see the cub.'

Saffie shook her head. 'I do not want to contaminate you, to spread disease.'

The young man nodded and sat down on the edge of the verge. It was not a modest angle, looking up at his nakedness, but a fortuitously-placed fern covered his modesty... He stared, unabashed, just as curious about her as she was of them. 'How is it that you have a black jaguar?' he asked.

Saffie sat as well, perched on one of the smaller boulders. 'Someone tipped off the police about a rich, fat granjero who had trapped two jaguars when they were cubs. He kept them illegally as pets for many years. The police seized them, and brought them to our animal sanctuary just a few months ago. Not long after, and to our surprise, one of them gave birth to a black cub. A miracle! But the granjero had kept the animals in dirty, squalid conditions, and both adults died soon after.' It was heartbreaking.

'I saw that the cub too is weak...' said the young man.

Saffie narrowed her eyes. 'How long have you been watching us?'

He smiled, and did not answer. 'What are you doing around this way? Where are you going?'

'I've been told about the golden flowers of a floating sky island...'

'Ah, I see. You've come for their healing properties, for the cub?'

She sat up. 'You know of them?'

'Yes, of course. The island is close, just around the river bend. You're almost there.'

'Have you... ever used the flowers?'

'No! I have only been told about them. They say it is impossible to reach them because of a particularly vicious kind of tarantula that colonised the island soon after the last dwellers left, many years ago. I'm told that others in my tribe have tried. But the spiders are numerous, their venom deadly, and they attack without provocation, without hesitation. Each one is massive – larger even than my hand.' He spread his fingers out to show her – they were particularly big hands, congruous with his wide, flat feet. Though his physique was slim and lithe. 'So we are unable to reach the flowers. But... *you* would have no problem.'

Saffie tilted her head, wondering why he would say this. 'You called me daughter of Mother Earth earlier...'

'We have heard of such a one. One that has a special way with animals. And I guessed that it might be you. Only she would dare venture out into the deepest jungle, alone. And only she would brave the tarantulas of the floating island. It's you, isn't it?'

It was Saffie's turn to smile and leave his question unanswered. 'I must go now. The cub is very sick... But I was pleased to meet you both.' She waved cordially at them and started to leave.

The girl turned to her brother and quickly told him something. The young man immediately shouted out. 'Wait! My sister just remembered something...'

Saffie stopped and turned back to them, impatient. 'What is it?'

'She wanted to tell you about an entrance.' He frowned as he turned to his sister for help. She explained the details to him, and he in turn relayed them to Saffie. 'She says that you must look for the face of the mountain that has the ancient tribal paintings... There is a picture of... of... an elephant!' He grinned, pleased that he remembered the word – elephants were no longer native to the Americas. 'A large elephant that has long horns. When you see that picture, you will find a dense swathe of hanging vine next to it. It covers an ancient entrance that has been cut through the sandstone – a shortcut to the top of the mountain. The other route, the path on the other side of the mountain, degraded and fell away many, many moons ago. So that is the only way. Though... the entrance hasn't been used for a long time.' He frowned as he thought of the number of animals and insects that must inhabit the tunnel by now. 'If you really are daughter of Mother Earth, the passage should be no problem. But if you're not...' – his eyebrows rose, expectant – '...you may never emerge from it.'

Saffie got up thoughtfully, and raised a hand in gratitude. 'Thank you!' She wondered if they might try to stop her, but the young man only sat back leisurely, and the girl just stared. It wasn't every day they saw a westerner passing through the jungle.

He called out to her. 'By the way, if the spiders don't kill you, the night cold will. So you must descend before nightfall. Remember, up there, without cover at night, you will almost certainly die.' He said this a little too light-heartedly for her liking.

Saffie nodded, 'Thanks again!' – and turned to leave.

Just as the young tribesman had told her, the moment she rounded a looping meander, she saw that the river straightened and divided, and the table-top mountain arose from between the two arms of water. A cloud of mist, the Aru, had rolled in from the jungle and surrounded it, dreamlike. The mesa's craggy, vertical escarpment of shale was capped by a stratum of sandstone, over which spilled a verdant mat of shrubbery.

When she reached the tepui, she skirted the river's edge, and the balmy water rushed over her feet, cleaning her muddy sandals. Saffie tried to ascertain the river's width and depth. It did not look overly wide, perhaps just eight metres, yet the water was dark and swirling into furious eddies, a sure sign that it was deep, and the bed uneven. The flow too was fast and treacherous, and downstream, several boulders were jutting haphazardly out of the water. It would be impossible to swim; the force of the river would instantly sweep her away and slam her into the jagged rocks – an almost certain death. On the opposite bank, there was a sandy beach, piled with tree trunks that had fallen from the edge of the summit. Overhead, tepui swifts flew in sweeping curves, screeching, gleeful, as they dove in and out of foliage.

She walked further along the river, assessing the best way to cross, ever-conscious of the need to hurry. As she followed its course, she came across several more fallen trees that had partway bridged the river onto boulders. Most of them were still thick with branches, but she came upon one that was traversable, and, she estimated, spanning about three-quarters of the way across the river.

She extracted a coil of rope from the bottom of her rucksack, tied one end to an arrow – the one with the barbed broadhead tip – and the other end she tied firmly around her waist. Climbing tentatively onto the log, she tested her footing to see how solid it was. It rocked this way and that by several inches, and she knew that a sudden surge of water would jolt it and tip her straight in. She had to be quick, and nimbly she edged along, one light foot criss-crossing over the other – shaky legs compensating for the precarious wobble of the tree. Heart thudded, adrenaline flowed, knowing that her life depended on the chance of factors beyond her control.

The end of the log was wedged loosely between two boulders, and, quick-as-a flash, she reached over her head for the bow, and deftly nocked the arrow. Squinting at a heavy, fallen tree, she pointed, aimed, released – hoping upon hope that it would take. Slicing the air, the arrow thwanged solidly into the wood. But before she had time to test that it was firmly embedded, a sudden surge of water jolted the tree and she was thrown into the river with a splash. The flow immediately whooshed her downstream, and she gasped and spluttered for breath, bobbing in and out of the frothing white waters, struggling to hold on to the rope. It felt like she was drowning, battling with the water for an age, until she found herself floundering on the sand of the beach.

When she got up, dribbles of blood tinted the run-off water pink, and she looked down to find grainy-brown leeches hooked onto her legs. Wriggling as they drank her blood. Saffie sucked air through her teeth from the pain, and she quickly took her machete and slid the blunt edge between their suckers and her skin. They dropped to the sand as writhing ribbons, and she stepped away after prizing off each one. Checking herself all over, in case she missed any, she moved across to a clear part of the beach, sat down, and carefully took off her rucksack to check on Sabu. He emerged squirming, no energy to shake himself dry. Saffie lifted him out, crying, 'I'm so sorry, baby!' She lay back and draped him across her torso. The rise and fall of his belly against hers was scattered and fainter than before. In direct sunlight, it did not take long for both of them to dry, a matter of minutes. But she was worried that the shock of the water had weakened him even more. As she lay, droplets of blood where the leeches had sucked dribbled slowly onto the white sand, staining it red; the anti-clotting enzyme that the leeches had secreted would mean that her blood would be dripping for a while. She felt a little dizzy, but there was no time to lose.

Gently brushing off the mud and sand from Sabu's fur, she placed him back in the rucksack, got up, and put the rucksack on her back. She set out once again, walking around the tepui, constantly looking up at the rock face for the ancient tribal paintings.

At last she came to an area of the mountainside that recessed into a darker hollow, and she tested and pulled on various vines before climbing up onto a narrow ledge. Closer now, the shadows dissolved to reveal faded pictographs, though they were still clear, still vibrant: a riot of random geometric shapes, patterns, and lines, in terracotta colours. As well as a smattering of hand prints, and child-like drawings of animals, birds, crabs, fish, humans – drawn crudely, disproportionately, and scattered randomly. Saffie's skin prickled as she imagined ancient tribesmen, not dissimilar to the ones she had met earlier, working for days on the artwork, hands daubed in red mud intensified perhaps by the seeds of the annatto shrub, which natives still used to this day for its berry-red dye. The curandero had told her the paintings were 1,000 years old, though that was likely an arbitrary number. There was no way they could know for sure. But what Saffie was seeing with her very eyes was evidence of a thriving ancient civilisation, perhaps numbering in the millions. That was until European invaders brutally slaughtered them – the natives' screams mingling with those of the jungle monkeys, as a sea of crimson blood spilled onto red soil... Whoever had escaped were killed off by the raging diseases that the foreigners brought with them – a deadly parting gift that crept and seeped insidiously through the jungle.

Whether it was from exhaustion, or because she was near the end of her journey, or from being in the presence of traces and remnants of a mysterious, long-dead people – Saffie's spine tingled in a rare moment of spirituality... The physical colliding and melding with the metaphysical... Her mind, her soul, elevated to a higher plane, like an epiphany...

Or perhaps it was just the coca leaves she'd been chewing to keep her alert. Either way, she began to feel very emotional as her eyes roved, searching, over the artwork. And then she saw it. A large picture of a mastodon – a smaller relative of the woolly mammoth. She shuffled to her right, along the foot-wide ledge, and hung onto a vine as she hacked away at the thick dangling bush next to the picture. The shrubbery dropped down bit by bit to reveal a heavily cobwebbed, pitch-black entrance. Clouds of dust billowing out made her cough.

Saffie jumped down to search for pieces of dry wood she could hack at to form clubs. Then she went back to the copal tree she had passed earlier, and lit a match underneath one of the white-grey globs of resin that seeped from its bark. It softened, like melted toffee, and she rolled it onto the top of a club, working her way through more resin, until she had covered three clubs with a good smattering of the substance. She put two of the makeshift torches in the side pouch of her rucksack, and lit the last. The flame flared brightly as she returned to the entrance of the mountain, wisps of lemon-pine from the copal filling her nostrils.

The tunnel was barely the height and width of an average human, and she imagined lines of diminutive tribesmen shuttling through it centuries before. The air smelled dank and musty, and drips of water fell on her as she walked. Or at least, that's what she thought it was...

The machete tore through thick wads of cobwebbing, and things scuttled away on the walls all around – the light too dim, the darkness too thick, for her to see what exactly they were. They buzzed and rattled, whirred and slithered, as they scurried off in every direction.

The incline was steep, but Saffie did not let up as she climbed for hours and hours, keenly aware of the urgency. When the wood of the torch burnt right down, she lit the next, and then the next. But the last one burnt out before she'd reached the end, and she had to trail a hand against the wall, in the pitch black, raw nerves on edge, until at last she felt whispers of cool air against her skin. Fatigue and the ache of every muscle in her body fell instantly away as the buzz of expectation excited her. Light filtered in, marking the end of the tunnel. And adrenaline coursed through her as she stepped out into a refreshing breeze, raising a weary hand over her eyes until she became accustomed to the bright light.

Her jaw dropped. The landscape was unlike anything she had ever seen. In between the shaded crevices of canyons, and pocked sinkholes, loomed towering and peculiar rock formations – everything covered in misted greenery. Birds swooped and called overhead. And as Saffie walked along a path that disappeared into a low canopy – spying hardy plants and flowers wedged between crevices, or eking out of bare sandstone – she could not help but gasp in wonderment again and again at the variety of plants and flowers she'd never seen before. She marvelled at the ability of life to grow and flourish in the harshest of conditions. The canopy, which was much lower than the jungle in the basin, soon dropped away, leading to the edge of the escarpment. And the view that appeared before her was like a miracle that made scales fall from her eyes, to see what nobody else in the world could.

The jungle sprawled below her like a lush carpet of green.

The fragile blue ceiling of a misted sky.

Grandfather Sun nestled low in a corner, like a stooping old man.

At his feet, the coiling silver snake of the Rio Negro.

And when Saffie tore her eyes away from the spectacular scene – so vast, and yet strangely intimate – she turned, and saw behind her a grove of wizened old dwarf trees. She held her breath as she drew closer.

The squat, pale, trunks, not much taller than her, flowed and swirled into stubby branches. Growing upwards from the soil, slithered tendrils of a climbing plant, interlaced through the trees' rather plain foliage. The climbers fireworked into a mass of globe-shaped flowers, of a yellow so deep it verged on gold.

She could see now that what she thought was a dark mist around the trees, turned out to be a swarm of wasps hovering around the flowers' syrupy nectar, and what she had mistaken for a carpet of decaying petals was in fact a widespread cluster of tarantulas, each one as large as a dinnerplate. Their bodies were brown velvet, their bristly legs fidgeting or stroking the undergrowth. One by one the arachnids turned toward her. And she gasped, holding her breath. Stiffly she advanced step by step. But the spiders – instead of rearing up on hind legs and baring their fangs to attack – scampered backwards, clearing a path, and Saffie walked on, eyes widening in amazement.

The wasps cascaded into the air, and formed a giant ball around her, hovering and zizzing, eclipsing the sun. Yet they did not withdraw stingers from sheaths, but simply followed her as she walked through them toward the trees. The sensation of a million vibrating wings thrumming through the air.

It was terrifying, yet awe-inspiring.

Her heart thundered within her chest.

When she reached the clearing in front of the first tree, she knelt down on a shaky knee and pulled the unconscious Sabu out of the rucksack. He seemed even lighter than before, his body a bag of bones beneath his fur. He was fading fast. His life, like the fleeting dew, was waning, evaporating, with every passing second. Saffie's trembling hand reached for one of the flowers, and she held it above Sabu's rasping mouth. The flower was dripping with light, sweet nectar, already pooling between her fingers and trickling to the ground.

The little cub lying weakly on her upper leg stirred, and, with great effort, turned to look at Saffie. His drowsy blue eyes were like mirrors to the balmy sky. Distractedly he lapped up the drizzle of nectar as they both examined each other in a moment of calm; precious seconds of serenity. He saw Saffie's beautiful face, smooth, tanned, with black eyes brimming with tears. She saw his striking black fur now clumped and sandy, little paws curled inward, shivering from the fever.

Saffie smiled sadly at him. 'Drink, Sabu,' she whispered, barely audible through the buzz of the wasps. She remembered what she had meant to tell him the other day. And his parents. What she wanted to say to every single jaguar that had come and gone before them. Sabu, their collective representative.

'I'm sorry that we could not protect you, niño. Sorry that we couldn't save you from being hunted and skinned by poachers. Killed by farmers, as if you were vermin. From loggers and ranchers destroying your home, your habitat – out of selfishness, greed. Stupidity.' She spoke softly, though every muscle was tense. 'Couldn't stop them from wiping out your entire species... And now, there is only you, Sabu. Only you. The last of the great black jaguars.' She bowed her head, overcome. The possibility of his death just did not bear thinking about. But think about it she must – as she cried for him, as each tear dripped down... If he died, memories would be his only legacy. And man's great shame. The thought of it made her ache, made her physically pained. But when she looked down at him, glimmers of hope were instantly crushed as she saw that he was fading. His body becoming limp on her leg. His head turning slowly sideways. Eyes closing. A long, last, laboured exhalation...

Saffie breathed hard and fast. Not believing. Shaking her head. Eyes creased with pain. 'No...' she said, tremulous fingers burying into his fur, jostling him gently. But he did not move. 'Please, no...'

But as seconds and minutes passed, with the small body draped loosely over her knee, Saffie tensed with despair and anger – and dug nails into the dry bark of the wood, splinters piercing into her skin. She crouched over him, sobbing. Burying her face into his little neck, breathing in his earthy warmth.

'Don't go, Sabu,' she begged, half whisper, half groan. 'Don't leave me.'

Gradually, the sun began to set.

But she did not notice.

It lowered slowly, casting dregs of light over the golden flowers.

And as it sank, it inhaled the heat of the day, and dragged it down into the earth with it.

By degrees, coldness set in.

The wasps faded, returning back to their nests.

And in time, darkness descended, like a harbinger of the blackest omen.

31 THE BOOK OF YOU

Calista Matheson was having an existential crisis. They had been in South America for just over three weeks now, and – as she sat on a passenger ferry chugging down the River Negro, two pounds lighter, bronzed, and covered in raging red mosquito bites, antihistamine cream her new best friend – it had only just dawned on her that every, single, insufferable day there, in the tropics, was going to be a bad hair day. It was the worst. And had she known the climate would have this effect on her usually perfectly-groomed hair, she might very well have stayed home.

She had tried everything to tame the frizzy mane brought on by the incessant humidity – and was, at that very moment, battling to tease it into a manageable ponytail. She had given up on make-up a long time ago; it simply melted from her skin within minutes. Thankfully the 'au naturel' look became her, especially since the sun had bleached her hair, and the tan gave her a svelte, even sophisticated, appearance. The rows of men sitting around watched her in silent fascination, both mesmerised by her beauty, and amused, as she huffed and tutted and grumbled about the infernal heat. That was, until their partners elbowed them to stop staring.

The boat was cram-full. People were napping in hammocks lined up in rows under a shaded deck, some were cooking freshly-caught piranha or crabs on makeshift barbecues which were nothing more than foil containers filled with coals, others were openly washing the sticky, sweaty grime from their bodies on deck. In the Amazonas, distances were so great, that most journeys took days – and with the ferry's basic amenities, passengers had to improvise eking out an existence wherever and however they could.

Calista, Jake, Jemima, Rory Sanderson, and his two men, had spent weeks in Manaus scouring for the missing Ingenious girl, both physically and digitally, hacking into local servers to see what they might discover. But they had come up with absolutely nothing, and having exhausted all avenues, were just about to get taxis to the airport, when their guide eventually plucked up the courage to ask them why their group – which stood out like a sore thumb – had come all this way. Calista, with her particular way with words, though not necessarily a good one, blurted out that they were following a clue to locate 'a girl from a government experiment' who lived 'where the black meets the white' – despite their mission being top secret. She couldn't understand why Sanderson kept giving her frigid glares. The young guide, who looked no more than 25, thought about this for a while. It's true, he told them, that Manaus is famous for the black waters of the Rio Negro marrying the white waters of the Solimões – but there is another possibility. The main tributary to the Rio Negro is called the Rio Branco, Portuguese for White River. The confluence of the two rivers is about 300 kilometres upstream, he told them, so about six or seven hours away by passenger ferry. When Sanderson afterwards researched the area, they discovered that there was a nature reserve with an animal sanctuary run by the Morales family, who had a teenage daughter. The group suddenly became very excited indeed, and immediately made plans to travel there. The guide was pleased with himself – his suggestion provided another day's work arranging their travel, for the gringos paid well for his services.

On the ferry, Jake and Jemima were sitting together on the port side of the boat, having a chat – a few rows back from Calista, who sat starboard. At Calista's side lay Acuzio, Professor Wolff's husky, dozing. His fur had been shaved right down. Even in the shade as they were, the heat was sweltering. They had stayed in Manaus, the large capital city of the Amazonas – a surprising metropolis gateway to the jungle. It contained luxury condos next to a sprawling shanty town of Indios – indigenous people who had relocated there to flee from civil strife, or to be close to medical help, or try for a better life. But the shanty was nothing more than a collection of rickety shacks on mud, festering with heaps of rubbish and disillusionment – with crime lords roving about, pulling the strings.

While the group stayed in the much more decent, tourist part of Manaus, Calista complained non-stop – and on the ferry Jemima was worried that she would not take well to the jungle. 'I just don't think she'll cope,' Jemima told Jake, widening her eyes so that they looked bluer than ever.

'I thought she'd been doing pretty well, considering,' said Jake. Right on cue, a series of high-pitched screeches startled them, and they looked over to find Calista manically batting at a flying bug with her fan, screaming.

Jemima turned back to Jake with raised eyebrows. 'You were saying...?'

Jake grinned and shrugged. 'On the whole, that is. Anyway, we couldn't very well leave her in Manaus.'

Jemima fidgeted awkwardly. 'Well, it's too late now,' she said, glancing over at Calista and crossing her arms. The bug that had been plaguing Calista flew, rattling, toward them, and then veered across the water – heading for the jungle. 'Fulgora Laternaria,' said Jemima, watching it disappear.

Jake frowned. 'Pardon?'

'The insect. Otherwise known as a flying lantern.'

'Oh, right.' But he was distracted, looking over at Calista.

Jemima sighed wearily. 'I can tell you want to go to her.'

'It's just that–'

'You don't have to explain,' she cut in. 'She's your girlfriend – so go! Don't worry about me, I've got this big guy to keep me company.' She turned and smiled sweetly at the man sitting directly behind them, Gerard, one of Sanderson's men.

Jake didn't need telling twice. 'I'm coming back later to check on you,' he told her as he got up. He shimmied past the rest of the row of people, and went back to Calista.

Jemima draped her elbow on the back of the empty seat. 'Now, Gerry,' she said, twisting round to look at the guard. He was stocky and well-built, yet had oddly delicate features and fine cheekbones. 'You're never going to tell me your surname, are you...? Top secret and all that.'

Gerard raised an enigmatic eyebrow. 'Would it make a difference if I did?' he said, his voice was surprisingly refined.

'It's just that... I don't think we can really be friends if I only know your first name,' said Jemima in earnest.

Gerard looked over the crowds of people, as if searching for a name. 'Smith,' he said eventually. 'My name's Gerard Smith.'

Jemima thought about it. 'Okay... and I'm guessing John over there,' she nodded toward the other bodyguard, sitting behind Calista. 'I'm guessing he's Smith too? John Smith.'

Gerard nodded enthusiastically. 'Not for nothing they call you kids ingenious!'

Jemima mock laughed, 'Ha-ha! Very funny.' She turned her back on him, and reached for her backpack, rummaging for her book, 'Probability and Our Wondrous Universe' by T.G. Evans. As she flicked through to the page she'd got to, she stole a glance at the couple. Calista was fanning Acuzio while resting her head on Jake's shoulder, and Jake had draped a reassuring arm around her. They were sitting in silence, or perhaps talking quietly – she couldn't tell. It was an endearing and perfect picture of two people in love, yet still, she felt a sudden pang in her heart. She tore her eyes away and looked down at the book, grappling with a raft of emotions that she barely understood. It took her several minutes before she was able to concentrate on reading.

Before long they arrived at the Rio Branco, where they disembarked to find a smaller boat waiting, organised by the guide to take them upriver. About two hours later, they arrived at the animal sanctuary just as the light was starting to fade, weary from the long day of travelling, and fighting off the tiny blue midges biting through their trousers. They came to a cluster of houses on three-metre-high stilts, with a warming light glowing through the windows of the largest one. There was even a chicken coop on stilts. By the time they climbed the steps to reach the main door of the lighted house, their presence had been noticed, and the door was already opening. A stout, round-faced man peaked out from behind the door, an expectant look on his face. He held up a torch, and it glared into each of their faces. A beautiful frizzy-haired girl, a younger girl, a good-looking young man, and three burly men. At their heels sat a stunning husky, panting.

The man broke out in a smile, shouting out to someone behind him, 'No te preocupes, Alma! It's them.' And then to the visitors, he said heartily, 'Come in, come in.' When he stepped aside, they saw that a woman was standing behind him with a loaded gun. Pointed right at them. She relaxed, smiled awkwardly, put the safety latch on, and quickly stashed it away. Then she went to a cupboard, and pulled out a book from a drawer. She held it to her chest as the teenagers and Sanderson entered. The other two men stayed outside, guarding the entrance.

Sanderson looked at them suspiciously. 'It sounds as if you've been expecting us?'

The couple looked at each other, and the woman said, 'Please, sit down. I'm sure you must be exhausted from your journey. We will get you something to drink.'

'Yes, yes,' said the man. 'I will get some drinks.' And he hobbled off purposefully.

The place was sparsely furnished, though chaotically messy, with clothes, bags, medical instruments, and equipment, scattered all over the place. The fug of citronella burners hung in the air. The woman quickly cleared some things away, and Calista and Jake sat next to each other on rattan chairs, while Jemima perched on a stool. Sanderson remained standing, casing out the place.

Ignacio returned with a tray full of Inca Kola bottles filled with bright yellow liquid. He flipped off the lids with an opener, and handed them out. Disappearing again, he returned with a bowl of water for the dog, who lapped it up immediately. Ignacio stroked him. 'My, what a handsome boy!'

The woman said to the visitors, 'My name is Alma, and that is my husband, Ignacio.' She sat down on a creaky old stool. She had a kindly face, framed by short black hair.

Jemima jumped up and went to shake their hands. 'Pleased to meet you, Alma, Ignacio,' she said, ever polite. But she looked around. 'Is... is there anyone else?'

Again, the couple glanced at each other, and Ignacio went to fetch a device from a sideboard. 'We have a daughter, Saffie. She's 17,' he told them. 'But... she went for a trek in the jungle, just over two days ago. We were tracking her with this,' he held up the little black instrument that looked like a walkie-talkie but with a large screen. Worry creased his face.

'Though, just a few hours earlier, her signal went dead… I checked the device, and it is working properly with other trackers, just not hers.'

'Who else was with her?' asked Sanderson.

Alma sighed. 'That's the thing… she went alone.'

Sanderson grimaced with disbelief. 'You let your 16-year-old daughter go into the jungle *alone*?!'

They looked at him strangely. 'You… don't know about Saffie then?' was all Alma said.

Puzzled, Jemima asked, 'What do you mean? What should we know about her?'

'We thought… we thought you knew about her… ways,' said Ignacio. He took a chair and set it down next to his wife.

'They don't know, Ignacio,' Alma said to her husband. 'You'd better tell them.'

Ignacio nodded, turning to them. 'Ever since she was a little girl, Saffie loved animals with a passion. A *passion*! And they always seemed to love her back. At first, we thought it was just domesticated animals, but then, when she was five, we'd left her playing outside,' he waved a hand toward the door. 'Our friend, Vivi, had brought her son, of a similar age to Saffie, and she was watching the two play together, while we worked inside. But… when I came out to check on them, I saw that Vivi had fallen asleep, and an army of bullet ants was marching across the ground…' He looked at Sanderson in earnest. 'By the time I ran to them, the ants had swarmed over the little boy, stinging him all over. He screamed so much! I… the only thing I could think of was hosing them off him with water, so that Vivi could grab him, and bring him into the house. That poor child! He was in agony for days.'

Alma stepped in. 'I'd run out as soon as I heard the screaming. And I saw… I saw with my own eyes as the ants marched completely around Saffie, while they attacked the other child, Lucas, who was sitting next to her. Vivi herself got multiple bites on her feet when she ran to pick him up. Ignacio too. But Saffie… not even one.'

The teenagers looked at each other in amazement.

Alma sighed. 'That was when we really understood how… special she was.'

They fell into silence for some time, until Ignacio said, 'We are naturalists, my wife and I. And we often go on long treks through the jungle, not just to observe and document the flora, the fauna, but also to help injured animals. When Saffie was old enough to go with us, we noticed that, while we came home covered in bites and stings, she wouldn't have a mark on her. She is somehow... infallible.'

'To *most* things,' Alma emphasised, looking from her husband to the visitors. 'And we still don't know if there are some animals she might not be okay with. Like snakes, for example... You understand it's not something we would wish to test. But to be honest, almost everything we've come across in the jungle gives her a wide berth, or is perfectly harmless to her. And – bless her! – from a very early age, Saffie learnt very quickly to "utilise" her... affinity with animals. Whenever people found injured wild animals, and brought them here for treatment, we discovered she had a calming effect on them. Sometimes, we didn't even need to tranquillise the creatures, we just let Saffie stroke them, and talk to them, and they would stop being afraid. Pretty soon, and behind our backs, she was going right into their cages to give the recovering animals food. We only found this out later. Once, she had gone inside the jaguars' cage, which we discovered only after, when we found her sleeping on one of them. Now, these were not tame jaguars. They had been kept in captivity most of their lives, and were almost... unstable, mentally. They were certainly unpredictable, which made them even more dangerous. But Saffie always fed them, and even hugged them. And they never, ever hurt her. Not once did they even growl at her.'

Jemima was bursting with excitement. 'We know someone else who is like your daughter,' she told them. 'His name is Tai, and he has a way with animals too.' She was certain now that this Saffie was an Ingenious child, and clasped her hands together, thrilled. 'We must find her!'

'Do you know where she went?' asked Sanderson.

'Yes, yes. There is a rough map that Saffie memorised before she left. I'll go get it...' He disappeared, and returned with a crumpled scrap of paper. On it were crudely-drawn directions in faint biro, made by the curandero. 'We were packing. Getting ready to go out to search for her first thing tomorrow morning. And then you came.'

Alma remembered the thing she was hugging to her chest, holding on to it for dear life. Her fingers loosened unwillingly from its edges. 'Here,' she said, passing it to Sanderson. 'She wanted us to give you this.'

Sanderson blinked at her, not understanding what she had just said. 'I'm sorry, but... how could she know we were coming? She doesn't know of us. And our mission was supposed to be top secret.' He glanced briefly at Calista, who he'd learnt couldn't keep a secret to save her life. Not even a government secret of national importance.

Alma pushed the book onto him. 'She told us you would ask that, and that you will need to read the book to understand.'

Jemima jumped up and stood next to Sanderson, holding out her hand. 'May I?' she asked sweetly. Sanderson nodded, and she took the book. Jake and Calista got up and huddled around her as she opened the dark brown leather cover. The first page read, 'The Book of You', and Jemima's skin tingled. She leafed through several pages, and saw a record of a series of dates and times, followed by frantic scribbles. Jemima spent a few minutes deciphering the handwriting, and then skimmed through several pages.

But Calista couldn't read a word. 'I thought *my* handwriting was bad!' she smirked. She glanced up at the parents. 'Sorry!'

'No problem,' smiled Ignacio. 'Even we have to stare at the words for quite a while before we can understand them. We love Saffie very much, but she never really took to academic studies, to writing or reading. She was always very slow that way.'

They fell into silence for some time, until Jemima eventually looked up from the book, saying, 'Oh. My. Goodness!' She glanced at Sanderson, Jake, and Calista. 'This is about us!! The Book of You. It's us!' She held out a page to show them, again bursting with excitement, which, to be fair, was most of the time. 'Look at this,' she said, stabbing the page. 'This entry talks about an evil boy who hides what he really is...'

'Karl,' said Calista, wide-eyed.

Jemima nodded. 'I think so too! And another entry talks about an old man who can't see, and his companion who can't hear.'

They all stared at her, astonished. A look of realisation appeared on Jemima's face, and she turned to Jake and Calista. 'I think I understand! Tai needs to touch people to find out what they're thinking and feeling, but Saffie… she doesn't need touch at all. She can do it over distances!'

'Can she do that for everybody. Like, for us?' asked Jake.

'No, I don't think so,' Jemima replied, leafing through the pages. 'The entries I read mentioned only the Ingenious children – and she only knew about the Professor and the Chauffeur through *our* interactions with them. What she writes down is quite ambiguous. Just abstract thoughts and feelings really. There are no specifics, no details. But I'd need to read the whole book to get a fuller picture.'

Sanderson turned to Alma and Ignacio. 'This is how you knew we were coming?'

They smiled. 'Yes, she told us about a handsome young couple, an angel-faced girl, and some security men, who were making a long trip to come find her. And here you are! She also told us we could trust you, because you were linked to the same scientific programme where she was born. That's why we thought you knew about her ways with animals. Actually, she's been scribbling things here and there for some time now. But, about three-four months ago, she started writing even more furiously, for long periods at a time. Did something happen to you then?'

Jemima nodded slowly, thoughtfully. That was when the Professor had gathered them together into Avernus, Karl had come into their lives, and the four Ingenious children had 'looked' into his disturbed mind, to try and find out about the cure. But with tragic consequences. 'Something bad happened,' was all she told them, looking away. She needed to change the subject. 'I think we should go with you to find her,' she told them. 'Especially now we know she has a special connection with us… with me.'

Alma thought of something. 'So, does it work both ways? Can *you* hear what she's thinking? That might help us find her.'

Jemima shook her head. 'I'm sorry, no. We were all born with different abilities.'

The couple waited, staring at her expectantly.

Jemima suddenly realised. 'Oh! What *I* can do is crazy! When I touch something, or someone, I can "feel" how long they've got to live…'

Ignacio gulped. 'My! That is… very unusual.'

'And very daunting,' said Alma, thinking she had best avoid touching the girl.

Sanderson said, 'Well, I suggest we prepare to go out into the jungle first thing tomorrow.'

Jemima glanced at Calista. 'Cal... do you think you're up for it? If not, it might be best if you stay here. I mean, it's going to be wild out there. Savage, in fact. The heat, the bugs, the snakes... Can't imagine what it'll do to your hair!'

Calista gulped, and turned to Jake. 'A-are you going?'

He nodded slowly at first, then more certainly as he thought about it. 'Yes, I will. I need to see this through.'

'That means I'm coming too,' said Calista. She turned to Jemima. 'The question is, are *you* up for it, shrimp?'

'Course I am,' she said, sniffing, and ignoring the name-calling. 'Me and Jake are a team...'

'Ladies!' said Jake, stepping forward.

Just then, a rooster crowed several times, and Ignacio looked at his watch. 'Henry's telling us it's time for bed... Whoever's coming with us tomorrow, we need to wake up at 5.30 to prepare for the journey, then leave at sunrise.'

'Henry?' asked Jake.

'Yes, the rooster. He crows every night at around 10pm, like clockwork. He's a night owl... actually, a chicken... well, you know what I mean!' He said.

'And will he wake us up tomorrow as well?' asked Calista.

The couple smiled at each other. 'Not quite,' said Ignacio. 'Henry's not a morning bird. In the morning, he kind of just crows like crazy at any time that takes his fancy. Sometimes 3 a.m., sometimes 6 or 8 a.m. So be warned!'

Calista tensed. She needed her beauty sleep, otherwise, like Henry, she too would be grisly and grumpy in the morning. She tried to remember where she had packed her earplugs.

'I'll prepare some beds for you,' said Alma, leaving the room.

Ignacio followed her, 'I'll help you, my dear.'

Just as predicted, Henry the rooster woke them up at around 4 a.m., crowing and screaming his head off manically, though Calista slept through it all with her earplugs and eye-mask. Sanderson, who had slept in a separate hut with his men, and took turns to keep night watch, was up straight away. And Jake, then Jemima, stirred awake too, having shared Calista's hut.

Alma and Ignacio were not quite adept with all of the curandero's ways, as was Saffie, so instead, they brought plenty of dry biscuits and water for the journey, kitting out the others with everything they would need too.

They left the sanctuary in the care of their hired workers, and Alma, Ignacio, and the others embarked on their journey – first by boat to the same point where they had left Saffie three days earlier, then hiking through the jungle, following the tracker's recorded trail. Acuzio panted constantly from the muggy heat, and on his back he wore a holster bearing his water bowl, dog biscuits, several bottles of water, and a first-aid kit. In time, they were led to the place where Saffie had camped for the night, and they camped there too.

In the morning they set off early again, so that by the afternoon they had reached the point where the signal was lost, at the first tepui, when Saffie had hidden from the natives. Fortunately the crudely-drawn map from the curandero showed that there was a second mountain, at the parting of the waters, and they continued walking on until it was reached. With more of them needing to cross the water safely, they searched for a sure way to cross, following the river that hugged the base of the mountain, and walking straight past the tree trunk that Saffie herself had used. About 600 metres further along, they discovered a trunk that straddled the full width of the water, and first Sanderson crossed, with a rope tied around him, eventually securing the rope to a tree on the other side. And then the rest of them walked over the tree, holding firmly onto the rope. But they did not know of the secret passage that the native and his sister had revealed to Saffie. Instead, they circumnavigated the base of the mountain, trudging through the undergrowth, and wondering how on earth she had climbed the mountain. They searched and searched for a way to ascend – a path, a track – but to no avail.

Alma was becoming more and more desperate, and she finally sat on a log, at last succumbing to tears. Ignacio tried to comfort her. 'We must pray, mi amor. Have faith that God will help us find her. She must be up there, and we will find a way.'

But Alma just kept crying.

Sanderson tilted his head back to look right up the vertical pitch of the escarpment, shading his eyes, and swatting at mosquitoes. Even he, a seasoned climber, would find it impossible to scale because of the crumbling sandstone. He scratched his head and looked around, dumbfounded. It was as if she had vanished completely.

Meanwhile, down by his feet, planted firmly in the undergrowth, millions of organisms in the soil's biome were at work. They were able, in a matter of hours, to remove any remnants of human traces. Saffie's traces. Her sweat, globs of spit, dead skin cells, urine, faeces. Every last vestige of her assimilated by armies of termites, butterflies, ants, beetles, flies, as well as bacteria and fungi, so that there was nothing left on the soil or foliage for Acuzio to sniff out.

Sanderson's feet paced up and down, aimless. Stirring the creatures that roamed, hidden, beneath him...

295

'Realise that everything connects to everything else.'

Leonardo da Vinci

32 A SAVAGE CHAIN REACTION

He ran through the undergrowth, breathless, and trembling with terror.

Tilting his triangular head, he tried to discern the huge creature that was chasing him with supernatural speed. The single ultrasonic ear buried in the middle of his chest prickled with sensitivity as he crashed and slid through the jungle. Frantically, he fluttered the small wings on his back, but they were useless for flying, and barely lifted four of his feet from the ground. Instead he jumped from leaves to twigs. Nervous, clumsy jumps. He could sense the predator was gaining ground. Twisting his neck, he just about discerned the menacing form of it with his bulbous, stereoscopic eyes. Long antennae twitching with fear.

But he was fast tiring. Having only just grown out of and moulted from his last exoskeleton, his legs and arms were still soft, his footing wobbly, unsure. He managed to stretch and heave himself onto a higher plane: a leaf that swayed uncertainly, arguing with the wind. To his surprise, he found there another of his kind. A female praying mantid. She was much larger than him, and serenely beautiful – glowing with green, the exact shade of the leaf on which she stood.

To his amazement, she turned toward the predator, and reared up on her hind legs, lifting forelegs above her head, outward, in a stance that unnerved even him. Her femurs, like jagged claws, rose threateningly into the air, and she swayed softly from side to side. She was all at once terrifying, hypnotic, ravishing.

His skittish feet jostled round to behold the immense jumping spider that had stopped right in front of them, and for the first time, he saw it in all its awful glory. Its two principal eyes, black and shiny, and level with the leaf, stared up at the female – alarmed. Its hairy pedipalp stroked the air with wariness. One of its tarsi had reached for the leaf they were on, tilting them, but now slowly withdrew. And with a whoosh the spider suddenly vanished, jumping off and away – not wanting to court disaster. Leaving them in favour of a less frightening meal.

Alone now, the male mantid turned toward his saviour, and watched as she gracefully descended from her defensive stance. Of course he knew that it was just a bluff. Mantids had no chemical defence, no poison to deter predators, so instead, and as a last resort, they reared themselves up, pretending to be more fearsome, more deadly, than they really were. Now that he had seen her do it, the image of that defence posture was burnt indelibly in his brain.

The two stood face to face. And he looked up at her with vague feelings of admiration, gratitude, relief... and a sudden desire to mate. Carefully, he manoeuvred around, and she did not move when he scrambled up onto her back, clutching her thorax. She froze, stiffened. And sensing her apprehension, he stroked long feelers on the back of her head to calm her as he mated.

In time, she stretched her flexible neck up and around, to see. Her palp extending, reaching for him. When their mouths touched, it seemed as though they were kissing – but her powerful mandibles soon tore into his face, jaws crunching into him with a ravenous appetite, clamping open and shut. Working her way through, devouring his entire head.

Yet he did not fight her, did not resist. And even as he was being decapitated, his body continued to mate – a smaller brain in his abdomen kicking in to complete the process. He had made the ultimate sacrifice, allowing himself to be eaten, for the greater good of producing offspring. For the good of his species.

With the headless body still on her back, the female began cleaning herself, for she was meticulous about cleanliness. Mandibles brushed over her femurs and tibiae – with palp, like external tongues, wiping her mouth clean. Her forearms extended over her triangular head and wiped that too, gliding over the hard chitin. Sated, she shed the body on her back, and rested. Over the next days, she gorged on more of him, fattening herself in readiness of fertilising her precious eggs with the dead mantid's carefully-stored sperm.

Eventually, the female praying mantid's abdomen swelled, and she knew that her due time had come. She turned and carefully worked her way along the stem that the leaf was connected to – in search for a good solid twig, to suspend herself upside-down from. Only then would she begin laying her eggs over the course of several days. Eggs made from the male mantid, and that had cost him his life......

The ogre-faced spider lay in wait – ravenous, but patient.

It did not sit at the side of a conventional wheel-shaped web, hiding itself under a leaf. Instead, it was suspended from a tree – in plain sight – within the scaffolding of an A-shaped frame of webbing. Still as a statue.

Usually, being out in the open in the jungle meant almost certain death. Predators were everywhere. From keen-sighted, feathery monsters that swooped and screeched through the air, to inky, shadow-like mammoths, pacing the jungle with eyes that glowed eerily in the dark. But the spider was confident of its camouflage: its spindly body was like a collection of dangling twigs – fading, invisibly, against a background of black-brown bark.

It kept its cool, hanging upside down.

Shorter back legs skated along a single line of silk that was still attached to its rear. Four long forelegs folding inward – each claw clasping tightly onto a corner of a pale-blue rectangular net. The spider was proud of the design of its ingenious web. For this, it had teased out multiple strands from its spinnerets, and combined them into one – meticulously back-brushing them into crinkled, fluffed lines that were highly elastic.

As it lay in waiting, two posterior median eyes glinted dully in the moonlight, like brown goggles – they were the largest eyes of any spider, hypersensitive to light, giving it excellent vision as it hunted at night.

When the female praying mantid crept quietly by, triggering a radial thread, the spider lunged downward in a forward strike, stretching its elastic net around her, bagging her up. The webbing silk was glueless, but the brushed fibres entangled the mantid's bristled legs as she fought back. It was impossible to break free.

The ogre-faced spider quickly scuttled in to inspect its prey, triumphant with the catch. The sight of food triggered hunger pangs, making it salivate a recipe for death, priming fangs with venom. It moved in, sinking those fangs into the mantid, and injecting the deadliest of poisons.

Slowly the venom took effect, and the mantid's futile struggling began to slow. The spider worked through the night, at top speed, spinning silk around the mantid in a neatly parcelled ball. Infinite patience and hours of hard work were soon to be rewarded. By now, its stomach growled with hunger. And when the mantid finally stilled, the spider lunged with terrifying voracity onto its prey and spat acid-like digestive juices onto it. At last, it was able to slurp up the delicious, liquified innards. Savouring each sip, and relishing its midnight feast.

When it was done, the spider slowly withdrew – swaying slightly, as though drunk, with a full stomach and fatigue. It crept underneath the curled leaf of a nearby orchid. The flower's scent was strong, its heady perfume filled the air, lulling it to sleep, just as the morning light began to ascend……

The orchid undulated enticingly in the breeze.

There was something beguiling about the delicate pinky-yellow of its petals, and the deep curves that shaped them. But mostly the scent, reminiscent of vanilla and nutmeg, that spilled out into the morning like a rousing perfume, calling for the only thing that could pollinate it. The male orchid bee. The flower's scent was designed to attract only that kind of insect.

When just such a bee zoomed nearby, the small creature was immediately drawn to the orchid, changing course to land on its waxy petals. The bee itself was beautiful, with compound eyes like domed mirrors, and fringes of hairs against a metallic blue-green body – a glinting jewel in the hazy morning sun. With its exceptionally long tongue that curled under the full length of its body, it had been collecting scent oils for weeks, storing them in spongey pouches on wide hind legs. A perfume mix that would enable it to attract a female, its one mission in life.

But the orchid flower was a cunning trap, storing the proffered scent oils below a domed hood. And when the bee moved under the hood to harvest them, the waxy surface made the insect slip into the bulbous bucket directly underneath, half-filled with fluid. Within it floated the carcasses of other bees before him...

The little bee fought and struggled with the viscous liquid, trying to climb back the way it came, but downward-pointing hairs on the orchid's inner surface made it impossible to backtrack. Instead, small, raised knobs, like steps, at the rear of the bucket, lured the bee into a spout-shaped chamber, just large enough for it to pass through. But the chamber contracted, holding the bee firmly in place. With the orchid in its male phase, it secreted just the right amount of glue onto the bee's back – too much would hinder the bee's ability to fly, and too little would defeat the purpose. Then, two small orange-coloured sacs packed with pollen were pressed onto it; a precious backpack. Yet still, the orchid did not relax its hold, it kept the bee hostage until the glue had set perfectly, the pollen sacs firmly stuck – it was the only pollen the flower would ever produce. And only after the allotted drying time did the orchid loosen, allowing the bee to fly off.

The little creature was undeterred by the trap, falling, literally, for the same species of orchid again and again. And when it chanced upon an orchid in its female phase, the flower hooked the pollen sacs from the bee's back, triggering fertilisation, and ensuring another generation of the plant. The orchid and the orchid bee were made for each other – partners in pollination.

The orchid bee continued on its merry way. Spending weeks collecting and mixing fragrances; the designer of its own brand of perfume. But it was overeager. It landed on the gnarled bark of a tree, and fanned the unique smells from its leg pouches into the air, buzzing constantly – veined wings a blur. Three or four female bees passed, but his perfume was not quite good enough, and they could not be tempted by his special scent. And so the little bee pottered off to collect more fragrance oils from flowers – for, to the females, his worth was defined by the scents he carried.

As it flew, the bee spied a particularly vicious kind of wasp, well-known for its carnivorous ferocity, heading its way. Quickly it changed course, cautiously giving the wasp a very wide berth......

The wasp only vaguely noticed the passing orchid bee – its attention had been caught by something else. It descended and circled some foliage that overhung the still backwaters of the river, keen eyes spying a clutch of frog's eggs clinging to a leaf. Glistening, transparent globs, almost invisible against the leaf-shine and the rippling reflections bouncing off the water's surface. Yet the wasp's large eyes, nearly as big as its head, had spied the wriggle of tasty tadpoles within. And so it buzzed around the tree several times, working up the courage to attack; there was no such thing as easy pickings in the jungle.

The male frog was the sole keeper of the spawn. Passing female frogs had appeared briefly, laying the newest egg clutches systematically above the previous ones on the vertically-dangling leaf – and when they were done, the females simply left with a shameless glint in their eyes, never to be seen again... The male frog eyed them as they came and went, without protest, except for the odd croak or ribbit – quietly taking up his position at the top of the leaf, where the youngest, most vulnerable eggs were. Strong suckers under his feet practically glued him to the spot, even as he slept.

The dappled circular markings on his back looked similar to the jelly-like eggs, making him a brave decoy; a single wasp sting could easily kill him. But he remained firm, holding his position valiantly – so that when the hungry wasp descended, landing on the frog instead of the spawn, in the blink of an eye the frog's powerful hind-legs kicked it off, catapulting the wasp in a downward spiral into the water.

But soon, more wasps came. Too many for the frog to deal with. One by one the assaulters landed on the precious eggs and dug into each globe of jelly with powerful mandibles, sucking out a floundering tadpole, devouring it whole. The tadpoles, triggered by the vibrations of the predatory attack, began shivering inside their cases – and in a desperate bid to survive, the tiny larvae wriggled free and dropped into the river – landing in the water like plinks of rainfall. Premature, but at least alive.

The lone tree frog battled the wasp strike with valour. And at last, in time, the attack subsided – and the lurching leaf eventually stilled.

Many of the tadpoles on it, and the male frog, had survived.

At least for now……

The tiny ant seemed lost and helpless, wandering by itself in the undergrowth.

It was oblivious to the two vicious margays that fought above it – their fawn fur, marbled with black, coalescing into a blur as they threw themselves at each other, hissing, spitting, yowling. Heedless, the ant sauntered carefree underneath them – narrowly missing being speared by unsheathed claws, or crushed by their thudding bodies.

The solitary ant found a good tree by the backwaters, and casually climbed it, stopping at a particular leaf. The male tree frog's leaf. The ant stroked the waxy cuticle with the tip of a tarsus, tilted its head, and caressed the air with its antennae – assessing the worth of the foliage, the location of the tree, the taste of the breeze. But it sensed that the tree was too open to the wind and rain, and too close to deep waters, for its colony to forage safely there. Reluctantly, the ant turned to go, for the leaves were good ones. And so the tiny insect descended to continue its search. The tree frog had no idea that its spawn had once again been spared.

In time, the ant found a sturdy tree, with fresh foliage – which it deemed to be just right. It went to one of the leaves, latched a hind leg on the edge, and pivoted round as its powerful, jagged-edged mandibles cut out a crescent. The sap of the leaf was sweet and fresh, and it drank in as much as it could into a secondary stomach, the social stomach, saving the juice for its colony.

Silently the tiny ant turned and made its way back to the nest, its rear dragging against the ground, laying down a scent trail that marked the way. When the scout descended into the hubbub of the underground nest, it was greeted by forager ants, who swarmed around it, eager to taste. One by one, the scout 'kissed' them, regurgitating the sap from its stomach for them to relish, gently tapping the top of their heads with its antennae, as if to say, 'There you are, now go'. The chemical communication gradually informed the thousands of foragers: the ritual was their instruction, the sap, a taste of what they were to forage, and the scent trail, their map.

Within minutes, lines of foragers spilled out from the holes of their nest, following the scout's laid-down pheromones. Pouring through the undergrowth. And within hours, ant superhighways were established, going back and forth from nest to tree, with no congestion, no hold-ups.

Each returning ant carried a sizeable piece of leaf, and some of them even had one of the smallest ants in the colony, a minim, riding on their backs. They fought off pesky hump-backed flies – horrific parasites that persisted on laying their eggs in the ants' necks. The larva would burrow right inside the ant's head, feed on it, and then pupate there, while the unfortunate host ant instinctively left to protect the nest, dying outside, alone. In time, a fully-formed fly would emerge from the dead ant's mouth. The tiny minim therefore, with a span of less than a millimetre, formed a brave first line of defence against the huge parasitic flies. Hefty soldier ants were the second defence, the largest of the workers, hovering protectively around the periphery of the nest, and toing and froing along the lines of foragers.

The colony consisted of millions of ants, yet they worked together as a single living, breathing, entity......

The pygmy antwrens swept along the undergrowth, following the lines of leafcutter ants with keen interest. Though it was not the ants themselves that held their attention.

The two bright-eyed birds were inseparable, and when they flew from their suspended nest each morning – creamy-orange bodies, with a black-and-white head, back, and wings – they called to each other shrilly, their voices chiming in concert with the dawn serenade. They even bathed together, dipping bright plumage in a pool of water, throwing up glittering showers as they fanned their wings dry. Sometimes they hopped onto a swell of ants, stretching their wings and dancing, as angered soldier ants squirted sprays of formic acid up at them in defence. The birds happily rubbed themselves onto the acid as it rid them of pesky parasites; the inevitable ant bites a small price to pay for such benefits.

The wrens were one of the smallest of the antbirds, barely larger than a golf-ball and weighing less than an ounce, yet their short, rounded wings gave them excellent flight manoeuvrability – and as they swooped low over the ground, following the trail of leafcutter ants, they soon reached the tree that the tiny foragers were systematically stripping of foliage. A tree that, by the end of the day, will have been decimated entirely. The two antwrens alighted on a nearby branch, watching keenly, not the ants, but the foliage – for the birds knew that wherever the ants foraged, a plethora of insects were bound to be flushed out. Soon they saw spiders, praying mantids, stick insects, and centipedes scurrying from the bush, driven out by the ant army. And the two tiny antwrens revelled in a feeding frenzy......

The lone butterfly meandered through the shadowy jungle, like the lightest of poetical emotions, like a flutter of petals thrown up and tossed on the breeze.

She found a patch of leaves aflame with sunshine that poured as golden streams through a gap in the canopy. The butterfly alighted on one of the leaves, and spread her wings flat in the spotlight, trembling and basking in the warmth. Warmth that would soon give her the energy to fly again. Wings of lilac fading into pale-blue, were spotted and edged with black. And her large compound eyes soaked in the ultraviolet light, enabling her to see in a spectrum of colours – the world around her blazing and glowing with brilliance.

The lone creature was a collector of chemicals, flitting from flower to plant, salivating onto leaves and licking up the sap, or uncoiling its long proboscis to needle deep into flowers' nectaries. Each chemical was a necessity: the sap of poisonous plants would in turn make her poisonous, a deterrent against predators, and other compounds would nourish and hydrate her.

She seemed elegantly serene, though every stage of her four lives – from egg to caterpillar, chrysalis to butterfly – was plagued by parasites, birds, insects, dehydration, disease.

Even now, as she rested, a pair of antwrens descended out of nowhere, screeching. One of them pecked at her, lifting her into the air. But the butterfly managed to struggle free, tearing the edge of her forewing from the bird's beak. She landed back on the leaf and quickly pressed both wings together, so that the dull colouring of her underwings camouflaged her. The birds swooped around in a circle, searching for her, but she had vanished. And so the antwrens left, leaving in their wake the gift of a smattering of droppings. When it was safe, the butterfly quietly fluttered down and alighted on one of the droppings, siphoning up the valuable nutrients and minerals, before flying off once more. The broken wing hardly hampered her flight.

Before long, she found herself courted by a flurry of males of her kind. They flew above her in a rainbow of colours, battling with each other, and shaking pheromone showers, laced with a powerful aphrodisiac, onto her. Her antennae smelled and tasted each individual scent chemical, and she suddenly felt an overwhelming urge to mate. The males needn't have fought, for she allowed them, one by one, to pair with her.

After that, she became obsessed with a single will: she must lay her eggs.

She fluttered up into the air to search for a safe place to deposit them, the underside of a branch, a sheltered leaf, or even a spider's web, knowing that her eggs would be safe there. But the wind was strong, and it carried her over a large, long body of fast-flowing water, that threw up rafts of air currents, making her careen this way and that – until she was halted by a rocky vertical incline that loomed so tall it disappeared into the sky. And so she fluttered and bounced and skirted along the mountainous wall. Before long, her eyes were dazzled by the bright white of a sandy beach, and as she floated down toward it, her long antennae found that the air was ripe with the promise of vital nutrients – minerals that she desperately needed, to give her energy to lay. She descended onto the sand, where she was rewarded with a smattering of sticky, dark-red droplets. By now exhausted, she stayed there for some time, licking up the food that was infused with the tang of iron. Soon other butterflies appeared and swarmed around her.

But there came the thundering roar of a giant furred creature, leaping and bounding toward her. The monster was followed by the rumble and boom of humans shouting. The ground beneath quaked, and her entire body juddered with vibrations. Quickly, she ascended into the air, flitting away from danger. Higher and higher. Flying as fast as her damaged wing would take her. She flew and flew for what seemed an age, not knowing where she was going, tossed and jostled by the wind.

When she dared to descend again, a snake uncoiled from the branch of a tree and snapped at her – and so the hapless butterfly arose once more. Flying on.

Eventually calm descended just as she grew faint with weakness. But her antennae twitched with the fear of something strange, something terrible, something completely out of the ordinary.

She drifted down, weighted by the ache of tired wings, and gravid with eggs. But the vivid colours of the jungle had suddenly dissolved away – replaced, instead, by an astonishing sight: an endless terrain of black, punctuated by columns of grey smoke, stinging her eyes. Flame-red sparks growled around her, confusing her. And as she alighted on a smoking leaf, intense heat singed her feet, and both the leaf and her feet disintegrated into ash. She tumbled onto the ground, her wings melting into charred earth. Her large eyes, orbs of delicately etched glass, darkened with foreboding.

Lying there, alone, a fleeting speck of colour in a vast blackness, she was unable to move as heat surged through her body. She could only gaze upwards – searching for the reassuring kaleidoscopic colours of the sky, and the sun that warmed her. But there were only swirling mists – all at once murky, and dark, and leaden. Billowing around. Engulfing her.

The scorched land had become her apocalypse. Her end of days. And as the helpless butterfly lay, dying, in the dirt – heat tearing through her, consciousness fading – she tried to make sense of what was happening. But there was no way she could even begin to understand. No way she could grasp how her world could have become so suddenly, so completely, and so horribly annihilated.

33 JOURNEY OF DISCOVERY

"Acuzio, heel!! Heel, Acuzio!!" shouted Sanderson.

But the dog had bolted away from them, running toward a swarm of butterflies that had alighted on the sandy white beach, in a cluster. When Acuzio jumped and barked at them, the butterflies burst upward, exploding into a spectrum of colour, and gently fluttering away. The dog watched one in particular, its lilac-blue wing torn on one edge, as it flew higher and higher into the sky.

By the time Sanderson had reached Acuzio, the dog was sniffing the ground with great interest, circling around. Sanderson stooped down to inspect the sand. Just discernible was a smattering of deep-red smudges. 'Blood,' he murmured to himself, standing up; the viscous liquid had not been exposed to the usual barrages of insects, fungi, and bacteria in the soil of the jungle, and had lain on the sand unnoticed, except for the butterflies. Sanderson turned to see that Acuzio had picked up a scent trail, and he followed him.

The others noticed what was happening, and trailed behind.

They were led to a tree, and Ignacio noticed something on the ground: a spent match and globs of dry yellow resin. His eyes lit up, and he picked them up, sniffing the hardened gum. 'It is copal resin,' he said, 'and this looks very much like a waterproof matchstick of the kind I gave Saffie.' He drew closer to the tree to inspect the bark. 'She has melted off the copal, which is particularly used for burning, for its aroma...'

'Like incense?' asked Calista.

'Yes, like incense,' he said.

Jake scratched his head. 'Why would she be burning incense out here?'

Jemima had an idea. 'Maybe she was burning it, not for the fragrance, but for heat? Or light?'

'That's it – she made a torch!' said Alma.

Ignacio scratched his head. 'But she wouldn't have gone up the mountain at night…'

Sanderson thought of something. 'Since we haven't found any kind of path up the mountain, maybe there's another way, that requires light?'

'Yes, yes! There might be some kind of entrance, rather than a path!' exclaimed Ignacio. He turned to watch Acuzio. The dog was still sniffing the ground keenly, then stopped to look at them, whining – wanting them to follow him. 'Our friend has caught her scent,' he told them. 'We must make some torches too. I would say four or five, given the height of the mesa – and then we should follow the dog to find the entrance.' He started looking around, and went off to pick up a dry piece of wood.

The others followed suit, searching for more broken branches, while Ignacio busied himself with melting off the copal onto the tip of his club, just as Saffie had done. In the end, they made two torches for each of them.

Soon they were able to trail behind Acuzio, who resumed following Saffie's scent. And in time, they came to the ledge, and the indented section of wall.

They drew closer, and as their eyes adjusted to the shade, the crude, ancient tribal paintings were revealed. They stared at them in awe. Meanwhile Acuzio had gone further ahead, and was jumping up on his hind legs and clawing at the ledge, barking excitedly.

When they crowded around him, they saw that the hanging bushes had been partly hacked away, revealing the corner of a recess. Ignacio took a long stick and struck the bushes several times, to scare away any creatures that might be hiding there – and then he used the stick to pull back the greenery to reveal the full entrance.

Alma gasped. 'It's a tunnel!'

Sanderson immediately began instructing John and Gerard, who nodded their consent. Then he turned to the others. 'I'll go ahead with Gerard. And you can form a line behind me, with John at the rear. Okay?'

Calista gulped, eyes wide with trepidation. She knew that the tunnel must be filled with every sort of creature imaginable. Just the thought of it made her skin crawl, and she shivered. Jake put a reassuring arm around her. 'You sure you're up for this? Do you want to wait down here, maybe with one of the guards?'

Sanderson frowned. 'Not a good idea! It's best we all stay together.'

Calista looked at the tunnel, then Sanderson, and lastly Jake. 'I can do this... I think. Anyway, I'm going wherever you go,' she told him, not sounding quite as resolved as she wanted to. 'I lost you once, I ain't losing you again.'

Jemima grimaced from their sickly-sweet exchange. 'It's very touching and all, but we should get a move on!!'

'Agreed!' said Ignacio.

Sanderson climbed up onto the ledge, and then Gerard and John hauled up Acuzio. The others followed suit. One by one they entered the dark, dank tunnel.

It was a place that tested nerves of steel. A revealer of one's true mettle. The tunnel was a long, winding vacuum that seemed to suck out even their most stalwart resolve, hushing them into nervous wrecks, as it went on and on. In the dark, they heard the scamper of fleeing insects, sliding slithery sounds, rattling, hisses, clicking, and trilling. All punctuated by the sound of their shuffling footsteps and Acuzio's heavy panting. Worse still, they felt things – small and large – drop on their heads, their arms and bodies, and then scurry away, in between water droplets plinking against their heads, like Chinese water torture. Nervous, girly screams echoed both up and down the tunnel, making Alma jump. But they weren't Calista's screams. They were Jemima's. Calista glanced back at her and then nudged Jake. Getting the hint, he hung back and held out his hand to Jemima, and she gripped it with both of hers. She was trembling like a leaf.

When they at last reached the top, Jemima stumbled out, still shaking, arms hugging herself – her eyes dewy.

Alma embraced her, and Jemima melted, bursting into tears. 'Poor child!' breathed Alma. 'It's over now.'

'Until we go back down...' murmured Sanderson, unmoved by her sobs. This was exactly why he hadn't wanted children on the mission.

'There is a path!' said Ignacio, pointing at it with what was left of his stick. He immediately followed it, and the others fell behind him.

It drew them into the canopy of the mountain-top jungle, and after some time, they emerged on the other side to be greeted with the spectacular view of the Amazon basin. But they had no time to revel in its beauty, as Ignacio led them further along the path, to the grove of trees that were wreathed in golden flowers. As they drew closer, this time it was Calista who screamed when she saw that the ground in front of the grove was moving. She hid behind one of the guards when they realised it was a carpet of tarantulas, twitching and fidgeting in the bright sun. Calista was horrified. 'They're... they're...'

'Amazing!' said Ignacio with fascination. He stooped down to inspect them, as close as he dared. 'They are Goliath birdeater tarantulas. The largest I've ever seen. Please, keep back. They flick bristles at intruders, which causes very bad irritation that can last for days, especially if caught in the eyes.'

Alma stooped down behind her husband. 'I've never seen them with such a rich colour, like orange velvet. And so many altogether.'

'Yes,' said Ignacio thoughtfully. 'It is quite unusual for tarantulas. They're normally solitary creatures. But I've heard that some have formed clusters of social groups, similar to ants or bees – made up of thousands. This looks like such a cluster.'

Alma straightened her aching back, but then noticed something just in front of the trees – and she grabbed her husband's arm. 'Look!' she said, pointing to a section where the tarantulas rose in a mound about three to four metres away. Several of the spiders shifted, revealing woven material – and Alma gasped. 'Is... is that Saffie's rucksack?!' she cried, lifting a trembling hand to her mouth. She turned to find Ignacio searching frantically for his matchsticks, and then lighting what was left of his torch. Sanderson and his men did the same, and Gerard and John stood protectively in front of the others, while Ignacio and Sanderson advanced forward, holding the fire close to the ground. Afraid of the flames, the army of tarantulas parted before them, and the two made their way to the small mound. Ignacio swept his torch over it several times, and the spiders scuttled away to reveal Saffie lying hunched on the floor, covered in a fine layer of grey dust. Her father cried out, and thrust his torch on Sanderson, as he bent down to inspect her. She lay perfectly still.

Alma called out to them, beside herself. 'I-is she alive...?'

Both stooping down, Ignacio and Sanderson did not answer for some time. Eventually, Ignacio said with a voice choked with emotion, 'I... I can't tell.' His shaky hands could not find a pulse, either on her wrist, or on her neck.

Jemima broke free from behind one of the guards, and ran to them. She knelt down on the ground and took Saffie's limp hand, closing her eyes – concentrating. She at last snapped them open. 'She's alive!!' she cried out to Alma, smiling. 'She's weak, but okay. She needs air, and some water.' She began wiping off the dust from her – it was like fine, grey ash.

By now, the tarantulas had moved further away, to another section of ground, free from disturbance – and so Alma ran over as well, falling to the ground on her knees next to her husband, eyes streaming with tears. She gently took her daughter's hand and kissed it. 'Thank you, God,' she prayed, overcome. 'Thank you!'

The others came over too, and Ignacio gently lifted his daughter up, so that she was leaning against his chest. Calista gave her flask to Alma, who took it and dripped water into Saffie's mouth. Saffie started coughing, and Alma quivered with relief.

Saffie at last opened her eyes to find her mother in front of her, and her father's arms around her, and she tried to say something, but only coughed some more.

'Do not speak, mi amor,' Alma told her. 'Just drink for now, try to regain your strength.'

Saffie did as she was told, and spat out a glob of dusty saliva, before slowly gulping down more water. But then she pushed the flask away, and felt for something on her lap. 'Sabu...' she murmured weakly. Tears came to her eyes as she brushed off the dust from the bundle on her lap. His body was limp as she cradled him in her arms. 'Sabu!' But then she realised. She could feel warmth from his body, and the rise and fall of his chest against hers. And then slowly, his eyes opened – resplendently blue.

Jemima kneeled down next to her, smiling kindly at Saffie, before taking the little cub's paw and stroking it absentmindedly as she concentrated again. At last, she sensed that life pulsated through him – strong, and bright, and unhindered. 'He's good too,' she beamed. 'In fact, he's got many years ahead of him!'

And Saffie, with wide, damp eyes, fell upon the little cub and sobbed uncontrollably, her entire body heaving. Ignacio and Alma in turn enveloped her. The three of them – mother, father, and daughter – huddled together and wept.

In time, they drew apart, and Ignacio and Alma went off to find a water source, both for Saffie and the cub to wash, and to refill their empty flasks. Meanwhile, Calista, Jake, and Jemima stayed with Saffie, putting her on a clean blanket, where she lay back against their rucksacks, as she recovered her energy. They couldn't help fussing over the little cub as well. He lapped up the last of their water, and was looking brighter by the minute. He lay on his stomach and was able to keep his head up. He made healthy noises – a light rumbling growl, and snuffling sounds. But he would not leave Saffie's side, and sat next to her on the soft blanket, resting his cheek on her legs.

Saffie stared at each of the teenagers' faces, as if she couldn't believe they were real. 'You came,' she said, smiling.

Jemima grinned. 'I think you always knew we would,' she said – she had been reading Saffie's book.

'Yes, I did!' said Saffie. 'But… it's great to see you in person.'

Calista was distracted by the cub, and couldn't stop stroking him. 'Sabu is just gorgeous!'

Saffie nodded. 'He is. Sadly, the very last of the black jaguars. And by the sounds of it, the spotted jaguar is headed in the same direction. That is why I risked everything to bring him here. To drink from the nectar of the golden flowers. It saved him.'

Jake peered behind Saffie, at the grove of trees, and looked doubtful. He got up and went over to examine the strange, globe-shaped flowers, as well as the tree where they had found her lying at the base. 'There's something that doesn't add up, though.' He told them. 'See, all the other trees look old but healthy, covered with loads of flowers. But what happened to this one?' He gently kicked the stump of the first tree, dislodging a puff of dust. 'It looks as if half of it's been burnt. Disintegrated.'

Jemima got up too and examined it. The base was held up by buttress roots, for the soil was shallow – but what was left was a burnt, blackened stump, less than half a metre high.

Saffie shuffled around to look at the tree she had picked the flower from, and her jaw dropped. 'I... don't understand...' she said with disbelief. 'It wasn't like that before. When I came here yesterday with Sabu it was just like the others. Fully grown, with lots of flowers.' She stared at the ground, trying to remember. 'I... I picked a flower, knelt down, and dripped the nectar into Sabu's mouth. But it wasn't working. He went limp. I... I thought he died.'

Jemima came back, and sat on the edge of the blanket. 'I think I know what happened,' she said, deep in thought. She looked at Saffie. 'Do you remember, you wrote in your book about a boy who saved his mother, just by touching her...'

Saffie blinked, struggling to comprehend. She shook her head. 'No. No. Sabu was cured by the nectar. It has special healing properties.'

Jemima looked her in the eye. 'I think... I think whatever Tai did to help his Mum, you did the same with Sabu. It wasn't the flower, Saffie. It was you.'

Saffie sat stock still, as if in a trance.

'I'm guessing,' continued Jemima, 'that you held Sabu with one hand, and was touching the tree with the other. Somehow – and don't ask me how! – but the energy was drained from the tree and transferred into Sabu. Though the process almost killed you.'

'It does make sense,' said Calista wide-eyed. 'In a weird and wonderful kinda way! In fact, that would explain why there's all this ash everywhere.'

Saffie looked down at herself, at the fine grey dust that still covered her. She took some between her fingers, and rubbed them together.

'Except,' said Jake, 'with Tai, he used his own energy, his own life force, on his Mum – without realising what he was doing.'

'Which made him old,' finished Calista.

They all thought about this for some time, until Jemima said, 'Just as I suspected since I started reading your book, Saffie, you have amazing powers. And like Tai, you had no idea what you were doing when you saved the cub.'

Jake raised an eyebrow. 'Wow! That's… what you did for Sabu… it's just amazing!'

'A real journey of discovery!' added Jemima.

Calista smirked. 'You can say that again. You kids don't even know what you can do!! Don't know your own strength…'

Saffie glanced down at Sabu, who was purring loudly and beginning to fall asleep – then held out her hands, staring at them. 'I can't believe it. But… I think you might be right.' Her hands began shaking heavily as she thought of what she had done… what she was able to do. And she wedged them between her legs. 'I have to be careful…'

'Too right!' spluttered Calista.

Just then, Ignacio, Alma, Acuzio, and Gerard returned. They had found a waterfall and river, and filled their flasks. They gave one to each of the four teenagers, who gulped it down. It was the freshest, purest water they had ever tasted. 'The headwater is not far from here,' said Ignacio, pointing in a south-easterly direction. 'There is a beautiful waterfall, and water to swim in. We can wash there, refill, and prepare to return.' He looked up at the sky, and the haze of the sun. 'We must descend before dark. We are not equipped for the freezing nights up here. In fact, it's a miracle you survived the night, niña!' he told Saffie.

Alma nodded in agreement. 'The tarantulas… they kept you warm.'

Saffie sat up, blinking. 'What do you mean?'

They realised she didn't know. 'We found you on the ground, covered by tarantulas!' Alma told her.

'Amazingly they somehow knew you needed warmth,' said Jemima. 'I guess Tai's not the only one with a special connection with animals.' She began to feel more at ease with the daunting journey back down the tunnel – with Saffie with them, all those awful, unseen creatures would surely be repelled.

'Do you feel able to walk, mi amor?' asked Alma.

'I'll try,' she said, and Jake and Ignacio helped her up. She paced around a little, supported by them, and in time she let go and walked by herself. 'I'm fine!' she said, pleased. 'And dying for a wash. This dust is everywhere.'

She walked over to pick up her rucksack which was leaning against the tree stump. And she stared wistfully at the charred wood, stooping down to touch it. The crackled bark disintegrated into dust beneath her fingers. 'I'm so sorry,' she whispered to the tree, brows creasing. She sighed, straightened, and turned to look at all the other wizened old trees, and the round, yellow flowers, one last time. And then she thought of something. Taking the matchstick container from her rucksack, she emptied the matches into a pouch, and then carefully took one of the flowers, and picked off each of the petals, until she reached the bulbous, inner column that contained the nectary, ovary, and stigma. She placed it gently inside the container, and then snapped off some powdery anthers, as well as a few petals, and placed them inside too. Screwing the top back on, she tucked it inside her rucksack.

By the time she turned back round, everybody had packed up and was ready to leave. Sanderson had placed the cub gently in the top of his own rucksack with its head sticking out, and one of Sanderson's men carried Saffie's rucksack.

They walked about half an hour until they reached a clearing in the dense foliage, that opened up to the most beautiful waterfall they had ever seen, cascading from an expansive rock formation that disappeared into the mist above. It was surrounded by lush greenery, bejewelled by exotic flowers and fruits. Alma stayed with Saffie and helped her wash, and then they cleaned the cub – revealing his thick, jet-black fur. The other teenagers ran right into the water and jumped around, splashing each other, and swimming – screaming with delight and laughing hysterically. Meanwhile Ignacio went round and picked the fruits and ferns that he knew were edible, and they feasted on them to their heart's content. Even Sabu ate some soft, sweet papaya, diced into small cubes. But they knew that their time was limited, and after about 45 minutes, they packed up and trekked back to the tunnel entrance – refreshed, and clean, and with renewed energy. Feeling less daunted by the descent, and ready to take on anything.

34 A FUTURE GLIMPSE

Cheered that their mission to find the sixth Ingenious child was a success, and not only that, that the girl they discovered had a special affinity with animals and insects, their descent down the infested tunnel went much faster, and seemed less daunting, than the ascent.

This time, Jemima held firmly on to Saffie's hand, and the two somehow sparked energy between each other that both calmed Jemima and gave Saffie renewed strength. Like dynamos feeding off each other. When they came to the exit, and jumped onto the ground, they blinked through the bright afternoon sun – disoriented, but gulping down the fresh though humid air, quietly glad to be alive.

Calista sniffed the air and smelled something out of the ordinary, crinkling her nose. 'I smell burning,' she said, looking round to see where it might be coming from.

Saffie sniffed too. 'It's the dry season, so it might be a fire that has started spontaneously – though that's rare. It's more likely to be caused by farmers and ranchers. They keep burning off large areas of land to grow crops, or to convert into grazing pastures for cattle.' She looked over the horizon, shading her eyes, and then pointed to the top of the canopy, south of the mesa. 'Over there. It's faint, but you can just about see the smoke...' She gritted her teeth, seething. 'Their burning's reduced huge amounts of habitat for biota, and animals like Sabu – not to mention the devastating effect it has on climate change.' She was getting more and more worked up as she thought about it, her nostrils flaring. 'All sanctioned by the government now – apparently in the name of development and progression. Can you believe it?!' she huffed, red-faced.

'Wow!' gasped Jemima. 'That's just stupid...'

'And incredibly short-sighted!' said Saffie. 'I heard it described like...

like being on a flight with a passenger who starts stripping out rivets and bolts from the body of the plane, because they don't think they're that important!'

Jemima gulped, looking very upset indeed – and Saffie softened. 'I'm sorry for ranting... it's just that it makes my blood boil!'

Alma came over and put an arm around each of them. 'We shouldn't give up hope though. Hope that there might be change someday, before it's too late.' She craned her neck to see the others, who were walking ahead. 'We'd better keep moving. We have a long way to go.'

They caught up with the others, who were waiting by the same tree they had used to cross the leech-infested river earlier. They traversed it one by one, and then trekked back as far along the river as they could.

When they reached a section of still backwaters, they rested a while and filtered water into their flasks, while Saffie searched for, and found, a particular kind of barbasco liana. She cut off two sections of a hanging stem, and then beat them with a club-like stick against a log. The liana splayed like a brush, dripping with sap, and when Saffie waded into the river and stirred the barbasco brushes into it, the milky juices seeped into the water. Before long, fish of all sizes and shapes began floating to the surface, stunned by the toxins that paralysed their gills – though it was harmless to the environment. They scooped up the fish, and folded them into freshly-picked banana leaves. And then they continued their journey – trekking into the forest for another few hours until the light began to wane.

By then, they had found a good configuration of trees, and so they busied themselves setting up camp and building fires. When the firewood had burnt, leaving just the coals, they placed the banana leaf packets on top, allowing the fish inside to steam in the heat – and for dinner they sat around the fire, picking off the sweet, tender flesh that flaked easily from the bone. Sabu was regaining a healthy appetite, and licked up a soup of fish mashed in water. Acuzio had a large fish, carefully de-boned, all to himself.

When the animals had done eating, a curious Acuzio went over to sniff Sabu, who was tiny in comparison. But the little cub raised his hackles, and growled at him, baring small, white teeth – a show of bravado more than anything. Startled, Acuzio back-tracked and hid behind Jake.

When everyone retired to their hammocks, exhausted, Sanderson came back from a patrol around the area, nodding to Gerard, who got up and took the next shift. Sanderson went over to stoke the near-dead fire – at the same time, Jemima hopped out of her hammock, rubbed the sleep from her eyes, and fetched her water flask from her rucksack. There was more water in it than she remembered, and she gulped it all down thirstily. But it still wasn't enough, and she shook it for every last drop. Sanderson reached for his flask, and offered it to her. Her messy hair and sleepy eyes made her look even more childlike, and she took the flask from Sanderson with a sheepish smile. Gulping down several swigs, she wiped her mouth with the back of her hand, and gave it back. 'Thanks,' she said, her thirst at last quenched.

She started to go back to her hammock, when Sanderson asked, 'What you did… when we found Saffie and the cub. What was that?' He sat down next to the coals that had hushed into a pale afterglow.

Jemima stopped and turned back to him. 'You mean, when I touched them?'

Sanderson nodded thoughtfully. 'She was barely warm, and we couldn't find a pulse – it must have been very weak. But you… you knew that she was alive. And the cub.'

Jemima lowered herself on the stump of wood opposite him, rubbed the sleep from her eyes, and stared at the dying coals. 'The only way I can think of explaining it… it's like when you're measuring conductivity using an ohmmeter.' Her passion for physics and mathematics sparked her to become fully awake. 'Electrical conductivity's calculated by dividing the length of the material, by the area, multiplied by the resistance. So, a simple equation: conductivity equals 1 over AR.' She glanced up at Sanderson, who looked baffled. 'Sorry!' she chimed. 'I'm a maths geek. Mummy's always telling me off for spouting equations all over the place. Anyway, simply put, the smoother and faster the flow of electricity within a given material, the higher the conductivity. And, *somehow*,' she said, 'I can feel how smoothly energy flows inside people. The less resistance means the more "life" they have left in them. And the higher the resistance… well, you can work out what that means.' She watched

Sanderson carefully, wondering how he might react. 'I know! It's crazy...' she said, tapering off.

Sanderson shifted in his seat, grappling with understanding. 'So... you know how long people have to live, just by touching them?'

Jemima nodded, wide-eyed, as if she herself found it hard to believe.

'How does it feel?'

She thought about it for a while. 'Like I've been zapped by a massive adrenaline rush! Not necessarily a good one. At the same time, inside, I sort of feel like... like I'm freaking out. I kind of don't want to know, but I do, if you know what I mean.'

'I... I think I do. Understand, that is.'

Jemima smiled. 'Of course, I can't predict. So you might be full of life one day, but then get struck by lightning tomorrow... Which, by the way, has a probability of about one in 138,850.' She glanced up at the canopy. 'Though it might be higher here.'

Sanderson started to say something, but hesitated – and Jemima looked at him expectantly. Eventually he said, 'Do you... take requests?'

Jemima blinked at him in disbelief. 'W-what do you mean?'

Sanderson held out his hands to her, over the coals. The mild, residual warmth that arose from them made the hair on his arms prickle. Or maybe they were prickling from fear, apprehension. He wasn't sure, wasn't even sure he knew what he was doing. Yet the palms of his hands remained spread out between them.

Jemima looked at them, looked at his face, shaking her head, puzzled. 'Why?' she breathed, eyes creasing. In that split second, she seemed suddenly mature beyond her years – and Sanderson saw a glimpse of what she might look like in the future, as a young woman. Her childish exuberance, mellowed by reticence, modesty, doubt.

'There's a rare disease that runs in my family...' he told her, unable to look her in the eye. 'My father died from it, and my older brother too, just three years ago. I may look tough, but... I haven't worked up the courage to get tested.' He stared at the dim light of the coals. They were so faint, the outlines of their forms vague – yet they threw out enough light for Jemima to see that his hands were shaking. And she suddenly grabbed them with both of hers, closing her eyes, squeezing out the tears that had welled up. She breathed deeply – in and out – several times. When she opened her eyes again, she simply smiled at him, happy and relieved – and let go.

He looked at her directly now, and nodded slowly. Unsure of how he felt. With his father and brother gone, he wondered how he could reconcile living his life, when they could not. 'My wife...' he said, choked. 'Maggie. She's going to be glad. My son too, though he's too little to understand.'

Jemima's expression softened. 'How old is he?'

'Just three. He was born after my brother died...' he said, catching his breath.

'I'm so sorry...' They both stared at the coals for some time, until Jemima broke the silence. 'Well,' she said, stifling a yawn, 'I'm sure your son is going to grow up to be a good and courageous man, just like his Dad.' She got up and turned, mumbling over her shoulder, 'And whatever you do, don't get struck by lightning!' before shuffling off, half asleep.

He couldn't help but smile as he watched the girl slouch back to her hammock, and climb in.

He sat thinking for a while, before throwing more wood on the fire, and stoking the coals with a stick. It suddenly caught aflame, and roared with life. He got up, weary now, but still went over to each of the hammocks, checking that they were all okay. When he got to Jemima's, he found her curled up, and already fast asleep. Sanderson remembered that glimpse of maturity he'd seen in her, though watching her now, snuffling like a baby, and sucking her thumb, made the image evaporate instantly. He thought of his son, relieved that he would have the chance now to watch him grow up into a young man, get married perhaps, have children of his own. And, with a thudding heart, he felt a sudden swell of determination – to cherish every single minute of it.

He noticed that Jemima had left the netting open, so he zipped it closed, and went off to check on his men.

321

'*Learning is the only thing the mind never exhausts,
never fears, and never regrets.*'

Leonardo da Vinci

35 TEARS FOR BUTTERFLIES

Early the next morning, Saffie woke with a start, gasping for breath.

She immediately felt for the notebook in her back pocket, but it wasn't there – and instead, she doubled over, upset.

Jemima was already up, and went over to her. 'Saffie, what's wrong?' she asked with alarm, unzipping the netting.

Startled, Saffie swung her legs out of the hammock. 'Something happened... back where you came from. Someone died.'

Jemima froze.

'I-I'm sorry,' said Saffie, beside herself. 'I don't know his name. But he was a brilliant scientist, though his mind was no longer as it was. His wife is inconsolable.'

'It must be Dr Kendra! He died?!' asked Jemima, wide-eyed. 'W-what happened?'

Saffie shook her head. 'I don't know exactly. I really wish I could speak to them! But I can't. I never know details, only feelings, and abstract thoughts. I think it was some sort of accident that happened a few days ago.'

'Oh no, that's awful! And we have no way of reaching them – Gerard said the batteries for the satellite phones ran out days ago. We didn't think we'd be coming into the jungle you see. Poor Gaia!'

'The boy, and the two girls...' started Saffie.

'Tai, Milly, and Mei?'

'Yes. They are sad, very sad. Already, the one who has only a father...'

'Milly.'

'Milly, yes – she was already very depressed. She is disturbed by death, and feels... haunted by it.'

Jemima thought about this, mumbling, 'Oh dear! Milly hasn't been herself since Karl died. She was spending an awful lot of time in V3's room. She's one of the agents who was horribly beaten up… been in a coma ever since. Milly just sits there, staring at her for hours.'

Saffie nodded thoughtfully. 'Yes, I felt Milly falling apart when something bad happened. I think that she *appears* okay generally, but her mind is very fragile. There are cracks… like… like glass that has been shattered. I am *very* worried about her.'

'Sounds bad,' said Jemima. 'We had better get back to London as soon as possible. Saffie, will you come back with us?'

Saffie threw a glance at the sleeping forms in the hammocks behind. 'I need to ask mami and papi first. But I really want to go with you, to meet the others too.'

'The Prof will be happy. He's been searching for you for a long time.'

'I know! There is a lot to talk about.' But Saffie paused, looking suddenly puzzled.

'What's wrong?' asked Jemima.

'I can feel that their grief is a few days old, but I don't know why I'm only sensing the death of Dr Kendra only now. Usually, I'm able to feel things instantly, if it's strong enough.'

'Well you *were* on the mountain and unconscious for about a day… and I imagine it takes time to recover, physically, mentally, and emotionally as well.'

'Yes, of course, that must be it.' Saffie slipped down onto the ground, her sandals sludging on the thick mud. She looked around for her notebook, and found it in the hammock, just under Sabu's fur. She gently slid it out, trying not to wake him. Then, taking the pencil from her pocket, she scribbled very quickly the date and description of her feelings.

Jemima watch her quietly. 'You have to write it all down?'

Saffie looked at her, baffled. 'Yes, how else can I remember?'

'Well, Milly, Mei, and I – we actually have a really good memory. Milly especially. She can learn entire languages in just a few days. Me and Mei can too, but not as good as Milly. Though Tai – he's empathic, same as you – his memory is more like normal people's. I think when you have an empathic ability, everything's concentrated into it, and that's your main strength. An amazing one too!'

'So, you can memorise everything?'

'More or less. Equations especially. Well, I love all the sciences, but mostly I'm mad about mathematics, physics, chemistry. I love learning about how the physical world is perfectly bound together by the most beautiful equations and laws. There's so much to learn from space, and time, and even our own bodies – and how we're intimately connected with the universe. Did you know, for example, that on average the number of atoms in a human body is around seven times ten to the power of 27? That's seven with 27 zeros after it! And around 99 percent of our bodies is made up of hydrogen, carbon, nitrogen, and oxygen atoms. Now the hydrogen atoms were made in the big bang, and the rest were made in burning stars – which means that many of the particles that make us have existed for millennia...'

Saffie raised an eyebrow, her eyes glazing over slightly. 'Wow, that's... fascinating. You've certainly found your passion. You probably guessed mine is nature.'

Jemima smiled. 'Yes, I did. Sorry for prattling on...'

'No problem! Actually, I'm used to it – both my parents are vets, so they're always "prattling on" about medical stuff.'

Just then, the hammock quivered, and they turned to find Sabu waking up. The little cub stretched and yawned, and tried to get onto his feet, but the netting was too shaky. After wobbling, he collapsed, and started making raspy noises, calling for Saffie's help. 'Niño!' breathed Saffie, and she picked him up, cradling him in her arms. 'Sleepy baby,' she said, kissing him.

'He must be thirsty,' said Jemima.

'He is. We're quite close to a fresh water source, so we should pack up and go there to fill our flasks. Then it will take most of the day to reach the main river, where we can head back home by boat.' She scanned the jungle, and looked up at the sky. It was grey and humid, and already baking hot. 'There was a torrential downpour last night, and the mists are heavy and thick today, which will make visibility difficult. So we should leave soon.' She sniffed the air again. 'And they are burning the forest somewhere. Which means the wild animals will be frightened, agitated, hungry. We need to be on our guard.'

Jemima blinked at her. 'I thought you had a way with animals?'

'Some of them, yes. But there are about 430 mammal species in the Amazon, and around 380 different types of reptile – not to mention the tens of thousands of different species of amphibia, birds, and insects. And my... ability hasn't been tried and tested on all of them. So we still have to be careful.'

'Oh...' said Jemima, disappointed.

'Can you look after Sabu while I get everything ready? You need to take him outside the camp to go to the toilet. And then just watch over him.' She held out the cub to her.

'Um, okay,' she said, and took Sabu, cradling him in her arms.

Before she left, Saffie placed a hand on Jemima's shoulder before leaving. 'Again, I'm so sorry about Dr Kendra.'

'Thanks, Saff.' Jemima looked around, and then walked over to a tree several metres away. When she put the little jaguar on the ground, he picked his way over the mud, sniffed the vegetation and tree roots, and circled round a few times before squatting to relieve himself. Then he looked around for Saffie, and immediately ran back to her. It was good to see that his energy was returning.

Jemima sighed as she walked back to the camp. She had to break the news of Dr Kendra's death to the others.

When she told Calista and Jake, they went very quiet indeed. 'That's awful,' said Jake.

'Yes, so sad...' said Calista. 'And it's bad news for finding the last Ingenious child. No way of finding where they are now...'

•••————————————————•••

For the first few hours of walking through the understorey together, Saffie, Ignacio, and Alma thrilled at spotting plants and wildlife – pointing them out enthusiastically to the others. Everything was different in the jungle – as if the swathes of verdant foliage blushed a potent spell over all that lived there. Brightly-coloured macaws squawked as they flew overhead in flocks of hundreds. Patinated spiders and long centipedes scuttled for their lives across the ground – even the odd titan beetle, the size of a human hand, clicked and clambered before them, its brown wing-cases fidgeting in the heat. Monkeys of every sort – howler, spider, tamarin, and squirrel monkeys with their creamy white faces and round eyes – stopped and stared from the safety of the treetops, some with young clinging to their backs, and others hissing at them, or howling, and catapulting themselves from tree to tree with long, spindly limbs.

'Look up there,' said Ignacio, pointing to a tree where there was a flash of azure winking between the leaves. 'It's a spangled continga bird. Can you see? And there! Its mate just landing next to it.'

Calista craned her neck to see. 'Woah, they're completely different.'

'They are!' beamed Ignacio. 'In this species of bird, males and females are what we call dimorphic...'

'Does that mean they mate for life?' asked Calista.

'Not quite, but good guess,' said Ignacio. 'It just means that the male looks very different from the female, as you noted. So the female is a rather dull brown, whereas the male has vivid turquoise feathers and a burgundy throat, with speckled wings. He's quite stunning, isn't he!'

Mildly interested, Jemima came to have a look.

Jake drew closer as well and stole a sideways glance at Calista. 'Beauty isn't everything, I suppose,' he said meaningfully, as he stared up at the birds. 'But I imagine the male bird can see beyond the feathers, and just really, *really* appreciate her for what she is inside...'

Ignacio looked at him oddly. 'Eh? Anyway, the cotinga are polygamous birds, which means they have more than one mate.'

Jake sidled even closer to Calista and crossed his arms – his elbow lightly resting against her arm. 'Though I'd understand if they did stay together for life...' he mused out loud to her. 'I mean, if they really loved each other...'

Jemima suddenly felt sick, and immediately turned and walked away – and Ignacio at last cottoned on. 'Ah!' he said, and winked at Jake with a smile.

'Nah!!' said Calista, batting away Jake's idea with her hand. She motioned toward the flocks of females in the surrounding trees. 'Look at all the others he's got to choose from. He can have as many mates as he wants. That bird's got it made!'

Jake glared at her, flummoxed.

Looking baffled, Calista glanced from Jake to Ignacio. 'I'm... just talking about the birds...' she said, trailing off.

Ignacio stood next to them. 'He is using the birds as a metaphor, Calista.'

Calista frowned. 'What's a *metaphor*?'

Just then, Saffie called out to them. 'Anaconda alert!' She was pointing excitedly toward the far side of a marshy swamp, waving at the others to come over. 'You've got to see this. It's fantastic!!'

Ignacio stumbled after his daughter, eager to see – and a disappointed Jake turned to follow. But then Calista grabbed his hand, and pulled him back. 'I know what a metaphor is, you dummy,' she told him with a twinkle in her eye. She pecked him on the cheek. 'But no more metaphors or innuendos, okay? If I'm perfectly honest, I can't stand them. I just like straightforward, simple, to the point.' She smiled softly. 'Come on, there's another thingummy to see!'

Hours later, the jungle and all it offered was soon losing its appeal.

It seemed as though they had been trudging through the understorey endlessly – the sun was two-faced, smiling wryly, at its zenith, yet it scourged them with stifling, unbearable heat. Sweat poured from their bodies, the taste of salt slipping into dry, raspy mouths.

The Aru mist rolled in and out in gentle bursts, so that one minute they were surrounded by thick fog, barely able to see further than a few metres, and the next, the Aru would dissipate. 'They are particularly dense mists today,' remarked Alma. 'I think because of the increased humidity from the long thunder storm we had last night.'

They walked on and on. It was slow-going trudging through the mud that squelched with every step.

Reaching at last a sparkling, clear river, the flow was slow enough for them to wade in and filter water into their flasks, before drinking down great gulps. Then they washed off all the grime and mud. The sandy beach was inviting too, and Jake and Calista lay down on their backs – to rest for a while – letting the direct sunlight dry them. Out of nowhere appeared a kaleidoscope of butterflies, mostly in an array of yellow shades, but other species with varying colours and patterns joined them too. They landed quietly on the couple.

'Don't move!' Alma cried. 'They are sulfur butterflies. They won't harm you. They're just licking the sweat from your skin – it contains much-needed minerals.'

Finding herself adorned in a blaze of yellow, Calista reached for Jake's hand, slowly, so as not to disturb the butterflies. 'It's like something out of a fairy-tale,' she breathed, filled with wonder.

Jake turned, and really looked at her. Her mud-stained beauty, sand sprinkled in thick tresses of hair, wreathed in fluttering amber, gold, and citrine. He suddenly got up, and pulled Calista onto her feet.

'Jake!' she cried.

She was about to say something, but he hushed her. 'Shut up and listen...' he said, a flicker of a smile at odds with furrowed brows.

The butterflies had dispersed, but then gradually descended back onto them; a confetti of wings, batting gossamer-soft against their skin – a thousand feather-light caresses.

He laced his hand in Calista's, as his eyes delved into hers. His breath became shallow, light – a precursor to the stream of consciousness that began tumbling out unexpectedly in a babble of words. 'I've been thinking, Cal. A lot. About you and me...

'I think you know that I felt alone for a long, long time after my sister disappeared. Until that day in college, when I saw you sitting there in the canteen, reading my favourite book. In fact, it *was* my book, the one you'd nicked! And just like that, you were in my life. And.. and... being with you has helped me through the uncertainty of not knowing about Kara, and then loss, and then coming to terms with her death. So... I just wanted to tell you, the way I feel about you... it's like *nothing* I've ever felt before. We've been together for two years now, and my heart still stops when you look at me. *Every* time. This thing between us... I don't think I'll ever figure out the why or how of it, except that's just the way it is. And to be honest, I don't want to understand it exactly – because I kind of love that. You're an enigma. And I never want to stop discovering you, unfolding you, for the rest of my life. And...' He searched her face for more. But she didn't let him say another word. Her lips melted onto his, in the softest kiss.

And then it happened. He got down on one knee pulling something from his back pocket.

She gasped. Heart thudding. Time froze.

'Calista Emily Matheson...' started Jake, looking up at her.

The others, who were scattered around the beach, noticed something happening, and they all stopped to find Jake kneeling on the sand in front of Calista, half obscured by a cloud of butterflies. Saffie gravitated to Jemima who was sitting on the sand, and she sat down, putting an arm around her as they watched silently, dumbfounded.

Calista burst into tears before Jake even finished the sentence.

He looked up at her. '...Will you marry me?' he asked. 'There. Is that straightforward enough for you?' he grinned nervously.

Calista nodded, delirious with happiness, despite aching limbs, sand everywhere, and the shock.

'I-is that a yes?' asked Jake, wide-eyed and hopeful. Even with frizzy hair and splatters of mud, she was still the most beautiful thing he had ever seen – and surrounded by a plethora of fluttering butterflies made her even more dreamlike.

'Yes, it's a yes!' she beamed. 'Of course it's a yes!!'

He took her trembling hand, and slipped a twisted, knotted piece of wood onto her ring finger. They couldn't hug, because of the butterflies. But they stood on the sand holding hands, staring at each other in between looking up at the butterflies, swooping and floating around them. Silenced by happiness. A butterfly or two soon descended onto their tears, licking up the precious minerals, so that the two could barely see.

At the side of the beach, Saffie squeezed Jemima's arm. 'You okay?' she asked, looking into her lowered eyes.

Jemima nodded, though she wasn't okay at all. She stated softly, 'You know...'

'Yeah, I know.' Saffie wasn't sure if she should say what she wanted to. In the end, she just came out with it. 'We have a hard time as teenagers, don't we? We're in-between. Not kids anymore, and not yet adults.'

Jemima dared to look at her, but quickly looked down again.

Saffie watched her glare intensely at her feet. 'I can understand the mixed feelings you have for Jake,' she told her. 'I mean, he's been a good friend to you – but at the same time, look at him! He's insanely good-looking... I'm guessing it's difficult trying to figure things out.'

Jemima snorted. 'Tell me about it! I can memorise entire books, and decipher complex equations in a heartbeat, but... I can't work out what's going on up here,' she said, rapping knuckles on her head.

'Believe me, most of us are struggling with something – trying to understand ourselves. We're a raging bag of nerves, mixed feelings, mood swings. Well, I am anyway. Actually, I was – I've improved a bit. So it gets better, believe me. It's a process. We're figuring stuff out. And you have to remember that it's usually only when we're lost, that we discover exciting new places. That's a quote from someone, somewhere, but don't ask me who. Anyway, I have every faith that you'll eventually find your way, Jemima. That you'll discover a beautiful new place... and by that, I mean, you.'

Jemima's eyes dared to float upward to look at Saffie – taking in her sympathetic, kind eyes. Her lingering smile. 'Have you?' she asked, her voice small and light. 'I mean, have you found your new place?'

'I wish I could say I have, but that would be a lie!' she grinned, eyebrows slanting.

Jemima nodded thoughtfully. 'I'm kind of getting there... slowly.'

'That... that's great. Really great.'

Jemima stole a glance at the couple on the beach. 'I've thought about it all the time we've been here. Seeing those two together. And chatting with Jake. But I think I know now that, yes, okay, I was jealous at first that Jake only has eyes for Cal – but... I get it. Calista's everything I'm not. She's so beautiful, and popular. And I wish... I wish I could be more like her.' She sighed. 'I don't know! I don't know how I feel... about Jake, and about Calista as well...' Absentmindedly, Jemima made circles in the sand with a finger, like a kind of reiki – swirls within swirls. 'It's obvious she hates me.'

Saffie frowned. 'I'm not sure about that.' She suddenly thought of something. 'You may not know this, and this is between me and you, okay? But Calista's really jealous of you.'

'What?!' she cried. She looked over her shoulder suddenly, and lowered her voice. 'She's jealous of me? No way!'

'It's true,' nodded Saffie emphatically. 'Maybe because you're super clever. I gotta say, I think it's funny you're both jealous of each other. And another thing, Calista's actually been looking out for you. She acts tough, and I think that's something to do with the way her parents treated her… they were pretty nasty, and that's putting it mildly. But even after a tough childhood, she really cares about people. She cares about you.'

Jemima remembered something. 'Come to think of it, when we were on the passenger ferry, I saw her look back at me, then she said something to Jake, and he came over for a chat. She must've sent him over, maybe because I was sitting by myself.'

'That sounds just like her,' said Saffie. 'And last night, when we camped, she put the rest of her water into your flask, while you were sleeping. I saw her do it.'

Jemima suddenly looked up. 'She did?'

'Yep. So, she's always looking out for you. And I really believe that even though they're together, all three of you can still be good friends… Another thing – like you, Cal's an only child. And she's always wanted a sister. A kid sister.'

Jemima thought about it. 'Funny,' she said quietly, almost to herself. 'I've always wanted a sister too…'

'Well,' Saffie bumped shoulders with her, 'you already have *three* sisters, and *two* brothers, you know.'

'I know,' said Jemima. 'We're DNA siblings…' And then she registered what Saffie said. 'Hang on! You said *two* brothers. I'm guessing that doesn't include Karl. Does that mean you know that the last Ingenious child is male?!'

Saffie nodded, grinning. 'Yes it does!'

Jemima squealed. 'Do you know where he is?'

'No, I haven't worked that out yet. That's why I've been jotting down the times of the feelings I can sense from him, to try and figure out the time zone at least, or the country.'

'I can help! I can help you figure it out.'

'Great!

Jemima looked across the sand, blinking, digesting everything, only to find the happy couple walking toward them, hand in hand, minus the butterflies. When they stopped in front of them, Jemima immediately got up and hugged Calista. 'Congratulations, Cal! I'm really happy for you. Both,' she said, parting.

Calista looked surprised. 'You are?'

'I am! Though…' Jemima punched Jake on the shoulder lightly. 'She's too good for you, you know.'

Jake laughed. 'I know! That's why I had to wait till she was worn down, before asking. Otherwise I didn't stand a chance.' He grinned, squeezing Cal's hand.

'Ah, young love!' said Alma, who had walked over with Ignacio. 'So beautiful!' she said, clasping hands at her chest.

'I can tell you will be very happy together,' said Ignacio, patting Jake energetically on the back. 'Well done. You know, I don't usually advocate young marriages, but I think, when you know, you know.' He placed a hand on his heart. 'Here. You know here, that you're meant for each other, no matter what age you are.' He looked lovingly at his wife. 'Alma and I, we got married quite young as well – and I've treasured every single day of our 25 years together.' Alma blushed.

'Papi!' cried Saffie.

'I'm just being honest,' he protested.

Sanderson had walked over and butted in, nodding at the newly engaged couple. 'This is all very lovely,' he said sarcastically, 'but we need to get a move on.' Before going off to make sure nothing was left behind.

'Well, that's the engagement party over,' Calista said dryly.

'Wait,' said Jemima. 'Can I see the ring?'

Calista held out her hand with, on her finger, a knotty piece of wood in a rough hexagon shape.

'Erm, what exactly is that?' asked Jemima, baffled.

Jake explained. 'We passed a kapok tree yesterday, and I found a fallen branch that had a natural hole in it. It was the perfect finger width, and I liked the markings, so Saffie helped me cut around it into a ring, of sorts.'

Saffie laughed nervously. 'A delicate job for a machete! But it's the best I could do.'

Jake turned to Calista, 'Of course it's just until we get back to London, when I'm taking you to Tiffany's to pick out your ring of choice.'

'Tiffany's?' gasped Calista. She vaguely knew that it was a high-end jewellers frequented by celebrities and the rich. The closest she ever got to it was "Tiffy Lee's" – a knock-off Chinese replica brand, from a stall at Shepherd's Bush market.

'Erm, with what money?' Jemima asked, doubtful.

'The Professor's of course! You think I've come on this mission for free? Once he settles my invoice, I'll have the money to buy Calista's ring.'

Saffie frowned. 'And I thought you came out here to rescue me...?'

'That too. But rescues don't come cheap.'

Saffie narrowed her eyes at him. 'Well then, I'll be sending you my invoice for shaping your wooden ring – okay?!'

The three of them wandered off, joking and laughing, to go pick up all their things – and Jemima held back to watch them. She turned to look at the beach for a few minutes, observing the ripple of sun-drenched water, and the butterflies that were resting on the sand. She locked the scene into her perfect memory with a stuttered sigh. She was going to remember that day forever, but for all the wrong reasons...

Just then, a single butterfly landed at the corner of her eye, batting its wings, and gently drinking from the flow of liquid that dripped from it. She pushed it off, before it gave her away.

Turning, she dabbed at her eyes and picked up her rucksack. She kicked the sand several times, obliterating the perfectly-drawn circles, before walking back to the others.

They were packed and ready to continue their trek, when Saffie suddenly gasped and stopped. She closed her eyes, raising her face to the sun, as if its warmth transmitted the feelings she was absorbing from the other side of the world.

'What's going on?' asked Sanderson, coming closer.

Alma noticed too, and put a finger to her mouth. 'I think it's a notebook moment,' she whispered.

When Saffie opened her eyes, she looked around at them. 'They're in danger!' she breathed, blinking, and struggling to understand.

Jemima heard what she said, and came over. 'Who?' she asked, looking from Saffie to Alma. 'Who's in danger?!'

Saffie gathered her thoughts. 'It's Milly, Tai, and Mei.' She shook her head, hardly believing what she was sensing. 'No no no!'

The teenagers crowded round her, waiting with bated breath.

Saffie's eyes were creased with worry, not really seeing them, lost in her thoughts. 'They... they're looking into someone's mind, someone who they think is close to them – but... it's a trick!' She stumbled, feeling suddenly faint. Sanderson grabbed her, holding her up. Saffie continued, 'They think they're looking into his mind, but instead, he is looking into theirs.'

Jemima gasped. 'Who? Whose mind?'

Saffie concentrated, trying to work it out. She tilted her head, puzzled. 'It seems that he is like us. But old. A relative, I think. Though... there is something about him that I can't understand.' She looked around at them, eyes wide with wonder. 'Though he is like us, I can't *feel* anything from him. As if... as if he has no soul.'

The others looked at each other, perplexed by such portentous revelations.

Saffie continued, grave. 'It's bad, very bad. They are trapped inside him, and they cannot break free.'

Jemima gasped, and looked very pale indeed.

'Not only that,' said Saffie. 'Perhaps worst of all, there is something new, something different planted inside Milly's mind. Like... like a seed. A dormant seed, that will soon grow.' She hugged arms around herself, and shivered, though the heat was stifling. 'Already Milly is so fragile. I'm scared for her. For all of them.'

Sanderson looked grim, wondering what on earth had been going on in London during their absence. He was frustrated at being incommunicado, and powerless to help. 'There's nothing we can do but keep moving,' he told them. 'The sooner we get back, the better.'

36 PAIRS OF FIREFLIES

The last part of the journey was the longest.

It should have taken an hour, but because of the muddy ground, they walked for three long, exhausting hours, with still another mile or so to go. After the jungle fell away, the landscape opened up into a marshy plain, then a swamp, as they neared the confluence of rivers. To make matters worse, a particularly thick mist rolled in unexpectedly, so that one end of the line of exhausted trekkers – with Saffie and Sanderson at the head, followed by Jemima and Gerard, Alma and Ignacio, then Calista and Jake, with John at the rear – was unable to see the other end, obscured as they were in a cloud of white.

They had descended into silence, suffering from extreme fatigue, yet somehow managing to remain stalwart.

To make matters worse, lightning shot out from the murky grey sky – though they saw it only as white flashes through the haze above them. Just as well they could not see the flares of electricity etching silver roots that seemed to be straining to reach them. Sudden and unstable air currents swirled and billowed, tugging their bodies this way and that, making them stagger as though intoxicated under the brute force of the wind. Sanderson turned to look back at the party, and Jemima's eyes locked briefly onto his, before looking away – both remembering their exchange about being struck by lightning. A delayed cracking sound exploded overhead, making her jump. Instinctively Jemima drew closer to Gerard, and gripped his hand with hers – and he took it without a word, holding on tightly as though she were his own daughter.

Before long, the strong wind blew the mist away, and the white gave way to a grey world, roiling and heaving with storm. They found too that the path had narrowed into a ridge that was surrounded on both sides by stagnant water – pools of black that glistered nervously when lightning blazed above. Jemima stared at the water's spiked surface, bombed by the downpour of rain. She blinked nervously, and tugged on Gerard's hand. 'Are those… fireflies?' she asked, already realising before she finished the sentence the unlikelihood of beetles flying in such a tempest.

Gerard squinted in the rain. 'I'm not sure. I don't think so.' He turned to look ahead, pulling her to keep moving. But she could not tear her eyes away from the water. And then she realised. The numerous faintly-glowing dots on the surface were in pairs…

A series of lightning bolts – sustained ones – illuminated the water briefly, revealing that the spikes were not splashes of rain, but bony ridges of hard black skin, adorned at one end by a set of glowing orbs. Eyes. Jemima caught her breath, opening her mouth to scream just as Saffie halted suddenly, turned back, and hissed in a low, urgent voice. 'Don't. Make. A sound!'

Jemima clamped a hand over her mouth, just in time.

Everybody stopped in their tracks, and they all followed Saffie's gaze as she looked across the water.

They were surrounded by vast numbers of huge black caimans, with the nearest one so close they could see curls of breath rising like steam from its nostrils. It was over five metres long, maybe even six, resting its jaws on the edge of the swamp, with the rest of it tapering into a long, scaly tail just below water – like something straight out of prehistory. Its large brown eyes, edged with red, hinted of evil.

The group concertinaed, instinctively huddling closer.

Saffie warned through clenched teeth, deadly serious, 'Don't make any sudden movements. Stay close, and keep moving.'

They did as they were told, quivering with fear, yet still unable to help twisting their heads to view the sea of black creatures on either side of them. Were the monstrous creatures inching closer? Were they watching their every move, poised, and on the brink of tearing them to shreds?… They did not know if the rising panic was playing tricks with their eyes, were not sure if their own terror played mind games. But the party moved on. Step, by shaky step.

Sanderson strained to see ahead through the lashing curtain of rain, and his mind seized with fear to find more black caimans congregating over the path in front of them. He glanced at Saffie, his eyes betraying cracks of raw despair. Turning to look back, he saw too that the creatures had closed in behind John, the last in line. They were completely surrounded. And he knew they could go no further. Yet Saffie walked on, heedless... her face grave, brow furrowed with concentration.

Sanderson had never cried on the job, ever. But this might be a first. Thought he might go mad from the impossibility of their situation. Surely they were defeated, there was nowhere to go. Yet his legs kept moving in time with the girl's. He saw the way she stared intently ahead, as if her eyes projected an invisible beam, sweeping before them, over the creatures.

Still, they inched forward.

The elemental maelstrom raging and whipping.

Black caimans lurking, like otherworldly creatures of darkness.

Sanderson and Saffie were within reach now of the first huge beast in their path. Within biting distance. Yet it started retreating backward into the swamp, its grin of ragged teeth closing shut, its thick skin submerging. It was followed by a second caiman retreating, then a third, until a clear path began opening up before them. The next minutes quivered and expanded into an eternity as the nightmare progressed.

But there came a sudden gust of wind, an outcry, a streak of movement – and they turned to find Jemima slipping in the mud, falling sideways. Limbs flailing as she landed with a splash in the water right next to a caiman. In the blink of an eye, the monster snapped at her – huge jaws opening and clamping down, the stench of putrid breath, incisors piercing her shoulder. And she screamed in pain. It clenched her rucksack between its teeth and immediately withdrew – webbed feet back-paddling in the water. Sinking, and dragging her down.

Somebody cried out, and Gerard frantically swiped her hands with his, but they kept slipping from the wet. He snatched her wrists instead, gritted his teeth, and heaved with all his might. Jemima's eyes were circles of primal fear. The others screaming, shouting, chaotic scrabbling to get hold of her and combine their strength. The dragon-like beast shook its head to prize her free, to pull away. Slipping into the water, with Jemima in tow. In desperation, Gerard swivelled round, and kicked the side of the caiman's huge jaws with his boot, again and again. Blood spattered. Rain pelted. The wind thrashed. And suddenly the ferocious beast let go, with the others still pulling so hard that Jemima's arms were nearly dislocated from their sockets. They all fell backwards, sludging and splashing into the muddy waters.

But in an instant the caiman jumped up and snapped onto Gerard's leg instead, and it retreated in a flash, dragging him down – disappearing into the water like a slick of black oil. By the time the others recovered just seconds later, they sat up to find empty space where Gerard had been, the water seething with ripples, a single hand clasping at air, dragged down, slipping under, and then gone. Only a froth of bubbles remained on the water's surface. The air pregnant with horror.

Jemima wrenched herself from the mud, and got up onto uncertain feet, staring with disbelief.

Her entire body shaking.

No, she thought in a dull daze.

Numb legs pulled her forward, to where Gerard had been. And she waded into the water.

'No!' she cried. She kept going after him, but someone's hand grabbed her arm. Saffie's. And she stopped, waist-deep.

The two girls held on to each other, arms entwined, and Jemima stretched out her other hand to where Gerard had been. Tears mingling with the rain. 'No!!!' she screamed, stamping her feet, again and again – the water hurtling up all around, drenching them in black mud. In her mind, a chaos of thoughts, emotions, anger. Broiling until she was a seething mass of energy, clenching her teeth, veins bulging, eyes bloodshot.

'Bring. Him. BACK!!!!' she yelled. Like the worst of childlike tantrums, she heaved, and snorted, and stamped, with animal rage. Her balled fist pounding and pummelling the water.

The others were pulling themselves up from the mud.

Calista was crying uncontrollably.

The legions of caiman, drawn by the ruckus, ambled ever closer.

And then, in front of her, the water began to heave. A bubble surfaced

– a perfect gleaming dome – followed by another, and another. And something was suddenly thrust up from the swamp, pushed with inhuman force. It was Gerard! Behind him the huge caiman still clenching his leg, swam toward them, and launched him forward so that he landed with a splash next to Jemima. Gerard doubled over, coughing and spluttering in the mud. Jemima fell upon him and pulled him into her, cradling him, and crying manically. He was dazed, but at least he was alive. His injured leg lay limp, half immersed in water, bleeding out.

The beast pulled away and clamped its jaws shut, yellow teeth interlocking. Red eyes stared coldly, as it retreated back into the water, and vanished.

Saffie acted quickly, and whipped a cord from her rucksack, tying it tightly below Gerard's knee, just above the teeth marks.

But the other caimans were still advancing closer to the rest of the group, and when Calista shrieked as they came for them, Jemima turned around, and stretched out her arm behind her. Eyes fiery. 'Leave us ALONE!!!' she screamed at the mass of creatures, her voice shrill with hysteria. 'JUST... GO!!!'

And the others could only watch in amazement as the caimans obeyed without hesitation, and sunk back into the marshy water – until at last they turned, one by one, and swam off. Flicking armoured tails behind them.

Finally, Jemima broke down, cradling Gerard's head, and sobbing into his tangle of wet, muddy hair. Her body heaving, her shoulder dribbling with pink water mixed with blood.

With a shaky hand, nails black with mud, Gerard gripped her arm and squeezed it weakly, before succumbing to waves of blinding pain, and passing out.

Above them, lightning and thunder raged.

And the rain pelted down, relentless.

340

'Savage is he
who saves himself.'

Leonardo da Vinci

341

PART 4

37 THE ART OF MORBIDITY

The cool, light air-conditioning of Avernus was like a breath of fresh air.

Having just returned to England, and been seen by Dr Fargo, Jemima sat in a recliner in the BC, her shoulder in a brace with the upper arm wrapped neatly in bandages. It still hurt, despite the painkillers – and her usually flawless skin was mottled black and blue with bruises. Yet she was happy. Happy to be alive and back in London. And happy that she'd been reunited with her parents, who had come, spent several hours with her, and then left to fetch some of her things from home.

Young Treacle was curled up in her lap, snuffling softly. He had grown since she last saw him, and his stripes had deepened into a richer shade of toffee. Jasmine had just announced a surprise visitor come to see her, and as she waited for him expectantly, Jemima stroked Treacle's soft, warm fur. The Chauffeur eventually appeared, with Gerard at his side – limping in with a walking stick, but in good spirits. She was so happy to see him, and they hugged. Without meaning to, she absorbed him, realising with relief that he was full of life.

He pulled up a chair and sat down in front of her, smiling wryly. 'You look like Blofeld and his cat from James Bond – except younger, and with hair.'

'Thanks!' She picked up the kitten and talked to it face to face. 'Did you hear that Treacle? He's been here two minutes, and he's already insulting me!'

The cat sleepily opened his eyes to see the scary bruises on her face for the first time, and he shrank back in fear. 'Silly cat! Calm down, it's only me...' She kissed him and returned him to her lap, whereupon drowsiness soon overcame his alarm, and he curled up once more to sleep.

The Chauffeur brought in a tray of things, and they settled down, exchanged pleasantries, drank tea and dipped digestives, and talked about how wonderful English weather was.

Another little cat wandered into the room, meowing loudly, and looking around. It was Missy Mop, never usually far away from her brother, Treacle. When she spotted him on Jemima's lap, she jumped up next to him, began licking his fur frantically, and then settled down for a nap as well.

Gerard leaned forward to stroke Missy Mop's pretty ginger fur, remembering something. 'By the way, do you still feel strongly about knowing my surname?' he asked Jemima.

Her first impulse was to say not at all, especially after everything they'd just been through. She realised now that it didn't matter. It was a label, given arbitrarily at birth. But for some reason, she only shrugged.

'You know, anonymity is vital for the special ops division – unlike Sanderson's public office job. Though you did save my life, so...' He lowered his voice and looked over his shoulder furtively, 'my name's Gibson. And yes, Gerard is my real first name. But don't tell a soul, okay?'

Jemima beamed, and held out her good hand. Her trademark handshake. '*Sooo* pleased to meet you, Gerard Gibson. My name's Jenkins. Jemima Jenkins.' When they shook hands, his grip was firm and assured. Jemima closed an imaginary zip over her mouth. 'And don't worry. I'm good at keeping Mum!'

He nodded. 'Glad to hear it. 'Cos if you told anyone, I'd have to kill you. And them.'

Jemima snorted. 'Huh! You could *try*!'

'Ah yes,' he said, sniffing. 'I have to be careful not to make you angry...'

Jemima spluttered on her tea. 'What do you mean?'

'Someone told me about your hissy fit, and the alligators.'

'Caimans. They're caimans, not alligators.'

'Anyway,' he glanced warily at the two dogs sitting on the sofa not far from them. 'Let's just say, I've been told that when you get angry, animals start doing strange things...'

Jemima narrowed her eyes, turned, and called out, 'Acuzio! Come, boy!' She patted the side of the chair, and Acuzio bounded over. Gerard flinched; he was a huge dog. Jemima pointed to Gerard, frowning, and told the dog, 'Attack, Acuzio. Attack!'

Suddenly the dog jumped up onto his chair and began licking him manically. Great big slobbers, all over. Jemima fell sideways, laughing her head off.

•••————————————————————•••

When Saffie was safely installed in Avernus, and introduced to the other Ingenious children, they gelled instantly. After their first meeting, non-stop chatter soon ignited as they learnt about each other, recounted life stories in brief, discovered each other's personalities. By lunchtime they were discussing general topics and cracking jokes. And by evening they had settled down to comfortable silence, rediscovering the connection they had through physical touch. They arranged the modular sofas in the middle of the library in a ring, and lounged around on them, connecting in one way or other: Mei Hui sitting up, reading the news on her tablet, with Milly's head resting on her lap, her feet on Saffie's back. Saffie lying on her front, half dozing and half playing with Sabu, who by now had returned to full health. Next to her, Jemima sitting back, glued to her laptop. Finally, Tai curled up between Jemima and Mei Hui, fast asleep and snoring – his feet tucked under Jemima's legs and his head resting on the other side of Mei Hui's lap. Closing the circle.

Being together was like a reset, discharging all the anxiety and angst that had built up when they were apart. And they were more relaxed and calmer when they connected. Though when Saffie met Tai for the first time, his appearance shocked her into stunned silence. He was just 15 years old she knew, yet he looked like a frail centenarian, with pure white hair, pale skin dappled with liver spots, and the joints of his knees and knuckles stiff and knobbly from arthritis. Most of the time he was sleeping, or being pushed in a wheelchair with a blanket tucked over him. And he hardly spoke, for his breathing was shallow and laboured.

Even Jemima was shocked by the difference in his appearance from before Brazil, and being the youngest, and the most volatile with her emotions, she immediately burst into tears when she hugged him for the first time since their return. The other teenagers stared at her, mortified, expectant, worried. When they parted, she shook her head, barely able to speak. Eventually she told them in a small, trembling voice, 'He has just a few days…' before she broke down and sobbed anew. That set off Saffie, who had been holding it in, and then Mei Hui as well. Only Milly held back from crying, staring with a blank expression as the three girls wept.

Milly's mind wasn't what it was, and slowly she had been losing her grip on reality – pacing up and down the corridors, openly writing on the walls, constantly mumbling to herself, mixing up days and time, and becoming increasingly forgetful. She would wake up at three o'clock in the morning, and sleepily plod barefoot into the dining room, only to find it empty, and wondering where everyone was – then asking Jasmine to fetch the Chauffeur for breakfast. An almost daily occurrence. And though the comatose V3's state hardly changed from day to day, Milly repeatedly asked everyone how the woman was – up to 30 times a day.

The Chauffeur initially bore Milly's eccentricities with silent deference, but in time, her constant forgetfulness and peculiar ways made him avoid her as much as possible. He had also given up cleaning the graffiti she wrote over the walls – and Avernus soon became littered with Da Vinci quotes, drawings, and diagrams, even though they had hidden all the markers; somehow she always managed to find something to write with.

Her father, Brian, with the kind of infinite patience and benevolence that only a father has for his daughter, was able to deal calmly with her on a daily and hourly basis. Inside, he was going out of his mind with worry, but to his credit, he never showed it, and never cracked in front of Milly. Not once.

Tyaishia, on the other hand, though she was a changed woman – after losing her father, and now on the verge of losing her son – could not help becoming angry and bitter at the world, and she was often found ranting with rage, or crying in a corner somewhere, or retreating unexpectedly to her room when Tai's imminent death got to her.

The Professor was hardly around, spending all of his time in the laboratories working together with Dr Vassiliev on the cure. Just when they thought it was almost complete, they would be hindered in some unexpected way, or discover something new that delayed progress.

Gaia, on the other hand, though still mourning the loss of her husband, had begun to show herself again – sometimes turning up at mealtimes, and sitting next to the Chauffeur to eat in silence. Slowly, and in time, she became the glue that kept everyone together, quietly going around and spending time with them, giving of herself when she could, in between disappearing for long walks alone. The fresh air braced her, gave her life – unlike the rather claustrophobic Avernus.

That evening, Mei Hui took Saffie around Avernus to explore. One of the rooms had been used as a store for all the artwork found in Fitzsimmons' house. And a reputable art historian had been called in to catalogue everything. He soon discovered that not all the paintings with F. Jaffrey's signature were authentic works by the 19th century painter – the picture depicting the burning house, he told them, as well as the one they had dubbed 'Dragonfly Girl on the River' – both painted with modern oils, on new canvas, tacked onto recently-constructed frames. Of course, they already knew this. And so the art historian excluded those pictures from the catalogue raisonné which listed all of F. Jaffrey's authentic and verified works, with respective descriptions.

When Saffie and Mei Hui entered the store room, they found that most of the paintings were boxed up, though some particularly beautiful pieces had been left out for show, leaning against the walls. Saffie found herself instantly drawn to the Dragonfly Girl. She did not know that when she reached out a hand to touch the thick layers of raised impasto paint, Fitzsimmons had done the same thing many times before her. The ridges of hard-dried paint swirled with each brush-stroke, and for Saffie, letting her fingers linger over each of them was like discovering the artist, how he painted, what he must have felt. But, to her shock, that was not all she discovered. She quickly withdrew her hand and stumbled back – a startled and disturbed expression on her face.

Mei Hui looked at her curiously. 'Is there something wrong?' She stopped, herself overcome by a feeling of déjà vu. Then she remembered when they'd discovered the painting for the first time, Milly too flicked her hand back after touching the picture, saying that she didn't like it.

Saffie tore her eyes from the artwork, and turned to her. 'Yes,' she said quietly, stiffly holding her hand away from her, as if she'd just touched something foul. 'Something is *very* wrong.' She glanced fearfully at the painting. 'Th-there's someone in the painting.'

Mei Hui blinked at her. 'Yes, I can see there is a girl–'

'No, that's not what I mean!' Saffie huffed, frustrated with herself, trying to find the words. 'There is… a part of a person in the paint. Like… like ashes or something, mixed in.'

Mei Hui's jaw dropped and the hairs on her neck bristled. 'Are you sure?!'

Saffie nodded. 'Yes! Though I wish I wasn't.' She looked down at her hand with disgust. 'I want to wash my hand!' she cried, feeling sick. 'I'm going to wash it…' And she ran out of the room.

Ten minutes later, Saffie arrived in the store room, pushing Tai in his wheelchair, followed by Milly and Jemima – with two of the kittens traipsing behind, Missy Mop and Treacle, who had become quite attached to Jemima. They crowded around Mei Hui. Tai lifted his head with great difficulty, raising cataract-filled eyes to look at the painting. The others were standing around him, silent and grim.

'I-I can touch it,' said Tai with a hoarse voice. Though all he saw was a foggy image in front of him. 'I can try to find out…' He raised a weak hand that shook involuntarily from old age.

'No!' cried Mei Hui, an usual outburst for her. She calmed herself, and said with a softer voice, 'Tai, it is too risky for you.'

Jemima turned to them. 'I agree. When I left for Brazil, you had four months left. But after we came back, a month later, you went right down to just a few days.' Her eyes brimming with damp.

Saffie put an arm around Jemima, but spoke to Tai. 'I wrote in my book that I could sense you do not have full control over your powers, Tai. Did you… did you touch someone recently?'

Tai's shaky head began drifting downward, as if it were too heavy to hold up.

'You touched the Professor, Tai, remember?' Mei Hui reminded him. 'And he woke up. It was after we came out of Fitzsimmons' mind.'

Tai blinked, his thoughts muddled. 'I… don't… remember.' He looked both confused and extremely tired, and then seemed to sink into himself.

Before they knew it, he was fast asleep.

Mei Hui sighed, gently stroking his downy white hair. It was so soft. 'I think he revived the Professor, though he did not realise what he was doing. I'm almost sure that's what made Tai worse, because he collapsed afterward...'

'Poor Tai!' cried Jemima, battling the tears.

The sound of buzzing distracted Milly, and she saw something land lightly on Tai's shoulder. 'Fly!' she cried out, and waved it off. She watched it waft into the air. It zig-zagged randomly, and then brushed her cheek before flying off. 'Eurgh,' she grimaced, wiping her face.

Mei Hui watched it go. 'Strange. I think that is the first time I've seen a fly in Avernus.'

'I thought the air-con kept them out,' added Jemima.

They shrugged it off, and turned back to the painting. Staring at it with quiet fascination.

Saffie shivered. 'This person... whoever painted it, he must be really twisted to put a dead body in the picture.'

'She left him,' stated Milly from behind them, still looking around the room for the fly.

'Huh?' said Jemima, but Milly did not respond.

Mei Hui answered for her, gesturing at the picture. 'Georgina Whyte. The girl in the painting. Jeremy Fitzsimmons fell in love with her. And this image is an exact replica of the first time he saw her, except for one difference. In real life she wore scruffy clothes, but as you can see, he painted her with a white dress...'

'White, like a sacrificial lamb,' mumbled Saffie, staring at the painting with both morbid interest and disgust.

Mei Hui raised an eyebrow. 'They were really in love, but when she discovered that his face was changing because of the Fitzsimmons curse, and it could not be reversed, she left him. And that was that.'

'There's motive right there,' said Jemima wide-eyed, her mind racing with possibilities. 'I bet... I bet he went after her, begged her to come back, but when she refused, he killed her and burnt her to ashes!'

Saffie grimaced. 'And to think we have his DNA in us!'

'Seas cannot be measured by cup,' muttered Mei Hui, almost to herself.

Jemima frowned. 'What does that mean?'

'It is a proverb. The full saying is: "Man cannot be judged by looks, seas cannot be measured by cup".'

'Ah,' said Saffie, nodding. 'We shouldn't judge by appearance, or judge something on very little evidence.'

Mei Hui turned to the painting, remembering. 'When we went into his mind, we saw the memory of him painting this picture. He was tormented, but afterward, painting it helped him realise that there was nothing he could have done to make her, Georgina, stay. He realised that the problem lay, not with him, despite his... grotesque appearance. The problem was with *her*. But...' she looked away, disturbed. 'What worries me even more is that we saw him paint the picture, almost as if we were there in the room with him. Yet we saw nothing untoward. Nothing sinister. Though we know now that there is a dead person in the painting. That means... that means that, when we were in his mind, Fitzsimmons had full and total control over which memories we saw. He allowed us to see only the good parts. And he purposefully did not let us see what happened just before, that is, how there came to be a dead person, and how he mixed them into the paints...'

She struggled to control her breathing, and closed her eyes momentarily to calm herself. Trying to banish the sickening thought that they had delved into the macabre mind of someone so twisted. When she opened her eyes again, she looked at each of them, unwavering. 'Just as he is masterful at painting, he has artfully configured the memories we watched, in a way that we saw only the good, and nothing... nothing at all, of the bad.'

They all thought about this for some time.

'He controlled everything that we saw,' said Mei Hui eventually, 'in order to make us feel sorry for him...'

Milly stopped. She had wandered off, looking over the walls in search of the fly. But when she heard Mei Hui's words, she turned to them. '*I* feel sorry for him,' she said, over-emphasising the 'I'. There was a resolute expression on her face, as if no-one could convince her otherwise.

They all stared at her, until Jemima said, 'But... why would he want to do that, make you feel sorry for him?'

Mei Hui shook her head. 'That, I do not know. I can only guess that he wanted us to come around to him, sympathise with him.' She remembered something else. 'Tai mentioned before that he could not see any colours coming from Fitzsimmons.' She turned to Saffie and explained. 'Tai can see thoughts and feelings of people, as colours glowing around them. Yet, strangely, he saw nothing around Fitzsimmons. As for me, I am able to discern a person's inner heart, their scruples, how good or bad they are. But with Fitzsimmons, I could not determine anything. All this is very suspicious, and makes me think he is hiding many, many things...'

'It also shows how powerful he is,' said Saffie. 'Really powerful.'

They looked at each other.

'I had better tell the Professor,' said Mei Hui seriously.

They all agreed, eager to get out of the room. The morbidity was stifling.

Jemima called out to the cats, who were delicately sniffing around the room. 'Come on Treacle, Missy Mop. Let's get out of here. It's too creepy.'

Saffie went over to Milly, who was looking slightly lost, and held out her hand to her. 'I'll take you to your room, Milly.'

Milly looked at her hand hesitantly... but eventually took it. 'I'm hungry!' she said as they followed the others into the corridor. 'I want a snack.' So they headed instead to the kitchen. Milly hummed quietly to herself, swinging their hands together in time with the rhythm. It was about 11 o'clock at night, with no-one around, and so they raided the fridge and the pantry. Milly found a bar of chocolate in the snack drawer, and poured herself a glass of milk, while Saffie took an apple, looking around to see where they might sit to eat.

'Let's go to the swimming room,' said Milly. 'I like looking at the fish.'

'Sounds good – you have to show me where it is though.'

Quietly they made their way, and when Milly pushed the door open with her back, a puff of warm air spilled out, immediately reminding Saffie of home. They walked inside, and the lights went on automatically. Milly looked around – the room seemed different. Night imbued it with the hint of the hidden, the dim lighting casting long, mysterious shadows.

Saffie on the other hand was blown away. 'Woah, this is crazy,' she said, staring at the feathery fronds of the palm plants, and then up at the lake above the pool. The water was dark and murky, though the soft glow of ambient light accented the gently swaying waterweed, starwort, long stems of pondweed, and spiked water milfoil. Here and there came a flash of orange, gold, or pearly scales, as koi fish flitted through slithers of light.

But something caught Milly's eye, and she put down what she was holding on one of the loungers, and rushed over to the other side of the pool. 'Oh no!' she cried. Saffie followed her, still holding her apple, and found Milly staring, mortified, at a dried-out plant on a ledge set in the wall. 'It's almost dead!' cried Milly.

The long stems had collapsed into a mass of dried leaves, scattered with faded and withered cornflower heads.

Milly was beside herself. 'Jake... he's gonna be so upset...'

Saffie quietly absorbed Milly's alarm. 'I-I'm sorry, Milly. But can't he just get some more?'

'No!' she sobbed. 'These are Kara's flowers. His sister. He found them growing where she was buried.'

Saffie at last understood, realising their importance, what they meant to Jake. Her heart suddenly fluttered with nerves as she looked slowly from the flowers, to the apple in her hand, to Milly's desperate, crying face. An abstract thought gently came to her... An impulse. One that was irresistible and impossible to ignore. Like an itch that she knew she just had to scratch. She carefully reached for the plant, stroking a finger over the dry leaves. Her thoughts churning a blizzard of emotions. Sabu... the mountain... golden flowers... a decayed tree stump. Her heart pounding furiously, remembering that burning question. Was it really her, or the flowers, that had healed the cub? She desperately needed to find out.

She stroked the flowers, for seconds, minutes, concentrating all her energies... Then, as if in a dream, the dried leaves began to tremble, and – like the sad ache of longing at last coming to gentle realisation – they started to unfurl. Softly, tenderly, slowly. One by one, stems stiffened, swaying and coiling as they straightened and stood tall. Delicate petals shivered with nascent life and blushed vibrantly purple. Each stalk restoring, firm and succulent. Each flowerhead surging with colour. The air wafting with the faint smell of fresh sap. Yet, at the same time, the apple in Saffie's hand gradually slumped, until, just as the flowers revived, the fruit greyed and disintegrated into a pile of ashy powder, trickling quietly between her fingers to the ground.

Milly watched with wide unbelieving eyes. Heard a spontaneous whisper in her ear. It was the voice of her mother, gasping, 'Unbelievable!! Except–'

Just then, Saffie emitted a sigh as her eyes closed – and she collapsed on the floor.

Milly froze. Staring at the crumpled body at her feet, hardly able to breathe. 'Do something!' urged her mother. But Milly could only shake her head. 'I... I can't.' 'You can, Milly, I know you can.' 'No, no, no...' She started swaying back and forth, hugging herself. 'Milly, what's got into you? You need to help her.' 'Stop it. Go away.' 'Don't talk like that, I'm your mother.' 'But... I don't understand. A-are you a ghost?' Milly whimpered, terrified. 'No. I'm not. I'm just a voice in your head, Milly, that's all.' 'S-so, you're dead.' Silence. 'You're dead!' 'Of course I am.' 'Then... why do you keep talking to me?' Again, silence. 'Why?!' 'Because–' 'Tell me!!' 'Because... it's not me, Milly. It's you. You're making me talk because you can't let go...'

Milly stumbled back, startling herself as she bumped into the wall. She turned into it, huddling next to the cornflowers, crying.

There came the sound of running footsteps.

Gaia burst in. Behind her appeared the Chauffeur, panting.

They stared at Milly, saw the body in a heap on the floor, and ran over to them.

Gaia fell to her knees, and looked over Saffie, eventually shouting out, 'Jasmine! Get Dr Fargo, urgently!!' She looked up at the Chauffeur and signed to him frantically. He nodded his understanding. She got up, stepped back, and he scooped Saffie up, and carried her swiftly to the medical room.

Meanwhile, Gaia looked over at the tearful Milly, who was pacing nervously around, muttering to herself a constant chatter of dialogue. 'Milly, what happened?' asked Gaia gently.

Milly stopped, a panicked look on her face. 'I-it wasn't my fault! I only told her about the flowers, how important they were to Jake. They were all shrivelled up and dry, nearly dead.'

Gaia looked at the flowers. She hadn't noticed them before. She touched one of the leaves, it was soft and supple.

'I only told her!' Milly insisted. 'I didn't know she was going to bring them back to life. And then she fainted. And… and I keep hearing voices in my head. And they won't go away!!' She started thumping her head with both fists, hard.

Gaia lunged forward and took hold of her wrists, pulling them down, stopping her from hurting herself. She put an arm around Milly's shoulders and led her toward the door. 'Don't worry,' said Gaia, in a soothing tone. 'I know it wasn't your fault, Milly. It wasn't your fault at all. You must be tired, my dear. Let's get you tucked up in bed, okay…'

They disappeared through the door, and walked down the corridor to Milly's room, all the time Gaia speaking consolingly to her.

Back in the swimming room, a single housefly emerged from the shadows and landed on one of the petals of the cornflowers. It hopped from place to place on the plant, the chemoreceptors in its feet tasting the sweet sap of a leaf. Settled now, it stopped to clean itself, rubbing bristled forelegs together and then pulling them over its head several times, over the three ocelli, wiping its antennae and mouthparts. Metallic-red compound eyes glittered in the light, it stopped to stare at the vivid purple of the flowers, absorbing the blaze of colour. Suddenly, it launched itself straight up into the air, and then shot off – flying between the narrow louvred slats of an air vent. The echo of its faint buzz fading down the chute…

38 TOUCH OF DEATH

Saffie woke up the next morning, groggy and disoriented. Something small and furry was licking her face with a rough tongue.

'Sabu...' she murmured, opening sleepy eyes. She reached out and pulled the little cub into her arms. He growled lightly.

Dr Fargo stepped forward, scribbling something into his tablet before tucking it under his arm. 'How are you feeling?' he asked, smiling sympathetically.

She sat up and carefully touched her head, groaning. There was a bandage around her forehead. 'My head hurts...'

'Well, fainting and hitting your head in the pool room will do that I'm afraid. But thankfully it's only mild concussion. Your vitals are good, stable – so I think you're going to be all right.'

She suddenly remembered, 'The cornflowers!' Or had she dreamed it? The bursts of pain in her head were telling her not. She tried to scramble out of bed – she wanted to see for herself.

'No way, young lady!' He stepped forward to stop her. 'You're to stay here so we can monitor you, at least for the rest of the morning. Doctor's orders!'

Saffie slumped back resignedly, and lay against the pillow. Sabu took the opportunity to jump up onto her shoulder, and drape himself around her neck, tail flicking against her arm. His purring permeated into her.

'Well done, Sabu,' said Dr Fargo. 'You must keep her from escaping.' The cub looked up at him with his sky-blue eyes, and replied with a scratchy mewl. 'Thank you!' Dr Fargo told him, smiling. He scratched the little jaguar's ear. 'Cute little fellow!' The doctor remembered something and spoke into the air. 'Jasmine, tell Jake that Saffie's awake will you?'

'Yes, Dr Fargo,' came her lilting voice from the loudspeakers. 'He has been told'

Fargo explained to Saffie. 'I was given strict instructions to let him know the minute you woke up...' He turned to leave. 'Just off to get you something for the headache. Won't be long.'

Several minutes later she heard footsteps along the corridor, and Jake walked in, clutching something to his chest. 'Saffie!' he breathed, happy to see her up. 'You're okay?'

Saffie started to nod, but then winced. 'Apart from a thumping headache.'

He placed the pot of cornflowers on the bedside cabinet, and Saffie's eyes followed him. 'Th-they're beautiful,' she said, overcome.

'Thanks to you,' he said quietly. He perched on the side of the bed. 'I gotta say, I was devastated when I saw the state they were in when we came back.' He stopped, checking himself. 'I can't believe what you did though!'

Saffie looked at the flowers again, and then down at her hands, fingering the raised lines of scratches across her knuckles. 'I needed to find out. Needed to know if it was really me who healed Sabu. Or the flowers.'

They lapsed into silence, until Jake said, 'Well, it's you. Definitely you.'

'To be honest, I also wanted to see if I could help Tai somehow,' Saffie admitted. 'I... I just can't believe what's happening to him. It's not right. Not fair!'

Jake looked at her, frowning lightly. 'Saff. What you can do, it's just unbelievable, amazing, staggering! But, when we found you on that mountain, I saw the state you were in. You were half dead. Almost killed yourself. And that was just for a little cub.' He looked at the plant. 'And then again last night with the cornflowers – you fainted.' He paused, shaking his head. 'Tai harmed himself helping his mother, and if you try and help Tai, the same could happen to you. Or even worse. So it's just too risky. I don't know exactly how your abilities, your powers, work, but I do know that when a computer's left plugged in, and there's a sudden surge of electric flux, it can completely overload and fry the internal electronics, the hardware. And most of the time, nothing I do, whether it's replacing the power supply unit, motherboard, CPU – whatever. Nothing can bring it back to life. And you and Tai… you don't have a circuit breaker, a surge-protector, to stop the damage. You're burning yourselves, every time.'

He sighed and stared at the vivid blue of the cornflowers, still amazed that they had been brought back to life. 'The irony is, I read somewhere that when this type of cornflower dies, they leave seeds in the soil, and the flowers grow back. Every year. So I was going to find a nice place somewhere in the garden at home to plant them. But at least we can enjoy them for a bit more, before they die again…'

Saffie smiled, nodding. 'Okay, so they're the perennial kind. That's good.' She heaved a deep sigh, realising her folly. 'I almost killed myself for a perennial!'

The next day, everyone in Avernus was woken by howling. Long, mournful animal cries, that kept on and on.

Tyaishia rushed immediately to Tai's room, to find Dr Fargo standing over the bed, preparing an injection. Dog and Acuzio were pacing around, throwing their heads back, howling. The young cats too, scattered around the bed, were mewling hysterically.

Despite the din, Tai was lying back in bed, semi-conscious. His chest, under the bedsheet, rose and fell rapidly. The outline of his body was painfully thin, almost skeletal.

Driven to distraction, Dr Fargo put down the syringe, grabbed the distraught dogs by their collars, and led them out of the room and down the corridor. Their crying gradually becoming fainter. When he returned, Tyaishia glimpsed the worried faces of the others who had gathered just outside, before the door closed on them. The doctor strode back in and continued seeing to Tai. 'He's caught pneumonia,' he said, glancing over at Tyaishia, 'and it's gone to his chest.' He took an oxygen mask and gently put it over Tai's mouth.

Tyaishia felt almost scared to draw closer. Scared of what she was going to find. But she crept next to the bed, and lowered herself slowly on the chair, reaching out a shaky hand to grip her son's. It was cold, and light as a feather. 'Tai,' she said, quivering. 'I… I'm so sorry.'

Despite being weak, he managed to squeeze her hand lightly, and Tyaishia burst into tears, lowering her head.

But the bedcovers rustled, and she looked up to find him taking off the oxygen mask, eyes opening slowly. He struggled to breathe, gulping in as much air as possible, but it was never enough. His lungs squeezing tight. He turned his head toward her, and just before he spoke, the cats suddenly quietened and stilled. 'Ma... it's time,' he said, his voice gravelly, frail, wheezing between the words. It's okay... I'm ready to go. I'm... really tired.'

Tyaishia shook her head. 'No! You have to fight it. Don't give up!! Please don't give up.'

He took several more breaths of oxygen from the mask, his bony hand shaking. 'You need... to accept it,' he said over the rim of plastic.

Tyaishia shook her head, distraught. 'I-I can't. I won't! Don't leave me.'

'Please...' whispered Tai, his energy fading.

Dr Fargo drew closer, his face grim with knowledge of the inevitable. 'Tyaishia,' he said gently. 'There's nothing more we can do except... make him as comfortable as possible. And prepare ourselves.'

She blinked at him, and at last her eyes softened. The doctor's words finally sinking in. She fell upon the bed, sobbing even more.

The doctor tried to put the mask back on Tai's face, but he pushed it away. 'One thing,' Tai told him, gasping for air. 'I want to die... outside. Next to my tree.'

The doctor hesitated, reluctant. It would be difficult to take all the medical equipment out there. It was his lifeline. But how long did he really have, he wondered... Eventually, he succumbed. 'Okay,' he nodded, ashen-faced. 'Okay.' He put a hand on Tai's shoulder, as if his touch cemented the promise. 'I'll arrange it,' Dr Fargo told him. 'I'll take you to your tree.' Gently he pushed the face-mask over his mouth.

Tai lay back, gasping for breath, resigning – feebly – to the inevitable.

••• ——————————————————————— •••

A hushed despondency descended on Avernus as they prepared for Tai's death, bracing themselves.

They set up a lounger in between the roots of the great old oak, with Dr Fargo waiting next to it. The Chauffeur wheeled Tai out, across the fields that surrounded the lake of Avernus, grappling with the inclines, bumpy grass, and exposed roots.

The others trailed behind him, grim. Everyone was there except for Milly. 'She doesn't want to come,' said Brian. 'She's too upset.' But he was in two minds. 'Maybe I should go and get her...'

Saffie touched his arm reassuringly. 'I'm not sure. I sense that her heart is breaking. Maybe it's best to leave her for now. She'll come when she's ready.'

Brian nodded, sniffing, trying to keep himself together.

The Professor walked stiffly, his eyes were empty and dark, staring into the distance. On one side, Calista held his hand tight, weeping quietly, and on the other, Gaia lightly held onto the crook of his arm, a nondescript expression on her face. Jake walked next to a pale-faced Jemima. Mei Hui was holding Tyaishia's hand, walking just behind the Chauffeur.

Both Dr Fargo and the Chauffeur helped Tai out of the wheelchair, and though he was barely able to stand, he managed to hobble over to the old oak, one shaky step at a time. He leaned into it, and spread out feeble arms – hugging the roughness of its trunk. Melting into it. He absorbed the centuries, the seasons, the history that seemed to be imbued within every ridge and wrinkle, engraved by time itself. Felt the balmy warmth of a spring sun on his back, smelled the freshness of new leaves, the mossy bloom of lichen. He listened appreciatively to the sweet, innocent, song of birds nestled, hidden, amongst its boughs. An insect hummed faintly, flying past his ear.

Irresistibly drawn, the teenagers walked over one by one, and joined Tai. First Jemima, who put her arm around his shoulders and hugged the tree too. Then Calista and Jake, entwining arms with each other, and Mei Hui. And lastly Saffie, who closed the circle by putting her arm around Tai's.

They closed their eyes, and Calista gasped as she felt an energy, like warm liquid, seeping through her fingertips, into veins, along her arm, flooding every cell of her body, and then passing out the other side into Jake. The energy vibrated, pulsed, and throbbed, like a living thing, taking her breath away, yet calming her despite the emotional turmoil. Like the eye of a storm, a serenity radiated through her body – for how long, she did not know.

Time stopped.

And they coalesced into each other.

Slowly, silently, they all came to understand Tai completely, in every way – who he was, what he was, and why. Until there was nothing they didn't know about him. Until he was emptied.

And finally, Tai exhaled his last breath, and the connection broke. Just like that, even though they were still touching.

An ice-cold dread gripped Jemima's heart as she opened her eyes to see Tai's body go limp, his legs buckling, falling to the ground in slow motion.

Tyaishia screamed, and ran to him.

•••———————————————————•••

Deep inside the underground shelter that was Avernus, a small black housefly buzzed through the slats of an air vent, bursting into a dimly-lit room in a heavily-secured section.

Jeremy Fitzsimmons sat behind the thick black bars of his cell, crouching in the dark, his facial hair grown longer and peppered with even more white streaks. His hand was extended under the only natural light in the room, surging through a sun tunnel. It cast a bright beam in the dusty blackness. And Fitzsimmons' hand glowed beneath it, bathed in amber – his palm turned upwards, fingers unfurled, as if holding a ball of sunlight.

The fly buzzed overhead, then dived and skimmed along his arm, finally landing on his hand. It stilled, basking in the warmth. And then another fly came, and another, until his fingers and palm were covered with fidgeting black bodies. The flies hopped this way and that, and then turned to face him, one after another. Large ruby eyes sparkling like metallic jewels in the light, fixing on his grotesque face. Fitzsimmons closed his eyes and absorbed their tiny little minds. Vague images... murmurs of sound, fleeting smells... dizzying sensations, and strange tastes. He slowly inhaled them. Hazy puzzle pieces. Coming together, to form a whole.

At last he understood. Realised what was happening. And he staggered forward, collapsing into a heap on the floor. Breath heaving, his whole body shaking.

The flies burst upwards, droning and darting in random directions – finally landing on the matt black prison bars.

From the corridor came the patter of light feet. A girl's.

Milly's head peered through the glass of the security door, her face milky-white, wisps of hair around her cheeks. She opened the door and stepped in, dull eyes roving through the dimness.

Fitzsimmons slowly sat up and turned his head away from her, numb, ashamed, distraught.

When Milly saw that he was on the floor, she rushed over to him, kneeling at the bars, fingers curling around the scuffed metal. Behind her came the faint sound of buzzing – several flies following in her wake. They too landed on the prison bars, joining and blending with the others.

The old man, still looking away, stretched his hand out and felt for a bar. Hesitantly, Milly cupped her hand over his.

You're too late, he told her, from his mind.

Milly gasped, tears brimming, though he could not see them. *Oh no. Tai!*

Hastily, she got up and fumbled for something in her pocket. A key. And stepped forward to open the lock, hands trembling. As soon as the catch was released with a click, Fitzsimmons jumped up and flew out, like a dark, malevolent shadow. The door was flung back, throwing Milly to the ground.

But he didn't even look back at her.

He was old, but he ran swiftly, with a force that did not seem real, did not even seem human. Hurtling past the bodies of the two guards that lay slumped on the ground by the door. He ran through corridors. Up winding stairs – jumping two steps at a time, sometimes three.

When he reached the furthermost security doors, he hammered the code into the digital lock, flung the door open, and raced through the maze of tunnels that surrounded Avernus. Knowing exactly which way to go.

At last coming to what seemed like a dead end, he looked up at the tunnel rising vertically above his head, and he jumped onto the ladder that clung to the wall. The rungs were cold and rough, as though unused for decades – but he gripped firmly onto them as he climbed and climbed, heedless of the punishing splinters that dug into his hands. As he ascended, the air turned colder and damper, so that his ragged breath exhaled as faint plumes. The sound of water outside lapping against the thick metal walls. At the top, he grappled with the hatch door, clenching teeth, as he twisted the wheel with all his might. At last it gave way with a screech, and he pushed the hatch upward, and burst out into the warm summer air. He squinted briefly in the light, before jumping out onto the verge of grass. Looking around, getting his bearings.

He thundered across the bridge that spanned the lake of Avernus, feet clattering on the wooden slats. Then he flew across the fields that led to the great old oak. The sound of his heavy breathing resonating in his ears.

In the distance, he saw a small group of people.

Recognised the teenagers, arms wrapped around the wide trunk of a tree.

Saw Tai falling to the ground.

His mother screaming.

Dogs turning in Fitzsimmons' direction, barking manically and shooting toward him. Bared teeth, vicious snarls. Ready and raring to attack.

Fitzsimmons slowed and held out a hand to them, and they suddenly stopped, quietened. They paced backwards, heads bowing, as if in submission. Emitting a faint whining sound.

The teenagers turned and saw him. Shouting, screaming. Panicked!

Out of nowhere appeared five men, masked and dressed in black. Jumping in front of the teenagers, shielding them. The smooth whoosh of metal on metal as swords were withdrawn from the sheaths on their backs, ready to fight to the death to protect their wards.

Fitzsimmons slowed. Catching his breath. Through a tangle of hair, fiery eyes glared hard and dark. He charged toward the ninjas. But they did not move. Could not move. Frozen into statues. Swords falling, clanging to the ground, and then their bodies collapsing in a heap, paralysed. The old man darted between them, and rushed toward Tai who was slumped on the grass against the tree, his mother bending over him. But she was soon torn off and flung away as if she were nothing. He fell upon Tai, and someone from the group screamed. But they hung back, agonised, not knowing what to do, not wanting to leave Tai, Tyaishia.

Fitzsimmons bent down and dug a hand underneath Tai's back, scraping him up like a limp ragdoll. The boy's spine arched backwards, head hanging loose, stick-like arms dangling. The old man planted his feet firmly on the ground between the roots, and pressed his other hand flat against the thick bark of the tree. He threw his head back and cried out – a thunderous bellow that was black, blood-curdling, raw with pain.

The ground began to shake.

The great oak quivered.

Its branches rustling.

Birds flying out in all directions, wings flapping, squawking.

Fitzsimmons continued screaming – his veins popping, eyes crazed with red.

The group huddled together, trying to keep their balance as the ground tremored. Watching, terrified. The Professor being shielded behind them, out of harm's way. The blind old man frantically turned his head this way and that, confused, alarmed, staggering around.

The group watched with disbelief as Fitzsimmons began draining energy from the huge tree.

One by one, the leaves of the old oak began to vibrate, then slowly turned grey – disintegrating into ash and vanishing into the air.

When all the foliage had gone, the branches began whittling away.

Overground roots whipped up, scourging the ground, and then dispersed into the air.

Finally the trunk cascaded outwards into waves of dust, thrown up in the sky, and swirled around by the wind.

In time, where the great old oak had been, there was nothing more than a stump, gradually sinking into a heap of ash. When the entire tree was razed to the ground, Fitzsimmons stopped, doubling over in pain, gasping for breath. Eventually he forced himself to move. Crouched low over the boy's body, his cheek grazing Tai's lips. But there was no breath. The form of him – frail, broken, limp – remained still and lifeless.

Fitzsimmons exploded with rage and frustration, screaming anew, his hoarse voice cracking. Doggedly, he refused to give up. The old man lifted his ashy hand and raised it high into the air above him, fiery with anger.

Contorted fingers reaching, pulling, drawing in.

They waited. Watched. Breathless.

Gradually the sky went dark.

The clouds blackened.

The sun disappeared.

A faint sound of buzzing grew stronger and louder by the second. Until the noise became deafening. A droning that reverberated inside their heads as billions and billions of flies poured in from above, funnelling down towards Fitzsimmons' outstretched hand. Pulverising into nothingness. His skin, a vacuum, pulling in and voiding everything it touched.

Energy seeped into him, rattling through his veins, his blood, turning his skin grey. Teeth clenching from the agonising pain.

Sabu squealed, glanced briefly at Saffie with wild eyes, his legs walking stiffly of their own accord – toward the dark, scary, screaming man. Helpless to his body moving against his will.

Jemima leapt forward and grabbed the cub, gripping him to her chest. But she heard yelping, and saw that Acuzio and Dog too were running involuntarily toward Fitzsimmons. Anger burst inside of her, and she reached a hand out toward them and kept them from being pulled in. A battle of strength. A tug of war. The dogs' bodies immobilised by equal and opposite forces.

But then the ninjas, lying on the grass, came to life – and they got up one by one and began walking toward Fitzsimmons, unable to fight the tremendous force controlling them, unable to do anything but accept their fate.... Sweat pouring as they walked toward certain death. Drawn into the vortex. Into him.

Someone screamed, and the Chauffeur rushed forward to grab one of the ninjas' arms. The others joined him, grabbing one of the five black-clad men, desperately trying to stop them. But the ninjas were stronger, and pulled them along as they advanced.

Gaia's grip was weak, her hands arthritic, and the ninja slipped out of her clutch. She screamed in horror as the man broke free, and suddenly ran into Fitzsimmons, disappearing in a puff of grey.

Fuming red with rage, Jemima shifted her arm, reaching twisted fingers toward them, and screeching through gritted teeth as she drew each of the ninjas back, inch by inch, with every fibre of her being.

Mei Hui and Saffie battled through the tornado-like wind, the quaking ground, and the onslaught of flies smacking into them – struggling to reach Jemima, hair whipping up around their heads. At last they made it, and Mei Hui entwined an arm around Jemima's, while Saffie gripped her shoulder. They absorbed her power, and reached out a hand too – holding the others back with all their might.

The flies kept on descending around them so that the entire world was filled with black.

Sucked right into Fitzsimmons. A raging, howling Grim Reaper.

After an age, the throng of flies at last began to peter out.

The ground stilled, and an uncanny silence descended.

Fitzsimmons slumped on the ground, on top of Tai's cold, still body.

The old man's limbs spasming, head twitching, ravaged by the firebolt of energy that had ripped right through him. His fingertips and lips were black, as if touched by death. His hoary skin streaked by dark veins. Pain tearing through his body, like rivulets of molten lava, so that every cell in his body seemed rent asunder.

The agony was unbearable.

And at last, he lost consciousness.

The world around him, evaporating into nothingness.

'Truly man is the king of beasts,
for his brutality exceeds them.
We live by the deaths of others.
We are burial places.'

Leonardo da Vinci

39 DARK ENERGY

'What on earth just happened??!!' shrieked Calista, hobbling into the BC.

Almost everyone else was already there, dazed and dishevelled – silently waiting for Brian, who was going around disinfecting and dressing scrapes and wounds, that were, thankfully, only superficial. Though Brian himself was in a state of shock.

Calista went over to Jake who was sitting in a chair. 'You okay, babe?' she asked, kissing the top of his head and hugging him.

Jake nodded, though he didn't look okay at all, still grappling with what had just happened. 'That man... his power...' he said, stupefied.

'Yes,' said Mei Hui, as she went around giving out bottles of water, trying to stop her hands from shaking, but failing. 'Th-there is no doubt about us being "related" – his abilities are the same as ours.'

'But to the nth degree,' Jemima muttered. She was sitting in the far corner, pale as a sheet, arms wrapped around herself.

'It was awful!' said Saffie, jostling in her seat. 'I hope... I hope Tai's okay.'

Brian stopped what he was doing. 'Dr Fargo's with him now,' he told them, lowering his head slightly. 'I'm sure he's doing everything he can.'

They had all seen Dr Fargo bundle Tai's limp body onto the wheelchair and rush him away, so none of them had any idea what state he was in.

After that, everything happened so fast: a mass of security men crowding around the twitching Fitzsimmons, collapsed on the floor. The shot of a tranquilliser gun. Heaving his body – with a thud – onto the canvas of a stretcher, careful not to touch his skin. Carrying him away, surrounded on all sides. The rest of them shuffling back silently, like the walking dead. Passing the large crater of blackened earth where the great oak once was. Even the roots that were once visible in the pitted earth, had disappeared.

'He wiped out that entire tree. And controlled people, and things, as if they were puppets on strings,' said Calista, wide-eyed. But she turned to the Professor, puzzled by something. 'But I don't get it, Prof. If he had all these... mind powers, how come your men were able to capture him in the first place?'

The Professor, his usually pristine appearance in tatters, came out of the daze he was in – fingering a glass, a stiff dram of whisky only half drunk, on the table next to him. 'That's what I've been wondering...' He shifted in his chair. 'I can only imagine that he must have let himself be captured.'

'But why?' Calista asked.

It was Mei Hui who responded. 'Possibly because he thought that was the only way to get closer to us. I believe he kidnapped Dr Vassiliev for that reason, though the doctor did not know the secret location of Avernus. But then, when he came back to the country house, and he chased me in the forest that night, he realised we were there...' She stopped, suddenly baffled herself.

'Which doesn't make sense,' said the Professor, voicing Mei Hui's own thoughts. 'Why didn't he just mind-control you, and the security men, and Dr Vassiliev for that matter?' He rubbed his chin, trying to work it out. 'Also, he had to drug Vassiliev's vodka to make him go with him. That doesn't add up either.'

Mei Hui nodded, blinking. 'That is true. Is it possible that he didn't have the ability then? And thinking about it, in his past, we did not see any displays of that ability at all. He had no control over Georgina, and could not stop her from leaving him. It therefore seems likely that his being able to control minds is something recent.'

Jemima shuffled forward on her chair. 'Like me. I had no idea that I could do that thing with the caimans.'

Saffie frowned. 'Also, what he did with the old tree outside, was exactly the same thing I did for Sabu. It's like... like he heard about everything that happened to us in Anavilhanas – how Jemima controlled the caimans, how Sabu was healed – and copied it.'

'You're right. It's all too similar,' said the Professor, deep in thought.

'The question is, how did he learn about these things, when he's been locked in his cell all this time? It is in a remote section of Avernus, and he has no access to Jasmine, or any kind of device.'

Saffie shivered. 'Are we even safe from him now?'

The Professor turned toward her. 'I can assure you we are. My men have drugged him so that mentally he's... incapacitated. He poses absolutely no threat to us. And he will soon be transferred to a much more secure location. However, I realise now, I should never have brought him here. To Avernus. Should never have allowed you to get so close to him. That was a regrettable mistake.'

Mei Hui sighed, shaking her head. 'It is I who have made a very bad mistake, Professor. We should not have connected with him.'

'Why did you do that?' asked Saffie, turning toward her. She had already told them about Milly, and the 'seed' of something that had been implanted in her during that connection, though she did not know exactly what it was.

Mei Hui answered her quietly. 'We thought... no, we *knew* he was our DNA father, and wanted to find out more about him.' She paused, admitting, 'And also because we were foolish!' Her cheeks burnt hot.

The Professor heard her voice cracking. 'Mei Hui,' he said softly. 'You were made... *we* made you with an incredible intelligence, an insatiable curiosity. And it's only natural that you wanted to find out about him. Only... I knew about his appearance, and also that he could potentially be very dangerous. That's why I wanted to protect you and keep you away until I knew more about him.'

'So his endgame,' said Calista to both Saffie and Mei Hui, 'was just to find you guys? That's it?'

'I think so,' said Mei Hui. 'We are his progeny. He poured his entire fortune into "creating" us, funding Project Ingenious to make us with the genius traits from his genes–'

'Minus the ugly mug,' said Calista, bluntly. 'Kind of like the monster, <u>Frankenstein</u>, but inside out. As in, your genes have been patched together from his, but you look normal thank goodness...' she trailed off, suddenly wondering if she'd thought that through.

Brian looked over at Calista. 'Actually, Frankenstein, Victor Frankenstein, was the scientist who brought the monster to life. The creature itself had no name. I read the book as a teenager. It's a common mistake.'

'No way!' said Calista, trying to get her head around that. 'So, the *Professor* is Frankenstein, and not the Ingenious kids?'

'There's no Frankenstein really, and I'm not sure there's even a monster,' said the Professor. 'What Fitzsimmons did out there... he tried to save Tai. Almost killing himself in the process. Can he really be such a monster?'

Mei Hui pondered this. 'It is true that he was willing to sacrifice himself to try and save Tai, but he also did not care what, or who, was destroyed in doing so.'

Brian tutted, shaking his head. 'Poor V8. He was a hero. An absolute hero. We didn't know who he was, didn't know him from Adam – yet he risked his life to protect us... Rest in peace,' he murmured.

A solemn chorus of 'Hear, hear' and 'rest in peace' echoed around the room, and they all thought about him quietly... thought too about how valiant all the agents were in trying to defend them.

Mei Hui remembered something. 'When we went inside Fitzsimmons' mind, he showed us the innocent side of him. But there is also a dark side. Though–'

Calista snorted. 'Too right he's dark!'

Mei Hui continued, deep in thought. 'Though when dark and light mix together, it becomes grey. He is grey.'

'I agree,' said Saffie. 'His moral compass is all over the place!'

Eventually Calista said, 'Well, thank goodness you only inherited the genius genes from your DNA psycho Dad...'

Saffie spluttered. 'DNA psycho Dad?!'

Calista circled her index finger next to her temple. 'He's not quite right in the head, is he? But, question: where did *he* get his powers from?'

'It was passed on through the generations of Fitzsimmonses,' said the Professor. 'But of course one wonders where *they* got their abilities from.'

'I guess we'll never know,' said Saffie. 'Unless anyone's got a time machine lying around anywhere.'

Mei Hui's eyes slid across to look at Saffie, the word 'time machine' echoing in her thoughts. 'When we went inside Karl König's mind,' she said, remembering, 'it was like being in a time machine. We saw his entire life. Right back to when he was a baby.'

Calista thought about it. 'Karl was very much alive when you did that though. Unlike the Fitzsimmons folk – I'm pretty sure they're all dead by now.'

'We do have one connection to the past though,' said Mei Hui. 'The portraits that F. Jaffrey painted. They are all stored here in Avernus. If we study them, we might be able to learn more about the painter himself, his life.'

Saffie suddenly thought of something. 'What about Dragonfly Girl? If you guys can get memories just by touching someone, do you think you could touch the painting? Find out who the ashes belong to, and what on earth happened?!'

Calista looked doubtful. 'Not sure you can get memories from a dead person, let alone the remains of a dead person... Or can you?'

No-one could answer that. Until Jemima's voice piped up from a corner of the room. She looked fragile, and spoke quietly, still dazed. 'Memories are made from sensory experiences which trigger changes in neuron molecules in your brain. That reshapes the way the neurons connect. So, when memories are laid down, the memories in turn re-make and re-wire your brain.' Jemima turned to Calista. 'So technically, your brain cells don't just store your memories... they *are* your memories.'

'So...?' Calista blinked at her, none the wiser.

Jemima shook her head. 'Saying that, I seriously doubt it. Because even if there are brain cells in the painting, they've been inanimate for decades. Decaying over all this time. I'm pretty sure it's not possible to "read" them.'

Calista suddenly noticed how pale Jemima was. 'You okay, shrimp?' she asked, genuinely concerned.

Jemima pinched her lips together, struggling to control herself. Eventually she shook her head, whimpering, 'No... I'm not! I wish... I wish I'd been fast enough. I could've saved V8!!' She said, bursting into tears.

A chair scraped back, and Calista went over and put an arm around her.

Jemima closed her eyes, remembering. 'I... I saw the look in his eyes, just before he ran to his death. He knew what was going to happen, but he still looked... noble, dignified.'

'That is the way of the ninja,' muttered Mei Hui, saddened.

Saffie sensed the crack of pain that tore through Jemima's chest, it ricocheted through hers. 'It wasn't your fault, Jemima,' she told her, smarting from the pain. 'You did your best. Actually, you saved everyone else, stopped them from running toward Fitzsimmons. If it wasn't for you, there would've been loads more casualties. Sabu and the animals included.'

But Jemima wasn't convinced. 'If *only* I'd been faster, I might have saved him!' she said, wiping her eyes.

'You can't blame yourself,' said Calista. 'It was psycho that did all that... that mind stuff. He probably wiped out every single fly in London.'

'Or maybe even the whole of England!' said Saffie, worried.

'Good riddance to them,' Calista retorted. 'They drive me mad.' She suddenly thought of something. 'By the way, how on earth did he manage to get out of his cell?'

Brian stiffened as he packed things away into the first aid kit, though no-one noticed.

'We're looking into that,' said the Professor. 'Might've been a security malfunction of some kind...'

Calista stroked Jemima's messy hair. 'You shouldn't be alone tonight, Jem. We can bunk down together in the den if you want, get some sleeping bags from somewhere...'

Jemima sniffed, wiping away the last of her tears. 'Thanks, but I'm going back home shortly. And anyway, if I have nightmares, mummy and daddy don't mind if I get into bed with them. Mum's not a great sleeper herself, so we keep each other company...'

'Good. That's good,' said Calista, satisfied.

Jake at last came to life after a long spell of silent mortification. 'I still can't believe what just happened...' he said with round eyes.

'I know!' chimed Saffie. 'His powers! They're much, much more than ours! Though, to be honest, I still don't really know how I healed Sabu exactly.'

'The first law of thermodynamics,' said Jemima.

They all turned to her. Saffie frowned. 'What's that?'

Jemima sat up. 'The first law of thermodynamics is the law of conservation of energy. It states that energy cannot be created or destroyed within a closed system. Which means that the total amount of energy in the universe never changes.' She sounded scholarly, like a little lecturer. Discussing science always grounded her – there was something about the solidity of the fundamental laws, the timeless, inalterable statements that can even predict the outcome of natural phenomena. Like coming home after a long journey – science was warm, reliable, always there.

The Professor nodded, adding, 'Although energy *can* change from one form to another, it never disappears.'

'Ever,' said Jemima. She glanced up at the ceiling lights. 'Light is a form of energy, there's also electrical energy, heat, sound, gravitational energy, etc. There's even one called "dark energy".'

'Sounds creepy,' Calista remarked.

'Well,' said Jemima, '"dark" just means it's something that's not fully understood or explainable by known science, like dark matter. We know that dark matter and dark energy exist, because the effects are clearly evident. But we just don't know what exactly they are. So for example, we know that the universe is expanding, at an accelerating rate of expansion, because astronomers can see galaxies moving away from us. And interestingly, the farthest galaxies are moving faster than the closest ones. But what we don't know is what *exactly* is causing the universe to expand, to accelerate. Something definitely is, because we can see the effects. So that's why they've come up with the term "dark energy", to describe the force that's accelerating the expansion of the universe. Because the energy had to come from somewhere.'

'I get it,' said Saffie, filled with wonder. 'When I healed Sabu, we found out that I'd got the energy from the tree. And Fitzsimmons too, he drew the energy from that old tree, as well as that mass of flies.' She turned to Jemima. 'So, if there's all sorts of different energy, what exactly is the energy that *we* used?'

Jemima shook her head. 'I don't know. And we might never really find out. I suspect it's unknowable, like the dark energy that's expanding the universe.'

Saffie thought about this. 'I wonder if it's really unknowable, that force? Or is it just that we don't *want* to know?' She thought of her parents, and how deeply religious they were.

'Wow,' said Jemima, 'now that's a question.'

'Well, one thing's for sure,' said Jake. 'You guys, and Fitzsimmons, have some crazy ability to manipulate this dark energy. Though I have to say that you really need to get it under control, and get a grip on whatever it is you can do. 'Cos at the moment, there's more harm being done than good.'

Jemima nodded, interested. 'I like that idea. We need training. Like Luke Skywalker learning the ways of the Force in the Jedi Order!'

Calista snorted.

Just then, Jasmine's voice came from the overhead speakers. 'Professor, you have a phone call from Dr Vassiliev. Where would you like to take it?'

The Professor sighed. His earpiece had fallen out somewhere, dislodged no doubt during Fitzsimmons' maelstrom of madness. Being exhausted, the old man could barely move. And he was pretty sure that the doctor was only calling to tell him about yet another setback with the cure. 'I'll take it here,' he said, blasé. And then he spoke louder, into the air. 'Hello, Vadim.'

Dr Vassiliev's voice boomed around the room. 'Kherry, my dear Kherry!' he said excitedly. 'How are you? Are you having good day?'

The Professor barely knew what to say. 'Not quite. I'm with the children. And it's been... a tough morning.'

'Understatement of the year,' splurted Calista under her breath.

'Well!' said Dr Vassiliev in high spirits. 'I'm going to make your day, Kherry! I'm going to make you very, very happy man!'

The Professor sat up. 'Is it...?'

'The cure! We have overcome last hurdle. It is finished. Finished!! But...'

'But what?' asked the Professor, his skin prickling with anticipation.

'Our trials with test animals have been promising. But as you know, with this kind of new experimental science, we need to try on humans now. One of children. Before giving it to others. We do not know exactly what effects–'

'Yes, thank you!' said the Professor quickly, cutting him off, keenly aware of the children listening. 'I will call you back shortly and we can discuss it more. But thank you very much! That is just excellent. Fantastic news!!' He motioned with his hands a sign to Jasmine: end call. And the line went dead.

Brian turned to the Professor. 'I'm hoping Tai is alive, so you can try it on him first. But if not...'

The Professor nodded. 'I understand, Brian. Let's hope and pray for Tai...' he sighed. 'But we can also try it on Milly, if you so wish. The cure has the ability to rid the brain of excessive amyloid plaque proteins that have built up in the space between neurons, as well as regrow any shrunken neurons. Which I am sure will help Milly immensely. But... you heard the doctor say that this is experimental science, which means that it's not without risk.'

'What risks are we talking about exactly?' asked Brian cautiously.

'We cannot say for sure,' the Professor told him. 'I'm sorry, I wish I could give you more definite answers, but we just don't know what will happen until we start the trial.'

Brian thought for a while, saying eventually, 'If it comes to it, I still want Milly to try it.'

'Okay, I hear you,' said the Professor solemnly. He forced himself to get up, grunting from aches and pains. 'By the way, where is she?'

'She's in her room,' said Brian. 'She... she's resting.' He turned away to click the first-aid kit shut, and then picked it up by the handle. 'I'll go and tell her the good news,' he said, before walking out of the room. They listened to his footsteps disappear down the corridor.

Jemima turned to the Professor. 'You mentioned risks, Professor. If you could quantify it, what's the likelihood of something going wrong?'

The Professor finished off his whisky, savouring the soothing burn of it down his gullet. Quietly he said, 'At a guess... fifty percent or so.'

Jemima stiffened. 'Like tossing a coin...' she muttered.

The Professor flicked out his walking stick. He'd heard what she said, but he tapped his way out of the room without replying.

Jemima herself did not say another word. She didn't like those odds. Yet she knew that, with science, there was much, much more that they didn't know, than they did. Human knowledge of life, the world, the universe, was really only scratching the surface. Humans would need an eternity to understand it all fully. She sighed and was about to get up herself when Missy Mop walked in, meowing loudly, looking around the room, lost – as if searching for something.

Jemima stared at her, and then gasped. 'Treacle's missing!'

'The cat?' said Saffie. 'How do you know. It could be anywhere.'

'Missy Mop and Treacle are inseparable. They go everywhere together,' said Jemima, and then she called out to the air. 'Jasmine, search for Treacle throughout the whole of Avernus. Now!'

'I am searching, Jemima,' came Jasmine's voice in reply. There were several seconds of silence, before she said, 'I am sorry, but Treacle cannot be found. I have scanned the entirety of Avernus 80 times, and there is no sign of him.'

Jemima burst into fresh tears. 'Oh no!' she cried. 'Oh no!!'

•••———————————————————•••

Tyaishia was waiting nervously outside the medical room, pacing up and down, wringing her hands, sometimes even putting her ear against the door. Suddenly the door opened, and the doctor appeared, looking exhausted. She fell upon him, grabbing his arms. Looking him directly in the eyes. 'Please,' she begged. 'Tell me he's okay.'

The look he gave her did not bode well. 'I've been battling to save him, Tyaishia. But in the end, as a last resort, I've had to medically induce a coma and put him on an ECMO machine. I-it's a kind of... life support, which is keeping him alive. For now. We just have to wait, and pray. Pray that he survives the night, though...' he sighed, 'his chances look slim, very slim.'

Tyaishia blinked at him. Not wanting to believe. Despite the awfulness of what had just happened outside, she couldn't help but hope it might have saved her son. She rushed into the room, but then slowed when she saw all the machinery – beeping and flashing, pumping and whirring. A tangled mass of wires, and tubing flowing red with blood, protruding from underneath the blanket that covered Tai, and connected the other end to the ECMO. At the heart of everything was her boy. Frail, unconscious, still. She went to the far side of the bed, where there was space for her to take his hand. She kissed it tenderly, but unlike last time, there was no rustle of bedsheets, and he did not move. Silently she sank down into the chair – one hand holding onto his, and the other touching his soft, white hair. Slowly she began picking out bits of leaves, twigs, dirt. Her hand trembling uncontrollably. Unable to hold it in any longer, she broke down and wept onto the bed.

She wanted to pray. Wanted to pour out everything that was crammed and packed inside of her, to her God. But there were no words that could express her feelings, or that could break through the tight choke in her throat and the fear that braided her chest. 'Please,' was all she managed to whisper, quivering like a leaf. 'Please, God,' she cried. Over and over again.

•••———————————————————•••

That night, deep in the heart of Avernus, Saffron Morales had a lot to think about.

She lay back in bed, reflecting on the awful events of the day and reading through her little notebook of thoughts, feelings, sensations. She marvelled at her special connection with the Ingenious children, how it spanned even continents, and how she could capture vague glimpses of what they felt, even though they were only fleeting, here and there. She thought too about the last Ingenious child – where on earth he could be. Literally. She didn't have much to go on. All she knew was that he was male, lived overseas somewhere, possibly in Asia, and was a powerhouse of held-in emotions. She didn't doubt it, being a teenager.

Soon, sleep overcame her. But she tossed and turned, captive to the throes of an epic dream that seemed to last for hours. Hearing voices. So many voices. Before long, the dream turned into a nightmare, and she battled with the pillow, the bedcovers, and herself.

Suddenly she sat up, shaking her head, eyes still shut, panicked. Pressing hands firmly against her ears.

A female voice echoed in her mind. 'Get out of my head!' shouted a girl so vociferously that Saffie could almost feel the spray of spit against her skin.

Saffie glowered, face creased with confusion. It wasn't the boy speaking to her. It was someone else. Someone closer. A new voice, she did not recognise.

The voice came again. 'I... I don't know who you are,' whimpered a young girl, 'b-but I just want you to leave me alone!' And then she screamed at Saffie with almost manic hysteria. 'JUST... GET OUT! PLEASE. GET OUT OF MY HEAD!!!'

EPILOGUE

The shadowy corners of Avernus seemed to quiver, dream-like.

Still corridors humming with the sound of electricity.

The girl walked quietly, alone, along one of them.

Nightlights turned on in front of her with faint plinking sounds as she floated forward – and turned off from behind. Bare feet making hardly a sound against the smooth cement. Her silky hair swished about her shoulders; a light rustle of cotton pyjamas.

She reached the store room and went inside, turning the corner to stop, finally, in front of the Dragonfly Girl painting. It looked different in the softness of night, though still incredibly beautiful. As she stared, the colours seemed even more real. Seemed to break solidly through the invisible wall between art and the material, between portrayal and reality. Between the imagined and the actual.

Her eyelids slid halfway closed as she reached a hand toward it.

Heart fluttering like a panicked bird in a bone cage.

Stuttered breath, trembling lips.

She forced herself to touch it, gulping down waves of nausea.

And when skin touched paint, she forced herself to linger. Her senses reaching right inside the painting. Searching.

She gasped. Her crescent eyes jolting open. And she stared at the painted girl.

The girl's dark eyes seemed to rise from their downward gaze and stare right back, directly into hers.

Seemed as if she were turning to face her.

Opening her mouth to speak.

Seemed as though, from death, she had been brought back to life.

'Mei Hui,' breathed Georgina Whyte.

Dear Reader,

I had great fun (as well as shedding some tears) as I wrote this next instalment in the Ingenious trilogy. Fitzsimmons' character intrigued me greatly, and the genesis and discovery of his powers is also a precursor to the Ingenious children's discovery of who they are, and what they can do.

It has taken me longer than expected to write, purely because I have poured my heart and soul into it, and I also wanted to develop and write the story to the best of my ability – no small feat when juggling with family, work, and other responsibilities.

If you enjoyed this book, I would very much appreciate it if you could write a review, either on Amazon, Goodreads, or any other online book store. Even if it's just a few words, it'd really mean a lot to me!

You are also welcome to get in touch with me@jysamofficial.com – I always enjoy hearing about my readers' experiences, or answering any questions.

Wishing you the very best.

Yours,
J.Y. Sam

www.jysamofficial.com